KENTUCKY HEAT

Also by Fern Michaels . . .

KENTUCKY RICH
CHARMING LILY
PLAIN JANE
WHAT YOU WISH FOR
THE GUEST LIST
LISTEN TO YOUR HEART
CELEBRATION
YESTERDAY
FINDERS KEEPERS
ANNIE'S RAINBOW
SARA'S SONG
VEGAS SUNRISE
VEGAS HEAT
VEGAS RICH
WHITEFIRE
WISH LIST
DEAR EMILY

TEXAS SUNRISE
TEXAS FURY
TEXAS HEAT
TEXAS RICH

FERN MICHAELS

KENTUCKY HEAT

KENSINGTON BOOKS
http://www.kensingtonbooks.com

KENSINGTON BOOKS are published by

Kensington Publishing Corp.
850 Third Avenue
New York, NY 10022

All Kensington titles, imprints and distributed lines are available at special quantity discounts for bulk purchases for sales promotion, premiums, fund-raising, educational or institutional use.

Special book excerpts or customized printings can also be created to fit specific needs. For details, write or phone the office of the Kensington Special Sales Manager: Kensington Publishing Corp., 850 Third Avenue, New York, NY 10022, Attn. Special Sales Department. Phone: 1-800-221-2647.

Kensington and the K logo Reg. U.S. Pat. & TM Off.

ISBN 0-7582-0357-8

First Trade Printing: May 2002
10 9 8 7 6 5 4 3 2 1

Printed in the United States of America

For my friend Douglas Charles Girton

Prologue

∽

Mitch Cunningham stood at the entrance to Blue Diamond Farms, his legs spread apart, his hands on his hips. He squared off his hands into a box to stare at the luscious Kentucky landscape in front of him. He adjusted his dark glasses, then took them off. The baseball cap, which said NY Yankees, was pushed farther back on his head so as not to obstruct his view. And what a view it was. Thick velvety bluegrass, miles of white board fencing, rolling hills, a colony of barns, and the main house, which looked like something out of a Thomas Kincaid painting. Perfect for an opening shot in a movie. Just perfect.

Cinematographer by profession, he could see the opening scene in the movie he hoped to film, thanks to his bosses at Triple-Star Pictures. He didn't have a doubt in the world that he could turn the film into another *Gone With the Wind*. What he did have doubts about, however, was getting Nealy Coleman Diamond Clay to okay the project and allow the film to be made there on Blue Diamond Farms.

NCDC, as his bosses called Nealy Coleman Diamond Clay, was going to be a hard nut to crack. A very private person, they said. The promise of big money wouldn't mean a thing to her. Find her Achilles' heel and home in on it, they suggested. Think major box office, think movie of the century had been their litany when they presented the idea to him. The head honcho, carried away with a possible Academy Awards sweep, had fixed his steely eyes on Mitch, and said, "I don't want to see your face in these offices until you have a signed deal. We're giving you six months to lock in the deal and another seven months to make the film. With full pay and your usual percentage."

Then the honcho with the steely eyes pointed to two cardboard cartons. "Those boxes contain background files on NCDC from the day she was born. And"—he'd wagged his finger—"background files on everyone who is, or ever was, involved in her life right up to the present. If NCDC takes home a second Triple Crown, we have a home run in the making."

He'd taken the job because he would have been a fool not to.

He was here now to scout it out and make his pitch to NCDC. He chuckled as he made his way back to his car. He'd never been up close and personal with a horse before. In fact, the only real live horses he'd ever seen were on studio lots and from a distance.

Mitch settled himself in the driver's seat of the customized Jag. He reached for the folder on the passenger seat. The previous night in his hotel room, he'd separated the wheat from the chaff, and what he had before him were his notes, which he knew by heart.

Three families intertwined. The Colemans of Texas, the Thorntons of Las Vegas, and this branch of the family, whose matriarch was Nealy Coleman Diamond Clay. His index finger went down the long list.

Texas. Seth Coleman, deceased. He, like his sister Sallie and his brother Josh, had come from humble beginnings. Struck it rich in oil, branched out to aeronautics, raised cattle. Home base, Sunbridge. They could shoot some scenes there, too, if this was going to be the epic he planned.

For many years it was thought old Seth only had two children, Moss and Amelia. Later in the movie, he would prove that wrong. Seth had disowned Amelia, and she went off to England. Later she married Cary Asante and died, never having reconciled with her father. Moss had married a girl named Billie from Philadelphia, who gave him three children, Maggie, Susan, and young Riley, who was killed in the war. Moss was a bounder. Mitch knew just the actor to play that part. Billie and Moss were estranged long before he died, but she took care of him at the end. That would tie in to a wonderful tear-jerking scene. He closed his eyes to picture a young Moss in his Navy whites standing next to one of the planes he flew during the war. Yeah, yeah, the actor he had in mind could really pull that off. The trials and tribulations of the family might eat into his time, but he could do it. A spin-off from the movie was not out of the question.

Somehow he was going to have to fit in the Japanese Hasegawas. He blinked at the net worth of that particular branch of the family. Production costs could get dicey if he had to shoot on location in Japan. He'd work that out, too.

Then came the Thorntons. Sallie Coleman Thornton, married to a schoolteacher from Boston. Saloon singer and lady of the night to a prospector named Cotton Easter, who died and left her everything he owned. He blinked again at the Thorntons' net worth. The casinos they owned would juice up the movie. Two sons born to that union, Ash and Simon. Navy whites again. Tomcats or whatever planes they flew in those days. He'd have to get some Navy approval along the way. He wondered where the USS *Enterprise* was these days. To be dealt with. Fanny Thornton, married to both brothers. On his deathbed, first husband shoots brother—and second husband—dead. Talk about drama!

Mitch's eyes rolled back in his head. Four children to that union, twins, Birch and Sage, Billie, and Sunny, who suffered from some debilitating disease. Another tearjerker. They lived on and owned a goddamn mountain that burned to the ground and was then replanted by one of the richest men in the world, Metaxas Parish. Metaxas Parish was married to Ruby Thornton, who had recently undergone a double mastectomy. If he did that right, he might be able to further the breast-cancer cause among women. Her mother was a lady of the evening like Sallie Thornton. Metaxas Parish would be bigger than life in the movie since he had the ear of presidents and queens. The scriptwriter was going to have a ball with the screenplay, which would probably go to four hundred pages or more. All the family interaction could be shown in the spin-off. Yeah, yeah, definitely a spin-off. He was clicking, his adrenaline flowing.

Nealy Coleman Diamond Clay booted out of her family home, SunStar Farms in Virginia. Booted out with a baby born out of wedlock. Suspected father is Dillon Roland but not confirmed. Gentleman farmer and horse owner. Land fight over SunStar, with Colemans of Texas battling NCDC. Two brothers, Rhy and Pyne, retained SunStar in the end, thanks to NCDC. Great character parts for the brothers.

Nealy Coleman Diamond Clay. The little seventeen-year-old unwed mother who stepped into a fortune and rode to a Triple Crown. Adopted by Maud and Jess Wooley, she kept the name Diamond at Maud's request. Married to Hunter Clay, who died too early in his life. A son Nick born to the marriage. Nealy had raised another horse who was a serious contender for a second Triple Crown, with Nealy up. A grandmother jockey! Women were going to love it. He could see her face splashed across the world. Disney would probably make Nealy Coleman Diamond Clay dolls.

Then there were the horses. Flyby and Shufly. Father and son. Thoroughbreds worth millions of dollars. Sleek, racing machines who lived to cross the finish line.

Mitch slapped the folder back onto the seat. All he needed was a solid gold sales pitch and Nealy Coleman Diamond Clay to sign on the dotted line. He settled his sunglasses and baseball cap more firmly on his head, started the engine, and headed down the road that would take him to Blue Diamond Farms.

PART I

1

Nealy staggered to the corner of Misty Blue's birthing stall, where she leaned against the slatted wall, then slid to the ground. She wrapped her arms around her knees to stop the trembling in her arms and legs. She'd had no sleep at all for the past forty-eight hours and was operating on pure adrenaline. She wanted to sleep, needed to sleep, but she didn't dare close her eyes in case the fragile newborn colt needed her. A wan smile tugged at the corners of her mouth when she heard Flyby nicker softly. "I hear you, big guy. Your son is doing just fine, and so is his mama. It was touch-and-go there for a while, but then I guess you know that. I don't want you worrying one little bit." A second nicker, this one softer, echoed in Nealy's ears. "All's right with your world, eh, Flyby?"

As if in answer, Flyby whinnied.

"Everything is all right with his world, but it sure isn't right with mine right now. I think this straw has bugs in it."

"Ruby! Are you awake? Are you okay?"

"I'm as okay as I can be for going without sleep for forty-eight hours," Ruby said in a hoarse voice as she peeked through the slats into Misty Blue's stall. "Ah, look at him, Nealy, he's so gorgeous he takes my breath away." She gazed at the colt adoringly. "Metaxas is going to go over the moon when he gets here later today."

Nealy smiled at Ruby. Ruby Thornton Parish, married to one of the richest men in the world, and here she was, virtually living in her barn, helping with the horses and having the time of her life. Metaxas Parish, Ruby's husband, had planted an entire mountain for Fanny Thornton years ago when it had burned to the ground. As Ruby said, all Metaxas did was good things for other people.

According to Ruby, Metaxas knew everyone in the world, and

everyone knew who Metaxas Parish was because of his philanthropies. Nealy knew it was all true one day when the phone rang and the call was for Metaxas from the president of the United States asking him for help in some third world country.

Metaxas had scoured the world to get Ruby the best of the best when she was diagnosed with cancer. It made no difference to him that she'd had both breasts removed. He just held her and cried and cried because he loved her so much.

The new foal was for Metaxas, a birthday present to the man who had everything in the world.

Nealy looked at Ruby. She was so alive, so healthy. Her hair had grown in curly red and was about two inches long. She looked like a middle-aged cherub with twinkling green eyes.

Nealy rolled her eyes. Ruby, one of the richest women in the world, mucked the stalls, brushed the horses, and pitched hay. And she loved every minute of it.

Nealy yawned. "I hope we're both awake to see his reaction," she said as she struggled to her feet. Every muscle in her body ached with the exertions of the last two days. She was getting too old to wrestle an eleven-hundred-pound mare to lie down or hold still. Even though she was still in good physical condition, it was too much. Still, it was the bed she'd chosen to lie in so to speak, so lie in it she would, straw and all, for as long as she could.

Nealy raised her arm toward the light so she could read her watch. "When I get my hands on my two kids, I am going to strangle them," she said, stretching her aching back. "They know the first rule of this farm is someone is always here. I let them convince me that a week's vacation for everyone wasn't going to make the world come to an end. Yes, we have good help, yes, we left everything in capable hands, but there are always the what-ifs. What if I had decided to stay an extra few days with Ken? It's a damn good thing I didn't. I had this really weird feeling I should come home early. Don't ask me why because I can't explain it. Am I the only responsible family member around here? If I hadn't come back when I did, God only knows what would have happened. I'm so angry I could chew nails and spit rust. Not even a phone call from either of them. Two weeks, Ruby. They each took an extra week and didn't say boo to me. No calls, no nothing. It's unconscionable."

"I'm sure there's a good reason," Ruby said wearily. "Why don't you go up to the house and take a shower. I'll call you if anything goes wrong. Will you trust me with the colt, Nealy?"

"Of course I trust you. I would trust you with my life for God's sake." Nealy picked up her Stetson out of the straw and hit it against her leg to shake off the straw cleaving to the soft felt. Ruby was right. A shower was just what she needed. A long, hot, wonderful shower. She'd always thought she did some of her best thinking in the shower, and right now there were some hard decisions she had to make.

"The vet will be back in about an hour. Just talk to them, Ruby. Try not to fall asleep till I get back, then I'll spell you. This is the most crucial time for this little guy. God, we almost lost this beautiful baby." She straightened her hat. "Look at him, curious as all get-out. Okay, I'm outta here for some clean clothes and fresh coffee."

A voice boomed from the far end of the barn. "Ma! We're home!"

Nealy froze. *Not now,* she thought. *Not now. I need to think things through a little more to know what I need to do.*

Ruby dashed out into the breezeway and caught Nealy just as she was leaving Misty Blue's stall. "Ask questions before you say anything," she said, wiggling her finger in warning. "You might be surprised at the answers. That means take it easy, Nealy."

Nealy took a deep breath, exhaling it in an angry *swoosh.* She jammed her hands into her pockets so they would stop shaking.

"Ma . . ." His eyes took in the blood on Nealy's shirt. "What happened? Oh my God, the colt came early. Jeez, Ma, I'm sorry I wasn't here." He was tall, his lanky form casting a shadow in the breezeway, Willow at his side. Nealy saw him squeeze Willow's hand and knew he realized he was in deep trouble. *Good,* she thought. His eyes took on a wary look as he shuffled his feet on the concrete.

"It's pretty obvious, isn't it, Nick? The colt came early, and we damn near lost him." She paused to let her words sink in before asking, "Where the hell have you been? You were supposed to be here a week ago. Wipe that sappy look off your face. This is a working farm in case you didn't know that. You have responsibilities like the rest of us. I let you talk me into a week, Nick. A week is seven days, not fourteen days. You knew the deal. The workers who spelled us got their time off the day after New Year's. That left us shorthanded. Did you know and do you care? Bradley broke a leg on New Year's Eve. Donald is in the hospital undergoing an emergency gallbladder operation, and we have six men out with the flu as of yesterday. Everyone has been pulling double shifts, and they're tired. We all did your work while you frolicked in the snow and your sister is on some luxury ocean liner God only knows where. If it wasn't for me and Ruby, this colt would be dead. Neither one of us has had any sleep for two days, and for days before that an hour here or there when we were able to snatch one. Why didn't you call me? This would be a very good time to offer up an explanation, Nick."

"I thought Emmie . . ."

"You thought Emmie would cover for you, I know. And she might have if she wasn't off sunning herself on God only knows what ocean." Her son's look of surprise told her he thought Emmie was at the farm. It was no excuse.

Ruby reached out to touch Nealy's shaking shoulder. Nealy shrugged it off as she stalked toward her son. Willow, the household cook and Nick's skiing companion, cowered behind him as Nealy jabbed a finger into her son's chest, forcing him backward. Flyby snorted his displeasure. Ruby cringed against the stall. "Is there a reason why you didn't call, Nick?" She sounded angry even to her own ears. Angry, hurt, and disappointed. He wasn't the young man she thought he was. Maybe someday he would be, but not now.

"I got married, Ma. Willow and I went to Vegas and tied the knot after our ski trip. That's why I'm late."

"You *what*?"

"We got married," Nick said, his eyes wary at the expression on his mother's face. Willow still cowered behind him.

Nealy closed her eyes to let his words sink in. If she'd been angry, hurt, and disappointed before, she was doubly so now.

Stung to the quick by her son's words, she retaliated. "Pack your bags and get out. Now!"

Nick's gaze ricocheted first to Willow and then to his mother. "Ma! What the hell? Ruby, do something? Say something."

"You heard me. What part of 'pack your bags and get out' don't you understand?" Her voice belied her inner turmoil. The only thing that could save her from breaking down was to walk away.

"You're fired, Willow," Nealy shot over her shoulder as she stalked out of the barn.

"Ruby . . ."

Ruby stared helplessly at the young man and his frightened bride. She shook her head as she tried to soothe Flyby, who was pawing the gate to his stall. She was only a few feet from his stall when he kicked the stall door so hard that splinters of wood flew in every direction. A second kick sent the door flying off its hinges. The big horse charged out into the breezeway, ears back, nostrils flaring.

Ruby screamed when she saw him heading for Nick. She'd learned enough about horses since coming here to Blue Diamond Farms to know that stallions could be extremely dangerous.

"Flyby!" Nick shouted in an attempt to control the horse, but Flyby wasn't listening. Snorting and tossing his head, the stallion pushed Nick into the tack room opposite his stall, pushed him so hard that Nick lost his balance and fell.

Willow screamed.

Ruby gasped.

Satisfied that he'd had his say, Flyby whinnied before he ran after Nealy.

"Son of a bitch!" Nick groaned as he struggled to pick himself up off the floor. "I think that damn horse broke my ribs."

"Then you better see a doctor," Ruby said, not unkindly. "The vet is due any minute. He can look you over and maybe strap up your chest."

"Ruby . . ."

"No, Nick, I can't intervene. Nealy told me the first time I met her that this farm, these horses, take precedence over everything. Maud and Jess instilled that creed in her, and she abides by it.

Otherwise, it doesn't work. She was always so proud of the way you and Emmie adapted to it. Your mother was right, there are telephones. If I were you, I'd do what she says until she cools down."

Nick's eyes almost popped from their sockets. "Are you saying I should leave here? This is my home. Where am I supposed to go?"

"It *was* your home," Ruby said quietly.

"I . . . I . . . have a contract," Willow whispered.

Ruby guffawed as she offered up a withering look. "I would imagine, knowing Nealy, that when you go up to the house, there will be a check waiting and your pots and pans will be on the porch. I don't think this is a good time to try to negotiate. What were you thinking, Nick? You don't get married and *not* tell your mother."

"I guess I . . . come on, Willow, let's get your stuff and get out of here. Thanks for nothing, Ruby."

"Just a damn minute, Nick. You're the one at fault here, not me. Don't take your anger out on me. Like everyone else on this farm, I covered for you and Emmie. In case you haven't noticed, your mother and I both look like death warmed over, as does every other person working here. I haven't had any sleep either. Your mother and I did what the four of us should have done because that's what you do when a crisis arises. Look to yourself before you start blaming others."

"Bullshit!" Nick snapped.

"Wrong animal," Ruby snapped in return. She brought her hand up to shield her eyes from the bright morning sun invading the breezeway to see Nealy trying to soothe Flyby as he gently pushed her toward the back porch steps that would allow her the height to heft herself onto his back. Ruby could only imagine what she was saying to her prize stallion.

She continued to watch as a Dodge Durango, Emmie and Buddy's 4-by-4, skidded to a stop in the courtyard next to the back porch. She continued to watch as Nick wrapped his arms around his middle and hobbled over to Emmie's SUV, Willow close behind. And then all hell broke loose. Flyby reared up as Nealy grabbed his mane to secure her seat on his back. Ruby could hear angry sounds but couldn't distinguish the words.

"I hope your excuse is a lot better than your brother's, Emmie. You're a week late. Misty Blue birthed early." Nealy took a deep, sobering breath so she could say what she needed to say. "Make it good, girl, because you aren't going to get up to bat again. I can't believe how irresponsible the two of you are. I'm waiting, Emmie."

"Buddy left me. He went back to Ohio. He left me stranded at the ship. Stranded, Mom."

Nealy clenched her teeth. "I gave you a week because you and your brother convinced me it would be okay. One week, not two. There are telephones. If you think so little of this farm and me, so be it. We have rules here, and you and your brother know what they are. You both broke those rules. If your husband left you, it is something you have to deal with. I have a farm to run here."

"Mom, didn't you hear what I just said? Buddy left me. He said I'm normal, and he can't handle it."

Nealy clenched and unclenched her teeth again, "When did this happen, Emmie?"

"Last week. I didn't know what to do."

Nealy nodded. Any other time she would have opened her arms to her daughter and offered comfort. Maybe that was part of the problem. Maybe she'd been too available through the years, offered a little too much comfort. "Last week, and you're just now getting around to coming here," she forced herself to say, knowing where the question would lead, wishing there was another way. "Doesn't your telephone work?"

"I . . . I spent the whole week crying. I didn't see this coming, Mom."

Nealy patted Flyby's neck to calm him. "I'll leave it up to your brother and his new wife to explain things to you," she said. "Your services are no longer required, Emmie. That means you're fired and off the payroll. If I can't depend on you, what good are you to me? Now, you have something to cry about." Her heels nudged the stallion gently as she headed back toward the foaling barn and Ruby.

"Mom . . ." Emmie wailed after her.

Nick put his arm around his sister's shoulder. "Save your breath, Emmie, and go home. She just booted my ass out of here, too. We broke the cardinal rule. Now we have to stand up and take our punishment like the big boys and girls we're supposed to be. Do you mind if Willow and I bunk with you until I can find someplace for us to live?"

Emmie nodded, her face miserable. "I have to get her to listen to me," she said, starting after her mother.

Nick pulled her back. "Don't even *think* about it. Jesus! She sure can work fast when she wants to," he said, referring to Smitty standing on the back porch with two white envelopes in her hands. Within minutes Willow's pots and pans appeared in cardboard cartons as if by magic, thanks to the efficiency of his mother's longtime office manager. "I'll drive, Emmie, but first I have to pack Willow's stuff in the cargo hold."

"What's wrong with her, Smitty?" Emmie sobbed.

Nick stopped long enough to hear the office manager's reply. "You both broke the rules. As far as I can see there is absolutely no excuse for your behavior. You're old enough to know better. There *are* telephones. If I were you, I wouldn't drag my feet," Smitty said coldly, before she turned to enter the house.

"I don't understand," Willow said.

"With my mother there are no second chances when it comes to the horses. She gave us an inch and we took a yard. In plain English, we fucked up. She won't bend either. Let's get out of here. Stop bawling, Emmie. Life is going to go on whether Buddy left you or not."

"But not without Mom. I'm not going until I talk to her."

"It's too late for talking. You should have called. I should have called. We didn't. She bent enough to give us a week. The horses always have to come first."

"Just like that, we're walking away?" Emmie asked.

"Unless you want to crawl. It's your call. Get in the truck, Emmie. We'll talk when we get to your house."

Emmie climbed into the truck and buckled her seat belt. She turned to look out the back window to see her mother and Ruby staring at the truck.

* * *

Nealy watched her children drive away, a lump in her throat. Did she do the right thing? Only time would tell, she thought. Time had a way of dealing with everything.

"Nealy, are you sure you didn't overreact?" Ruby said, putting her arm around Nealy's shoulders.

"To your way of thinking, I suppose I did. The farm runs as well as it does because of the rules. When Maud and Jess were alive, my ass would have been on the road in seconds if I had done what those two did. I accepted those rules going in, and I made damn sure I never broke them. Emmie and Nick learned that same rule from the minute they were able to walk and talk. I gave us all a week. I realize now I shouldn't even have done that."

"Is your heart breaking, Nealy?"

"No," Nealy lied. "I'm going up for that shower now. I won't be long."

"What will they do?"

Nealy stopped and stared down at the ground. "I have no idea. Don't ask me that again, Ruby."

"Okay. Don't forget the coffee when you come back."

"I'll remember."

In the kitchen, Nealy headed to Smitty, who held out her arms. She stepped into them as the tears started to flow. "Don't say it, okay, Smitty?"

"You did what you had to do, Nealy. Now you have to live with it. I know what you're thinking and how hard it was for you to do. This isn't like when you lit out with Emmie at the age of seventeen. There was no love back there. You moved from darkness to sunshine. Don't start comparing. It's over, it's done with, and you don't look back. If you look back, Nealy, it's all over."

"It hurts, Smitty. I feel like those two ripped my heart out. Nick got married. He got married, Smitty, and he didn't even think enough of me to invite me to his wedding or to even call to tell me. I had no clue that he was even serious about Willow. Flirting is one thing, marrying her is something else entirely. And yes, I fired her. I had to. I sent my son packing, so how could I keep his wife around to cook for me? As for Emmie, we've always been so very close, and yet the one time when I could have consoled her, been with her, what does she do? She hangs me out to dry and stays home crying. I don't understand that either. I don't understand, Smitty, why she didn't come to me this time. At Thanksgiving they were talking about having a baby, they went on this second honeymoon cruise, and then he dumps her and leaves her stranded when they got off the ship. What's wrong with this picture, Smitty? Don't answer that. I probably couldn't handle it right now. I'd appreciate it if you would make some fresh coffee, and if you have time, call an agency and see about getting us a new cook. An all-around housekeeper might be better."

In the shower, with the water beating down on her weary body, Nealy cried, her tears mingling with the water cascading all about her. She'd broken one of Jess's rules, one of the rules he said it was okay to break from time to time: never let them see you sweat. She'd let Smitty and Ruby see her bruised heart, let them see her tears. *Well, that was then and this is now.* She stepped from the shower, towel dried her hair, dressed in clean clothes and was back in the kitchen just as the percolator made its last plopping sound. She filled a thermos for Ruby and one for herself. She was back in the barn in less than fifteen minutes.

"You okay, Nealy?" Ruby asked as she reached for her thermos.

"No. But I will be." The door to Flyby's stall lay at her feet. "He really did a number on that stall, didn't he?"

"Yes, he did. He didn't like your tone of voice, didn't like what was going on. And they say these guys are stupid lumps. Not this guy. You should have seen what he did, Nealy. He burst out of his stall and pushed Nick into the tack room. It was almost funny the way he did it, like he was trying to make your point for you. Nick said he hurt him, but I think he just scared the hell out of him. I know it scared the hell out of me, and he wasn't even after me. I put him in a new stall. He's fine, so don't worry."

"I know you might find this hard to believe, but that horse understands everything that goes on where I'm concerned. His daddy, Stardancer, was the same way." Nealy opened Misty Blue's stall door and smiled when she saw that the colt was nursing. "So, what do you think of our little Shufly?" she asked, shifting mental gears.

"Nealy, he is so gorgeous, he takes my breath away. He's just what Metaxas needs. I don't know how I can ever thank you for him. And for allowing me to be a part of all this. In my life, I've never been happier. I'm sorry about the kids. Things will get better."

Nealy waved her hand in dismissal. "Look, it's your turn to hit the shower. Take all the time you need. If you can, try to get a couple of hours' sleep. Be sure you take your medicine while you're up at the house." Nealy tried for a light tone, but she could hardly bear to think about Ruby's cancer. "I'm okay, Ruby," she went on. "Over the years, I've learned how to sleep with one eye open. I mean it, I'm okay. I have to see about getting this gate fixed before Himself decides to pitch another fit."

"Okay, Nealy. Things will work out. I want to say just one thing before I go up to the house. I want you to listen to me, Nealy, and we will never talk about this again. It isn't all that hard to say those two little words, I'm sorry. But, only if you are sorry in your heart. If you don't mean the words, don't say them. You are a mother. A mother is supposed to love and love and love. A mother will stand by her child even if he or she is an ax murderer. Never having been a mother, I can't know what you are feeling. To have a child must be the most wonderful thing in the world. I don't want to see you throw away the relationship you have with Nick and Emmie."

"I didn't throw it away, Ruby. They did. Maud and Jess used to say, for every action there is a reaction and you go on from there. Let's not talk about this anymore."

"You got it. See you later."

"Yes, later," Nealy said, leaning over the door of Misty Blue's stall to watch the colt suckle from its mother.

She wished she could cry. When had she become so hard, and yes, bitter? Hunt always said she had a black heart, and it always bothered her. She didn't have a black heart. Maybe it was hard and cold, but it wasn't black. She dropped her head between her knees and willed herself to tears. Her eyes remained dry. Everything always came at a price. Now she was going to lose the two people she loved most in the whole world.

Nick was just a boy, and now he was married. She struggled to remember how much older than Nick Willow was, but she couldn't remember. In the end, it didn't matter. *Her age isn't going to change the fact that she married my son. And he didn't think enough of me to call and share his news. Or wait to have a wedding here at the farm.* It hurt that he thought so little of her not to want to share one of the happiest days of his life.

Hot tears pricked her eyelids. Was there another way to handle things? If there was, she didn't know what it was. How could she? She knuckled her eyes. Maybe she should have been more caring, more gentle, more . . . *something.* The plain simple truth was, she didn't know how to be that way. An inner voice demanded an answer. *Then how can you be so caring and gentle with the horses and not your own flesh and blood?* "I don't know," she wailed. "I don't know."

Nealy lifted her head and stared ahead of her. Her adopted mother Maud's words rang in her ears loud and clear. "No matter what, the horses always have to come first." Jess had echoed those same words. Even hateful Josh Coleman had said the same thing. She'd lived by those words all her life because she'd been so grateful to Maud and Jess for taking her and Emmie into their lives and giving her a good life and then adopting her. In death they had provided for her by leaving Blue Diamond Farms to her and Emmie. To this day she felt she had to prove herself worthy of their love and unselfishness by making Blue Diamond Farms the best horse farm in the state of Kentucky. She'd done that, too. But the price had come high.

She thought about Emmie and how much she loved her. Back then in the early days, everything was for Emmie. Everything. Emmie was hers, her flesh and blood, and it was up to her to provide for her. She'd done that the only way she knew how. By working from four in the morning till eight at night. To prove to Maud and Jess that she was as good as any man. And to thank them, and to pay for their keep.

And now this. The one time when Emmie really needed her

mother, she'd gone it alone. "I would have found the right words to say to her. Maybe they wouldn't have been pretty or flowery, but they would have come from my heart. My arms would have circled her. Together we could have cried. Like Nick, she didn't want me. Didn't trust me to do the right thing. I would have. I know I would have. You just didn't give me the chance."

Hot, scalding tears rolled down her cheeks. "I love you both so much." She cried into the flannel sleeve of her shirt. "So very, very much."

"Make yourself at home, Nick. You've been here often enough to know where everything is. You, too, Willow. Take any room you want on the second floor. Before you can say it, Nick, Buddy must have had someone come in and move all his things out while we were on the cruise. It doesn't look like he ever lived here. I was so shocked, I just caved in. I wish you could have seen me. I was like a maniac going through everything for some little scrap of something that was left behind. There was nothing, not even an empty shaving-cream can. Not even a stray sock. I just don't understand how he could do this to me."

"Do you want me to go to Ohio and kill him?" Nick asked. He grimaced when Willow jerked her head sideways to indicate he should go upstairs while she talked to Emmie.

"He planned it very thoroughly," Emmie said, flopping down on the couch. "He let me talk and plan for a baby, he arranged the cruise, said it would be like a second honeymoon and then wham bam, he dumps me on the gangplank when the ship docked. He said he doesn't want anything. The house is mine, our joint bank account, everything. He just wanted out."

"I'm so sorry, Emmie. I wish there was something I could do for you. I need to ask, why did you wait so long to go to the farm and tell your mother?"

"I was too ashamed, Willow. Do you know what I did? Right there on the gangplank with people watching us, I begged him, I held on to his arm and tried to hang on to him. He shook me off like he would shake off a stray dog. And if that wasn't bad enough, I told him I would stop talking and go back to signing if he'd stay.

He laughed in my face. I was too ashamed to tell that to my mother. I just holed up here and cried all week. I didn't think about Mom, the farm, or the horses. All I thought about was Buddy. I turned on the computer and watched it until I thought my eyeballs would explode out of my head. I was so sure he would e-mail me and tell me . . . something . . . anything. Like maybe he was temporarily insane. Today, I finally realized it wasn't going to happen. How could I have been so stupid? How, Willow?"

"You loved him. Love doesn't come with an intelligence quotient."

"I feel terrible that you and Nick came home to such a mess. You just got married, and already there are problems. My brother is a great guy, but then I guess you already knew that or you wouldn't have married him. Mom won't bend. Things are either black or white with her. There are no gray areas anywhere in her life."

"I can't believe that, Emmie. Mothers are very forgiving. They love their children unconditionally. I'm sure you and Nick will be able to work things out with her once she calms down."

Emmie laughed, a bitter sound to Willow's ears. "Maybe other mothers are like that, but ours isn't. We learned early on, almost as soon as we could walk, that the horses always came first. We were raised that way. I'm not saying it's wrong, it's the way it is, and we knew that, accepted it. Mom is very loving, very generous and kind with us. As soon as we hit our teens she told us we could take care of ourselves. She stopped that motherly hovering thing all mothers do. I don't know how Nick is going to handle this. All he knows are the horses, and yet I can't see him signing on with another farm. I'm glad he has you, Willow. I'm glad you're both here. I'm a terrible hostess. Would you like some coffee? Yes, coffee's good. I'll make some. Why don't you go upstairs and freshen up. I'll call you when the coffee is ready."

"That sounds like a splendid idea. Emmie?"

"Yes."

"Would you really have stopped talking if Buddy agreed to stay with you?"

"I guess I meant it when I said it. I know that doesn't say much for me, now does it? He dumped me because I'm normal now. He hated it when people talked to me and I responded. He wanted me to keep signing. I got so used to talking I would forget to sign. Then he would grab my arm and swing me around and make me sign. I guess that should have been my first clue. I don't know what to do without him. All I do is walk around in circles."

"This is a pretty kitchen," Willow said, changing the subject.

"Mom helped me decorate it. The breakfast nook gets the full morning sun. I like to curl up in the wing chair in my pajamas on Sunday morning and read the paper and drink a whole pot of coffee. Nick and I used to alternate Sundays. I always looked forward to that time. It was special. I guess I can do that every day now for the rest of my life. Do you want to hear something strange, Willow? When my stepfather, Nick's dad, died, Mom never once cried. He was dead, and she didn't cry. Buddy leaves me, and I fall apart and can't stop crying. Can you explain that to me?"

"No, Emmie, I can't. Each of us grieves in our own way." She gave Emmie a hug. "I'm going to go upstairs and freshen up. I'll be down soon. Are you sure you're okay?"

Emmie nodded as she measured coffee into the silver basket.

Satisfied that the coffee was perking, Emmie curled up in the wing chair in the breakfast nook. Maybe she should have told Willow and Nick the rest of her sorry tale. To what end? Some things were just better left alone. She looked out the window to watch her two favorite squirrels, Lizzie and Dizzy, scamper across the deck railing to the huge bowl of pecans she kept on the picnic table on the deck. She'd tamed them to a degree. Oftentimes when she sat out on the deck with a book they'd come right up to her chair and beg for the nuts. They always scampered away and watched from a distance when Buddy would join her. She wondered why that was. Did they sense something in him that wasn't right? Were squirrels like dogs, good judges of character? Did it matter? Right now, nothing mattered, not the loss of Buddy or her mother's ugly decision to banish her.

Lizzie and Dizzy scurried across the railing, hopped onto the back of one of the deck chairs, and then onto the windowsill outside the breakfast nook. Their eyes shiny bright, their bushy tails swinging from side to side, they watched the sleeping girl who fed them every day and changed their daily water bowl on the steps of the deck. They chattered to one another as their little paws tapped on the glass for recognition. When none was forthcoming, they scampered away.

Upstairs, Nick perched on the edge of the bed, his head between his hands. He wanted to bawl, to kick and scream the way he'd done when he was a little boy. Always be responsible for your own actions. Words his father had taught him early on. Words he'd always heeded. Until now. How could he make this all come out right? He couldn't.

His mother had looked so tired, so weary. Ruby, too. Ruby had undergone chemotherapy and radiation treatments for a whole year. On the road to recovery, she still had to take her meds, still had to get plenty of rest, and he'd failed her, too. He should have called. Why hadn't he? Because he didn't want to hear a lecture, didn't want to hear his mother say he was too young to marry someone he barely knew. He knew what he felt, knew what Willow felt, and that was enough for him. If only Misty Blue hadn't foaled early. If only Buddy hadn't left Emmie. If only, if only, if only. One week, one miserable goddamn week, and his whole life changed in a matter of minutes. Did it matter that he'd never, ever, taken a vacation? Did it matter that up until now he'd given his life to Blue Diamond Farms and the horses? What mattered was the week he'd taken for himself to get married. No matter what, he should have called. Somewhere far back in his mind he'd had the thought that when he and Willow returned there would be a second marriage like both his mother and Maud had, with a reception for the farm workers. A tradition of sorts.

From the time he'd been able to understand, he'd heard stories about how wonderful Maud and Jess were, how they'd been together all their lives and only married when they were older because Maud wanted the piece of paper that said she belonged to someone. His mother had said theirs was a real lifelong love affair.

As a youngster, he'd thought his parents were happy. But only at the end of the day when all the farm work was done. They'd had so little time to spend with one another and with their children. Maybe the marriage hadn't been so wonderful after all. Maybe he was wearing rose-colored glasses. Maybe he didn't want a marriage like theirs after all. Maybe that was why he'd done things the way he had. Maybe a lot of things.

One stinking, lousy phone call, and he wouldn't be sitting here ready to bawl his head off.

Bottom line . . . he should have called.

"We'll work this out, Nick," Willow said, sitting down next to him on the bed. "I'm going to send the check back. Maybe I should take it back and try to talk to your mother. She used to like me. Maybe we can talk, woman to woman. It's worth a try, Nick. I hate seeing you so miserable."

"I'm not just miserable. I'm fucking miserable, and it's my own fault. I'm in shock. I knew I should have called. Some small part of me wanted to, but the larger part of me said no, she'll demand I come home. Our trip was special in so many ways, my first-ever vacation, making love to you, getting married. I wanted to keep it close for as long as I could. I didn't want to share it with anyone but you. This is the result."

"You aren't selfish, honey. And you can't take all the blame. I should have insisted you call your mother. I know your mom. I should have known how she'd react." She cradled him against her. "First thing tomorrow, I'll take the check back and then drive into town and look for a job. There's that new hotel. They were advertising for a chef. We won't starve, Nick."

Nick flopped backward onto the bed and laughed bitterly. "Money is the least of my problems, Willow. I'm fixed financially for the rest of my life. Emmie is, too. Hell, between us we could buy and operate our own farm. Maybe that's what we'll do if Emmie is agreeable. I want your promise that you won't go to my mother. If you want to send the check back, that's okay, and it is your decision. Just so you know, my mother never backs down. Never."

"She's not like that, Nick. I used to talk to her for hours in the kitchen. It's like we're talking about two different people here. The woman I know is nothing like what you're describing."

"Don't delude yourself. I'm her son. I should know. Everyone wears two faces. There's the family side where it all hangs loose and you know someone inside and out, and then there is the public side, where that person lets you see only what they want you to see. You do it, I do it, everyone does it. Sometimes we do it consciously and sometimes we do it unconsciously. How is Emmie?"

"She's hurting, Nick. How do you expect her to feel? She said she didn't see it coming. What kind of man would do something like that? And in public." She told him about Emmie's confession.

"Jesus. I'm just spoiling for a fight. I should get on the next plane to Ohio and beat the crap out of that sorry son of a bitch. I don't care if he is deaf. I don't understand why he would go back to Ohio anyway. His parents did come from there, but as far as I know he only has an uncle left, and he must be pretty old by now. By the way, that uncle couldn't wait to unload Buddy when his parents were killed. He allowed my mother to take him in and Mom raised him. I really should go there and beat the living crap out of him."

"That's not what you're going to do, Nick. This is Emmie's problem and we aren't going to do anything unless she asks us to intervene, which she isn't going to do. Right now we are going to go downstairs and have some coffee and talk about our future. We have to start making plans."

"I don't know if I can leave here, Willow. I have to be around horses. It's my life. It's all I know."

"I didn't say anything about leaving or you not being around horses. I said we need to talk about what we're going to do. That includes Emmie."

"Okay. Listen, I just want to shower and change. I'll be down in a few minutes."

"Take your time. I'll unpack our suitcases and meet you downstairs."

In the bathroom with the door closed and locked, Nick broke down and sobbed, his shoulders shaking uncontrollably. "I'm sorry I let you down, *Dad*."

In the foyer, Willow reached for her jacket. A breath of fresh air might be just what she needed. A walk around the yard might clear her head a little. She was on her second lap when she noticed the mailman trying to jam mail into Emmie's box and having a hard time of it. She jogged forward and held out her hand. The after-

Christmas sale catalogs were heavy. She staggered under their weight and on into the house, where she shrugged out of her jacket. She called out to Emmie as she entered the kitchen. "I brought your mail in. Guess in the excitement of going on the cruise you forgot to notify the post office to hold your mail. Nick thinks you might have some bills that need to be paid. Oh, Emmie, I'm sorry. I didn't know you were asleep."

"I guess I dozed off. It's not a problem. Our coffee is ready. I've been meaning to go out and pick up the mail, but I simply didn't want to make the effort. I guess it did pile up. Two weeks' worth from the looks of things. I'll go through it later."

"No, let's go through it now," Nick said, entering the kitchen. "I don't want to see you get a bad credit rating. You need to pay your bills on time. I would like some coffee, ladies."

"Oh yes, sir, kind sir, it will be my pleasure to serve you some coffee. Would you like me to whip you up a double chocolate cake while I'm at it?" Willow teased.

"Nope. We ate too much rich food on vacation. Coffee will do just fine." Nick sorted through the first-class mail. "You have a certified letter one of your neighbors signed for. Guess they just stuck it back in your box. It came sometime last week. It's from Josh Coleman's lawyer, the one Mom sent packing. You remember, the ornery, dumb one who couldn't get anything right. Do you want me to open it?"

"Be my guest, then chuck it. I don't want anything to do with those people and all those crazy lawyers. All lawyers do is bleed you dry."

"Well, lookee here, Emmie. Don't be so quick to chuck this one. Seems that ornery old buzzard we all thought was on the dumb side is suffering from Alzheimer's. This letter is from his son informing us and apologizing at the same time for the mistakes his father made. Remember the day you signed off on SunStar Farms, Josh Coleman's horse farm in Virginia? You signed it over to Ma's brothers. Right?"

"Yes, my uncles. So what?"

"So what is this? The filings were never made in the timely manner the courts require. They are now null and void, and you have to sign a new set, which is enclosed. Do you want to sign these, Emmie? You don't have to, you know."

"Why wouldn't I want to sign them?"

"Think about it. Ma just booted our asses out of Blue Diamond Farms. You own a farm. We can go there and take it over. Between the two of us we could bring that farm up to snuff."

"What about Uncle Rhy and Uncle Pyne?"

"What about them?"

"If we take it over, even though it was willed to me, what will happen to them?"

"I don't know. I suppose they could work with us. I heard Ma say she would make them full partners at Blue Diamond Farms if they wanted to join her. I don't know how anyone in his right mind could turn down an offer like that."

"Isn't SunStar tied up in that legal mess Mom is dealing with?"

"I don't know, Emmie. Mom never said much about it to me. The lawyers are handling it all. Look, it's the answer to our futures. Do you want to stay here and cry yourself to death over Buddy and Mom, or do you want to get on with your life?"

"Don't we need a lawyer? We can't use the one Mom uses because it will be a conflict of interest. The whole thing is so messy I'm not sure I want to get involved. Can we think about it?"

"Hey, I know a lawyer. Dad had these two friends he went to law school with. They still call me on a regular basis. The one named Hatch is an Indian and bigger than life. According to Dad, his billable hours are through the roof. Dad loved that big guy. If he hadn't married Mom, he would have joined the firm. Another friend of Dad's is Bode Jessup. Dad said if I ever needed a good lawyer, to call Hatch. According to Dad he's the best of the best. His first name is Shunpus. Guess it's an Indian name. He's our man. Dad used to talk about those guys all the time. Sometimes I think he thought he made a mistake by not going into the firm with them. What do you think, Emmie?"

"Mom . . ."

"Emmie, for God's sake, we aren't doing anything illegal.

SunStar was left to you. It's yours. Where is it written you have to give it to Rhy and Pyne? Mom told you to sign off on it, and you did. Did you even think about it when she told you to do it? No, you just signed the documents because she told you to sign them. Did you ever think about what you did and the why of it?"

"A few times," Emmie mumbled. "Buddy said I was stupid for doing it. He called Mom a dictator sometimes. Let's think about it before we make a decision. I don't see anything wrong with getting in touch with your father's friend. See what he thinks. If he thinks it's the right thing to do, we'll do it. You know, of course, that Mom will have a fit."

"That's a given. Guess we'll have to live with that, too. If you two fine young women think you can manage without me, I'd like to fly out to Santa Fe and talk to Hatch in person. I'm not comfortable discussing something like this on the phone. I could fly out early tomorrow, stay overnight, and be back the following morning. You okay with that?"

Willow nodded. "Okay, Nick."

"Then it's a go. I'll go upstairs, pack, and make a reservation. An early dinner would be good or I could take you ladies out to eat. Decide and tell me the verdict when I come back down."

"Okay, honey. We want to go out."

"That was quick."

"You know us women. We can make snap decisions. Right, Emmie?"

"You bet." Emmie smiled.

"I think I'm going to change my clothes if we're going out to dinner. Do you need me to do anything?"

"No. Go up with Nick and change. I need to sit here and do some thinking."

Nick was right, Emmie thought. She'd blindly signed off on SunStar Farms when her grandfather died because her mother told her to do it. It never occurred to her to question her mother's orders. It was all done to make sure her brothers always had a place to live. "You don't need that farm, Emmie," was what she'd said. "There are too many bad memories attached to SunStar Farms.

Besides, you can't uproot your uncles from the only home they've ever known." So, she'd signed off on it because she was a good, dutiful daughter and always did what she was told.

Now, according to Nick, the legal papers she'd signed were null and void. She still owned the farm. If she wanted to, she could take possession of it like Nick said. If she wanted to.

2

Nick looked around the busy airport for some sign of Hatch Littletree. A grin as wide as all outdoors stretched across his face the moment he spotted the big man. They exchanged grins as Hatch lumbered toward him, opened his arms, and gave him a body-crunching, manly hug.

His father had told him Shunpus Littletree, nicknamed Hatch, because of an extraordinary feat back in college, was as big as a grizzly bear but as gentle as a pussycat. According to his father, Hatch was a full-blooded Indian who worshiped success and fine things. He was also generous to a fault, with one of the biggest, most lucrative law practices in the West. The last time Nick had seen the big man was at his father's funeral. He'd watched in awe when the gentle giant wept as his father's casket was lowered into the ground.

Hatch had called a lot those first months, just to talk, to reminisce. The calls tapered off later on, to be followed with e-mails and short, handwritten notes. To this day they continued.

"You look so much like your dad you're spooking me, boy. You have any luggage?" The big man boomed so loud people turned around to see where the sound was coming from. "How's your mother?"

"She's fine, Hatch. She's part of the reason I'm here. Dad always said if he was in trouble, you were the first person he would go to. He told me to remember your name and to call you if I ever needed a smart attorney."

"Hunt was right. I'm the best. I don't believe in being modest. I'm so damn good at what I do I can hardly believe it myself sometimes. Your dad hated the law, but he would have made a damn fine attorney. I couldn't believe it when he said he wanted to stay on the farm and work with horses. I don't know if you know this or not, but during the last year of his life, he came out here and we hung out together for five straight days. He asked me if the job offer was still good, and I said yes. He said he had some things to work out first, and he'd let me know. He never did. I knew even then something was wrong, but I also knew better than to stick my nose where it didn't belong. I wish I had. That hindsight thing, you know. So, Nick, how's it going down on the farm?"

Nick increased the length of his stride to keep up. "It isn't. I got married last week in Vegas. That's part of my problem. My mother ... can we talk about all that later? Tell me about my dad. How'd you all get to be such good friends? What was he like when he was my age? I know you and Dad were really close. I envy you that."

Hatch's expression turned thoughtful. "We were all full of piss and vinegar back then. We were so high on life we thought we could fly. There wasn't one ounce of fear in any of us. By us I mean Bode Jessup, your dad, me, and Hank Mitchum. We were supposed to be a four-man law office, but your dad bugged out. We kept an office for him just in case he ever changed his mind. None of us could bear to take on another partner, so his offices are still the way they were the day we started out. The door, our letterhead, our corporation papers still read, Littletree, Jessup, Clay, and Mitchum. When you were born, Nick, we set up a trust for you. Hunt didn't want us to do it, but hell, we did it anyway. You're old enough now so that you can start hitting it anytime you want. You do know about it, don't you?"

"No. Dad never said anything. Did Mom know? I guess my next question should be, why?"

"Because it was the right thing to do. As to your mother, I don't know, Nick. Probably not would be my guess. All the statements come to our office. I'd call Hunt after the first of the year and give him a rundown. I think he was embarrassed about it all and felt like he let me down by not joining the firm. Hell, Nick, life is to be lived, and I live every single minute of every day. I'm good to myself and to those I love. Hell, I'm even good to those I don't love.

Life is just too damn short to be unhappy. Hop in, kid. You hungry?"

A plane passed overhead. Nick looked up to see the landing gear drop. He would have loved to learn to fly, but he'd never gotten around to taking flying lessons. He'd never gotten around to a lot of things he would like to do. His life had been horses and only horses.

"No, not really. I'd like to see the office where . . . you know. Did you know about my dad's affairs, Hatch?"

"Yeah. He told me about them. It was like he needed a kind of absolution, and by telling me it made it all right. It didn't, but that's okay, too. One of my main rules in life is never to judge another."

Nick settled back in the comfortable seat of the Range Rover. "Nice country." He found himself eager to see Santa Fe. He'd heard it was a quaint little town, catering to tourists looking for high-end jewelry, Western clothing, art, and furniture.

"Yeah, it is. How's the horse business?" Hatch cackled.

"Pretty much as usual. Misty Blue dropped her foal night before last. I didn't get a chance to see it but . . ." He sighed.

Hatch slapped at his forehead. "That reminds me, I don't think I ever told you, the partners, myself included, put down half a mil on Flyby at the Derby. With those crazy odds and your father's hype, how could we go wrong? We did the same thing with the Preakness and the Belmont. We used the money to start your trust fund, kid. When your mother ran the Belmont the second time, we put down a cool mil and donated it to charity in your father's name. We divvied it up among animal shelters where they don't put the animals to sleep, battered women's shelters, and children's charities."

Nick's jaw dropped. "Why?" he asked, awestruck. "Why didn't you keep it, have some fun with it? At least a part of it."

Hatch bellowed with laughter. "We did have fun with it." He glanced over at Nick. "What good is having money if you can't do good with it? When we were in school none of us had a pot to piss in, and I mean that literally. One whole semester we lived on macaroni and cheese and mustard and ketchup sandwiches. The rich kids used to thumb their noses at our circumstances, but they damn well couldn't thumb their noses at our brains. When you get, you gotta give back. The firm gives away more than it keeps. We do a lot of *pro bono,* too. I think that's why we were put on this earth."

Nick screwed up his face and shook his head. "My dad said you were a crazy son of a bitch. He meant it as a compliment."

Hatch laughed, the car literally rocking beneath his solid body. "You look real miserable, kid. You wanna talk about it now?"

Nick shook his head as he stared off into the distance, the hot, dry wind ruffling his dark hair. He focused on the scenery. He'd been born and raised in Kentucky. He hadn't done much traveling, so the flora and fauna of New Mexico were completely foreign to him. The architecture, too. A lot of earth colors and red-tile roofs, nothing like Kentucky.

They drove in companionable silence for several miles. Nick's thoughts turned to his problem—his mother. He'd been thoughtless and irresponsible by not returning home on time. And he'd made it worse by getting married and telling her after the fact. But did his actions justify such a harsh punishment?

"I need to talk to someone, Hatch."

"I'm as good as the next person. I shoot straight from the hip, Nick. Spit it out."

Nick sucked in his breath and then let it out in a long sigh. "It's like this. I took a vacation, my first ever . . ."

Twenty minutes later, Hatch swerved into the parking lot and screeched to a stop. "Great timing," he grunted as he got out of the truck. "Let's go inside where it's cool and have a nice cold beer. I'll show you around, let you see the suite of offices that were meant for your dad. When we started out we were in a two-room shack. This fine edifice," he said, pointing to a large adobe-brick-and-glass building that was exquisitely landscaped, "is the result of a lot of hard work, brainpower, and believing in ourselves. Believe it or not, I do some of my best thinking while I'm talking. It's an old Indian thing," he said by way of explanation. "That's some heavy-duty shit you just laid on me, kid. Come, I want you to meet Medusa. She runs this place."

Nick wasn't sure what to make of Hatch. He hadn't said a word the whole time he'd been telling him his sorry story and hadn't said anything afterward either. It was as if he hadn't heard a thing he'd said. Maybe his father was wrong, and Hatch wasn't the right person to help him after all.

"Dad told me about her. He said she was like Bode Jessup's Mama Pearl. Once, when I was about eight and I was pestering him to tell me how many stars there were in the sky, he told me about Medusa and Mama Pearl. He said if he could have just one wish, it would be to have someone like that in his life. Grandpa, my dad's father, loved him, but he was a hard man. I think Mom loved him, but she's hard, too. He wasn't a happy camper those last few years, but there was nothing anyone could do."

"Yeah, kid, he was unhappy during the last years of his life. We all tried to help, but happiness comes from within. There comes a point where you have to back off and hope for the best. All that other stuff, the outer trappings we think of as happiness, that's just the frosting on the cake.

"Medusa, I'd like you to meet . . ."

"Hunter's son. You look just like your father, young man," Medusa said, holding out a birdlike hand with six silver bracelets on her tiny wrist.

She wasn't just a tiny woman, she was a miniature . . . of what, Nick didn't know. Seventy-nine pounds tops. A tiny little lady with a smile as big as the world. Soft, brown eyes flecked with gold matched the long, thick braid that hung down to her waist. A cluster of tiny, silver bells hung from her ears. They hung around her neck and wrist, too. So, if they tinkled, how come he hadn't heard a sound? He was about to look down to see if she had them on her ankles when she said, "No, I don't wear ankle bracelets."

"You have to stop reading people's minds, Medusa. You're spooking this boy. One of these days you're going to give us Indians a bad name."

"You look just the way your dad said you looked. He said you were prettier than the first foal born in the New Year." Medusa smiled.

"That was a high compliment coming from Dad," Nick said softly.

"I know that, Nicholas, and yes, at times we send up smoke signals. Mostly when I want to get Shunpus's attention. He ignores the telephone, you see."

Jesus, he thought, *she really can read my mind.* Embarrassed, he concentrated on the bells she was wearing. Why didn't they tinkle or give off some kind of sound?

Medusa smiled. "They only tinkle when I want them to tinkle."

"Enough!" Hatch boomed.

"Come with me, young man. I will show you your father's offices. My best friend's son here," she said, pointing to Hatch, "has kept it like a shrine to what might have been. Would you like some coffee or a drink?"

"I'd like a cold beer if it isn't too much trouble."

Hatch's right hand reached out. "Why don't you just give me that folder you have and I'll look at it while you're perusing Hunt's offices," he said.

Nick was awestruck by the lavishness that surrounded him. Everything looked and felt expensive. Hatch's office was decorated in bright, primary colors with Native American art and artifacts covering the walls and furniture tops that carried through to the main lobby and various hallways.

He moved in a trancelike state as he walked from room to room. In his father's office he tried to picture his father behind the ornate mahogany desk, but the image wouldn't appear behind his eyelids.

"Your father wouldn't have been happy here, Nicholas. These are just rooms. I wish Shunpus would let go of the past. For some reason he won't allow himself to do that. Sometimes when he thinks I'm not looking, he comes in here and smokes a cigar and drinks a bottle of beer. I think he talks to your father's spirit. We Indians do that, you know."

Nick turned around. "You seem to know everything, ma'am. Does . . . does my father answer him?"

She smiled. Her smile was her best feature because it was so wide and beautiful and gentle at the same time. "I think Shunpus believes he does. That's the main reason the firm has never taken on a new partner. There are spirits in here, Nicholas. Who they are, I do not know."

"Uh-huh," Nick said uneasily.

"Does the spirit world frighten you, Nicholas?"

Nick whirled around to the sound of tinkling bells. He could feel his heart take on an extra beat. "Are you trying to tell me something?"

Medusa smiled, but she didn't respond to the question. "I will fetch your beer."

The offices were state-of-the-art, complete with the DVD widescreen television, VCR, and a CD system. A bar was snuggled underneath the breakfront that housed the sound system, and it was stocked with every drink imaginable. Hell, he could have popped his own beer. Then again, if this was a shrine, maybe only Hatch was allowed to drink from the bar. For clients there was grape soda, snacks, potato chips, pretzels, and an assortment of See's chocolates and gumdrops, all his father's favorites.

A huge round table held the latest law periodicals and a monstrous bowl of fresh fruit. He found himself grinning when he saw a copy of *People* magazine. Hatch did love Hollywood gossip, his father had said once. A sofa that looked comfortable enough to nap in and two deep, comfortable chairs flanked the round table. Nick tried them out, bouncing on each of them. Comfortable but not so comfortable clients would want to stay beyond a reasonable length of time. At six hundred bucks an hour, why would they even want to sit down? He laughed.

Nick was still laughing when he walked the length and breadth of the new-looking office that still had his father's name on the door. It was, according to the walk off, thirty feet by twenty-five feet. A monster room.

He loved the rich paneling, the perfectly hung drapes, the matching fabric on the furniture that complemented the deep, chocolate carpet. The green plants added a human touch, as did the ornate and colorful fish tank in the corner. Hatch had deliberately put four fish in the tank. A tiny plaque glued to the side said, *Bode, Hunt, Hatch, Hank.* He stared at the fish swimming so gracefully in their tank.

The bookshelves were elegant and matched the burnished paneling. It all smelled so new. So unused. Nick knew that had his father moved into these offices, he would have made a mess of it within minutes. A working mess that only he understood.

Right then, right that very second, Nick wished with all his heart that he had gone to college as his father wanted him to do. "Go to college, son, get your degree, and then you can decide what you want to do." He'd gone on to say there was a world beyond the farm and the horses. A world he needed to explore before he committed to a life of horse breeding.

Nick squeezed his eyes shut as he tried to bring the memory into sharper focus. His father had looked so sad that day. His voice wasn't like his usual voice either. It had been sad, too. He blinked the memory away.

He stared ahead at a door carved into the paneling across the room. He was like a little kid when he stood before it, his hand on the brass knob. Inside was a bathroom so elegantly appointed he found himself sucking in his breath. A glass-enclosed shower, thick, thirsty-looking towels, a toilet raised off the floor. He bent over to peer under it before he gingerly sat down. The vanity basin with its walled mirror would be the envy of any woman. He preened in front of it, running his fingers through his dark curls. He looked down then and saw the yellow wall-to-wall carpeting. Hatch did love yellow according to his father. It had something to do with corn and reservations.

A second door in the bathroom led to a closet that was bigger than his room and bath back at Blue Diamond Farms. Everything was built-in—shoe racks, drawers for everything imaginable. A chair, table, and lamp, and a small kitchen that was so perfectly camouflaged he did a double take. A hideout, for when his father didn't want to sit in his office or maybe wished to hide from Hatch. The guy did have a wacky sense of humor. The same intricate phone system was on a long table with stacks and stacks of yellow legal pads. Cups of pencils, pens, trays of paper clips and rubber bands were neatly lined up. But it was the picture on the wall, blown up to ten times its original size, that made him double over and roll all the way across the room. Laughing and gasping for breath he finally managed to get up and salute the picture in the elegant gold frame. "Here's to you, Miss Priceless," Nick said smartly.

The name Miss Priceless belonged to a duck. On a bet, Hatch had kept a duck egg between his thighs for five days. The morning of the sixth day, a baby duck broke its way through the shell and proclaimed Hatch as its mother. Hence the name Hatch. The story, the way his father had told it over and over, was one of Nick's favorite memories.

An identical picture was hanging in the attic back at the farm. His mother had refused to allow it to be hung in the house.

"I miss you, Dad. Seeing all this makes me wonder if you made a mistake. In a way I can see you here, and in another way I can't. Bet you never thought those guys would make a shrine to you. It must have been nice to have friends like that. Friends that would do all this in your memory. Guess you know I never had any real friends. No time. I feel close to you here for some reason. Back at the farm the feeling isn't so strong." Absentmindedly, Nick reached down for the beer that was sitting on a tiny white napkin. He hadn't heard Medusa come in. Spooky.

Beer in hand, Nick walked around to the back of the desk and sat down in his father's chair. He wondered what it would feel like actually to be a lawyer sitting here waiting for a client. "I can see you sitting here, Dad. I really can."

"It's not too late, Nick. You can always go to college. Hatch and the others will help you. You wouldn't have to sweat your ass off working and studying like we did. You could go first class, Nick. I bet if you went to school summers, you could ace the whole thing in half the time it took us."

Nick whirled around, his face a mask of panic. "Am I dreaming or did you just talk to me?"

"What do you think? I like to mosey on over here every so often to see how the guys are doing. I get an itch in my git-along if you know what I mean."

"Yeah, yeah, Dad, I know what you mean. I miss you, Dad. Are you . . . you know, keeping up with what's going on at the farm?"

"Of course."

"Did I do wrong coming here? You said if I ever found myself needing a lawyer, this was the place to come."

"I did say that. Trust Hatch. I'm sorry I never told you about the trust fund those guys set up for you. I wanted to, but the time never seemed

right. I want you to have it all, Nick, but I want you to earn it. You'll know when the time is right to use it. The time has to be exactly right. Do you understand what I'm telling you?"

"I understand, Dad. How much money are we talking about? Do you know?"

"Of course I know. The last time I checked it was right around fifteen million. Hatch started it with Flyby's winnings after taxes. Those guys are something else. The trust has been growing from the day you were born. Among other things, that big Indian has a streak of luck in him two miles long. Everything he touches turns to gold. He would have made an excellent stockbroker. By the way, that chair fits you perfectly. Better than it would ever have fit me."

Nick heard the tinkling bells and sat up. "I guess I fell asleep."

"I guess you did. Did you have a nice conversation with Hunter?"

"Ma'am?"

"Your father, Nicholas. Did you enjoy speaking with him?"

"How . . ."

Medusa smiled as she picked up the beer bottle. "Shunpus is waiting for you in his office. Come along."

His brain felt fuzzy as he staggered after Medusa to Hatch's office, where he sat down in a deep comfortable chair. The big man stared at him with sad eyes as he waited for Nick to speak, the contents of the folder spread out in front of him.

Nick struggled to clear his throat. "That . . . those papers . . . I think . . . they were just an excuse to come here. Right now I feel like my world has been turned inside out. I wanted to come here many times when things piled up on me. I know I could have called, but it isn't the same. Mom . . . Mom doesn't . . . she won't ask for help. Dad was different in that respect. When I think back I don't know if I was a good son to him or not. I was torn between the two of them. Don't get me wrong here, Dad loved the farm and the horses. My mother loved them more, *loves* them more. They consumed her. They still do. In trying to please both of them I shortchanged all three of us.

"I've been thinking a lot about the past, the present, and what the future holds," he continued. "It all came to a head when I got back home yesterday morning. After the disbelief, I got pissed. Royally pissed. I was looking for something, anything to, you know, fight back. And there it was," he said, pointing to the papers in front of Hatch. "I realized something else on the plane coming here. I want a life. A real life. I have a wife, and I want kids someday. I love the farm, the horses. Why do I have to make a choice? Dad did that. What did it get him? Unhappiness and an early death. While I was sitting in his offices, I must have dozed off, and I had this dream about him. It was weird. It felt real. Like he was right there. I even thought I smelled his aftershave. Do you think I'm losing my mind, Hatch?"

"No." Hatch smiled. "I go in there from time to time and, like you, end up dozing off and dreaming about him, too. He was a hell of a friend. The kind you never forget."

Nick fidgeted in his chair. "It wasn't a dream, was it?"

Hatch shrugged. "Your guess is as good as mine. Tell me what you want me to do. Do you want me to kick your uncles' asses off their farm? I can do that in a heartbeat. All your sister has to do is sign the papers. This other stuff, your mother's suits and countersuits, that's a different ball game. I can tell you right now, nothing good is going to come of that. When family starts attacking family, it's all over. No one wins."

Nick nodded. He jerked his head sideways. "It felt good in there."

Hatch grinned. "Did it now?"

"Yeah. Dad said the chair fit me better than it ever fit him. What do you suppose he meant?"

"What do you think it meant?"

"That maybe I belong here. That maybe if I'm good enough, I could sit in that chair for real."

"Well hot damn, boy, that's a real good assumption. It would take a hell of a lot of commitment for someone to take on a challenge like that. Hard work, no sleep, eating on the fly, nose to the grindstone seven days a week, twenty-four hours a day. I don't know too many people who would commit to something like that. I know some people who could help you if you're one of those dedicated people. Are you?"

Am I? Nick closed his eyes before heaving a mighty sigh. "Yeah, I am." He felt good. The words sounded just right to his ears.

"What about your new wife, your sister, and, of course, your mother and the farm? And what do you want me to do with all of this?" Hatch asked as he rustled the papers on his desk.

Funny, he thought. "I . . . I don't know. I thought I did, but now I don't." He gave Hatch a sheepish smile. "Dad always used to say when you don't know what to do about something, do nothing." He sat back in his chair, his emotions churning. "I have thirty-eight credits. I took night classes over my mother's objections. Then it got to be too much, and I couldn't continue. What do you suggest?"

Hatch rubbed his hands together, his face gleeful. "Open the door, Nick." His voice boomed through the building. "Emergency meeting!"

Nick looked around at the angry-sounding tinkling bells. "We have a twenty-five-thousand-dollar communication system so there is no need to bellow like a wild bull, Shunpus," Medusa chastised, as her tiny hands clapped shut over her equally tiny ears.

"Got your attention, didn't it? Take a seat, gentlemen. This is Nick Clay, Hunt's son. I know you know that, I just want to start off right," Hatch boomed. "This boy has decided he wants to finish up his undergraduate education and go on to law school so he can sit in his father's chair. I say we make this happen. Between the three of us we can whittle his time down to almost nothing. We'll get him accepted, registered, office school him twenty-four hours a day. As of Monday morning of next week, the three of us shut down. The associates can take over. Nick is our top priority. What'ya say, guys? Let's get on the stick and start making some calls. Call in every favor that's owed us. If we have to endow, we endow. Whatever it takes to get the okay to do this. Medusa, find him a place to live. He's not going to be there much, but he needs an address. You okay with this, kid?"

Nick's tongue felt twice its normal size. All he could do was nod.

"Does it feel right?" Bode Jessup asked, clapping him on the back.

Nick nodded a second time.

Hank Mitchum pumped his hand up and down. "Jesus, I can't believe we're finally going to get a real Clay in the office. Good move, Nick. Your dad would be real proud of you."

"Then let's get to it, people. Medusa, call the car service and have them pick up Nick. Call the airport and have our pilot file a flight plan. Nick, he'll wait till you have all your ducks lined up and fly you and your wife back. Now, get the hell out of here so we can get to work. Oh, bring all your transcripts with you. Have a good flight."

He was dismissed. His eyes bugging from his head, he allowed Medusa to lead him from the office. "They can do this? They can actually . . . you know . . . teach me, help me. Law professors will actually come here and do it all one-on-one? That boggles the mind."

"You sweet, darling boy, of course they can do it. The word *endowment* is a very powerful word to law schools. It is Shunpus's favorite word when he wants something. For some reason, it always works. More important, they *want* to do this for you. You will have to work very hard, for they will not let up on you. When they said twenty-four hours a day, they meant twenty-four hours a day."

"But the firm. The billable hours . . . They'll lose a lot of money."

The little bells tinkled, a cheerful sound this time. "Yes, millions and millions. It makes no mind, for they would have given most of it away anyway. Shunpus is guided by the Mountain Spirits."

"Mountain Spirits?" Nick looked back toward his father's office. "Are you serious?"

"Nah. It's a crock, but we like to pull out the Indian stuff every now and then to get people riled." The tiny bells tinkled again. To Nick's ears it sounded like an entire symphony.

An alarm button went off in Nick's head the moment he opened the door to Emmie's house. It was too quiet. Too still. He shouted to Willow and his sister. When there was no response he bounded up the stairs to the second floor. He poked his head into the room he'd chosen for Willow and himself. Other than his backpack and suitcase, there was nothing else to see. The bed was made, but there was no sign of Willow or her luggage. He saw the note then, propped up on the dresser. His hands shook so badly he could hardly get the single sheet of paper out of the envelope.

My Dearest Nick,

I am so sorry, Nick. I went to see your mother even though you told me not to go. She was very cold, very angry. She said many things, most of them ugly and hurtful. I can't be the cause of a rift between you and your mother, so I'm going away. I hope the two of you can patch up your differences. I will always love you. I want you to know that. If you love me, don't try to find me. It can never work for us. Take care of yourself and try to be happy. All my love forever.

Willow

Nick sat down on the edge of the bed. He looked up as Emmie came into the room.

"She left right after you did, Nick. She said she was going to ride around for a while to clear her head. I didn't dream she'd go to see Mom. I fell into a deep sleep and didn't hear her when she got back. Either she called a taxi or a car service. She took all her pots and pans. No, no, that's not what she did. She must have taken a taxi out to the farm and then took her truck. That's why she went out there. I guess she figured as long as she was picking up her truck, why not talk to Mom. She left me a note, but it just thanked me and told me to convince you not to look for her. I'm so sorry, Nick. I really am. What are we going to do now?"

"Jesus, Emmie, I don't know. I am going out to the farm, though. You can come with me if you promise not to cry and carry on." In a choked voice brimming with emotion, he told her about his visit with Hatch and the outcome. His hands folded and unfolded the letter from his wife as he talked.

"Nick, that's wonderful. I always thought you'd make a good lawyer. I think that's what Hunt wanted for you. Willow doesn't want you to look for her, Nick."

"Willow would have loved Santa Fe," he said, trying to absorb the news of his wife's leaving. He wrapped his arms around his middle. "I feel like someone just ripped out my guts. Emmie, I love her so much. She made all this . . . this life we've led more bearable. I wanted to give her the moon and the stars all wrapped up with a big silver bow. She didn't want that. She liked to go for walks and hold my hand. She's just a plain, simple girl who was dumb enough to fall in love with me. Where will she go, what will she do?"

"She'll be fine, Nick. Willow is a fantastic chef. She can get a job anywhere. She didn't say anything about a divorce, so there is hope she'll change her mind at some point. I have to tell you something, Nick. I'm pregnant. Before you can ask, Buddy doesn't know. I wasn't sure when we went on the cruise. Then when I passed the third month and knew for sure, I decided to tell him after the cruise but . . . I don't want him to know. You're the only one I've told. I don't know what to do, Nick."

"I'll tell you what you're going to do. You're going to go with me to New Mexico. You'll stay with me if you're okay with that. I don't think either one of us should be alone right now. Family has to stick together. But, Emmie, you should try to talk to Mom before you make that decision. She fired you, but she told me to pack my bags and get out. I see negotiating room there for you if you want it."

"You already sound like a lawyer, Nick. I'll go out and say good-bye, but that's it. I'm really sorry about Willow. I truly liked her. She was good for you."

"Sometimes things aren't meant to be. We had two great weeks. Some people don't even get that. I'll do what she wants for now, but I'm not giving up on her. I love her, she's my wife."

"I can make you some bacon and eggs, Nick. I'm too tired to go out for something to eat. Tomorrow is another day, and you look awful. Let's eat and call it a night. All our problems will be here in the morning. You didn't say anything about the baby, Nick."

"Sometimes wonderful things come out of chaos. A baby is a wondrous thing. I get to be an uncle. I'll be a good one, Emmie. I swear I will. A baby needs a father figure. I think you're going to make a wonderful mother. I have a feeling we're both stepping into a new and wonderful life. Hatch told me about his wife and son and the accident that killed them both. Bode and his wife Brie have twin girls. Hank isn't married. The proverbial bachelor. I think Brie will take you under her wing. It's a good thing, Emmie. Let's eat so we can go to bed."

"You aren't going to sleep, and you know it. We have to decide what to do about SunStar Farms."

"For now, don't do anything, Emmie. Neither one of us is in the right frame of mind to make any kind of important decision that pertains to other people. For ourselves, yes, but not for the uncles. That was Mom's doing anyway."

"You sound like you hate her, Nick," Emmie said, slapping bacon into the frying pan.

"There's a fine line between love and hate. I love her, but I don't like her right now." His voice was anxious when he said, "Is that how you feel, too?"

Emmie's head bobbed up and down. Tears dripped down her cheeks.

Emmie waited until she knew Nick was busy with other things before she went out to her SUV. She climbed in and started the engine. She drove off with no destination in mind. Her mind whirled and twirled as she drove along. Eventually she ended up at the entrance of Blue Diamond Farms. She parked along the side of the road and stared at the place she'd called home for most of her life. She looked up at the bronze sculpture of Flyby that graced the entrance. Flyby, her mother's beloved horse, the horse Nealy had ridden to victory in the Kentucky Derby, the Preakness, and the Belmont to make her a Triple Crown winner. If Emmie lived to be a hundred, she didn't think she would ever see a more magnificent horse.

She made a tent out of the palm of her hand to stare across the Blue Diamond spread. It was so breathtaking with its miles of white board fencing, fencing she'd helped paint every year of her life. The little hills and valleys of the dark blue-green grass stretched for miles and miles. When she was little her mother had shown her how to take a blade of grass and put it between both thumbs and whistle. Her mother had always laughed and laughed when she was able to do it.

Emmie sat down on the rich, velvety grass that was like a soft carpet and hugged her knees. She needed to feast her eyes on what she considered the most beautiful place on earth.

By squinting and shielding her eyes, she could see the old fieldstone house with the glorious front porch where she'd played as a child. She remembered her mother rocking her on Maud's old rocker and telling her stories about a mermaid named Emmie. She narrowed her eyes even more and was able to see her bedroom window on the second floor.

It was a pretty room, with a bedspread full of tulips. Even the drapes had tulips on them. Tulips were her mother's favorite flower. Hers, too. Once she'd made her mother a picture with a square basket full of the colorful blooms. She was seven that year. Her mother framed it and hung it in her bedroom. She'd been so proud that day.

"I'm going to miss this place," she murmured, her voice cracking. She would miss driving here each morning, working with the horses, talking with her mother and Smitty, her mother's friend and office manager.

Emmie plucked at the grass until she had a handful. She lowered her head to sniff the fragrance. It was sweet and pungent.

She stared into the distance, remembering when she'd left after marrying Buddy and moving into her own house. She'd tried to make it a home, but she knew now she'd been unsuccessful. Her heart was at Blue Diamond Farms, not in a house off a dirt road in the middle of nowhere.

Some things were just not meant to be.

A second later, she was running to the SUV, where she pulled out a Tupperware container from the cargo hold. She ran back to the spot where she'd been sitting. She used the small pocketknife attached to her key ring to cut out a square patch of grass. She scooped out a handful of dirt and dropped it into the container. She set the grass plug on top of it. If she watered it every day, would it thrive or would it die? She didn't know.

She ran over to the board fencing, dropped to her knees, and sliced a wedge of wood from the bottom rail. Just a small piece that wouldn't be missed. She added it to the container. She held it like the rare jewel it was and carried it back to the SUV. She climbed in and positioned it between her legs so the dirt wouldn't spill out.

She backed up the truck, stared up at the sculpture of Flyby, and waved. "I'll be back someday. I don't know when, but I'll be back." She drove off in a storm of tears.

A lump the size of a golf ball settled in Nick's throat as he brought Emmie's car to a full stop by the back steps that led to the porch. "Are you coming in or are you going to sit here in the truck?"

"I'll sit here and wait till you pack your things. We can walk down to the barn together. Strength in numbers, that kind of thing."

"Fifteen minutes at the most. I'm not taking everything, just what I need. I'll tell Smitty to throw the rest of the stuff out."

Nick was as good as his word. Thirteen minutes later he shoved two suitcases into the back of the 4-by-4. He poked his head into the passenger-side window. "We don't have to go down to the barn. We can write a note and leave it on the kitchen table."

"I'm not that gutless, Nick. Let's go." There was no point in telling her half brother she'd already been to the farm. Besides, it was a private thing between her and the farm. She wanted to keep it that way.

Nealy had seen the car and watched from the barn window. What would they say? More importantly, what would she say? And where was Willow? She felt jittery, out of sorts. *He looks so much like his father,* she thought. She knew then, in that instant, that her children were not there to apologize.

"Mom, we came to say good-bye."

Nealy nodded, not trusting herself to speak. She finally managed to get her tongue to work when she saw they were turning around to leave. "Where are you going?"

"Are you asking because you care, or are you asking because it's the right thing to say so you can tell yourself later you did care enough to ask? Don't answer, Mom. I'll save you the trouble and tell you. We're going to Santa Fe. I'm going to college and law school. Dad's old friends are going to help me. It's what Dad wanted for me. I'm sorry I listened to you. Willow left me. Is that funny, Mom? Because of you my wife left me. Just so you know, I'll never forgive you for that. Emmie's pregnant. Isn't that funny, too, Mom? You can just have yourself a real good laugh now. By the way, we both want to apologize to you for fucking up and thinking we deserved a life of our own, not one created from your mold. You have yourself a good life now, you hear?"

Emmie bit down on her tongue so she wouldn't cry. With Nick's hand on her elbow she managed to turn around and walk back to the car.

"Thanks for not crying, Emmie. I would have caved in if you'd started to bawl. Christ, did you see the look on her face? You're a woman, what the hell was *that*?"

"Disbelief. Hatred that we're going to your dad's friends. What's that picture in the back?"

"That's Miss Priceless. I'll tell you all about her later. Smitty saw me carrying it out. Don't look back, Emmie. Now you can cry. We're on the highway."

"I'm not going to cry, Nick."

"Attagirl."

3

Nealy reached out to grab hold of the gated door to Misty Blue's stall to steady herself. Ruby ran to her. "Did . . . did you hear, Ruby?"

"Yes. I wasn't eavesdropping. Voices carry in the barn. I'm so sorry, Nealy. Look, it's never too late to say you're sorry. Go after them. They're your children. You can't let them go in anger."

Nealy made no move to go after her children. Instead, she stared at the car until it was out of sight. "They're really *leaving*," she said, giving a voice to her thoughts.

"You told Nick to pack his bags. You fired Emmie. Did you really think either one of them would come crawling back? Your blood runs in their veins. You put it to the test. Willow tried to make it right, but you booted her ass out of here so fast her head must have been spinning."

"You're saying I'm wrong," Nealy said, rubbing her cheek against the mare's head. Misty Blue snorted with pleasure. Nealy's hand automatically went to her pocket for a mint. "He got married, Ruby. My son, my *only* son, didn't think enough of me to tell me. That's unforgivable in my book." There were other things she wanted to say, but she didn't trust herself to voice them aloud.

A look of weary patience settled on Ruby's face. "Nealy. The boy is young. He's in love. Probably for the first time in his life. He made a mistake in your eyes. Everyone makes mistakes. That's how you learn and grow and turn into the person you're meant to be. Up to this point, Blue Diamond Farms and you have been his whole life. When does he get a turn? When you say so? Life isn't like that, Nealy. And Emmie is going to have a baby. You'll be a grandmother! How can you give that up? Two words, Nealy. That's all it will take to bring them back. Say them. Now, before it's too late."

"No, I won't do that. Besides, it's too late."

"You don't know that for certain. You can't know that unless you try," Ruby pleaded.

"I do know that, Ruby. They're my children. I could shout those words from the rooftop, and they'd say, 'Too late, Mom.' Nick's never forgiven me for his father's death. He never said the words, but I knew. He idolized his father, and Hunt wanted him to go to college, get a degree so he could make his own choices. I put every obstacle in his path so he wouldn't do that. He belongs here, with the horses. He has it, Ruby. He's got the touch."

Sudden anger sparked in Ruby's eyes. "Guess what, Nealy!" The boy doesn't want the touch. From everything you've shared with me about Nick and now his own actions, it appears the boy wants what his father wanted for him, an education and a career in law. It doesn't matter if he has the touch or not. It's not what he wants."

Nealy ignored Ruby. "He just *thinks* that's what he wants," she returned doggedly. "The truth is he's been bamboozled by those Midas-touching bastards in Santa Fe. They tried every trick in the book to get Hunt into the firm and when that didn't work, did they give up? No, they never give up. Now they have my son. It was one of the biggest sore points between Hunt and me. He was going to go. He made the decision the year he died. I never told anyone because I didn't think he'd go through with it. Nick might have known. He could have heard us fighting over it. He never said a word, but I think he knew. For months now I think he was just looking for an excuse to leave here. He didn't have the guts just to come out and tell me. He chose this way. It doesn't matter now. He got what he wanted."

"And Emmie? What about her?"

Nealy smiled as she stroked the foal. "A break from me and the farm will be the best thing that ever happened to her," she said for lack of a more reasonable explanation. "I don't know if you know it or not, but Emmie has never been alone. Not even for a second. She doesn't know what it is to live outside the farm. First it was me, Maud, Jess, and then Buddy, but their marriage went sour.

"Things like that happen sometimes. It happened to Hunt and me. I think it happened to Emmie because she was finally coming into her own and Buddy couldn't handle the normalcy of it when she was finally able to speak again. There was trouble in the marriage a year ago. I saw it, and so did Smitty. Even Nick commented on it." Nealy moved out of the stall into the breezeway. "Emmie will make a wonderful mother. The minute she stands on those independent legs of hers it will be look out world, here I come!"

Ruby's eyes narrowed with suspicion. "Nealy Coleman Diamond Clay, look at me. Dammit, you set them up, didn't you? This was all a big brouhaha so they'd leave just to save face. Damn, you did it on purpose! What an actress you are. You almost had me fooled with that routine you just went through." Ruby slapped at her forehead as she headed for the wrought-iron bench on the other side of the breezeway. "There was a moment there, Nealy, when I wanted to shake the living daylights out of you."

Nealy smiled, relieved that Ruby now knew the truth. "I did, Ruby. It almost killed me, but I did it. I didn't think you would catch on so quick. If I hadn't done it this way, neither one of them would have gone. They never thought they had choices before, and that's my fault. They're like me in a lot of ways, but Nick is like his father. Emmie wants to be Emmie, but she thinks she has to be like me. This is the only way they're going to be who they should be. I just want whatever makes them happy. Don't for one minute think this isn't killing me. It was the hardest thing I've ever had to do." She leaned against the door, her face a mask of misery.

Ruby pressed her back against the wall and stared at Nealy. "I don't understand. Why did you have to drive them away? Why couldn't you have just said they were free to go?"

"Because they wouldn't have gone. They wouldn't have gone. I know that in my heart. I did what I thought was best, and there's no turning back."

"Why do you hate Hunt's old friends?"

"I don't hate them. I don't much care for them. One of them

hatched a duck egg between his legs and called the chick Miss Priceless. After that, they called him Hatch. Hunt thought that was the greatest thing in the world. The bunch of them are mega, mega, mega millionaires. They work for all the casinos in Vegas, Atlantic City, and all those Indian casinos, then give most of the money away. Hunt was in awe of that. I guess I was jealous of their lives, how successful they all became and how they kept after Hunt to join them. They stayed friends all these years. After Hunt's death, Hatch called Nick at least once a month. The year Hunt died, Hatch's wife was killed in a car accident. Nick went to Santa Fe and stayed for six weeks. When he got back, he called Hatch two or three times a day. That's the kind of friendship they all had. There was no room in that world for me, and I guess I resented it. What I didn't count on was Willow leaving Nick because of me. I'll have to make that right somehow."

"You're okay with all of this then?"

"No, not really, but I can live with it. Keep your eye on the foal. I'm going to take Flyby out to the stallion cemetery. I need some Nealy time with Maud and Jess. By the way, what do you think it would take to get you and Metaxas to sign on with me for a while? We're going to need all the help we can get with Nick and Emmie gone. I was even thinking of asking Ken to join up."

Metaxas and Ruby had introduced Nealy to Kendrick Bell the day she won the last leg of the Triple Crown, hoping she'd fall in love with him. It hadn't happened. Ken was a friend, nothing more. She'd gone to his home in the Watchung Mountains in New Jersey for the holidays trying to see if there was a possibility of a relationship developing. Recovering from a triple bypass, Ken sat glued to his chair, afraid to move, afraid to do anything but vegetate. She'd tried and done everything she could think of to shake him out of his fear, a fear his doctors were concerned about. Nothing worked. Simply put, Ken was afraid to live. She'd returned home, disappointed and saddened that a man like Ken would sit around doing nothing for the rest of his life.

"Dover Wilkie is a really good guy and a great farm manager," Nealy went on, as if talking to herself. "We were lucky to find him after Nick's grandfather retired. Nick taught him everything. He's so good with the horses I rest easy when he's around them. Dover is the main reason I agreed to the Christmas vacation. Still, he's just one person."

"A kiss on the cheek will probably do it for Metaxas, and off the top of my head, I'd say a full-blown kiss on the lips for Ken would seal the deal. That's only if you're interested. Go on, I'll keep my eye on this baby. It's okay for me to tie a red ribbon around his neck, isn't it? Metaxas likes his gifts wrapped. I cannot wait to see his face."

"I can't wait to see his face, too, and no, you cannot tie a red ribbon around his neck," Nealy said, leading Flyby out of his stall. "Misty Blue would eat it. I won't be long."

"Take all the time you need," Ruby said. "I'm just going to sit here and look at this beautiful baby."

Nealy led Flyby outside to the mounting block. With the ease of an experienced horsewoman, she mounted his bare back and, using only his mane to guide him, trotted him out to the stallion cemetery and the little cemetery next to it. Instinctively, the big horse came to a halt in front of Maud's and Jess's graves. As always, Nealy could only shake her head and marvel at his intelligence and intuitiveness.

The minute Nealy slid from his back he turned around and headed toward his sire's grave. Nealy watched as he pawed the ground and reared back, snorting and puffing loudly. His duty done, he waited patiently for his owner.

Nealy shivered inside her warm jacket as she hunched her shoulders for added warmth. "This is rough, Maud," she said, her eyes on Hunt's gravestone. "I feel like I'm going to collapse. I'm trying to do the right thing here. Maybe it's too late. Maybe I should have done it sooner but . . . I just couldn't make myself do it. The circumstances were just right this time, so I had no excuses. My mind tells me they're going to be fine. They're both hard workers, not a lazy bone in their bodies. They care about the animals and people. They're financially secure. My heart just feels bruised and battered right now. I made a mess of it, didn't I, Maud?" Nealy looked around, then cast her gaze upward as though looking for a sign. When none was forthcoming, she sighed.

"I guess that means I have to do the best I can under the circumstances. What will be, will be." She whistled softly for Flyby, who trotted over to her. "Did you have a nice visit, big boy?" Flyby gently nosed her shoulder until she stroked his big head. "I hope I can handle all of this. It's going to be strange around here for a while without Nick and Emmie. I don't know if I'll ever get used to it. You know what, Flyby, I'm going to sit here on this bench for a few minutes. I need to do some hard thinking." Her legs stretched out in front of her, Nealy leaned back on the iron bench.

"It's too cold out here, Nealy. You're going to fall asleep. Go up to the house and take a nap. Nothing's going to happen."

"Hunt. Gee, I haven't heard from you in years. You're angry with me, aren't you?"

"No. I admire you for what you just did. It took guts. You always had a bushelful of those. I'm glad you finally let them go. I'm real proud of you."

"Really, Hunt. You sound different. Are you finally happy? We got married for all the wrong reasons. I'm sorry about a lot of things. How about you?"

"The past is prologue, Nealy. Only the present counts for you. You'll be okay. I just wanted to thank you for letting him go. I know it was hard."

"I wish you were here, Hunt. I really do. I learned so much since you . . . you went away. If I only knew then what I know now."

"Don't do that to yourself, Nealy. Life will go on. Life, Nealy. Live your life. Be happy. All I ever wanted for you was to be happy. I wanted the same thing for Nick. It seemed there was never enough time to be happy. All our time was spent with the horses until there was nothing left for anyone else. It's getting colder, Nealy, and the wind is whipping up. Take Flyby back to his stall. By the way, that foal is a beauty. I'm going to keep my eye on him."

Nealy opened her eyes and smiled as Flyby nudged her shoulder. "Yeah, I know it's cold. I was just resting my eyes a little. I think I'll walk you back and let the wind whip me along. I had a dream. Actually, it was kind of nice. I haven't dreamed of Hunt in years. I wonder if it means something."

Nealy turned for a last look at the cemetery. For one tiny second she thought she saw a vision of Maud pointing to Hunt's gravestone. She blinked, and the vision was gone. A trick of light? The wind? She was on overload, and her mind was playing tricks on her. Maybe she should go up to the house and take a nap. Better yet, she'd make a bed for herself in the barn and sleep there and let Ruby go up to the house and get some rest.

Dover Wilkie rubbed at his stubble of beard as he stared at Nealy, who was sound asleep in the stall next to Misty Blue's. He hated to wake her, but she'd told him she was expecting an important phone call, and he had no way of knowing if the call that had just come through was the important one or not. "Nealy, wake up, you have a phone call. No one else is here to take it. Ruby is up at the house. Do you want me to tell them to call back or tell them to hold on?"

"No, that's okay, Dover. I'll take it. I just need a minute." She looked down at her watch and blinked. She'd slept for four hours. She felt more tired now than when she'd curled into a ball and closed her eyes. "I must have tired blood or something," she muttered.

"No real sleep in four days will do that to you," the burly farm manager muttered in return.

Nealy picked up the phone in the tack room. "This is Nealy Clay."

"Nealy, it's Ken. I'm returning your call."

"Ken. Thanks for calling me back. How are you? How are the dogs? Do you miss me? Do the dogs miss me?"

"You bet. What's happening?"

"Misty Blue dropped her foal. It was touch-and-go there for a little while, but everything is fine now. I had to fire Nick and Emmie." She followed up with a brief explanation. "Metaxas is due any minute now. Ruby is so happy. There just aren't any words to tell you how far she's come. She looks great, says she feels great, and her world is right side up."

"You fired your own kids! Why, Nealy?"

Was that condemnation she was hearing in Ken's voice? Hunt had used the same tone of voice with her whenever he disapproved of something she'd done or said. She could feel herself start to bristle. Out of the corner of her eye she could see Ruby entering the barn. She mouthed the words *It's Ken.* "Because they deserved to be fired. They broke the rules."

"Don't you believe in second chances, Nealy?"

"Sometimes. This wasn't one of those times."

"I guess that's your way of telling me it's none of my business."

"I didn't mean it like that. I called you for a reason, Ken. I was wondering if you would mind coming to Kentucky and signing on for a brief spell to help out a little. We've had a few emergencies and are shorthanded. I wouldn't expect you to do anything really strenuous."

"Well . . . I . . ."

"I'll take that as a no," Nealy said coolly. "Thanks for returning my call."

"Nealy, wait. Don't hang up. You caught me by surprise. It's not that I don't want to go to Kentucky. I . . . we talked about this, Nealy."

"Right. You're afraid if you raise your arms, you're going to drop dead. You're afraid to have sex because you think you might die in the act. You're afraid to go for a walk because you think you'll keel over. Never mind that your heart specialist warned you that inactivity will do you *more* harm. Right now, right this minute, I'm thinking you are a *wuss*, and that's one thing I do not need. All four of your doctors said you were fit, Ken. They said you were in better shape than some thirty-year-olds. I don't know why I'm even talking about this. I have things to do, so I'm going to hang up. Before I do that, though, I'd like to make a suggestion. Go talk to a shrink. Bye, Ken."

"My God, Nealy, what the hell was that all about?" Ruby demanded. "You're like a runaway bulldozer. What did he say?"

"It's what he didn't say. You heard my end. He didn't say anything. He's afraid to live, Ruby. All he does is move from one chair to the other. He gets up, he sits down. He goes to the bathroom. He brings in the mail and the newspaper. Those are his activities. The day before I left to come home from my visit up there, he hired a car service to drive him into the city to his doctor's appointments. I went with him. By the way, there are four of them. They all told him the same thing. They also suggested a shrink. He just stood there looking sheepish and shrugging his shoulders. One of the doctors finally said, 'You aren't going to follow our advice, are you, Mr. Bell?' Do you know what Ken's response was? 'Probably not, Dr. Quinn.' End of quote. His mother called a dozen times while I was there. She kept asking him if he was getting out and doing things. He lied to her and said yes just to get her off the phone. I don't have time for nonsense like that. If he wants to sit on two dozen different chairs a day and die from boredom, don't expect me to help him along. I'd be an accessory to his eventual death. He doesn't even cook. How hard or strenuous is cooking? He orders all his food prepared and delivered. I have a farm to run and horses to see to. Maybe Metaxas can get through to him because I sure couldn't."

"Guess you just crossed him off your possibility list."

"Yes, I guess I did. I wonder where Metaxas is."

"He's running late. He called to say he'd be here by four." Ruby clasped her hands in front of her. "You okay with the Ken thing?"

"I'm okay with it. I had a few fantasies about him for a while, but I can't picture myself with him. You know what I mean. I know this isn't going to sound good, but I know you'll understand. I haven't been with a man since Hunt died. I went to Ken's over the holidays to see if I could . . . you know . . . I was prepared to try him out. Me, too, for that matter. You get to be a certain age and you just aren't comfortable taking off your clothes in front of anyone, especially a man. I was going to do it, though. In order to have sex you need to have two players. He didn't want to play. He wanted that big-brother routine, a walk, hold hands, a kiss here or there, and that was it. Hey, I have two brothers. I don't need another one. We're moving on here, Ruby."

"I guess we are. Oh, Smitty said to tell you your lawyer called and will be out around seven. Said she needs to talk to you."

"Just what I need today. I hope my eyes are still open at seven o'clock. We have work to do, Ruby."

"I hear you, boss," Ruby quipped.

* * *

They hid out in the tack room, watching Metaxas make his way from the house to the barn, calling his wife's name as he walked along.

"Isn't this where you shout surprise, surprise!" Nealy whispered.

"I want him to get to the barn first. Oh, I can hardly stand this. I love that man so much it hurts. Here he comes! He looks so lost. He needs me. He really does, Nealy."

"I know that, Ruby. Someday I hope I can find someone to love me the way that man loves you."

"You will. Trust me."

"Ruby! Sweet baby, are you in here?" Metaxas boomed, all 230 pounds of his being quivering with his greeting.

"I'm here, honey. Ohhh, it's good to see you. I really missed you."

"You smell like horse poop, Ruby."

"I know. Isn't it heavenly? Is everything okay? You look . . . I don't know . . . sad somehow. No crisis anywhere in the world that you had to fix?"

"Nope."

"I can fix that right up. C'mere, I have something I want to show you. I have a present for you."

"For me!"

"It is your birthday, honey. Listen, I know you have everything in the world. It's always so hard for me to buy you a present, Metaxas. I agonize over it every single year. This year, though, I bought the biggest red bow I could find and was going to stick it on your present, but instead I'm going to hand it to you. The bow I mean. I hope you like it. If you don't, you'll tell me, won't you?"

"Did you get me a John Deere tractor, Ruby? You did, didn't you! Hot damn. I always wanted one of those."

"Not exactly, honey. It's a mover, though," Ruby said, inching her way to Misty Blue's stall. She used her index finger to point to the foal nursing at his mother's side. "His name is Shufly, and he's all yours, honey!"

"Mine!" Metaxas boomed, his face full of awe. "Mine!"

"He's yours, Metaxas," Nealy said, unlatching the gate. "Go take a look. Misty knows you. Flyby's watching you, so keep your hands in your pockets."

"Jesus God, I can't believe this." He grabbed Ruby and hugged her. "Ah, sweet baby, how'd you do this?"

"Misty did it. Flyby played a big part. Nealy and I just helped. Do you love him, honey? Did I surprise you?"

Metaxas raised his hands and clenched them. "Love him! I want to pick him up and hold him." He started to shake with his declaration. Nealy smiled. Ruby whooped with laughter. Flyby whinnied loudly.

"God Almighty, sweet baby, where'd you get this kind of money?"

"No, no, no, honey. I didn't pay for him. This baby is a gift from Nealy. I'm going to give her chickens for the rest of her life," Ruby said. She smiled, realizing how long it had been since she'd even thought about her Thornton Chicken farm in Las Vegas.

"Is he . . . do you think . . . ? Is he Derby material?" Metaxas asked.

Nealy lifted her shoulders. "It's too soon to tell, but it's a strong possibility. He's got the breeding, and he's certainly got the legs for it."

"We are going to move here for the next three years, honey," Ruby said. "Nealy is going to show us what to do. Are you okay with that, honey? Nick and Emmie are gone, so we have to help out. You don't have anything earth-shattering you have to deal with, do you?"

Metaxas shook his head. "If I did, I'd put it on the back burner. I don't believe this! That little four-legged baby is the most beautiful creature I've ever seen in my entire life. It's right up there with . . ."

"Rebuilding and planting an entire mountain for Fanny Thornton?" Nealy quipped.

Metaxas waved away Nealy's words as he put his arm around Ruby's shoulders. "No. I was going to say the day Ruby got news of her clean bill of health."

Nealy felt a lump start to grow in her throat. This wonderful man didn't care one whit about his wife losing both her breasts. This wonderful man who loved and loved and gave and gave twenty-four hours a day—like Hunt's old friends. Suddenly she felt inferior, a regular Scrooge in comparison. She didn't like the feeling at all. Her shoulders slumped as she watched Ruby and Metaxas stare at the newborn foal. She knew she wouldn't be missed if she went up to the house.

Smitty greeted her with a cup of coffee. Today she was as bejeweled and bejangled as usual. Smitty had style and grit, and Nealy adored her.

"What say we sit down here at the kitchen table and talk, Nealy. Want a cigarette, or did you quit again?"

"I quit, but I'll take one and quit again tomorrow. Do you think I'm nuts, Smitty?"

Smitty blew a perfect smoke ring. "If you're nuts, then that makes me nuts, too. No, Nealy. What surprises me the most is you thought we'd all fall for your little charade. We've been together twenty-five years. I know you as well as you know me. I also know you're hurting real bad right now."

"I'll get over it," she said with more confidence than she felt. "Did Clementine say what she wanted?"

"Not to me she didn't. You know how I hate that legal crap. What would you say if I told you I'm thinking about getting married?"

Nealy leaned back and crossed one leg over the other. She was never more relaxed than when she was smoking a cigarette. "I'd say it's about time. Is Dover Wilkie the lucky man?"

"You know he is, but don't get carried away and start planning a wedding, Nealy. I'm just thinking about it. It's not that my biological clock is ticking. It stopped a long time ago. Believe it or not, I get lonely sometimes. I don't want to give up my independence, and I don't want to do that housework slash cooking thing. I'm probably not good marriage material. See how easy I can talk myself out of things."

Nealy nodded. She looked around at the cozy, comfortable kitchen she'd done over years before. She loved sitting here drinking coffee and musing about what each new day would bring. Out of the corner of her eye she saw pots of brilliant poinsettias all along the baseboards. How festive they looked even though the holidays were officially over.

"They were half price at the supermarket, so I bought them all," Smitty said, pointing to the red flowers in their foil-covered pots. "I thought we could use some color in here. If we take care of them, they should last another month. It's okay to cry, Nealy. Go upstairs and bawl your head off and get it out of your system. You remember how to cry, don't you?"

"Crying is a luxury I can't afford. If I give in now, I'll run after both of them. Did Ruby tell you about Ken?"

Smitty shrugged. "I always said men were strange creatures. Put them all in a bag and shake it up, and you know what, they all come out the same. You don't look particularly heartbroken. That's just an assumption on my part. Feel free to jump in and correct me, Nealy."

"I would if there was something to correct, but there isn't. I think I'm being punished. I went to New Jersey to . . . you know . . . sort of, kind of, check him out. I went there for my own personal . . . You know what I'm talking about, Smitty. In a way I was actually relieved when nothing happened. There weren't any bells or whistles. He didn't rock the ground beneath my feet. Somewhere, someplace in this world is a man who can do that for me. I just haven't found him yet. I will, though."

Long years of familiarity allowed Smitty to speak her mind. "No you won't!" Smitty snapped as she tugged at the yellow-leather vest stretched tight across her chest. "If you stay here on this farm twenty-four hours a day, there is no way in hell you are going to find such a man. You know what else, Nealy Coleman Diamond Clay? You wouldn't know what the hell to do with a *real* man. So there."

"You're a wiseass, Smitty. I have more important things to think about than getting a *real* man in the sack. I'm going upstairs to take a nap."

"That's probably the smartest thing you've said since coming back from New Jersey. What should I tell Mr. Bell if he calls again?"

"He won't call. It takes a certain amount of energy to pick up the phone and dial a number, and he's not willing to expend that energy."

"You're a rip, Nealy."

"Among other things. Thanks for getting the poinsettias. They really perk up the kitchen. If I'm not up by five, will you wake me, Smitty?"

"Sure, kiddo. By the way, with all the excitement going on around here I forgot to tell you I hired on four brothers. Do you remember Scully Mitchel?" Nealy nodded. "Well, he croaked the day after Christmas and his sisters are selling everything off. The boys are looking for work. Nice young men. Nick knows them. Fully licensed. They know how to work hard. I hired them on and gave them a raise in the bargain. All four of them will give you an honest day's work for a day's pay. They start tomorrow or the next day. Soon as they finish up for Scully's sisters. You okay with it?"

"More than okay. My shoulders feel lighter already. Thanks, Smitty."

Smitty's brow furrowed in worry as she watched Nealy's retreating back.

In her room with the door closed, Nealy walked over to Maud's old rocker and gently lowered herself into the softness of the cushions. She was tired, but she wasn't sleepy. She just wanted to sit and think about what she'd just done. She wished she could cry. Why couldn't she? When was the last time she'd really cried? She couldn't remember. Maybe when her dog Charlie died, and then Stardancer. Maybe. Why couldn't she remember? Did she cry when Maud and Jess died? She couldn't remember that either.

Her arm reached out to the day-planner Smitty had given her a year ago. She tried to write in it each night, but for the most part she forgot or was too tired even to pick up a pencil to jot down a few notes. Every damn day of her life was the same, so what was the point of making entries that said the same thing over and over again? There were no surprises, no events, nothing out of the ordinary. Maybe Smitty was right. She needed a life outside of the farm. Interests, hobbies. The thought made her throat muscles tighten.

Nealy's gaze swept across the room to the pictures on her

dresser. Her gaze lingered on a picture of Hunt and Nick with their arms around each other, big smiles on their faces. She remembered vividly the day Smitty had taken the picture. She'd been about to join her husband and son when Nick said, "No, Mom, this is just me and Dad." There was no picture of her with Nick. No one had ever asked to take one. When Hunt died, she'd gone through all the photos and brought this one into her room. Nick had one in his room. She wondered if Nick had taken his picture with him. Of course he had. It was one of his most treasured possessions.

Before she could stop to think, Nealy dropped the daily planner on the floor and bolted out of the room and down the hall to her son's room. Her hand trembled so badly she could barely open the door. Her heart beating trip-hammer fast, she stepped over the threshold and took a deep breath. What had she expected to see in here? The room was neat and tidy just like Nick himself. A young man's room done in earth tones. Once it had been a little boy's room. Even back when he was a little boy she had never come into the room unless she was invited. It was Hunt and Nick's domain. There were no pictures anywhere. Where were all the baseball bats, the mitt, the skis? Where were the posters young men always hung on their closet doors? Maybe inside.

Nealy reached out to open the closet door. Two flannel shirts on hangers. A pair of old boots, the heel loose on one. There was nothing on the overhead shelf. She slid one of the flannel shirts off the hanger and brought it close to her face. It smelled like Nick, clean and crisp. She peered again into the depth of the closet. Of course there was no baseball bat or glove. Nick never had time for extra activities. All he did was work and read and study. And if she'd had her way, he wouldn't have read or studied at all. Because . . . because . . . she'd wanted him to be like her, not like Hunt. And to that end, she'd worked him like a mule, the same way Josh Coleman had worked her. What kind of mother did that make her? Not a very good one. Where had she lost her way? Was it when she married Hunt? She wasn't a good mother, and she hadn't been a good wife either. She felt dizzy with the thought.

Emmie. Emmie was different. All those years when she couldn't talk, all those years of coddling her were different. Different because Emmie was different. Nick had been a sturdy little boy and an even sturdier teenager. And he was a hard worker. Because she made him work. Someday Blue Diamond Farms would be his and Emmie's to run. They had to be prepared to run it the way she'd had to learn. She could never have progressed to where she was now if she'd gone to college. And because she didn't go to college, she'd always felt inferior to Hunt. Had she taken that and dumped it on Nick and Emmie? Of course she had.

Hunt overrode her so many times when it came to Nick. He home-schooled him a lot. A quick study, all Nick had to do was show up and take a test. And he always passed. She knew that because Smitty told her, not because Hunt and Nick did.

That was when she trenched in and made Nick work harder. She knew now that Emmie had carried half his load just so he could study. Just the way her brothers had stepped in to help her when she lived at SunStar Farms. She knew that, too, because Smitty told her. Long after the fact.

Nealy dropped her head into her hands. This was all because of what happened with that hateful old man Josh Coleman back in Virginia. He'd left a mark on her soul, and she didn't know how to erase it. God help her, she was just like him.

Her single-minded goal in life had been to tie her children to her so they would never leave the farm the way she'd been forced to leave SunStar Farms.

She wasn't fit to carry the name of Mother.

She knew she was going to cry when she felt the hot tears behind her eyelids. With her son's shirt pressed to her cheek she let the tears flow, red-hot against her cheeks. Her shoulders shook, and her body trembled. "I'm sorry, Nick. I'm so very sorry. Forgive me, Emmie."

Nealy closed the door behind her and walked back to her room, the shirt clutched tightly in her hands. This time she locked the door behind her. Still crying, she climbed up onto the big four-poster and curled into a tight ball. She was asleep within minutes, her dreams full of sorrow and regrets.

*   *   *

"Nealy, it's six o'clock. Wake up, kiddo." Smitty was banging on the door.

"I thought you were going to wake me at five. We'll be eating dinner when Clementine gets here," Nealy muttered as she stuffed Nick's shirt under her pillow. "I just want to wash my face and comb my hair. I'll be down in a minute. What's for dinner?"

"Thornton Chicken frozen potpies. I made a salad," Smitty called through the door. "Ruby and Metaxas are in the kitchen. He says he's going to find us a housekeeper who can cook. I don't think he likes Thorntons, and Ruby is having peanut butter and jelly because she won't eat chicken. Shake it, Nealy. Dover and I have plans to take in a movie this evening."

"Okay. Okay. I'll be right down."

Nealy looked at her reflection in the bathroom mirror. She looked haggard and old, and her eyes were red and puffy. Everyone was going to know she'd been crying. According to Smitty it wasn't such a terrible thing to cry. The only problem was, she didn't feel one bit better.

She sighed. Life would go on regardless of how she looked or what she did.

4

Nealy stood at the kitchen sink, her hands in soapy dishwater. A long frond from the fern hanging over the sink tickled her ear. She gazed out the window at the steady drizzle that would, according to the weatherman, turn into an all-night hard rain. She shivered inside her wool sweater.

Her hands fumbled in the soapy water for the plug. The dishwater gurgling down the drain sounded ominous to her ears. She could have loaded the cups and silverware into the dishwasher but felt the need to keep herself busy so she wouldn't think. It wasn't working. Maybe after the meeting with Clementine Fox she would drive over to Emmie's house. Maybe. She knew she wouldn't do it because going to Emmie's house, seeing her things, would only make her feel worse than she already felt. It would be better if she sent Smitty, but even that could wait till tomorrow. She'd burned her bridges and had to live with her loss. For now anyway.

A smile tugged at the corners of her mouth. Emmie with a baby. She was going to be a grandmother. Would Emmie send pictures from time to time? She hoped so, but she doubted her daughter would want to share her precious child with someone like her. *Someone like her.* The words danced around inside her head. What was wrong with her? Why couldn't she have called her children into the kitchen and said something like, "Listen, I'm sorry I've been so hard on you. You're now free to do whatever it is you want to do with your lives." Why couldn't she have done it like that? Maybe someday she would come up with an answer that she could make sense of. Then again, maybe she would never come up with the answer.

Nealy dried her hands and stood at the counter watching the

fresh coffee dripping into the glass pot. Clem might want a cup. She grinned. Clementine Fox, according to Metaxas, was the best damn lawyer in the country. A real kick-ass attorney who didn't think twice about taking on the big boys and coming out a winner.

Clem liked bourbon straight up the same way Smitty did. Nealy opened the cabinet and brought down a bottle of hundred-proof bourbon and a squat glass with a turkey on the front. It belonged to a set of bourbon glasses Danny Clay, her father-in-law, had given her one year. There were six, and so far none had broken. She closed her eyes and conjured up a mental picture of Danny. She should call and tell him about Nick on the off chance her son hadn't gotten around to calling his grandfather. She was about to reach for the phone when the back door opened and Clementine Fox blew into the kitchen with a strong gust of rainy wind.

Nealy blinked. How could anyone look so ravishing, so elegant, so professional in a rainstorm? She eyed the shimmery pink raincoat in awe. Even the attorney's umbrella was of the same shimmery pink material. The briefcase in her hand was a Gucci. It looked new and crisp, just the way the raincoat and umbrella looked.

"I'm dripping all over your floor, Nealy," Clem apologized, her voice calm as usual. "If that's coffee I smell, I'd like a cup."

"No bourbon?" Nealy asked in surprise.

"Not tonight, honey. It's bad out there, and I don't need liquor running in my veins if I'm driving. Just coffee, no cream or sugar. "Where is everyone?" she asked hanging her raincoat and hat on the rack by the door. She walked over to the sink and plopped the pink umbrella against the side.

"Smitty said she was going to the movies with Dover. Ruby and Metaxas are down at the barn. Nick and Emmie have moved out to experience life on their own. End of subject, okay?"

Clem's expression remained passive. "Okay with me, Nealy. I'll just leave the papers that concern Emmie, and you can forward them to her. It seems a set was sent to her, but she hasn't responded. It really doesn't have anything to do with you, but Emmie is going to have to get off the stick and make a decision here."

"What papers? What are you talking about?" Nealy asked, setting a cup of coffee down in front of the attorney.

"The papers regarding your . . . ah . . . father . . . Josh Coleman's farm that Emmie signed off on for your brothers. The papers were never filed in a timely manner. The attorney, according to his son, suffers from Alzheimer's and simply forgot. The papers have to be redone. Emmie has to sign again. If she doesn't, the farm is up for grabs. It is very complicated, Nealy. If it isn't done properly, I don't think I have to tell you the Colemans will be right there, pen in hand. Right now your brothers are considered squatters by the Colemans, and they want that farm. We go to court in two weeks."

Nealy blinked and shook her head to ward off a wave of dizziness. She slumped into a straight-backed chair across from Clem and gulped at the hot coffee, sorry she hadn't put a jolt of Jess's favorite bourbon in it. There wouldn't be a problem if she could call Emmie and tell her to hop in the car and come right over, but Emmie was gone. "I thought you said their lawyer wanted to sit down and work something out. Are you saying that offer is off the table?"

"It was never *on* the table, Nealy. It was just something Valentine Mitchell said in passing. Let me remind you, Valentine Mitchell is the *legendary* Valentine Mitchell. The one who used to make the headlines once a month. The Colemans of Texas were her biggest clients, and she let the world know it. They dragged her out of retirement to handle all of this. The Colemans never okayed the deal. They want SunStar Farms, and they want those horses. It's the only thing that can save them if you prevail and take Sunbridge. We need to get our ducks in a row here, Nealy."

Nealy leaned forward, eyeing the lawyer narrowly. "What horses are you talking about, Clem?"

Clem stared at Nealy over the rim of her coffe cup, then slowly lowered it to its saucer. Her facial expression was that of someone no longer sure of her position. "For starters," she said, keeping her eyes on Nealy, "the horse you rode to victory in the Belmont. I can't remember its name. And all the other horses at SunStar."

Nealy felt her body grow still. "My brothers don't own any

horses. The day I left for New York to ride in the Belmont, my brothers sold off all the horses. Every single one. They're just being boarded at SunStar Farms. Guess no one told you that, huh?"

"No, I guess no one did," Clem snapped, pulling a legal pad and pen out of her briefcase. "Do you want to tell me how that happened? If it's true, it's a good thing for you, but it is something I should have known about. I think you just won this case."

Nealy smiled.

"I need the particulars," Clem said, pen poised to write.

"That's easy enough. Metaxas bought the horses. My brothers filed the papers the day after the Belmont, before there was any lawsuit. It was all legal. I didn't know anything about it till after the race. I think he paid a whopping five bucks for each horse, so there is no money in the coffers for the Colemans to take. And, Clem, read my lips, they aren't taking my brothers' house, either. It will be over my dead body. You need to call your opposing counsel and tell them that. I suggest you do it now, so I know what's going on. We don't have a lot of time if we're going to court."

Clem scribbled on the legal pad and then threw her pen down on the table. "If you have any more little surprises you haven't shared with me, now is the time, Nealy. You're taking this all very well, so that tells me there are other surprises." Her face was stony cold, her eyes narrowed slits.

Nealy fiddled with her spoon. "I have one more," she said quietly. Clem crossed one shapely leg over the other and sat back. "Not to change the subject, but what does a pair of shoes like that cost?"

"Five hundred and sixty dollars," Clem replied without blinking an eye. "What's the other surprise, Nealy?"

"I bought up all of Riley Coleman's loans. I paid two points above what the bank was charging. They couldn't wait to take my money. I did it over the phone, wired the money to cover all the loans, and got the papers the next day by overnight mail. It didn't even take twenty-four hours. I can boot Riley Coleman's ass out of Sunbridge in minutes. I know how the game works. I might look stupid, Clem, but I'm not. I take care of my own."

"And you would do that?" Clem asked tightly. "Boot him out?"

"In a heartbeat. Now, where do we stand?"

Clem picked up Nealy's pencil, which had rolled across the table, and snapped it in two. "I don't know. I really don't know. It's raining in Texas. Actually, it's been raining for ten straight days. Their drought is over. The Japanese stock market is healthy again or appears to be healthy. Throw those two ditties into your equation before you make any rash moves."

"You're copping an attitiude with me, Clem. Why is that?"

"It's the nature of the beast. When I came into this, I admired you. Right now I don't much like you. Don't worry, that won't color my defense. I guess I was hoping it wouldn't get down and dirty. That's always wishful thinking on my part when I get involved in a case." She stood up and smoothed down the tight-fitting cranberry suit over her hips. "There's no guarantee Val will be home to take my call."

"Try," Nealy said, the single word edged with steel.

Clem reached into the side pocket of her Chanel handbag to withdraw a small black Palm Pilot and her cell phone. She punched in the numbers and waited. "It's her answering machine," she said, covering the phone with her hand. "Do you want me to leave a message?" Nealy nodded. "Val, it's Clem Fox. I need to talk with you. Give me a call," she said, rattling off the hotel number as well as her room number. "I should be there in, say, an hour. We're having some real bad weather. Kind of like what you are getting there in Texas. I'll wait for your call."

"Do you want me to fix you a thermos with coffee, Clem? It really is bad out there." Nealy stood up and tugged at her jeans, smoothing them down over her hips. For the first time she realized she and Clem were about the same height and weight. But that was where the resemblance ended. For one crazy moment, she tried to imagine what she would look like wearing Clem's cranberry-silk suit and lizardskin shoes. The first word that came to her mind was ridiculous. But not as ridiculous, she thought, as what Clem would look like wearing her jeans and boots.

Clem walked over to the coatrack. "No thanks. I don't have that far to drive to my hotel."

"I'm sorry if I disappointed you. I can't be anything but what I am. I wish I could be more refined, more feminine, more like you, but that's not who I am. I feel, I hurt, and I bleed. My family is all I have. They belong to me. I appointed myself my brothers' protector, and I'll use any means available to me to see to it that no one takes away what belongs to them. They started this. For God's sake, I didn't even know we *had* a family until all those Colemans and Thorntons showed up at SunStar Farms." She let her breath out in a *swoosh*. "If I could have just one wish, it would be that none of this had ever happened. But it did happen, and I have to deal with it." She looked Clem straight in the eye. "If you want out, I'll pay you off, and you'll never hear from me again. It's your call." She inched her way around the attorney to reach for her yellow slicker on the coatrack. "It's pretty nasty out there. You might want to consider spending the night. You can take the room at the top of the stairs on the right. Think about it before you head out into that mess. I'll say good night. I want to go down to the barn."

"Nealy . . ."

Nealy shrugged into her slicker as she stared down at the attorney's pricey shoes. "Yes?"

"A few minutes ago when I said I didn't like *you*, what I meant was I don't like what you're doing. When this first started you said it wasn't right for family to sue family. I felt the same way. I never had a family, Nealy. I grew up in one foster home after another. All those people wanted was the money the state paid them for my keep. I was lucky if I had enough to eat most times. I was married for a short while to a real louse. He believed I should work and he should gamble. That ended real quick, so I never got to have a family of my own." She set her cup down on the counter. "I try, with my clients, to make things come out right for their families. I can't stand to see a family torn apart. What I'm trying to say here is sometimes life isn't fair. Look, you have money to burn. Literally. And yes, you busted your ass to get here just the way I busted my ass to buy these shoes on my feet. I didn't step on anyone, though. All I did was work my ass off. You don't need that Texas spread. In your heart you don't want it either. I understand you going to the wall and fighting with your last breath for your brothers, but you don't have to destroy the Colemans in the process. That isn't who you are, Nealy. At least I don't think it is. You don't have to be like your father. What he did was unconscionable. Don't compound it."

Nealy snapped up the front of her slicker. "Thanks for your vote of confidence. To me, there's nothing more important than family. I've made mistakes. Everyone makes mistakes. It's what you learn from those mistakes that counts. Not having a family of your own should make you understand where I'm coming from. One more time, I did not start this. You can't blame me for a drought in Texas or the Japanese stock market sliding downward. When things like that happen you don't pull the plug and go after someone else's home and threaten to take away their livelihood so your good life can continue. I would never do something like that, and I won't tolerate someone else doing it to my family. Like I said, I take care of my own. I don't expect anyone else to do it for me. I really have to get down to the barn. See you, Clem. I really like those shoes and that rain gear. You look good."

"Okay, Nealy. I'll call you if Val calls me."

Pulling the hood of the slicker over her head, Nealy ran out into the black, rainy night.

As soon as she entered the barn's breezeway, Flyby started pawing at the floor of his stall. Nealy walked over and gave him a mint. "Good boy," she said, patting his muzzle. The next stall down was Misty Blue's. She nickered softly. Ruby and Metaxas were still where she had left them hours ago. "Your eyes are going to pop out of your heads," she chided gently. "You really don't have to stand guard. Misty Blue knows what to do with her baby."

"Oh yes, we do, Nealy. I've been staring at this baby ever since I got here. He is beyond gorgeous. I don't know what to say, Nealy. No one has ever given me a gift like this. Don't misunderstand. People give me gifts all the time. And I appreciate all of them because they're given from their hearts. This . . . this little guy is different. He walks and he breathes. He's *alive*. I feel like I should do something. You know, something memorable to . . . to preserve this moment."

"Go into the stall, Metaxas. I want to show you something. Just walk slowly and talk softly. I'll come with you. Misty won't hurt you." Once they were in the stall, Nealy said, "Now I want you to rub your hands over the foal's body, just like you were giving him a massage. That's right. Do his head and ears. Good. Now, stick your fingers into his mouth and rub his gums. What you're doing is called imprinting. It's sort of like bonding. If you do this and the other things I'm going to show you every day, he'll be as imprinted to you as he is to his mother and me. It'll make him easier to work with as he grows older." Nealy demonstrated how to pick up the colt's legs. "A racehorse's feet and legs are his most important assets. It's important not only for you to be well acquainted with how they should look and feel but for the horse to be relaxed when the farrier, vet, and other people examine them." One by one she had Metaxas pick up his legs, massage them, then lightly tap each tiny hoof. "You have to do this every day without fail, Metaxas."

"Not a problem, Nealy. I'll do everything you say. He feels wonderful. He's mine. This little guy is really mine."

"You sound like you won't be here to oversee things," Ruby said, a note of anxiousness in her voice. "Are you going somewhere?"

With an effort to keep her voice steady, Nealy said, "Clementine was just here as you know. We go to court soon. She told me she didn't much like me. That's okay. She doesn't approve of a few things she called surprises. Like for instance, Metaxas telling my brothers to sell the horses to him for five bucks each. And she didn't approve of me buying up the Coleman bank loans. The way I look at it is this. They started it. They didn't care about my brothers. Their plan was to snatch that farm right out from under them. And the horses. They didn't count on me, though. I have to do what I have to do. If I'm wrong, I'll be held accountable, and I'll deal with it. I won't beg or whine or cry."

Ruby drew Nealy to her and cradled her head on her shoulder. "Honey, do what your heart tells you to do, and if you can live with what you're doing, it's okay. You gotta do what you gotta do. Just be sure to think things through and don't go off like Metaxas says, half-cocked. Pick your battles and map out your strategy. I think that's the same advice Metaxas would give you."

"Am I wrong, Ruby? Tell me the truth."

"You know me and my feelings about family. I know that I

would kill for mine. I know that sounds terrible, and if it ever came to that, I'd try to find another way. But know this—I am capable of killing to protect my own. Us women have this . . . this fierce protective thing in us when it comes to family. The Thorntons, my family, have it. It doesn't matter that I was born on the wrong side of the blanket. I'm one of them, and it is to that family that I pledge my loyalties. Why else would I have taken over the business of running Thornton Chickens? Fanny Thornton is not only the matriarch of the family, she's one of my dearest friends. I'm not sure about the Colemans. They're an aloof bunch to my way of thinking. I've never taken the time to get to know them because they aren't of my blood. So, where are you going and what are you going to do?"

Nealy shrugged. "I won't be doing anything till after the court case. If it all gets settled, I'm going to search out my mother's people. And I'm going to look into finding Sallie Thornton's sisters. I need to do all this. I've put it off too long. Maybe I won't think and hurt so much if I keep busy. Not to worry, I'll be here when it's time to start training Shufly."

"What about Kendrick Bell?"

"He's not the one, Ruby. I guess what I'm trying to say is he didn't measure up in my eyes. I would go out of my mind sitting around like he does. I'm not ready for a sedentary life. He isn't going to change. He's too frightened. Like you said, Ruby, you gotta do what you gotta do. What does Metaxas say?"

Ruby laughed. "You don't want to know."

"You're an incredible woman, Ruby. The best thing that ever happened to me was you coming into my life."

Ruby blushed.

"I'm going to check the stallion barn and call it a night. You two don't have to sleep here in the barn, you know."

"I know. We want to. Besides, I don't think you could pry Metaxas away from here. He is in seventh heaven. I've never seen the man so happy. To my dying day, Nealy, I will be grateful to you for this."

"I'll say good night then," Nealy said, hugging her. "Night, Metaxas."

Ruby rolled her eyes when her husband muttered something that sounded like good night. "Go!"

"I'm gone. See you in the morning."

"Yeah, in the morning."

She knew she was dreaming because she knew it was impossible for dead people to parade before her. They were angry with her and yet kind at the same time, forcing her to wonder how that could be. Off in the distance, standing on a hill, or maybe it was a mountain, was a sign that she could read if she squinted. FIND THE ANSWERS. What answers? A dream was supposed to *give* you answers. Didn't the subconscious provide you with responses to things that bothered you during the day? Didn't those questions lie in wait until you closed your eyes and then manifest themselves in crazy dreams? Somewhere she'd read that Gypsies believed dreams were a special knowledge presented to us by our ancestors. Upon awakening, one was to write down the dream and try to interpret its meaning. But this dream wasn't giving her any knowledge or any answers. It was just a crazy, mixed-up mess.

Nealy rolled over and stretched out her legs and immediately a solid cramp in the flesh of her calf caused pain. She hobbled around the room, her gaze swerving to the clock on the dresser—4:10. When the cramp in her leg eased, she sat down in Maud's old rocker. She was wide-awake. Pain would do that to you, she decided. She found herself clenching and unclenching her hands, a sure sign that she was in turmoil.

Life was so complicated. Dealing with horses, employees, and the farm was totally different from real life. God, how had she come to this miserable patch in the road? Was she deaf, dumb, *and* blind? Obviously she was, or she wouldn't be in this predicament. And what exactly *was* this particular predicament that was making her so damn miserable she had nightmares? The kids? Ken? Her past? All of the above. "Your problem, Nealy, is you ignore any and all things that don't pertain to the well-being of the horses."

There! She'd said it, and this time she would take it to heart and do something about it. This time she wouldn't ignore it.

The past. Deal with that, lay it to rest. Ken isn't going to play any kind of role in your life, so put all thoughts of him behind you. The kids will be okay. If they need you, they'll call. It won't matter that harsh words passed between you. Love between a mother and a child can never be broken. Let them go to do what they have to do to make their lives whole and rich. The horses, the farm, all was okay on that front. Ruby and Metaxas would take care of the foal for now. Dover could make things work, take up her slack, and, with the four brothers Smitty hired on as grooms, she could leave the farm for a few days at a time, possibly as long as a week. If she wanted to. The big question was, did she want to go on a quest whose ending she might not like. Maud always said, "If it ain't broke, don't try to fix it." Maybe she should just let things alone. What good would it do to resurrect her mother's family? She might upset their lives if she was successful in finding them. Maybe it would be enough to know there was family out there. She could observe, check it out, weigh the pros and cons and then make a decision. Perhaps just knowing would be enough.

For long moments she sat there, still and silent, and reflected on her thoughts. It was strange, but she felt better already, as if a heavy weight had been lifted from her shoulders.

A sense of relief enveloped her, and she sat back. She had pinpointed the three trouble spots in her life. Blue Diamond Farms, while a great deal of work, was not complicated. It was her joy, but it was also her excuse for not making a life for herself. Things would eventually work out with Nick and Emmie. Kendrick Bell was no longer an issue.

Nealy closed her eyes and tried to formulate a plan. The court case loomed, pushing everything else to the side. Okay, she would deal with that and Clem on a day-to-day basis. When she wasn't dealing with the legal end of things, she could go through the files the private detectives she'd hired had handed over to her. She could go to Austin, Texas, check the court records, put notices in local papers. Surely something would surface to give her a clue to her mother's family. Plus, Pyne had sent on all the boxes and folders of records he'd found in the attic. She'd go through each box, each file, each slip of paper. Smitty could help her. All she needed was a starting point, something to dig into, something to follow through on. If there was family out there, she wanted to find them. And she would.

She heaved a sigh as she struggled out of Maud's rocker to head for the shower, then stopped in mid-stride when she thought about Hatch Littletree. She had to corral her thoughts where the big Indian was concerned. If he was going to be the protector of her children, their guiding star, she needed to rethink her feelings about him. Hunt always said Hatch had the purest of hearts. Whereas he had called her heart black. Her step faltered. "Oh, God!"

Dressed, her hair still wet from the shower, Nealy made her way downstairs. She wrinkled her nose. Was that bacon and coffee she smelled? She grinned when she saw Metaxas flipping bacon at the stove. "Coffee's ready, Nealy."

"I am so hungry I could chew the doorknob," Nealy said.

"Me, too," Ruby chirped. "Smell him, Nealy. He smells just like us. Doncha love it, honey?"

"I sure do, sweet baby. What will you have, Nealy?"

"One egg, some bacon, toast, and lots of coffee." She reached for her bottle of multivitamins at the back of the table.

"Coming up. Nealy, is it okay that a lot of my business mail, my calls and faxes come through here? I don't want your people bogged down with my business. I can just as easily bring some of my people here if you have a room where I can set things up."

"You can use the cottage Danny and Hunt used to live in. Which reminds me, I have to call Danny sometime today. Dover didn't want to stay in the cottage, so it's empty. Feel free to use it. The office here in the house isn't big enough for what I imagine will be coming in for you. And then there's the entire garage and the apartment on top of it. Take your pick."

Ruby sat sipping her coffee, looking like the second happiest person Nealy had ever seen. "The four brothers showed up this morning, Nealy. They were nice and clean, had haircuts, and they're respectful. I like all four of them. They know horses, too. Gentle hands. It's amazing, isn't it, Nealy, that I can spot a good worker. I learned a lot hanging around you. You're going to like all four of them, and they like each other. It's nice to see that. Billy, the youngest one, took to Metaxas right away. I think it was that role model/father image thing. Dover took over, and they hustled. Smitty did real good on that one. I'd give her a raise if I were you. Your new housekeeper arrives tomorrow. Good food for a change. Not that what we've been eating isn't good but it can be improved upon," Ruby added hastily, her eyes on her husband standing at the stove.

Nealy stifled her laughter. "Sounds like things are moving along smoothly. No problems, no crisis, just smooth sailing. Until the court case comes up."

"Are you worried about that, Nealy?" Metaxas asked.

"Yes and no. I don't want to see my brothers lose the farm. They aren't fighters. Rhy and Pyne can't even comprehend any of this. All they've ever done is work. They just want to be left alone in peace. They never even got married for God's sake. They don't understand how family can do this. Hell, I don't understand it either. What I do understand for certain is, the Colemans are not going to get away with it."

"Eat up, ladies. I won't be doing this after today, so enjoy it now. By the way, Nealy, did you dump Ken?"

Nealy blinked. "Well, that's one way of putting it, I guess. I hope he changes and starts to do what the doctors tell him to do. I tried my best when I was there to get him to take walks, to do things, but he was always so anxious and kept wanting to go back to the house, where he felt safe and secure. I can't live like that. I won't live like that. He's your friend, Metaxas, maybe you can get him to get off his duff and join the world."

"I tried," Metaxas said, sitting down next to Nealy. "I know where you're coming from because I tried, too. He wants to sell me his interest in the restaurants. I agreed because I don't want his apathy to ruin the business. The deal should close in a few weeks. I'll stay in touch and do what I can, but don't look for any miracles. They ain't gonna happen where he's concerned. I feel bad because he's such a nice guy."

"What are you going to do today, Nealy?" Ruby asked as she stacked her dishes on the counter.

"I'm going to exercise Flyby, and I've got a full load on my plate. If you guys can handle Misty and Shufly, I'm good to go. I'll clean up here, you cooked. Go on, I know you want to get back to the barn. I'll call you for lunch."

"Let's go, sweet baby," Metaxas chortled.

Nealy smiled as Metaxas wrapped his arm around his wife's shoulder. Would she ever be as happy as the two of them? The smiled stayed with her as she loaded the dishwasher and wiped off the counter and table. Satisfied that the kitchen was spic-and-span, she sat down with a fresh cup of coffee to wait for Smitty.

The minute the office manager walked through the kitchen door, Nealy bombarded her with a list of things to be done for the day. "And, Smitty, call Dagmar Doolittle and get us some press for that big Derby Ball you said I should throw. Since this is going to be my first, so-called, coming-out ball, I want to make sure we really make a splash. Have some of the office girls work on it. Invitation only. Figure out what we can realistically charge, with all the monies going to the Best Friends Animal Sanctuary in Kanab, Utah. Work it up so people *beg* to be invited. Dagmar will be good at that. And, I think you should limit the number of people we invite. Get the biggest hall, the best band, the best caterer around. In fact, I know of a set of twins, Kitty and Josie Dupré, who run a catering business in New Orleans that would be just perfect. Pay them whatever they want to come here. And you might want to hire the Butterfuncks, a band from New Orleans, too. Hire a decorator. I'll pay for all of it. Just get the ball rolling."

"Okay, boss. Anything else?"

"Plenty. I'll feed it to you as I go along. I'll be in the dining room with all my stuff spread out. If it's the last thing I do, I'm going to find my mother's people."

Smitty whistled. "Attagirl! Call me if you need me. Hey, our new housekeeper arrives today, right?"

"Tomorrow."

"Oh, shit!"

"So, what are you telling me, Clem?" Nealy asked three days before she was scheduled to appear in court.

"I'm saying Valentine Mitchell says the Colemans are not interested in settling the case out of court. Val said her clients are willing to take their chances in a court of law in front of a judge. She could have something or she could have nothing and be bluffing. Up until the minute we walk into court it could change. And she doesn't know about those two little surprises you sprang on me two weeks ago. If you have any other aces up your sleeve, this would be a good time to bring them out so I can look at them. The way it stands right now, your old Virginia homestead is going to the Colemans—lock, stock, and barrel. I can almost guarantee they won't want it when they find out there are no horses to sell. However, you and your brothers will get a percentage of Sunbridge since we can prove through DNA that you are indeed Seth Coleman's children. Your children will also receive a share. Since you and your brothers are the only three blood children remaining, the percentage will be higher. The others are grandchildren and great-grandchildren. As far as SunStar Farms go, the Colemans still think they're getting horses. It's a damn mess no matter how you look at it."

"How is it those horses didn't show up on discovery?"

"They did. Val got a little cocky and wasn't careful enough in her wording. All it asked was the name of each horse and the value placed on it. It didn't say anything about ownership. I'm having a hard time believing she was that sloppy. The flip side to all of this is she probably doesn't approve of this suit any more than I do. Are you sure, Nealy, absolutely sure, that Metaxas has receipts for board for all those horses, not to mention the bills of sale?"

Nealy rummaged through the stacks and files on the dining-room table. "Got them right here. Smitty can make copies for you."

"When do your brothers plan on leaving for Texas? I have to go over their testimony with them."

"They're leaving the night before. I'm leaving late this afternoon. I'll meet up with all of you at the hotel in the morning. Don't worry about my brothers. All they can do is tell the truth. There's no need to rehearse them. If you do, they'll get nervous."

"And you are going to do . . . what when you get there? Is there a reason why you're going early?"

"As a matter of fact there is. I have a lead on my mother's family I want to follow up on. Smitty came across it, and, strangely enough, it wasn't all that hard to find, according to her. It makes me wonder why both those detectives I hired earlier couldn't find this family. With my suspicious mind I'm thinking there was some kind of intervention. Then again, maybe not. I'll get to the bottom of it. I guess I'll see you in the Austin courthouse two days from now."

Nealy's eyes were hard and cold when she leaned over to tweak Clem's cheek. "Think about all those high-end shoes you can buy when you send me your bill."

"Nealy . . . I know what you're planning. At least I think I do. And I know you didn't ask for my advice, but I'm going to give it to you anyway. Don't do it."

Nealy clucked her tongue. "You're right, I didn't ask for your advice. See you in Texas, and make sure you wear a Stetson or they won't take you seriously."

Nealy watched the lawyer from the kitchen window as she started up her car, the wheels spinning in the gravel.

"What's she got her panties in a wad over?" Smitty asked.

"She doesn't like what I'm doing. In the beginning she couldn't wait to sink her teeth into this case. She saw dollar signs, and that was all she saw. Somewhere along the way she switched up on me. She likes and favors compromise. She knows I don't need the money; therefore, I should cave in and suck it up. Her idea would be for me to buy my brothers a new farm and let them run it. She doesn't understand, Smitty. I don't know if anyone but my brothers or I understand what's going on. I'm not doing this for me; I'm doing it for them. For Nick and Emmie, too. That old man in Texas just threw us away. Threw us away, Smitty. It was like we weren't human. He turned us over to that ugly, hateful man we thought was our father. He didn't care if we lived or died. We weren't good enough to be part of his fine upstanding *legitimate* family. We were just a dirty little secret that he palmed off on his hateful brother. It's my turn now. If you don't approve of what I'm doing, don't tell me because I'm going to do it anyway."

"Kiddo, go for the jugular and kick some ass. You're right, it's your turn. You just make damn sure you can live with whatever you do. Call me and let me know how it's going, okay?"

"I will. You never judged me, Smitty. Why is that?"

"Because you never judged me. You always took my side with Carmela, and you always listened when I had something to say. By the way, calls have been coming in thick and fast. Everyone wants to be invited to your Derby Ball. I told Dagmar ten thousand a ticket and somehow or other it turned into twenty-five thousand. It doesn't seem to make a difference. It's like a presidential ball or something."

"Dollars?" Nealy gasped.

Smitty laughed. "Yep, dollars. You can make a lot of animals happy with that contribution. Multiply that by one hundred people. We'll be able to save a lot of animals with all that money. Very worthy cause, Nealy. You did good. What's it going to be next year?"

"Spousal abuse. If this flies, hike the price next year. There are a lot of women's shelters in this state that can use the money. You're working on all those good charities you said I needed to donate to, right?"

"I'm donating your money left and right, Nealy."

"Good. I feel better already," Nealy muttered, her thoughts on Hatch Littletree and his philanthropic activities. "So, I'm a little slow at this. I'm getting there," she continued to mutter as she made her way upstairs.

5

They sat around the dining-room table, their faces solemn, coffee cups and whiskey glasses at their elbows. In the center of the table were legal pads and legal papers. Piles and piles of legal papers.

"This is just a guess on my part, but I'd say there's at least fifty pounds of legalese in the center of this table. And for all this we get to pay money. On top of that we're going to boot our relatives' asses out of their home. Does that about sum it up, family?" the ever-blunt Sawyer demanded angrily.

"Shut up, Sawyer. None of us likes what's going on. In this world you do what you have to do to survive. It's too late for recriminations. You voted along with the rest of us," Riley said, his face haggard and gaunt. "Do you believe this rain?"

Cole Tanner stood up. He shoved his hands into his pockets. "Look, this is how I see it. Once we get Sunbridge back on its feet and the market stays steady, we can give back the farm and the money. We won't feel any better, but it's something maybe we can live with."

Maggie Coleman Tanaka stared up at her son as though he'd lost his mind. "Earth to Cole," she said, waving her hand in front of her son. "Are you the one who is going to stand up there in court and say, hey, listen, we're stealing your home out from under you and your horses that we plan to sell to the highest bidder and when we're satisfied that we have enough money we'll start to pay you back? That has to be the dumbest, the stupidest thing I've ever heard of. No."

Cole sat down and poured whiskey into his coffee cup. He gulped at it, his eyes watering. "Then what's our answer?"

"There is no answer, you asshole," Sawyer shot back. "I hate all of us for this. I do. I'm going to work for Lockheed Martin. They made me an offer I can't refuse. Adam and I gave you every last cent we had and you pissed it away on interest for all those goddamn loans you took out, Riley. I'm outta here. You can go to the slaughter by yourself."

"Will you just shut the hell up, Sawyer? That mouth of yours is always running. You have to appear in court. You were subpoenaed. None of us wants to do this. We have no other choice. Legal is legal."

"You're an asshole, too, Riley. You started this damn mess. I just hate it. Do you hear me, I hate it. I want out. I don't care if I have to pick shit with the chickens, I want out."

"After tomorrow you're out," Riley roared. "Now just shut up."

"Your doorbell is ringing, Riley," Sawyer sniped. "That means you have company. It's probably someone else with papers to serve us. Us. All of us. Don't recognize the car," she said, peering out the kitchen window. "Oh, Jesus, God, it's Nealy Clay!"

They rushed from the table to peer out the window.

"She looks like a woman with a mission," Sawyer sniped again. "Just for the fucking record, I like her. Isn't somebody going to go to the door?"

"I'll go," Maggie said quietly.

Nealy's heart started to pound the moment she turned off the ignition. The windshield wipers squeaked to a halt as rain continued to roll down the window. Within seconds, outside visibility was practically zero. Without the sound of the radio and the hum of the heater, the now-silent car took on an ominous silence. She shivered inside her suede jacket. She wished for an umbrella, knowing she was going to get soaked the moment she stepped out of the rental car. She had to run across the compound to the wide back porch with its green-and-white-striped awning. Six hundred feet at least. She looked down at the thick yellow envelope on the seat next to her, wondering again what she hoped to gain by coming here.

Get out of the damn car, Nealy, and do what you came here to do, a voice inside her head prompted.

Through the pouring rain she could almost make out a neat line of cars. That had to mean the whole family was here, and ready to go to court to strip her and her family of what belonged to them. She clenched her jaw so tight she thought she heard it crack. "That's why *I'm* here," she muttered.

Clem had been dead set against her doing anything but fighting things out in court. Ruby, even though she'd said, "Do what you gotta do," didn't really mean it. Nealy could read the disappointment in her eyes.

Black heart.

How many times had her husband told her she had a black heart? Hundreds, probably, in the years before his death. For reasons she never quite understood, she had been a great disappointment to him. More than once it had occurred to her that he had expected too much of her. It had also occurred to her that she usually expected too much of herself. How had that happened? *You're procrastinating. Get out of the damn car, Nealy, and do what you came here to do. Just do it.*

Her hand was on the latch that would open the door when a different voice, Smitty's, thundered in her ears. "Just make damn sure you can live with whatever you do." Could she? Hell, yes, she could. She grabbed for the yellow envelope.

Somehow the door opened. She couldn't remember exerting any pressure to make it swing wide on its hinges. She wished it was a bright, sunny day so she could really see this place called Sunbridge that was now hers, thanks to the contents of the envelope in her hand. According to the papers she was carrying, everything belonged to her, Sunbridge with all its thousands of acres and all the other Coleman enterprises.

Black heart.

Nealy ran across the compound, counting the line of cars. Five.

Black heart.

The door opened before she had a chance to ring the bell on the side of the screen door. "Come in, Nealy," Maggie Tanaka said. She held out a green-and-white-checkered hand towel. Nealy shrugged aside the offering. Rain dripped off the Stetson. She reached up to remove her hat, gave it a gentle shake, then settled it more firmly on her head.

She saw it all in one wide glance, the dust bunnies under the table, the coffee cups, the whiskey bottles, half-eaten sandwiches. She saw the sick, miserable expressions on all their faces, the slump of their shoulders.

Maggie Tanaka cleared her throat. "Would you like some coffee, Nealy? It's fresh."

Black heart.

"No thank you. I won't be here long enough to drink it."

"Why *are* you here, Nealy?" Sawyer asked.

She had rehearsed the answer to that question all day. "That smart-ass lawyer you all hired to file suit against me made a little mistake," she said, pausing to create a moment of tension. "The horses at SunStar Farms belong to Metaxas Parish. In your lawyer's discovery, she asked the value of the horses, not who owned them. I hold a multimillion lien on SunStar Farms. So you see, you get nothing but land, barns, and a house." If she'd said the Devil himself was dancing with the Archangel in the middle of the Houston Astrodome, she couldn't have hoped for a better reaction. As one they shrank before her very eyes.

Blackheartblackheartblackheart.

Nealy took a step forward and slid the padded yellow envelope across the table. All eyes followed it until it came to rest in front of Riley Coleman. He made no move to touch it. One by one, they raised their eyes to stare directly at her.

Black heart.

Anger roiling inside her, Nealy was hard-pressed to maintain a calm, even voice, as she said, "You might want to think twice before you open that envelope, *Mister* Coleman, and show everyone just how much in debt you really were." Riley raised his eyes to meet hers. "I'll give you credit for one thing. You sure do have a knack for making poor investments."

A surge of gratification ran through Nealy at his anxious look. "That envelope contains paid-in-full receipts for *all* your outstanding loans. I, Nealy Clay, paid them off." She gave him a cold, hard smile. "Legally," she added, opening her arms wide, "everything you have belongs to me now." The magnitude of her words washed over her with such force it made her light-headed. "But since I don't want to be like you, like any of you," she said, giving her con-science a chance to speak, "I'm giving it all back, free and clear." She stepped away from the table and blinked back the threatening tears. "I thought I wanted to belong to this family. I know now that isn't what I wanted at all. I don't like you people. And I hate what you tried to do to my brothers. Someday, someone far wiser than I will hold you all accountable. This is the end of it, do you hear me? The end. I hope I never have to set eyes on any of you again!"

In the time it took her heart to beat twice, she was outside in the pouring rain. It felt cold and wonderful. So wonderful she drove away with her windows rolled down, the rain pelting her through the window. She wished she could tell someone what she'd just done. "Hey, Hunt, if you're up there, can you hear me?"

"*I hear you, Nealy. You did good back there. I'm proud of you.*"

"Do you still think I have a black heart, Hunt?"

"*You aren't out of the woods yet. One good deed isn't going to cut it.*"

Nealy laughed, a joyous sound. "Now why did I know you were going to say that?"

"*You okay with all of this, Nealy?*"

"I'm okay with it, Hunt. Anything else you want me to do?"

"*Now that you mention it, you could make nice to my buddy Hatch.*"

Nealy laughed aloud. "Don't push it, Hunt."

"*Think about it, Nealy. That's all I ask. Just think about it. Give old Hatch the benefit of the doubt. For me. For old times' sake.*"

Nealy nodded. "I'll think about it."

The laughter was warm and intimate. Nealy flushed all the way down to her toes.

"*See ya, Nealy.*"

"Yeah. You're watching the kids, right?"

"*Every minute.*"

"Thanks."

"*My pleasure.*"

The smile stayed on Nealy's face all the way back to the hotel.

Inside her room, which was toasty warm, Nealy shed her wet clothes and availed herself of the thirsty robe folded neatly on top of the long vanity, compliments of the hotel. Within seconds she had the phone in one hand, a cigarette in the other. Her brother

Pyne picked up the phone on the third ring. He sounded stressed. "It's Nealy, Pyne. Listen, you don't have to go to court. Cancel your flights. I'm here, and I've taken care of everything. No one is going to take the farm. No one. Do you hear what I'm saying? We're in the clear."

"Jesus, Nealy, how'd you manage that? You sure they aren't going to pull some more of their magic tricks? Wait a minute, what did you have to give up to get them to agree?"

Nealy laughed. She heard the anxiousness in his voice and explained what she had done. "Their homestead. I wish you could have seen them, Pyne. They couldn't believe it. Hell, I don't believe I did it either, but it feels good. This is going to sound strange, but I felt sorry for them. They looked so . . . so beaten. I think we would have won in court, but I decided that wasn't good for any of us. It's over. How's everything?"

"Thank God. Things are pretty good. No complaints. Be nice if you came for a visit."

Hearing the relief in Pyne's voice was all the proof she needed that she'd done the right thing. "We can move on now, Pyne. All of us. You can get back to making SunStar Farms everything it can be and I . . . I'm going to go in search of Mama's people. I've got some leads on Mama I'm going to follow up on today. I'll call you tonight if anything pans out. Hug Rhy for me, okay?"

"I'm not hugging Rhy, Nealy," Pyne grumbled.

"Okay, okay, slap him on the back for me."

"Nealy?"

"Yes."

"Thanks. I guess I should say more, but I don't know the words."

Nealy's eyes misted. "Thanks is enough. I'll call you later."

Nealy looked around. It was a beautiful hotel room, almost like someone's private apartment. It was tastefully decorated with a small sofa and two wing chairs that matched the drapes and carried through to the thick comforter and designer pillows on the king-size bed. She eyed the bed. Maybe she needed a nap to drive away the drained feeling that seemed to be taking over her body. What was it Maud used to say? Oh yes, "I'll just sit here and get forty winks and then I'll be good to go." *Forty winks it is. Not yet though.* She had one more phone call to make.

Nealy listened to the phone ring on the other end of the line. Seven rings later the breathless attorney said, "Hello, Clementine Fox speaking."

"Clem, it's Nealy Clay," she said cheerfully.

"Nealy, can this wait, I'm going to miss my flight if I don't leave right this second."

"That's why I'm calling you, Clem. You don't have to leave. It's over and done with. I took care of everything. The Colemans and I have settled up so to speak. Send me your bill, and we'll call it a day."

The attorney's voice dropped to a whisper. "Nealy, what did you do?"

"I just came back from Sunbridge. I gave them back their homestead. I signed off on all the loans. It's over." For some reason she still couldn't believe she'd done it. It had been a last-second decision but the right one for all concerned.

"And . . ."

"There is no 'and.' It's done. It was the right thing to do. I think I might still be angry deep inside, but the anger will go away at some point. I did feel good when I did it. I don't want to be like them. I don't want to belong to that family. Thanks for everything. See you around."

"Nealy, I'm not sending you a bill. It was a pleasure doing business with you. For whatever it's worth, I'm proud of you."

A smile tugged at the corners of Nealy's mouth as she hung up the phone.

Nealy smacked her hands together in satisfaction. Now it was *really* over.

Feeling good about herself, Nealy curled into a ball on the big bed and was asleep within minutes.

Forty miles away in the Coleman kitchen at Sunbridge, the occupants stared at one another, their faces registering shock, dismay, and shame.

An ugly look on her face, Sawyer slammed the coffeepot on the counter. "Now that the roof over your head is secure and the hallowed ground once more belongs to you, I think I'll head back home to my husband and my new job that I shouldn't have to work at."

"I can pay you and Adam back now, Sawyer," Riley said, a desperate look on his face.

She glared at him. "That's pretty funny, Riley. You're going to pay me back with Nealy Clay's money. No thanks. Get off your ass and make this ranch profitable. The drought's over. Don't call me, I'll call you." She slammed the door behind her.

Cole clicked his tongue in disgust. "She's a hothead, always was, always will be," Cole said, his eyes on his mother, Maggie. "Mom, what do you think?"

"What I think is that Nealy Clay is like Mam used to be—one tough cookie when the chips were down," Maggie said, referring to Billie Coleman, the matriarch of the Coleman clan. "I don't care what any of you think; I, for one, admire Nealy Clay. I'm sorry it all ended like this. Somewhere, someplace, somehow, all of us came to believe this placed called Sunbridge was something special. It's like thousands of other places. It's brick and mortar and acreage. It's not sacred. Home is wherever you are. Home is where your things are with the people you love and care about. A trailer, a tent, an apartment can be home. I'll be leaving now, too. If I were you, Riley, I'd call Ivy and ask her to come home. I am just sick over this. And no, like Sawyer, I don't want you paying Henry and me back with Nealy Clay's money." Her gaze narrowed as she homed in on her son and nephew. "Mam thought you were man enough to take over Sunbridge, Riley. You failed her, and don't blame it all on the drought either. Cole, Shad turned over a multi*billion* dollar aeronautics empire to you, and you're in the hopper. If you had been on top of things, this wouldn't have happened. You were both asleep at the switch. I want to leave you both with this thought. Coleman Aviation with Sawyer at the helm was thriving until you mortgaged it to the hilt. Billie Limited is alive and well thanks to me. We're women. If we can do it, why can't you? One last thing, don't either one of you *ever* forget that Nealy Clay and her brothers rightfully belong here. More so than any of us. Illegitimate or not, they are Seth Coleman's children. Children. *Not* grandchildren, *not* nieces and nephews. His children. It was all in the papers the attorneys gave to us. We could never dispute it. Good-bye everyone."

"Guess she told us," Cole mumbled as he reached for the bottle of Jim Beam. He poured a healthy jolt into Riley's cup, then filled his own. "What should we drink to, cousin?"

"How about shame?" Riley said, holding out his cup.

"I got a bellyful of that. To shame. Ours. We can never make this right, Riley."

"I know."

Cole poured again. "We need to talk. Let's go up to the hill and hash it out the way Colemans always do when they have problems."

"That's the best idea I've heard in a coon's age." Riley reached for the Jim Beam. Cole reached for the other bottle.

Together they walked up to the hill to the family cemetery, their hearts troubled, their eyes downcast. Other family members who had made the same trek thousands of times over the years had worn the round medallions of stone on the pathway to a smooth, satiny finish.

"See that tree, Cole," Riley said, pointing to an ancient cottonwood. "That's what Ivy and I hung on to when the tornado whipped through here. I thought that day was the worst day of my life. I was wrong. This is the worst day of my life. In minutes it was all gone. Ivy said in a way it was a good thing. It was a new beginning for all of us. He was a bastard, Cole," Riley said, waving the whiskey bottle in the general direction of Seth Coleman's grave. "I don't know if I want to be buried up here with *him*. If you stay in Japan, are you going to want to be buried on the Cherry Blossom Hill?"

"I don't know. I don't know anything anymore. I feel like bawling. We fucked up, Riley. We didn't just fuck up, we *really* fucked up. I want your permission to go back to Japan and boot those black suits the hell out of there."

Riley took a long pull from the bottle. "You shoulda listened to me a long time ago. I told you the old ways don't work anymore," he said, slurring his words. "Fire them all. Kick ass and take names later. Do it! You don't need my permission."

"Maybe I don't need it. I want it. You okay with it?"

"Yeah. Tell me what to do, Cole. I'm swimming upstream here."

"If you trust me, if you give me six months, I can bring Rising Sun around to where it was. What's mine is yours. There's oil here, Riley, I can smell it."

"I can smell it, too. Bankers don't go by smells. Six months it is, cousin."

"There's a glitch, Riley."

"There always is," Riley said, tilting the bottle.

"You need to go back to Japan with me. The black suits will take it better with you standing next to me."

"Okay."

"You gave in too easily, cuz. I thought I would have to fight you to agree."

"It's time for me to go back. I have to clean up all my loose ends before I can ask Ivy to come home. Whatever it takes. I wish I was a kid again. We can pull it together, can't we, Cole?"

"Hey, we've been through a lot of shit together. This should be a walk in the park compared to that plane rescue in the Alps." Cole stared up at the old cottonwood tree, remembering the time he and Riley had flown to Switzerland to save the passengers on a downed airliner because his mother Maggie's stepdaughter was on board. "That was a nightmare from hell, but we did it and no one died," he said, clapping Riley on the shoulder. "We'll leave in the morning."

Riley nodded. "Do you miss them, Cole?" he said, pointing to the line of gravestones.

"More than you know."

"Do you think *he's* in hell?"

"Yeah. 'Cause that's where he belongs. Let's say our prayer and go back to the house. We're soaked to the skin. We must be nuts standing out here like this. Hell, I didn't even realize it was raining until just now. I guess we really are drunk."

"Our Father, who art . . ."

* * *

Nealy rolled over in the large bed. She was groggy but alert enough to realize she wasn't in her own bed at Blue Diamond Farms. She squinted when she brought up her arm to look at the hands on her watch. Could it be 10:05 when it was light out? She blinked and then blinked again. How could it possibly be morning? She'd slept almost around the clock. Maybe doing good deeds allowed one to relax to the point of being comatose. She struggled out of bed, reached for the phone to call room service. "A pot of coffee, toast, and a pack of cigarettes," she said into the phone. "Thirty minutes! Can't you bring it any quicker than that?" Assured they would try, Nealy headed for the bathroom, where she brushed her teeth, showered, washed her hair. She was wrapping her head in a towel when her breakfast order arrived.

She scribbled her name on the charge slip, ripped open the package of cigarettes, then poured coffee. She gulped at it, surprised how good it was for a hotel's.

The envelope she'd brought with her was directly in her line of vision. Maybe she'd open it with her third cup of coffee. A perfect smoke ring escaped her lips. She savored the smoke, knowing full well how bad it was for her. She was going to have to quit smoking very soon if she started training Shufly. She wondered if, at her age, she was up to the three years of gut-wrenching work. She wasn't a kid anymore. Her joints could attest to that. If she pulled this off, she would be riding the Derby when she was fifty-two. The press would have a field day with her. Let them.

She poured more coffee into her cup as her thoughts shifted to her children and the Colemans. Her heart fluttered in her chest. *Let it all go, Nealy. Don't go there. That was yesterday. The kids will be fine. The Colemans will be like the phoenix, they'll rise again from the ashes.*

Nealy reached for the thick yellow envelope. It contained complements of the various detective agencies she'd hired, photocopies of old newspaper articles about the Colemans. She'd read them all and had found nothing of help until Smitty pointed out an old picture of Seth Coleman eating lunch in what looked like a diner named the Horseshoe. A waitress with a long braid hanging down her back was smiling at the rancher. The caption underneath the picture said the waitress's name was Martha Ridley. Nealy's mother's name was Martha Ridley.

Smitty had written to the Austin courthouse and, for twenty dollars, secured Nealy's mother's birth certificate as well as birth certificates for Pyne, Rhy, and herself. The birth certificates back home—the ones Pyne had sent on with all the boxes belonging to Josh Coleman—had the last name of Coleman on all three of them. The three certificates spread out in front of her said the last name was Ridley.

There was only one Ridley in the local phone book. Carl Ridley Mortuary. There was no home listing for Carl Ridley. Still, it was a place to start.

Nealy shuffled the papers, the local maps Smitty had stuffed into the envelope, as well as a local telephone book. All she needed was a beginning. Maybe all the lost pieces would surface and fall into place.

Forty minutes later, Nealy was dressed and in the rental car, the map spread out on the passenger seat. It was eleven-thirty when she parked in the mortuary's empty lot. Two long, shiny, black hearses sat under a canopy. She shivered as she made her way around to the front of the building.

Inside, she flinched. The scent of flowers was sickeningly sweet and overpowering. Somber music seemed to waft from the ceiling. She itched to return to her car.

"May I help you, Miss?" asked a young man, so perfectly attired, so hushed, so somber as he approached her, his hands folded in front of him, that Nealy thought he looked like one of his own customers.

She cleared her throat. "Are you Mr. Ridley?"

"There is no Mr. Ridley. He passed away several years ago. I handled the remains myself since I was his partner. I'm Jason Lyons, the owner."

"Well, Mr. Lyons, I'm trying to locate my mother's people. My mother's name was Martha Ridley. She used to live here. Do you know anything about your partner's family?"

"Not much, I'm afraid. Carl never talked about his family. He never had children; his wife passed away many years ago, and he never remarried. I do know that he had a brother who is also deceased. It seems to me there were three sisters. Two of them lived in Dallas but I remember Carl going to both of their funerals some years back. He never said what the sisters' married names were or if there were children. Carl wasn't one for sharing his private life. I think the other sister moved away to someplace where there were horses. I don't know why I say that. Carl must have mentioned horses at some point. I'm sorry I can't be of more help."

"Did Mr. Ridley have any friends I can talk to?"

"He belonged to the Chamber of Commerce, the Kiwanis, and all the town's organizations since he was a local businessman. I took over in that regard about five years ago when he lost interest in civic activities. The truth is he buried just about everyone he ever met or worked with. You might try talking to the lady who took care of him the last couple of years. She might know something. I can give you her address and phone number if you like."

"I would appreciate that very much," Nealy said, looking around at all the burgundy furniture, the dark blue carpets, and the heavy velvet draperies hanging over the windows. She hated the furnishings, the atmosphere, and the pasty white man writing down the address behind a highly polished desk. Why couldn't the room be light and airy? Why did they have to have brass lamps with dark green shades and lightbulbs that burned during the day? Her skin itched, and her eyes started to water with the heavy flower scent. She started to breathe through her mouth.

"It's not far from here. I made you a rough sketch. Catherine Nolan is her name. Give her my regards when you speak with her."

"How . . . how old is Miss Nolan?"

"Oh, she's up there in years but quite spry," Lyons said.

He can't wait to get his hands on her, Nealy thought. *Bastard. What a way to earn a living, sitting around waiting for people to die.* She fled.

Jason Lyons was right; Catherine Nolan's house was less than fifteen minutes away. Nealy parked on the street and stared at the small white house with a large front yard. It looked well maintained. She wondered what "up there in years" meant. Was Catherine Nolan really old? If so, who kept the house painted and who maintained the yard?

She liked the small front porch with the two cane rockers. The heavy door behind the glass storm door was shiny red and held a Christmas wreath that was still fresh and green and gave off a scent. She rang the bell and waited. It opened almost immediately. Nealy introduced herself and was invited inside.

Catherine Nolan looked just the way a grandmother was supposed to look. She was plump and wore an apron. Her cheeks were plump and pink, and her eyes twinkled behind wire-rimmed spectacles. Her hair was snow-white and fashioned into a topknot on the middle of her head.

"Come in, come in," she said when Nealy introduced herself. "Can I offer you some coffee and gingerbread? It's fresh out of the oven. Today is my baking day. I hope you don't mind if we visit in the kitchen. I have to watch the oven."

"I'd like that very much, Miss Nolan."

"Call me Rinney. Everyone calls me Rinney. Sometimes I forget my name is Catherine. Tell me why you're here, Miss Clay."

Nealy told her. "Mr. Lyons said you might be able to help. He also said to give you his regards."

"*Don't be needing his* regards just yet. He'll be getting me soon enough. Got my plot all picked out, even my casket. Got me one of those fancy Springfield jobs from a mail-order house with lots and lots of shiny brass. All paid for, too. I have it stored away in the garage. Mercy, I don't know what I can be telling you. Mr. Ridley was very close-mouthed. When he passed on, I packed up his things. No one wanted them, so I fetched them here and they're still in the cellar. Didn't seem right to throw a man's life away like that. There wasn't any family left in these parts, and no one knew where to look for any distant relatives. I asked everyone in town, and the police chief said it was all right to store the things here in case anyone ever did come looking. Good thing I did, too, since here you are." She set a flowered plate with a generous slice of gingerbread in front of Nealy. "Would you be liking some fresh whipped cream with your cake?"

"I do have a sweet tooth, ma'am. Yes, I would. This coffee is delicious."

"I grind the beans. Makes all the difference."

"Miss . . . Rinney did you know Seth Coleman, or any of the Colemans for that matter?"

Rinney Nolan looked like she'd just swallowed a lemon. "Everyone in these parts knows the Colemans. Heard they fell on hard times. I know it isn't Christian of me to be saying this, but I'm glad. I don't know, maybe the young'uns aren't too bad, but old Seth, he's a legend around here."

"He was my father," Nealy said.

"Fancy that. If you had told me that when you first came here, I would have sent you packing instead of offering you my fresh cake."

"No, no. It's not what you think. I hate his guts. I really do. I'm here because of my mother. I want to know about her. Can you tell me anything?"

Still bristly in spite of Nealy's confusing confession, Rinney said, "I can tell you plenty. She took up with that rancher, and it was the end of her. She was a fun-loving girl, Marty was. Worked hard over at the Horseshoe. That's where she met Seth Coleman. He was smitten with her. Everyone in town knew. Carl, Mr. Ridley, was beside himself, thinking the townspeople would go off and die somewhere else. Said it wasn't good for his business." She clucked her tongue to show what she thought of that statement. "It wasn't like people were going to go out of town to die. In the end it didn't hurt his business at all. Your grandparents took the shame really bad and became reclusive. They stopped going to church, and the Reverend, he would stop by and talk from time to time. Marty moved out of her parents' house and Seth set her up in an apartment. Paid all the bills. Gave her spending money and bought her clothes. He even bought her a car. Then the second baby came along and then a third. I guess you were the third one. I was a nurse back then. Your mama got very good care, I can tell you that. She was a good mother, too, from what I heard. Loved her babies she did."

"Yes, I was the third one."

"Then it all went wrong. Marty's car was gone. At first she thought someone stole it. Wasn't so. Then the whole town started buzzing about Seth Coleman's brother that came for a visit. Seth never went to the Horseshoe after that. Then Marty was gone. By that time her other two sisters had married and gone off to the Lord only knows where. Carl Ridley was the only one left. He didn't talk about his sister after that. Not that he talked about her much before. He felt too shamed to even bring up her name."

"What . . . what did the townspeople think when . . . when she left?"

"Just about what you would think they would think. What they *knew* was more like it. That Seth paid his brother to take Marty and the young'uns off his hands. He got tired of her and was seen chasing Melba Winerose, but nothing ever did come of that. That's all I know. Now, did you like my cake?"

"It was very good. Do you mind me asking how old you are, Rinney?"

"I'm eighty-four. The reason I'm eighty-four is I never got married. Didn't have some man telling me what to do and when to do it. I had peace of mind. And I had money in the bank and my own little house, and I did have a car for a long time. Sold it off a while back. My neighbors take me to the store and to church. Sometimes I miss not having children, but I've had my share of dogs and cats. Gave them a good home, and they snuggled with me at night. Now"—she held up a warning finger—"that's not to say there were never any men in my life. There were several, but I made sure they went home at night to their own beds. I'd like for you to tell me what happened to your mama, child."

"She died. That old man Josh worked her to death. I never knew her. The only picture I have of her is this one," Nealy said, pulling the photocopy out of the yellow envelope.

Rinney peered down through her bifocals. "She was pretty, that's for sure. I'm sorry she died so young."

"Do you remember anything about her, Rinney? Anything she might have said when she was in the hospital, maybe something she said to someone. My brothers and I don't really know anything about her."

The little woman's face puckered up. "She liked violets. Someone brought her some when she delivered one of the little boys. Come to think of it, she had violets on her little table every single time. She liked to needlepoint. She made me a pincushion once. I still have it. It was to thank me for taking care of her when she was in the hospital. I forgot about that until just now. It had a bluebird on it. She said something about bluebirds and happiness. To my way of thinking that meant she liked birds and bluebirds in particular. You wait right here, and I'll fetch the pincushion."

When Rinney returned, Nealy reached for the small, round tufted cushion. Tears burned her eyes as she stared down at the pincushion. She was holding something in her hands that her very own mother had made with her hands many, many years ago. A gift of gratitude to another human being.

"If you want it, child, keep it."

"Thank you. Thank you so very much."

"If you like, you can go down to the cellar and look through Carl's things. It's warm down there, but you best put on one of my aprons so you don't get your clothes dirty. There's only three or four boxes. Some of the things belonged to your grandparents, small things Carl kept as memories. There might be something there of Marty's. I didn't go through the things, just packed them up. By rights, I guess those boxes now belong to you. You can take them with you."

"You don't mind?" Nealy asked, incredulous that at last she had something she could sink her teeth into. She held the bluebird pincushion over her heart.

"Be glad to get them out of the cellar. I just keep moving them from one spot to the other. Sometimes when it rains hard the cellar gets wet."

"I don't know how to thank you, Rinney."

"You can thank me by not thinking harshly of your mother. She was young, and she did love that man. She truly did. He broke her heart. I think she loved you young'uns more, though. You go ahead downstairs. The light switch is on the right. If you bring the boxes up here, I'll tape them up for you. They're right there under the steps."

Nealy stood at the bottom of the steps, her heart thumping in her chest. She walked around behind the steps and stared down at four huge cartons. The mother lode! She felt light-headed, almost giddy with what lay before her. She would carry them out to the car and back to the hotel, where she would ask them to label the boxes and ship them UPS to SunStar Farms. Instead of heading back to Kentucky, she would go to Virginia first, and be there with her brothers so they could open the boxes together.

Her knuckles were pure white as she continued to clutch the bluebird pincushion.

"You've been very kind," Nealy said when she had secured the last box in the trunk of her car. "I will treasure this pincushion all the rest of my life. I didn't have one thing, not one little thing, not a scrap of paper, not a hairpin to prove to me I really had a mother. Is there anything I can do for you, anything at all to show my gratitude?"

"I'd like it if the next time you visit Marty's grave, you put a bunch of violets there for me. Tell her I remembered."

"I'll be sure to do that, Rinney. Maybe I'll get some seeds and plant them all over her grave. In the spring, when they bloom, it will be like a carpet. A beautiful, violet carpet planted with love from her daughter and her nurse. If you ever find yourself in Kentucky, be sure to visit." She hugged the little woman, who hugged her in return.

"You drive safely, young woman," Rinney said, and smiled.

6

Dusk was settling over SunStar Farms as Nealy watched her brothers carry the four cartons of Carl Ridley's belongings into the living room. Rhy had his bowie knife ready to slice through the thick tape Catherine Nolan had used to seal the boxes. Nealy had her fingers crossed, the pincushion in her hands. She'd carried it with her, either in her hand or in her pocket, since the old nurse had given it to her. Her brothers' expressions tugged at her heart. *Please,* she prayed, *let there be something in these boxes that will show us we were loved and wanted. I don't care if it's a scrap of paper, just so it's something.*

"I don't know if I'm ready for this," Rhy said gruffly, his expression apprehensive. "We're going to be mighty disappointed if there's nothing in here but funeral books and sympathy cards."

"There's only one way to find out." Nealy looked at Pyne, whose eyes appeared glazed. "You open the first one, Pyne."

Pyne's hands trembled as he pulled the sturdy carton toward him. Everything in the box belonged to their uncle Carl Ridley— old bank statements, ledgers, a paperweight, an assortment of odds and ends from a desk. Nothing personal, nothing intimate.

"Rhy, you go next," Nealy said, her fingers tracing the outline of the bluebird on the pincushion.

Rhy ran his fingers through his graying hair, a determined look on his face. He yanked at the carton and opened it. "Books and pictures. Old-fashioned pictures." He held up a handful of pictures. "They're so old they've started to turn brown."

"No, that's the way they were back then," Nealy said, reaching for the pictures. "They call it sepia. Oh, look, this must be our uncle and his wife. You look like him, Pyne," Nealy said, as Rhy held up a framed photograph. "You really do. Who's that?"

"Must be our grandparents," Rhy said quietly. "They look like nice people. Stiff but nice. Oh, God, look, here's a family picture. Which one is Mom, Nealy?"

Nealy peered at the picture. "This one," she said, pointing out a young woman of about seventeen. "See, she has the braid going down her back. She had the braid in the diner picture. I bet she never cut her hair. Oh, she was pretty. Are there any more?"

Rhy screwed up his face. "Just pictures of the mortuary. One of a line of coffins. His first dollar I guess, since it's framed. Who gets the picture of Mom?"

"We all get one. I'll take it home with me and have a copy made for each of you. I can order an extra one or maybe have it blown up so you can hang it over the mantel. Would you like me to do that?"

"Yes," the brothers said simultaneously. "Yes. Do we look like her, Nealy?"

"Damn straight we look like her. We have her bone structure, her high cheekbones, and that glorious hair. We might have Coleman blood in our veins, but we don't look anything like those bastards. Just goes to show who had the best gene pool. Are there any others?"

Suddenly the hateful words Rhy had spoken to her the previous spring came to the forefront of her mind. "We really don't know what *he* was like so I can't honestly say we aren't like him. But I do know that if things had gone differently, we wouldn't be the people we are today, and we might not be sitting here."

"That's it for the pictures. Some magazines with new methods for embalming."

Pyne shuddered.

"Your turn, sis," Pyne said, pushing a carton toward her with his booted foot. "Wait, let's have a beer and a cigarette. This . . . this . . . shakes up your insides. I'll fetch it."

"I bet she was just like you, Nealy," Rhy said as he stared down at the picture of his mother. "You're her daughter, so it stands to reason you would take after her. We aren't like that . . . our father, are we, Nealy? What I said before about not knowing what he was like . . . Sons are supposed to take after their fathers."

Nealy placed a comforting hand on her brother's shoulder. "All we have to remember now is that our mother loved us. He doesn't matter. Sons do not always take after their fathers. Sometimes they take after their mothers."

Pyne returned with the beer. "Let's make a toast to our pretty mother," he said in a choked voice.

Nealy bit down on her lip, her eyes filling with hot tears. "To you, Mom," she said, holding up her bottle to clink it against Rhy's and Pyne's.

"She had a nickname. They called her Marty. We never knew that before. She liked violets. Before I leave, I want to plant some violets on her grave. You two will have to tend it and weed it. You'll do that, won't you?"

"It will be a privilege," Pyne said softly.

"Nealy," Rhy said, sitting his beer down next to him, "I've been meaning to tell you this for the past couple of days but kept forgetting. Dillon Roland has a new foal. Heard in town last week that he was boasting it was Derby material. Born same time Shufly was born. He calls him Navigator. Says this time he's going to go all the way to the Triple Crown."

Nealy laughed aloud. "Not in this lifetime. There are no words to tell you how much I hate that man."

"So does everyone else around here. I know you registered Shufly for the Derby the day he was born, but do you think he's Derby material? Do you have any sense of it yet?" Rhy asked.

"You know the answer to that question yourself, Rhy. It's too soon to tell. But I will tell you he's got everything going for him. If I had to take a guess, and it's just a wild guess, I'd say yes. Shufly isn't the problem. I'm the problem. I'm pretty old to be running the Derby."

Both brothers whooped with laughter to show what they thought of that idea. Nealy grinned. How wonderful it was to sit with her brothers, laughing and talking like a real family. *Please, God, don't ever let this change.*

"Okay, your turn, Nealy. Let's see what you have there," Pyne said.

Nealy took a long, deep breath and felt her nerves spike. Would this be the box that finally put to rest all her old longings? *Don't have high expectations, Nealy.* Childishly she crossed her fingers and bent over to bend back the flaps of the cardboard carton. "It's clothes!" she said in dismay. "Socks and underwear, a wool sweater and some gloves."

Her brothers looked at one another. Both of them dropped to their knees to put their arms around her. "It's okay, Nealy. You have the pincushion and the picture. A few days ago we never expected even that. Just be grateful, and we have one more box to go through. It might turn out to be the best one yet. Why don't we go outside and walk down to the barn. We need to clear our heads. This is powerful stuff we're doing here. Come on, Nealy," Pyne said, helping his sister to her feet.

They were back in the house within the hour, their faces hopeful but resigned.

"Nealy, you open this last one. You're the only daughter, so it should be you. Let's just agree that whatever it is, it's more than we had when we started out. We need to be grateful for this little bit," Pyne said.

"You're right. Well, here goes." Gingerly, Nealy folded back the flaps of the box, then bent them downward. A piece of yellow paper lay across the contents of the box. In dark ink, the huge printed words proclaimed MARTY'S THINGS. "Oh, God, oh, God!" Nealy said, clapping her hands to her cheeks. "It's Mama's things. How did he get them if she went away? Did that hateful old man send them to Carl Ridley?"

"*Maybe* the answers to your questions are in the box, Nealy. See what it is," Rhy said, sitting down on the floor next to his sister. Pyne settled himself in the space on the other side of Nealy.

"It's her things. Her personal things. Things she either left behind or . . . or, I don't know what. Here's a bracelet, but it's tarnished. A book. Oh, look, it's *Little Women*. Here's another one, *Jane Eyre*. That means Mama liked to read. Oh, isn't this wonderful. Oh, look at this, it's pressed violets in a little silver frame. It's tarnished, too, but I can polish it up. Violets must have had some special kind of meaning to her." Nealy opened a small wooden box whose lid was on hinges. "It's her recipes. Recipes she wrote. In her own handwriting. Look how pretty her writing is. All swirly and flowery. You can hardly read my handwriting." Tears dripped down her cheeks as she reached for a packet of faded photographs tied with a violet-colored ribbon. She handed the packet to her brothers.

Rhy undid the ribbon, his eyes wet. "It's us when we were little. Damn, we were good-looking kids. She wrote our ages and names on the back." He passed the snapshots to Pyne, who passed them to Nealy. They cried openly then, brothers and sister. It was the last picture that brought Nealy to her feet. "Well, if there was ever any doubt, this erases it. It says, Rhy, Pyne, Cornelia, and their daddy, Seth Coleman. I know our first instinct is to burn this, but it is the only picture we have that's proof. If neither of you mind, I'd like to keep this. I won't look at it or anything like that, but I do think we need to preserve it. Don't ask me why I think this, I just do. Do you agree?"

"Sure," Pyne said.

"It's okay with me."

"Good. How about if I take all these pictures with me, get new negatives and prints made. Then we'll each have a set. Look how cute you two are. You can see by the look on Mama's face that she adored you both. You can't even see me, I'm so bundled up. This is the only picture of me from that time. It proves I'm me. Do you have any idea how important that is to me? Maud and Jess took pictures of me, but I was seventeen then. These are *real*."

"What else is in there?" Rhy asked, peering into the box.

"That's because you bundle up babies," Pyne said gruffly. "I can see your face."

"A scarf wrapped in tissue paper. It feels like silk. A snood. That's to keep your hair in place. Here's a jeweler's box! Mama had jewelry!" Nestled inside the velvet box was a single strand of pearls and a silver ring that looked like a wedding ring.

Three pairs of eyes stared down at the pearls and the ring.

"These pearls are older than I am. Why would Mama have a wedding ring? Do you think it was a pretend ring? You know, to make her feel better about her relationship with Seth Coleman."

"That would be my guess," Pyne said. "It doesn't matter anymore, Nealy. It really doesn't."

"It matters to me, Pyne. It always will, too." Nealy handed the box to Rhy, who dropped it. The silver ring rolled across the floor. Nealy scrambled on all fours to capture it. Pyne picked up the pearls. Rhy reached for the box, dropped it a second time, and watched as the velvet lining fell loose. A square of brittle paper, folded over to match the size of the lining, fell out.

Nealy sucked in her breath. "What is it?"

"I don't know," Rhy said.

"Maybe it's one of those things none of us wants to know. If our mother hid it in this box, she must have done it for a reason," Pyne said. "Maybe we don't have any right to look at it."

Nealy gave her brother a long-suffering look. "She's gone, Pyne. We *have* to look at it. When people hide things they always expect those things to be found someday. Maud told me that. You're the closest, Rhy, you see what it is."

"You're a girl. You do it," Pyne said.

"All right. But if it turns out to be something none of us likes or that we can't handle, we put it back and never mention it again. We have to agree, or I'm not touching it."

"We agree, we agree. Just do it already," Rhy said loudly, his voice booming all around the room.

Nealy's touch was reverent as she unfolded the fragile square of paper. "It's . . . it's a . . . what it is is . . ."

"For God's sake, Nealy, what the hell is it?" Pyne exploded.

"It's a marriage license! Mama was married to Seth Coleman. It says so right here. Look for yourself!"

"Just tell me one thing, are we legitimate or illegitimate?" Pyne demanded hoarsely.

"You are *legitimate!* We all are. Look at the dates! Just look at those dates!" Nealy screamed at the top of her lungs. "There is a God after all! I knew there was, but this . . . this makes it all right. I can't believe this! If they were married, why did they let everyone think . . . those awful things?"

"Who knows the way that ugly man's mind worked? More to the point, if Seth Coleman was married to our mother, did he divorce her? How could he have sold us off to his brother?"

"I don't know, Pyne. We'll probably never know. I don't know about you two, but I am in total shock. I simply can't believe this."

"Are you sure it's real? You said the ring might be a pretend ring. Maybe this is a pretend marriage license," Rhy said.

"No, it's real. As real as my marriage certificate to Hunt. See, here's the raised seal. We can always check it out. They were married in Nevada. I don't think it would be hard to check. I can have Ruby ask the Thorntons to do it for us. It's just all so unbelievable."

"Is there anything else in the box, Nealy?" Pyne asked.

"Some letters. I guess they're from her sisters. And a book. No, it's not a book. Well, it is a book but it's a diary. Mama's diary. Oh, my God! Mama kept a diary. Now we'll know everything. Everything we ever wanted to know about her. Look, it's late. Let's make some dinner since it's your cook's day off. Some fresh coffee. We'll build up the fire and sit in here, and I'll read her life to us this evening. I want to think about all this for a little while. You know, kind of hug it to me. Is that okay with you both?"

"Sure, but you have to do the cooking. I have some things to check on at the barn. Rhy, you bring in a load of firewood. Bring lots of it. I have a feeling it's going to be a long night. You might need to bring in some beer from the back porch."

Nealy settled herself in the corner of the deep, comfortable sofa. Next to her on a small table was a thermos of coffee. Beer bottles in a bucket of ice rested on the coffee table between her brothers' recliners. It was nine-thirty when Nealy opened her mother's diary. Once it had been bright red. Now it was faded to a dusty pink. The small brass key was pinned in place with a thumbtack.

"This is a five-year diary. What that means is there are just a few lines for each day of the year. I never had one of these, but I gave one to Emmie when she was about ten. We used to laugh at how she could only get a few words on each page because she wrote her letters so big. She would . . . what she would do was write her secrets on a piece of paper and then Scotch tape it to the page. At the end of the first year that diary was ten inches thick with extra sheets of paper. This diary," she said, looking at her brothers, "was probably never meant to be read. I have mixed feelings about reading it. Maybe if we'd had a normal life and came across this by accident at some point, I want to think I would have returned it to wherever I found it. I hope we're doing the right thing by reading it."

"Is the book full? Did she use up all the pages?" Rhy said.

"No. There's about thirty pages with nothing written on them. Sometimes, she skipped whole weeks and months. I guess she just wrote what she thought was important. The first entry is the one where she met Seth Coleman. This is what it says. . . ."

I met the most dashing man today at the diner. He kept ordering food just so I would keep coming back to his table. He told me my hair was beautiful and that my complexion was like fresh cream. I tried to hide my hands because they're so rough and red. I wonder if he'll come back. He left me a wonderful tip. I'm going to buy some of that glycerine and rosewater. Maybe even a pair of rubber gloves for when it's my turn to do the dishes. I hope he comes back.

"The next entry is two weeks later."

He came back. He asked if I'd like to go for a walk with him after my shift was over. I said yes. He told me again how pretty I was. He told me he thought about me every day for the whole two weeks. He's so virile. We walked over to the park and sat on one of those hard wooden benches. I let him kiss me. I thought my heart would pound right out of my chest. He told me he was a widower. He likes me a lot. I can tell. He asked if he could see me again. I said yes.

"It goes on like that for a while. Mostly just one line here or there. Then at the end of the month she writes a summary. At least I think it's a summary. Here's the first one."

* * *

This has been a month to end all months. I think I'm falling in love. Seth says he already loves me. He wants me to have sex with him. I said no. He comes by every single day. They're starting to tease me at the diner about snagging a rich rancher. I asked him if he was rich, and he said yes. He brings me flowers every single day. Little bunches of violets. He's very kind and gentle with me. He says pretty things that I like to hear.

"There aren't any entries for the next few months. This is the next one, four months later."

I'm beside myself. I don't know what to do. Seth wants to go to bed with me. I keep saying no. Mama would skin me alive if she knew I was even thinking about going to bed with a man I wasn't married to. All my girlfriends have had sex, and they tell me to go ahead. Seth said we could take a trip. He worked up this fancy story for me to get away. I'm thinking about it. I want to, but I'm afraid someone will find out.

"There's not another entry for an entire year. This is the first one."

I asked Seth point-blank if he intended to marry me. He said, not yet. Mama won't even look at me. She called me a harlot. Daddy won't look at me either. They won't sit at the table with me. They stopped going to church because everyone is talking about me. Seth said he loves me and that sex with me is so wonderful all he does is dream about me. I told him how things are at home, and he agreed to get me my own apartment so he can come over anytime he feels like it. He said he would buy me my own car. Imagine that! He gives me spending money, too, as he put it, to buy myself some pretties. He means fancy underwear and silky nightgowns. I do it because I love him. He never talks about his other life but I asked around and I know he has children. I think he's ashamed of me. I started to cry when I asked him that and he said no, he wasn't ashamed of me. I want to get married because I love him so much it hurts when I can't see him.

"No more entries for seven months."

* * *

I've made up my mind. I'm moving out of the apartment and giving back the car. I can't live like this. My friend Melba said I could stay with her for a while. I'm not even going to tell Seth. I'll leave him a note. I can get a job waitressing anywhere. I don't have any willpower where he is concerned. This will be a good way to find out if he truly does love me or if he just wants a cookie on the side.

"There aren't any real entries, a line here or there saying she hasn't seen him or heard from him. She got a new job at someplace called the Sweet Grass Cafe. The next entry is four months later."

He found me. He looked awful. Sad and his eyes filled up. He said he loved me more than he loved his horse. I guess that's a good thing. He said he would marry me, but we couldn't tell anyone for legal reasons. I don't care about reasons. I just want to marry him and be happy. I hope we have a baby.

"Well, she got her wish. The next entry is two weeks later."

We got married. Seth wanted to keep the marriage license, but I wanted to keep it. He said no, he's the man, and he should keep it. He stuck it in his pocket and when he fell asleep, I took it out and hid it. He thought he lost it. He was so upset. He never asked me if I took it, so I didn't have to lie. He said he could get a copy of it by paying more money. I never in my wildest dreams thought I could be so happy. I now have a beautiful two-bedroom apartment with a marvelous kitchen. Seth bought me a fancy yellow car, a brand-new one. He said it was a wedding present. He gave me a string of pearls. He is so kind to me. He comes every day. He gives me more money now so I won't have to work. My hands are starting to look real nice now. I even polish my nails.

"The next time she wrote was a full year later."

Merciful God, I'm pregnant. I thought it would never happen. Seth was furious at first. Then when he saw how happy I was, he smiled. He said he was going to have to move me again. To Dallas. I cried for days because that means I won't see him every day. He said he would visit week-

ends. He said he would find a nice house with a backyard for our firstborn. I pray that it will be a boy. I asked him today if he was ever going to take me to the ranch, and he straight out said no. He said our life had to be kept separate and secret. I did agree to that, so I cannot complain.

"There are other one-line entries mostly dealing with her morning sickness and Seth not showing up every weekend the way he promised."

I have a beautiful baby son. He is so precious he takes my breath away. Seth is mesmerized with him. I think he truly loves him. Rhy coos for him and grabs his finger. Seth says he is going to grow up to be a sturdy lad. I sit for hours just watching him or else I rock and sing to him. He is the most beautiful thing that has ever happened to me. I sent Mama a letter telling her, and she sent it back. I sent one to Carl, and he said it would be better if I didn't write him again. I don't know where my sisters are. When Mama and Daddy got so angry they moved out. I feel sometimes like I broke up our family. Seth says that's nonsense and said I don't need anyone but him. He forgot to leave money for me today. I don't know what to do. I'm afraid to call him at the ranch to remind him. He warned me never to do that. Maybe I can think of something clever.

"She wrote six months later."

I'm pregnant again. And I'm still nursing Rhy. I'm afraid to tell Seth, but I know I have to. I haven't seen him in over a month. There is barely enough food. I've been watching one of the neighbor's children just for pin money. Pin money that buys bread and peanut butter. I'm so sick of it I could throw up. I have to find a way to get some money even if I have to take it out of his trousers while he's asleep. This is a fine mess I find myself in.

Nealy's anger mounted as she read on. "There's more of the same. No money, he isn't visiting. Just a line here or there. He was furious when she told him. She writes that she cried for weeks at a time until Rhy came down with colic because he wasn't getting enough milk. Oh-oh, what have we here."

* * *

Well, I got my spunk together and told Mr. Seth Coleman what I thought of him. I made demands. Threatened to go to the ranch if he didn't leave me enough money to live. He looked like he was ready to strike me. I dared him to lay a hand on me. Something in me died right then and there. He left me fifty dollars. I took another twenty out of his trousers while he was taking a shower. Then I went back and took two more twenties. I'm going to buy some fresh meat and vegetables. The baby is due any day now. My neighbor has promised to watch Rhy for me. I promised her twenty dollars, and she jumped at it. All the sunshine seems to have gone out of my life.

"The next entry is the day she came home from the hospital with you, Pyne."

I have another son. He is just as beautiful as his brother. I'm surprised he is as big as he is and as healthy seeing how I didn't eat well during the nine months. He's a good baby, eats and sleeps. Rhy loves him. Seth said he was a strapping little boy. He brought me violets and tried to make peace with me. He left me $200. I took another fifty out of his trousers. Just in case. I hope he doesn't visit for a while. We do much better when he isn't around. I'm starting to dislike my husband.

Nealy sat quietly for ten minutes, reading her mother's words to herself. What would she have done in her position? She wondered. She couldn't imagine herself ever being in that kind of fix and yet . . . She thought back to what her life had been like before leaving SunStar Farms and realized she *had* been in a very similar position. The only reason she had left was because Josh threatened to send Emmie to an orphanage. But for that, God only knows how long she might have stayed. Maybe forever, like her brothers.

"There are a few more entries over the next year, mostly to do with lack of money and her growing dislike for Seth Coleman. Here's one where she talks about the two of you."

My two precious little boys. They are the sunshine, my only sunshine. I played outside with them all day today and had a picnic under the trees.

They still take my breath away. To think that I could make such beautiful little creatures. I don't know what I would do if anything happened to either one of them. My heart almost bursts with happiness when I settle them at night. When they wake in the morning my heart melts as their little arms circle my neck. God smiled on me when he gave me these two angels. I hope I live long enough to see them raised with their own families. Seth sent money through the mail. That's good. That means he won't be here for a while.

"The next entry is just a week later. Something's up here."

I'm so upset. Seth is here and will be here for the entire month. He said he has business in Dallas. We're eating wonderfully. He wants steak and roast beef every single day, and baked goods. My pantry is so full I just stand there and stare at it. He's good with the boys and they like him. My neighbor loaned me her camera and we took some pictures. At first Seth balked, but there wasn't too much he could do in front of my neighbor. My heart doesn't sing anymore when he's around. I'm sad to say I'm counting the days until he leaves. Every single day I take twenty dollars out of his trousers. He carries enough money around to choke a horse. Tomorrow I'm going to take more and hide it away. I'm going to do that every day until he leaves.

She glanced up to see that her brothers were both sitting forward in their chairs, looking as if they were expecting a bomb to explode.

"The next entry is a month later."

He's gone! Even the boys seem relieved. They are so good. They sit by themselves and color or play with their toys. I'm so grateful they have each other. I now have a little over $500. I feel so much better with this little nest egg. The larder is full, Seth made sure of that. The boys have a roomful of new toys, and their father didn't forget me either. I think he left me with another baby. I can't be sure but I'm almost sure. I haven't been feeling well lately. It will be a good reason to go to the doctor for a checkup. My heart is lighter. Seth said he wouldn't be back for several months. What kind of marriage is this?

* * *

"I want to cry for this woman who was our mother," Nealy said. "Maybe she'll get enough money to make her move." Her brothers could only shrug.

"The next time she wrote was four months later."

The doctor confirmed it. I'm pregnant. Maybe I'll be lucky and have a little girl this time. I pray to God I do. The doctor told me my heart isn't as strong as it should be. It beats irregularly or something like that. He told me not to overtire myself and to take vitamins. I do get tired easily and lately when the boys go down for their naps, I take one, too. One day they both climbed in bed with me and covered me up. They tell me I smell like sugar cookies. Pyne likes to kiss me on the ear and Rhy pretends to nibble on my nose. Dear God, how I love those two little men of mine. Seth will be coming this weekend. I dread seeing him, dread having to tell him. But my little nest egg will increase if he comes.

"She wrote five days later."

Seth's reaction was just what I expected. He was furious and stormed out. He came back hours later all liquored up and wanted to go to bed. Thank God the boys were already asleep. I suffered through it all. This time I took the whole wad of cash he had on him and hid it in the coffee bag. When he looked for it in the morning I was all innocent. I told him how drunk he was when he got here. I even cried when I asked if he wouldn't be able to leave me money. He said he would send me a check. Then he told me his brother was coming for a visit soon. Sometime during the next few months. I was surprised since he never talks about his other family. All I wanted was for him to leave. I now have $2000.

"There's a bunch of blank pages after that entry. It looks like maybe she wrote something and then tore out the pages. Anyway, the next entry is when she comes home in November with me. I'm finally born," Nealy said, wiping her eyes.

She is so very beautiful. And so healthy. She's just as good as Rhy and Pyne were when I brought them home. I'm going to call her Cornelia after

my grandmother. The boys adore her and take turns holding her and rock-
ing her. Rhy sings to her. Pyne makes faces to make her laugh. He doesn't
understand that newborn babies don't laugh. I don't want to share this lit-
tle miracle with Seth. I know his opinion of women and female babies. He
won't be kind to Cornelia the way he is to the boys. I will have to be her
champion, and I will do that lovingly every single day of my life. I just
want to hold her against my breast forever and ever. Seth is coming this
weekend and bringing his brother with him. I'm anxious about this visit.
While I was in the hospital I was thinking about Seth and how he was
never around for any of the children's births. I had to go through it all my-
self. I had to get myself to the hospital and I had to get myself home. Thank
God for nice neighbors. The nurse Seth hired for me was very sweet. Her
name was Rinney. He fetched her from Austin just for me. Seth did send
flowers each time, but it would have been nice if he had been there in per-
son. I now have $3000 in my nest egg. God is watching over me.

Nealy licked at her dry lips. "There's one more entry and that's
the end of the diary. I'm almost afraid to read it. Pop me one of
those beers, Rhy. I think I'm going to need it. We know one thing,
boys, our mama did love us. She really and truly loved us. God, I
wish I had known her even if it was just for one day. One day! Here
goes."

Rhy nodded.

Her brothers turned to look at her and she knew what they were
thinking, that she wasn't at all like them or like their mother, that
she was strong, strong like her father, Seth Coleman.

She felt the bile rise in her throat. She didn't want to be anything
like any of the Colemans, especially her father. With an effort she
continued to read.

I don't expect I'll be writing in this little diary again. My life has come
to an end. At least the life I had. Seth brought his brother here. He looks
just like Seth. But he's a mean, hard man. I could tell. But then Seth
turned mean, too. Seth is packing us off with his brother to Virginia. He
said he can't take care of us anymore. He said his brother would take care
of us from now on. Said he gave him money for our keep. I think he sold us
is what I think. There was no mention of a divorce. Thank God I hid that

marriage license. We're to take nothing with us, not even the children's toys. Just our clothes. I called my brother Carl and asked him if he would come by and pack up our things and keep them for us until I needed them. He said he would. I don't want to go, but I'm realistic enough to know that my $3000 wouldn't keep us for long. We have no other choice. Seth made me cook a big dinner to show his brother I knew my way around the kitchen. Then they both left without eating anything. Seth looked at me and said good-bye. He didn't kiss me, didn't touch me. He just said good-bye. I simply stood there and looked at him. His brother will be by tomorrow to pick us up. I'm going to spend all of this last night on my knees praying to God that this man is good to my children. I don't expect him to love them. I just want him to be good to them. I will pray until the moment we all walk through the door for the last time.

"Oh, God!" Nealy sobbed into her hands. Her brothers broke down and joined her. When she couldn't cry anymore, Nealy struggled to her feet. "Does Hank Meyers still own the feed store?"

"He died a long time ago, Nealy. His son Hank Jr. runs it now."

"Get on the phone with him. Tell him I'm on the way and I want to buy some flower seeds. Pay him whatever he wants. A thousand, ten thousand, a hundred. I don't give a shit. Say please. Sometimes that helps. I'm on my way. You boys get the shovels and some manure. We've got plenty of that for sure. We are going to plant us some violets."

"It's winter, Nealy. The ground is frozen, and it's the middle of the night."

"It might be winter but the ground isn't frozen. If it is, we'll thaw it out. We're doing it! Do you think any of us are going to sleep tonight? We aren't. I'll be back in thirty minutes."

She was as good as her word. "Hank Jr. thinks I'm nuts. I told him he was probably right. What did it cost to get him to open the store?"

"A month's free board for his horse."

"Let's go, boys."

Two hours later, Nealy covered the grave with a thick layer of hay and then watched as her brothers tacked down the burlap cover she'd spread across the entire grave.

"Now what?" Rhy asked gruffly.

"Now we can rest easy. We each say a prayer, and go back to the house, and cry in each other's arms. She loved us with all her heart. That's what we carry away from all of this. No more and no less. Race you to the house!"

PART II

7

Emmie crept down the steps tying the belt on her robe as she went along. Nick, she knew, was studying in the dining room, and she didn't want to disturb him. She skirted the room and made her way to the kitchen. She peeked in and frowned. Nick was sound asleep, with his head and arms on the table. She wanted to cry for him. He was so ragged these last weeks, but he was coming into the homestretch—only a year to go—and it would be worth all the sleepless hours, all the anxiety.

She knew she had to wake him up but hated to do it. First she rinsed the coffeepot, knowing she would need to make fresh coffee for Nick.

She looked around, delaying the moment when she would have to wake Nick. *I hate this place,* she thought. *I really hate it.* She knew she could go home, back to Kentucky. She could go back to the house she'd shared with Buddy, but she didn't like that house because of the bad memories. She wanted to go *home* where she belonged. Back to Blue Diamond Farms.

She'd run away like a coward, following Nick blindly because at the time it seemed like the thing to do.

She tiptoed over to the sliding door and walked out onto the patio. She looked down at the patch of Kentucky bluegrass growing inside the small greenhouse she'd purchased at a local hardware store. She tended it as carefully as she tended to her daughter. The grass was thick and luxurious and perfect in color. She thought about all the times she'd stood over it and cried. Maybe her tears helped it to thrive. She was tempted to snip off a blade, and put it between her thumbs and whistle. She had been tempted hundreds of times, but she'd never done it. She wanted, needed, to preserve each blade. A lone tear dropped onto one of the slivers of grass. In the dim patio light she could see that it looked like a small, bright diamond. She swiped at her tears and walked back into the house.

Inside the house, Emmie made her way to the dining room, where she gently shook Nick's shoulders. "Wake up, Nick."

"Oh, God, did I fall asleep? How long have I been asleep? What time is it?"

"It's almost two o'clock. I went to bed at midnight and you were awake then. I guess maybe an hour, Nick. Would you like me to make some coffee for you? I can fix you a ham sandwich if you like."

"Yeah, do that, Emmie. Make that two sandwiches. Pickles if you have them, and make the coffee really strong. What are you doing up at this time? Is Gabby okay?"

"She's fine. I couldn't sleep."

Nick tossed his pen on the table. "Were you outside watching your grass grow? By the way, how's it doing?"

Emmie beamed. "I have five squares now. Each one is as big as a doormat. I can't plant it here, it would never survive. Just seeing it every day is all I need."

"You really miss home and Mom, don't you?"

"Yes, I do. I was missing Mom tonight. That's why I couldn't sleep. Do you think she misses us, Nick?"

"I don't know. I hope so. I sure as hell miss her. I'd give anything to hear her yell at me for something or other. I want to show you something, Emmie. C'mere," he said, leading her to the breakfront, where he opened the bottom cabinet where he kept his books. "See this box. It's letters I wrote to Mom. Letters I never mailed. Sometimes when I think I can't do this one more minute, I stop what I'm doing and write her a letter. I always feel better afterward. Did you ever do that?"

There had to be hundreds of letters in the box. "A few times, but all I did was cry and make myself feel worse so I stopped. The grass makes me cry, too. Somehow, it's different, though. The grass represents a place. The letters to Mom were . . . I don't want to talk about it. I'll make the coffee and sandwiches."

Nick followed Emmie into the kitchen. It was probably the most pleasant room in the whole house because Emmie had wallpapered it herself with strawberry-patch-patterned paper that made the room bright and cheerful. She'd even painted strawberry decals on the white window shades. Thick green plants whose names he didn't know, sat on the counter along with a bright red sugar bowl where she kept change and dollar bills for the paperboy and the youngster who mowed the lawn. Just last month she'd made red cushions for the two benches that curled around the table in the breakfast nook. She called it busy stuff to keep her mind off things.

"Do you ever think about calling, Emmie?"

"Every single day. I actually did, once or twice but I always hung up before anyone could answer. One time I wasn't quick enough and I heard Smitty say hello. I cried all day. Did you do that, too, Nick?"

Nick nodded. "So many times I lost count."

"This was all worth it for you, Nick. You're going to be a lawyer. You're following your dream. I'm just existing. I have no goals, and that silly book I'm pretending to write is never going to go anywhere. It's just something to do. I lost all my direction. I don't have any goals, nothing to strive toward."

"You have Gabby. That's a miracle in itself," Nick said, reaching for the thick ham sandwich Emmie had made for him. He wolfed it down. He grabbed the second one and ate it just as fast. He munched on sour pickles until the coffee was ready.

"I wish we had more time to talk to each other," Emmie said wistfully as she cleared off the counter.

"It's just a little longer, Emmie. Just hang on until I finish, okay. Listen, maybe I don't tell you often enough how much I appreciate you being here. We're family. At the moment, all we have is each other. We need to stick together."

"I know, Nick." Hoping to delay him just a minute longer, she asked, "I hardly ever see Hatch. How is he?"

"That's one busy guy. He's here, he's there, he's everywhere. What's really amazing is the guy gets everything done and done on time. I'm a slug compared to him. I have to get to work. It's late, Emmie, you should go to bed."

"I will as soon as I finish cleaning up the kitchen. Will you be here for breakfast? If you don't have to leave early, I can make you those blueberry buttermilk pancakes you like so much."

"Sorry, Emmie, I have to be in the office by seven. Sleep in. I can grab some sweet rolls and coffee when I get to the office."

Emmie looked around the tidy kitchen before she scribbled a note to herself and left it by the phone. Call Hatch, ask him to go to lunch. Remember to take the latest pictures of Gabby to show him.

She poked her head into the dining room for one last look at Nick. He was bent over a thick law book, a yellow legal pad next to it. She crossed her fingers and smiled. Nick would do well. When you put your heart and soul into something, it had to work out well.

Upstairs, she crossed her fingers again. *Please, don't let Hatch be busy tomorrow. Please.*

Across town, Hatch Littletree popped two bottles of beer and carried them out to the balcony. He set one on the little round metal table and kept one in his hand. Tonight was another one of those nights when his memories wouldn't allow for sleep. His shoulders slumped as he stared off into the dark night, the stars above twinkling down on him.

He thought about his dead wife and son because no matter what he did, they were always with him in his mind. Would it always be this way? Was it that way for Nick and his mother when Hunt Clay died? Maybe for Nick, but not for Nealy. Hunt said Nealy had fallen out of love with him. Then he'd gone on to say he doubted if she ever loved him. Death was always hardest on those left behind. *Don't go there, Hatch.*

The big Indian had never listened to his conscience, so why should he start, he thought. Life was a bitch sometimes.

He flopped down on one of the chaise longues and stretched his legs out in front of him. He blinked when he realized he was barefoot. He didn't remember taking his shoes off. Ah, one of those little mysteries of life that would never be solved.

He gulped at the beer in the bottle. Once, after his wife and son died, he'd consumed twelve bottles of beer in a little less than an hour. The alcohol had not dulled his brain one bit. If anything, it intensified his rage and grief. *Don't go there either, Hatch. The past is gone, you can't bring it back.*

His eyes burned unbearably. "I need a goddamn life is what I need." He choked up with the words. Like it was so easy to do. Just go out on the street and say, hey, do you want to be my friend? I need a life, and in order to have a life I need friends and people around me. I need someone to hold and someone to love. I need someone to care about, and I want someone to care about me.

He switched his mental gears and was that skinny, raggedy-ass kid, back on the reservation, running wild. The good old days when he was young, dumb, and stupid. He roll-called his life until it brought him back to his chair on the balcony.

It was a good life, and he wouldn't change even one day of it, right up until the day the hospital called to tell him his wife and son were dead.

You're going there again. I told you not to go there, an inner voice warned.

Maybe he needed a cause, a project. Nick was a cause of sorts. Maybe a payback to his friend Hunt. Whatever it was, it was coming to an end. Nick was only a year away from taking the bar. When Nick passed, and he knew the kid would pass, Hatch would be at loose ends again.

He thought about Emmie and her little girl. A smile worked its way to his lips. He loved holding the little one in his arms. Loved the feel of her and the way she smelled, all sweet and powdery just the way his son had felt and smelled. *You aren't supposed to go there, you dumb schmuck.*

"Then where in the damn hell am I supposed to go?" he cried in a tormented voice.

Try Kentucky, the inner voice suggested. *Go there and make peace with Nealy Clay for her kids' sakes. Call it a mission. Bring her up short. Tell her how wonderful her kids are. Tell her how she screwed things up. Tell her life is too short and tell her she's in danger of losing her children altogether if she doesn't do something.*

Yeah, right, like I'm an authority and she's going to listen to me. Hunt told me many times she hated my guts.

So charm her. You're good at that. Nothing ventured, nothing gained. What's wrong with trying? the voice inside his head pressed.

Hatch stared down at his toes. He wiggled them to have something to do.

He leaned his head back into the soft padding on the chaise. Within minutes he was asleep.

He woke with a start at six o'clock when his cell phone rang. He mumbled a greeting. "Emmie! What's wrong? Is the baby all right? Lunch? Absolutely. I'll meet you at Carson's at twelve sharp. I'll look forward to it, Emmie. Thanks for inviting me."

Hatch was on his feet a second later, stretching his arms upward to follow his gaze. "I'm definitely taking this as a sign that I'm to go to Kentucky." He waited to see if a lightning bolt would descend in either acceptance or rejection of his idea. When nothing happened, he marched into the house and headed for the bathroom.

"Look out, Nealy Clay, here I come!" He whistled. A sure sign that something in his world was coming up right.

8

It was a beautiful day, Nealy thought as she hooked the heel of her boot on the board fencing to stare about her. She liked this time of day just after the sun came up when the dew sparkled on the bluegrass and the farm took on life. She liked it almost as much as she liked the end of the day when the sun set, especially when she knew the day had been a productive one.

Today, though, she was off her feed. She knew why but didn't want to think about it. Hunt had always said that was one of her main problems. She liked to shelve things and force herself to forget about them.

She couldn't forget this, though. It had been two and a half years since Emmie and Nick drove away from Blue Diamond Farms. There hadn't been so much as a word from Nick. Emmie had sent a birth announcement and a newborn picture of the baby. Other than that, there had been no communication. She hadn't heard one word from Nick. The birth announcement was of the drugstore variety, just a little fold-over card that said baby Gabriella Coleman was born on June 28 and weighed seven pounds nine ounces and was twenty inches long.

Coleman. That had to mean Emmie divorced Buddy and took back her maiden name. She should have known that, but she didn't. Did Emmie tell Buddy about the baby? Did she call the baby Gabby?

When Emmie was seven, Maud had given her a doll that she christened Gabriella and proceeded to call it Gabby. That doll had been Emmie's constant companion for more years than she cared to remember.

Dover Wilkie approached. "Nice morning, Nealy. Whatcha doing out here by yourself?"

"Thinking, Dover. Just thinking. I wish I had a cigarette." She looked up at him from under the brim of her hat.

"Thinking will get you into all kinds of trouble." He shook loose a cigarette from his breast pocket and handed it over. "This is the only one you're getting. You quit, remember? Besides, you're in training."

"I know, Dover. Sometimes I just *need* a cigarette. I was just thinking that I don't even know what my granddaughter looks like." She inhaled deeply and blew out a long stream of smoke. "The way things are going I may never get an opportunity to see her." A glazed look spread across her face. Up until now she'd been able to camouflage her feelings and her loneliness. She'd done it so well, she'd even camouflaged them from herself.

The lines of concentration deepened around Dover's eyes. "This is just a thought now, Nealy, but you could get up real early, get on a plane, go see that granddaughter of yours, say some pretty words, and be back here before the sun sets. If you want to, that is." Dover fired up a cigarette and watched the smoke circle Nealy's head.

"Yes, I could do that, Dover. My heart and my gut tell me this isn't the time." Nealy stared out across the pasture. "What do you think of Shufly, Dover?"

"Best horse I've ever seen. Perfect configuration. Perfect in every way. He's just like his daddy but stronger and faster. I didn't think that was possible, but he is. He's not just Derby material, he's Triple Crown material. We all know that. Beats the pure hell out of me how you've managed to keep this horse under wraps these past two years."

"I don't mean how he looks. I mean, you know . . ."

The vet and farm manager smiled. "I'm not a trainer, Nealy, but I am a pretty good judge of horseflesh, and the most important thing to me besides a colt's physical soundness is balance. If he's got good balance, his racing motion will be fluid, which means his stride will be even when his hooves hit the ground. It's just my opinion, but I think being fluid helps keep a horse sound. I've watched Shufly train, and he definitely has good balance. He also has a good, big eye. He's curious about everything that goes on around him and he's always bright-eyed and alert. In other words, he's interested in life. And that's a major asset."

Nealy took a deep breath. She trusted Dover's judgment even more than her own. "Maud always used to say, and Jess agreed with her, that you keep the best close to your chest until the time is right."

"You aren't going to enter Shufly in any prep races, then?"

"I gave it a lot of thought and decided not to. It's not entirely unheard of, you know. I figure he can race right here on the Blue Diamond track. That's what it's for."

"But he needs to know what it's like to compete against other horses, Nealy."

"I know that. That's why I bought a four-horse starting gate and had the track revamped. I'm going to start him out at six furlongs against Darcy's Dream, our last year's Breeders Cup winner. Then against Apache, who prepped in the Blue Grass Stakes last spring. Then . . ."

"Okay, okay," Dover said, holding up his hands to silence his boss. "I should have known you would cover all the bases. You always do." He put his hand on her shoulder and followed her gaze to the pasture. "Just be ready for all the flak you're going to get," he warned. "They're going to say you haven't done enough with Shufly to prepare him."

"I'm well aware of that, and I'm also aware that's not all they're going to be saying."

"What's that supposed to mean, Nealy?"

"You know the Thoroughbred racing business as well as I do, Dover. It's a man's world. Once it becomes public knowledge that Shufly is going to be running for the roses, there is going to be a buzz of gossip about his breeding, how he trained, and . . ."

"His jockey," Dover finished for her. "You. A woman."

"That's right. Me. A woman." She offered up a sideways smile. "I thought I had loosened things up a bit with Flyby's Triple Crown win, but I was just kidding myself. Someday things will be different, but I have a feeling that's still a long way off. You know as well as I do that every farm owner in the state of Kentucky resents me. Smitty tells me what's going on and who is saying what. They still, after all these years, refer to me as the stranger who stepped into the golden pile of horse shit. Every damn one of them wants to see me fail, and they want to see me fail because I'm a woman. That's the bottom line, and don't try to tell me different, Dover."

"Wouldn't think of it, Nealy, girl. I suppose the positive side to all this is that Shufly will be the dark horse entry, which should give him some pretty terrific odds."

They stood in silence for a few minutes watching the grooms turning the horses out into the pastures. Nealy never ceased to be awed by the sight of a magnificent horse tossing its head and galloping from one end of the pasture to the other. There was something purely magical about it for her.

"Listen, Dover, just between us, do you think I have the spit to pull this off at my age? I worry about that. My checking account statement says I'm a senior citizen."

Dover laughed so hard he started to choke. "Sometimes you are downright pitiful, Nealy. You're in your prime. You still have what it takes and then some. I see you out there every day exercising Shufly and Flyby. You're as alert and agile as a twenty-one-year-old. I mean that, Nealy, girl. Everyone on this farm says the same thing." He patted her on the back. "I'm moving on here, and no more cigarettes. You hear me, Nealy?"

"I hear you, Dover. Today is just a bad day. I'm going up to the house for some coffee and breakfast. Can I fetch you anything?"

"Nope. Swear on Shufly you ain't gonna smoke any more cigarettes."

"I swear, Dover. Get out of here before I kick you all the way back to the barn." Nealy laughed.

Nealy settled the Stetson more firmly on her head as she started the walk up to the house. Even though she was heading into the sun, she could see the outline of a man walking toward her. A giant of a man. She tilted the brim of the Stetson and squinted.

"Hatch!"

"Nealy, it's good to see you again. It's been a long time."

"You . . . you lost weight." What a stupid thing to say, Nealy thought, clearly flustered.

Hatch laughed, a great booming sound. "Hard work will do that to you. I forgot how great this place was. Of course I only saw it that once, and . . ."

"A funeral isn't the best time to pay attention to other things. What are you doing here? Are the kids okay?"

"The kids are fine. In my wildest dreams I never thought Nick could do what he's been doing. The firm pulled every string we could, and he did the rest. He's acing everything. Works twenty hours out of every day. He expected it going in, and he buckled down. You can be proud of him, Nealy. He's going to be one wild-ass lawyer. That's another way of saying he's a natural."

Nealy swirled her tongue around the inside of her mouth. "He was a natural with the horses, too," she said quietly.

"That may be, Nealy, but the kid *loves* the law. Just because you're good at something doesn't mean you have to love it. Hunt was the perfect example. He was a damn fine attorney but he loved horses more. I guess you're wondering what I'm doing here."

"Kind of," Nealy said. *He looks great,* Nealy thought. Her heart gave a little lurch inside her chest.

"It's like this. On the eve of my son's first birthday, Sela and I were getting ready for bed and suddenly she started to cry. She said she would give everything she owned if only her mother, our son's grandmother, could attend his first birthday party. I was thinking about that last night and realized you've never even seen a picture of Gabby except her birth picture." He reached inside his coat pocket and took out a handful of snapshots. "I hope I wasn't wrong thinking you would like to see what Gabby looks like. I can tell you all about her, too," he said eagerly. "I'm her godfather. Well, actually Nick and I are both her godfathers. Emmie wanted both of us. Gabby has two godmothers, too." He held out the pictures.

A cry of joy escaped Nealy's lips. "Oh, Hatch, thank you," she said, rushing to him to put her arms around his waist and hug him. He smelled good, all clean and *citrusy. Whoa, Nealy.* Flustered with her actions, she backed up, and said, "Come up to the house and have some coffee and breakfast. Listen, I . . . I am so very sorry about Sela and your son. I wanted . . ."

"Shhhh," Hatch said, placing his index finger against her lips. "It still hurts to talk about it. They aren't here any longer, and life goes on."

He had his big hands on her shoulders, a gentle touch for a man his size. He looked down into her eyes, and something happened to Nealy Diamond Clay. Something so strange, so alien, so foreign to her she was unable to tear her eyes away. She saw herself drowning in his dark eyes, saw him pulling her free, then holding out his hand to her to lead her away. Hunt, his fist shooting in the air, stood on the sidelines.

"What's wrong, Nealy? Are you okay?"

"I . . . ah . . . I don't know. You have beautiful eyes," she blurted.

It was Hatch's turn to look befuddled. The best he could manage to say was, "Do I now?"

"I was jealous of you," she blurted a second time.

"I know," Hatch said gently. "I was jealous of you, too. My partners, too. We wanted Hunt, and you snagged him away from us. It hurt. He was like a brother that deserted me. We all felt like that."

"All those years I worried that you would show up and drag him away. I spent a lot of time worrying about the wrong things. I often wonder if I had it to do over again if I would make the same mistakes. It wasn't meant to be. I think Hunt realized that before I did. He had Nick for consolation. I had the horses. Not exactly the way it should be. This sun is hot, and it isn't even midmorning. I hope you have time for me to show you around before you leave."

"I'll make the time, Nealy. I love all this bluegrass. I'd like to see the colt. Nick talked to me about him. Is he a winner?"

"Damn right he's a winner!" Nealy said, opening the screen door that led into the kitchen.

"Smitty, we have company for breakfast. Come out here, I want you to meet someone. Hatch, this is Matilda our cook and housekeeper. And this, you remember, is my right hand, Smitty. Matilda, Smitty, this is Hunt's old friend, Hatch Littletree."

Hatch swiveled around, shaking hands with the cook and then swiveling back in one easy, fluid motion to shake Smitty's hand.

"I'm so glad to see you again, in happier circumstances. I want you to tell me again how you hatched that egg," Smitty said.

Hatch grinned. "Very carefully."

Smitty grinned in return. "I already ate, Nealy. I have a lot of work piled up, so I won't be joining you. Nice meeting you, Mr. Littletree."

"Likewise."

"There's a bathroom off the kitchen if you want to wash your hands. I'll go upstairs and be right down. Just pancakes for me, Matilda. Hatch, give her your order."

Nealy galloped up the steps, breathless with the effort. She ran down the hall to the bathroom, where she leaned against the wall, struggling to take deep breaths. Something was happening to her. She looked in the mirror and groaned. She didn't look anything like Hatch's beautiful wife. Would he compare her to Sela? She clapped her hands against her fiery red cheeks. All she could do was splash some cold water on her face and brush her hair. She looked longingly at her cosmetic bag. Nick always said, "You clean up good, Mom. You should fix yourself up more often."

Nealy leaned against the vanity and closed her eyes. What was it Jess always said, "A day late and a dollar short." *Now what does that have to do with anything?*

"He's worth it, Nealy."

"Hunt?"

"You finally met the right one. You know it, don't you?"

"The one what? You spook me, Hunt."

"If you play your cards right, you could land the big guy. They don't come any better than Hatch."

"Don't go trying to fix me up with a surrogate duck, Hunt. Go back on your cloud or . . . or . . . you aren't going to . . . you can't . . . can you?"

"Oh yeah. You only have a year to the Derby. After that, maybe you should think about . . . other things. Like finally maybe trying to be happy. He can make you happy, Nealy."

"This is obscene. You're my husband and you're dead and you're trying to fix me up with some guy who hatches duck eggs between his legs. I don't want your help. Go away. Stop spying on me. You are, you know."

His laugh was warm and intimate, the same way it had been back in Texas years earlier. Nealy shivered as she opened her eyes. Damn, she really needed to get more sleep. How could she possibly lean against the vanity and doze off. She shook her head to clear her thoughts and raced downstairs.

"I like this kitchen. It's warm and cozy. You can tell people live here. I moved out of the house, sold it, and moved into a condo after . . . afterward. It's all stainless steel and chrome. I'm talking about my kitchen. Lately, any spare time I have I spend with Emmie in her kitchen. She's a terrific cook."

Nealy envied Hatch his relationship with her daughter. "Yes, Emmie was always a good cook." She walked over to the counter and poured herself a cup of coffee. Over her shoulder, she asked, "Did she ever tell Buddy about the baby?"

"No. I want her to, but she's adamantly against it at this time. I didn't push it. She's a very good mother." He spread the pictures across the table. "Sit down, Nealy, and have a look at your beautiful granddaughter. These are yours to keep. I had this set made for you."

Nealy's hands shook as she picked up first one picture and then another. Tears gathered in her eyes. "She looks just like Emmie did when she was her age. How chubby she is. Emmie looks wonderful. Nick looks tired," she said accusingly.

"Tired doesn't quite cut it. He's dead tired. More like exhausted. We make sure he eats right, exercises, and sleeps just enough to get by. It's the way it is, Nealy. He knew the ground rules going in and agreed to everything. He's holding up his end of the bargain. The law comes so naturally to him. He aces all of it with very little sweat. Your son has a phenomenal memory."

"What you're saying without saying the words is I screwed over my son for my own selfish reasons. Is that the way you see it?" Nealy asked.

"It doesn't matter what I think, Nealy," he said. "I'm sure you had your reasons for doing what you did." He smiled at her. "He's a fine young man, Nealy. One you can be proud of."

Nealy leaned across the table, determined to get all her questions answered. "You never liked me, did you?"

There was a spark of some undefinable emotion in his eyes. "I didn't know you well enough to like or dislike you. All I could go on was what Hunt said. I suppose along the way I formed some opinions. He told me you didn't like me."

"That's not exactly true. I was jealous. I told you that before. I suppose I still am. First you have my husband tied to you, and then my son and daughter run to you for safeguarding. You opened your arms wide to both of them. For that I'm grateful. I can't comprehend your generosity. You live in a big, wide world. My own is narrow by comparison. All I've ever known are horses and the land. And racing. I like to think that I'm a good person, but stacked up against you, I failed in Hunt's eyes. For a time you and I were the two most important people to him. In the end, you won and I lost. It's that simple."

Hatch reached for Nealy's hand. His eyes bored into hers. "Nothing in life is simple, Nealy. We all make mistakes and I've made my share just as you have. We learn from those mistakes. If we don't, we're lost. Life is never easy. Giving is what makes my life whole. When Sela and my son died I didn't think I could go on. That was the selfish part of me. I wanted to see my son grow into a fine young man. I wanted to grow old with Sela. I stuck my snoot in a bottle for a few months. Bode, Hank, Medusa, and Clay were there to pick up the pieces. They didn't try to stop me because it was something I had to work through on my own. Sela told me that if anything ever happened to her she wanted me to pack her away, all the pictures, all the memories, and get on with my life. I've been trying to do that because it's what she wanted. Some days are harder than others. Is that how it was with you when Hunt died?"

"No. It wasn't like that at all. We'd grown too far apart by then. I grieved, but life went on. I think I was in shock for a long time. He was way too young to die the way he did. Sela and your son were too young, too. I had the horses. It always comes back to the horses." The warmth and the strength of his big hand surprised her. She made no move to withdraw her hand, content for some strange reason with the closeness.

She didn't want to ask the question, but she did anyway because she needed to know. "Do the kids ever talk about me?" Her voice was so sad-sounding to her ears she wanted to cry.

"No. At least not to me. I won't lie to you, Nealy."

Nealy forced a smile. "I'm grateful for that, Hatch. If you're finished with your coffee, I'd like to show you the farm. Do you have the time?" She made a move to withdraw her hand, and Hatch squeezed it before he let it go.

"I have two hours before I have to be at the airport. Do you have anything else you want to ask me about the kids or Gabby?"

Nealy jammed her hands into the pockets of her jeans. "I don't think I have a right to ask anything. Circumstances aren't the best right now. Perhaps one day in the not-too-distant future things will change. I hope so. Oh, look, there's Ruby and Metaxas. I want you to meet them."

"Hatch, you son of a gun! What the hell are you doing here! It's been years! How are you, you big Indian?" Metaxas bellowed.

Ruby and Nealy watched in amazement as the two men slapped and clapped one another on the back, pushed each other away so they could eyeball one another before they met again in a bone-crushing hug.

"You two know each other?" Nealy asked in surprise.

"Hell, we're like two peas in a pod." Metaxas laughed. "Do you know what this guy did? He ripped a city right from under my nose. He built an entire community for his people. I had the contract, and he did it for free. I knew then I wanted to meet this guy. Then he charged me fifty bucks for the tour when it was finished. He's good people, Nealy."

"Yes. Yes, he is," Nealy agreed. "Nick and Emmie are with him in Santa Fe as you know. I don't know why I said that," Nealy dithered.

"Like I told you, Nealy, if they're with Hatch, then they're in good hands," Metaxas said. "Come on, I want to show you my horse. Not another one like it in the world."

Hatch looked questioningly at Nealy, who smiled and nodded.

"Now that's a man!" Ruby giggled, as she playfully nudged Nealy on the shoulder. "Good-looking in a rugged way. Muscles up the kazoo. Rich, too. Can't beat rich and good-looking. He's got eyes for you, Nealy. I see something in you that's different than it was before you went up for breakfast. What do you suppose that is?"

Nealy giggled. "Your imagination. He brought pictures of Gabby. Ruby, she is so very beautiful. He said the kids are well, and Nick will be taking the bar next year. I felt so proud I wanted to bust. I played the game, though. He . . . ah . . . he never remarried."

"Fancy that." Ruby smirked. She led Nealy over to the bench in the breezeway and sat down. "You should tell him the truth, Nealy."

"No. It's better this way. He didn't say, but I don't think the kids know he's here. He came on his own to give me pictures of Gabby. It was very considerate of him to come here like this. I guess he really is a nice man. I was always jealous of him. That's the bottom line."

Ruby sighed with happiness, her eyes on Metaxas and Hatch. "Oh, Nealy, I am so very happy, and I owe it all to you. I go to sleep with a smile on my face and wake up with a smile. I have never seen Metaxas so happy. You will never know what a wonderful thing you did by giving him that horse. Everything else in life suddenly paled for him. He goes to sleep with a smile and wakes up with one, too. We will be forever grateful. The best part of all is Shufly loves him. Yesterday when you went up to the house for something he was playing with Metaxas. He bent down, got a mouthful of grass, and when Metaxas called him pretty boy he blew it right at him and then snorted and pawed the ground like he'd just one-upped his owner. Metaxas laughed until his stomach was sore. They bonded, that's for sure. The horse is a ham, Nealy."

"You're telling me. Every time I want to take his picture he *poses.* He sees the camera and he wants you to get his best side, which is his right side. Then he does that snorting, pawing thing to show you he's having a high old time. My blood just boils every time I hear someone refer to horses as big, dumb, and stupid."

"So, Nealy, tell me, what do you think of that big Indian?"

"Don't go there, Ruby. He just came here to bring the pictures and to tell me about the kids."

"He could have called to tell you that, and he could have sent the pictures by overnight mail. Flying here . . . now that tells me this man is something special. Really special. You aren't going to screw this up, are you, Nealy?"

Nealy's face bunched itself into a grimace. "There's nothing to screw up. I need a dye job," she said, running her fingers through her hair.

"And you need to pluck your eyebrows. A nice French manicure would look good. I have some really sinful perfume that goes great with the smell of horse manure."

"Enough!" Nealy hissed. "He lives in Santa Fe, for God's sake."

Ruby shifted her weight from one side to the other. "Would you just listen to the two of them. You'll never need a PR person with Metaxas around. He thinks the sun rises and sets on you, woman. Listen."

"I'm telling you, Hatch, I've never seen anything like it in my life. This is a whole new world to me. This creature here who is busy chewing the buttons off my shirt is alive and breathing. He's all mine. Mine. He can pitch a fit with the best of them, and he can be as gentle as a pussycat. He likes to play. It's Nealy that got him to this point. She's got magic in her hands and voice. You should hang around here for a few days and just watch. You'll never be the same again. One of a kind. There will never be another one like . . ."

"I can see that. He is beautiful," Hatch said.

"You dumb *schmuck*, I'm talking about Nealy, not this horse. *She's* one of a kind. She's riding this baby in the Derby. Honest to good God, Hatch, I feel like a father."

"Oh. Yeah, yeah, I guess she is one of a kind. I don't mean this to sound sexist but isn't she kind of . . . you know, *old* to be riding in a Derby full of male jockeys?"

"Age is a number, Hatch. I know people who are seventy and are young, and by the same token I know people who are fifty who damn well dodder. It's a mind-set. She's training. Knowing what I know now, and that isn't a whole hell of a lot, I wouldn't trust this horse to anyone but her. When she's on his back they are *one*. Make no mistake. She knows this horse, and he knows her. Here, give him a mint, and he'll love you," Metaxas said, slipping Hatch a peppermint.

Hatch grinned as the horse lapped up the mint, then tossed his head in thanks.

"Told you he was a ham. Hey, nice seeing you again. It's been a long time. Since Sela's funeral actually. I'm glad you're out and about. Let's make a pact not to let so much time go by before we meet again. Old friends need to stay close."

"It's a deal."

"Listen, if we go to the Derby, how about sharing my box?"

"I'd like that. I gotta get going. Nealy wants to show me the farm, and I'm eating into my time. Gotta get back home."

"Great seeing you again."

"You, too, Metaxas. I'm ready for the rest of the tour, Nealy," Hatch said, striding over to the bench.

"Then let's do it!"

"Nice meeting you, Ruby."

"Likewise," Ruby called over her shoulder as she scampered across the breezeway to join her husband.

They walked the farm until Hatch looked down at his watch. "Gotta go, Nealy. This was nice, real nice. I enjoyed myself."

"I did, too. Thanks for bringing the pictures. I was having a bum day when you got here. You made it better."

They were at the car. Hatch climbed in. "Maybe we could have dinner sometime."

"Sure, anytime you're in town, just call." Dinner. She felt flustered at the thought. Didn't he see the gray in her hair, the wrinkles around her eyes and mouth? Not to mention the bushy eyebrows that Ruby said needed to be plucked. He was probably just being polite.

"How about tomorrow?"

"Tomorrow?" Her stomach rushed up to her throat.

"Yeah, tomorrow. I can be here by six."

"Six. Well . . . okay." A little more than twenty-four hours. Dye job, French manicure. Eyebrow waxing. Shopping. Smitty said you always needed new underwear for a first date.

"Good. It's a date then. Do you want dress up or casual? I'm asking because I own a couple of suits and some white shirts."

Nealy burst out laughing. "Let's do casual. We can go to the Jockey Club for dinner. I'm assuming you'll want to stay over."

"Yep."

Nealy sucked in her breath. Damn, the sun was bright. Where did all those chittering birds come from all of a sudden?

"See you tomorrow at six then. Have a safe trip. Thanks again, Hatch."

"My pleasure."

Nealy stood rooted to the driveway until Hatch's car was out of sight. She had to tell someone.

"Rubyyyyy!" she yelled at the top of her lungs as she sprinted for the barn.

Metaxas and Ruby came to the doorway on the run. "My God, Nealy, what's wrong?"

"Wrong? Nothing's wrong. I have a *date!* He's coming back tomorrow. Six o'clock!"

"No!" Ruby screeched. "That's great! Oh, my God, I'm so excited! Did you hear that, Metaxas? Nealy has a date tomorrow! We were just talking about the possibility a few minutes ago. Life is certainly strange. I knew it! I knew I saw something in his eyes. That doesn't give us much time. Just a little over twenty-four hours. Oh, Lord, there's so much to do. Honey, you're on your own. Tell Dover he has to take over with Shufly until Thursday morning. Better make that Thursday afternoon. Yes, yes, Thursday afternoon sounds right. You can do this, honey. You're good in emergencies. None better. Nealy has a date. This is so wonderful! Isn't it wonderful, honey?"

Metaxas stared wide-eyed at his wife and Nealy. "Wonderful. Women!" he muttered as he made his way back to the barn.

"Okay, okay, this is what we're going to do. We're going up to the house to shower and then we're going to town. I know just what to do and what to buy. Bring lots of money, Nealy."

"It's a casual date, Ruby. Smitty said all I need is new underwear."

"That, too. Oh, I'm so excited. I can see you with him, Nealy. I really can."

"Yeah, well try this on for size. Can you see me carrying on a conversation with him? I'm no good in social situations. I get tongue-tied. I can't hold my own off the farm. Talking to a man is different from talking to you or Metaxas and the horses."

"That's why we're going to do all this stuff today. Tomorrow we're going to *practice*. Will you trust me?"

Nealy sighed. "I'm not sure I like him, Ruby. How can I suddenly like him when I've hated him for so long?"

"You never *really* hated him. You were jealous of him. How do you think he'll be in bed?" Ruby whispered.

Nealy giggled. "I'm only going to dinner with him."

"Then why are you going to buy new underwear?"

"Because Smitty said that's what you do when you have a date. It's for me, so I feel good from the skin out. I'm not going to go to bed with him."

"We'll see." Ruby smiled.

Smitty brought the golf cart to a stop, the mail piled on the seat next to her. The moment she saw Hatch's car she flagged him down. "Mr. Littletree, do you have a minute?"

"Sure. Is something wrong?"

"No. I just want to tell you something. Normally I don't stick my nose into other people's business, especially Nealy's business. There's something you need to know. I don't want you leaving here thinking bad things about Nealy. But I want what I tell you to be just between the two of us. Is it a deal?"

"Yes."

"Nealy didn't send those kids off in anger. She picked her time and did what she had to do so Nick would run to you. The same goes for Emmie. She didn't count on the girl being pregnant, though. What I'm trying to tell you is, she knew the kids would never have left her otherwise. Emmie would have kept on clinging to her. I hope I said all this right. You understand what I'm saying, don't you?"

"Yes. Well, I'll be damned. And of course the kids have no idea?"

"None. She thinks they hate her. Are they really doing okay, Mr. Littletree?"

"They're doing just fine. Before you know it, Nick is going to be one wild-ass attorney. Emmie is a wonderful mother. It's working. Thanks for clueing me in. I won't say a word. See you tomorrow."

Smitty was halfway to the house before the word *tomorrow* registered fully. "Well, hot damn!"

"Smitty, Smitty, guess what! Nealy has a date tomorrow with Hatch. He's flying back tomorrow. Six o'clock is the zero hour," Ruby shouted.

"That doesn't give us much time," Smitty said, tossing the mail on the kitchen table. "Tell me what you want me to do."

9

Nealy propped her feet up on the porch railing. She closed her eyes, and mumbled, "This just isn't worth it. It's only a dinner. Why do I have to go through all this?" Her eyes snapped open to plead with Ruby and Smitty.

"The man is flying here from New Mexico to take you to dinner, so it's more than a dinner. It's an *event*. A happy event. It's a happening. You need to get with the program here, Nealy," Smitty chastised.

Nealy turned to Ruby as if for support. "You have to do this because," Ruby said patiently, "your social skills are not the best. You have to learn to relax. I think a good stiff drink before you leave, another one before dinner at the club, and you should be loose enough to carry on a conversation. What do you think, Smitty?"

Smitty nodded. She started to sweep the front porch, more to have something to do than anything else. "You're supposed to be excited, Nealy. You look positively miserable."

"That's because I am miserable. Look, I can hold up my end of the conversation if the talk is about horses. I can talk about the kids. You made me read yesterday's paper and the one that came this morning. I know them by heart. What do you really think the chances are of Hatch wanting to talk about what's in the paper? Zip, that's what. And you can forget about trying to get me to wear high heels. I'd probably fall and break my neck. I have a nice dress, new underwear. I'm going to wear makeup. My eyebrows are plucked, my hair has been styled, I have perfume. Okay, okay. What's next?"

Ruby refolded the shawl she'd brought down from Nealy's closet. "It must be ninety degrees today. Even so, you're still going to need to take a shawl because the air-conditioning at the club is cold. That means you'll shiver and be uncomfortable. When you're uncomfortable conversation becomes difficult, you tend to get cold, and then you have to go to the bathroom a lot. Let me see you smile like you mean it."

Nealy grimaced for Ruby's benefit. "Damn it, why can't I just be me? I'm not even sure I like this man. He's not coming here for me, he's coming because of the kids. He probably thinks he has to do this out of some misguided feeling for Hunt. I truly believe he was just being polite when he asked me to dinner."

Ruby crossed her arms and gave Nealy a long-suffering look. "You can't be just you because, you, Nealy, are boring as hell," she said, her bluntness raising both Nealy's and Smitty's eyebrows. In spite of their shocked expressions, she maintained her stance. "He wasn't being polite. The kids might have a small part to do with it but not a whole lot. I think he wants to get to know you. He's a widower and you're a widow. I rest my case," Ruby said as she plucked a yellow leaf off a crimson geranium.

"Another thing, Nealy, don't order six desserts to 'taste test' like you usually do. If you think you're going to be nervous, order something soft so you don't have to chew. That way you can just swallow. *One* dessert," Smitty said firmly.

Nealy grimaced again. "Soft food. One dessert. I think I can handle that."

"And don't offer to pay half." Ruby grinned.

"Not a chance," Nealy quipped. "Look at that sun. It's a beautiful day today, just like yesterday. No humidity even though it's hot. We should water these geraniums, they're starting to wilt. The porch is pretty in the summer. Why can't we just have dinner here and sit on the porch and watch the stars? That to me is the perfect date."

Smitty shook her head in disgust.

"Because that's not a date." Ruby sighed. "You can sit out here when you get back from your date. You can sit here all night in your new underwear if you like. Oh, Smitty, I wish you could have seen her in Victoria's Secret yesterday. For the first five minutes she looked like she stepped into hell. Then she bought one of everything. There's nothing like lacy underwear. I used to have a ton of it. Not anymore, though. Now I wear undershirts."

Nealy paled at the meaning behind Ruby's words. "Oh, Ruby, I'm so sorry," she said, leaping off her chair. "I swear to God, I didn't give that . . . you . . . a thought. How could I have been so stupid? See, that's what I mean. You want me to be one of those folderol women, and it isn't me. I wear cotton underwear because it's comfortable and I sweat a lot. It must have been awful for you when I was buying all those bras."

Ruby took Nealy's hands in hers and smiled. "No, Nealy, it wasn't awful at all. I had one little pang, and that's the truth. I'm just so damn grateful to be alive that lacy bras are the least of my worries. Things like that are not important."

Nealy eyed Ruby and knew in her heart she was speaking the truth. She nodded. "I'm not sure of the dress. It's sleeveless, and my arms are so muscular."

"Your arms aren't muscular, they're like steel rods," Smitty shot back. "You're wearing the dress, and that's final. It looks good on you. It makes your eyes more brilliant. You're wearing those diamond earrings Ruby gave you a few years ago, too. They aren't too big, and with your new haircut they'll go perfectly. We're going to make a lady out of you yet."

Nealy gasped. "Am I *that* bad? You make me sound like a scrubwoman. You told me I was okay at the first Derby Ball I went to, Smitty."

"You were okay looks-wise, but if you remember, you were there for five whole minutes and then you hightailed it out of there. You should have stuck it out and mingled. Because you didn't, people are saying you think you're too good to associate with them."

Nealy gasped again. It seemed this was her day for reality checks. "Who said that?"

"Everyone, that's who," Smitty sniped. "Now buckle down and let's get on with it. It's almost lunchtime, and you have to take a nice, long, scented bubble bath and then a little nap so you're raring to go."

"Yeah, right," she said, shooting Smitty a twisted smile. She threw her hands up in the air. "God, the things I let you two talk me into. This better be worth all this effort," Nealy said, sitting down again and crossing her ankles the way Ruby instructed. "A lady does not cross her legs nor does she prop her feet on the banister," she muttered over and over until both Smitty and Ruby collapsed laughing.

"Oh, my God, he's here! I just heard his car door slam," Nealy said, running into the bedroom. "I am so jittery. I can't believe this." She held up her shaking hands for Ruby and Smitty to see. "That damn drink didn't help at all."

Ruby didn't bother to try to hide her smile. "Nealy, why are you getting so upset? He's just a man. A man! Not God. Not the president of the United States. You're just going out to dinner. No world-altering decisions are going to be made over the table."

Nealy plopped down on Maud's old rocker. She wished she could just take root and stay in the chair all night long. She shrugged. "I guess I want him to like me. He didn't. At least Hunt said he didn't like me. I didn't like him either, and here I am going to dinner with him. I have a right to be nervous. I have a right to be full of anxiety. In case you've forgotten there have only been three men in my life, and Kendrick Bell doesn't count. That leaves two: Dillon Roland, Emmie's father, and Hunt. A lot of years have gone by. I am not one for small talk. I say what I have to say and that's it. All those words, all that energy to utter them, and they mean nothing."

Ruby crossed her arms over her chest in a no-nonsense pose. "Shut *up*, Nealy! Go downstairs and greet your guest. We'll stay up here and watch from the window. Have a good time. Don't swear if you can help it. Remember, one dessert and soft food. Order bourbon on the rocks as your before-dinner drink. Don't drink any of those silly sweet drinks, or you'll get sick." Ruby paused. "You're still sitting here, Nealy. Get going. I can see him from here. He's on the porch. Don't trip on the steps going down."

Nealy stood up on quivering legs to smooth the wrinkles out of her dress before she marched out of the room, her back ramrod stiff.

Smitty plopped down on the rocker. "This is not a good thing. That drink should have kicked in. How much did you give her?"

"A triple. She downed it in two gulps. You're right, it should be kicking in any second now. Oh, God, I hope it all works out. We might have screwed her up more. She'll do just fine. She will, won't she, Smitty?"

"I don't know. I guess. I hope so," Smitty said, pushing herself out of the chair. "I'm exhausted."

"Me, too. We're the ones who need a drink. As soon as they leave, let's belt a few on the front porch."

"Sounds like a plan to me. How's she doing? Can you see anything?"

Nealy smiled when she opened the screen door to admit Hatch. "Well, I'm ready if you are!"

"Then let's go." Hatch grinned.

The bourbon kicked in somewhere between the third and last step leading down from the front porch. It increased her ability to communicate to such a degree she started to babble about wining and dining as she executed a magnificent pirouette at the same time for Hatch's benefit.

Hatch's eyebrows shot upward as he clapped his hands. "What do you do for an encore?" He grinned.

Nealy's laughter rippled in the evening air. "Any number of things. You'll just have to wait and see."

Grinning from ear to ear, Hatch opened the door. Nealy fell forward into the seat. "Ooops," she said, looking back at him. "Don't close the door yet. I have to cross my ankles. Ladies are supposed to cross their ankles, not their legs. Do you know why that is, Hatch? Okay, batten down the hatches!" She started to laugh and couldn't stop. "Didya get it? Hatches, Hatch?"

Hatch bent down to pick the end of her shawl up off the ground. "Uh-huh. I got it. Is it okay to close the door now? Did you cross your ankles?"

Nealy wiggled her rear end in the seat until she was comfortable. "Yep. I'm good to go," she said, struggling with one long end of the shawl. "Oh, shit," she muttered.

Hatch struggled with his laughter. "Is something wrong?"

"It's this damn shawl. They said I needed it. I don't need it. I wanted to wear a dress with sleeves so you wouldn't see how muscular my arms are. Smitty said they looked like steel rods. I'm just nervous," she said, yanking at the scarf again. "Shit, it's half out the door. It's probably dragging on the ground. I'm just nervous. I said that, didn't I? People say the same thing over and over when they're nervous."

"I can tell." Hatch gurgled with laughter.

Nealy struggled with her seat belt. "Oh, what gave it away? I know why. It was because I said shit. They told me not to swear. It just sort of came out if you know what I mean. I never do anything right."

"I've always been good at guessing things. It's an old Indian trait." Hatch adjusted the seat to accommodate his long legs. "You don't have to watch what you say around me. I have a few bad habits of my own."

"Imagine that," Nealy said, giving him a wide-eyed look. "We can go now, Hatch. I'm buckled up. The hell with the shawl. I'll just throw it away. You already saw my arms, and if I freeze, I freeze. Right?"

"Yeah, yeah, that sounds right. You have nice arms."

"Doya think so? You mean I worried for nothing?"

Hatch blinked. "I don't understand. Why were you worried?"

"Women worry. It's what makes us tick. It separates us from you men. Women have worried since the beginning of time. I'm not all glitzy and glamorous. I'm plain. I usually smell like horses. I'm not . . . womanly. Perfume doesn't do it. I wanted you to like me for me. You didn't like me, and I didn't like you. I thought we could start over. I didn't know I was going to get so nervous. Smitty and Ruby gave me a drink, and here I am. I might be kind of drunk. I've never been drunk before. Maybe I'm just feeling, you know, good, because I don't . . . well, sometimes I do . . . this damn shawl is strangling me. Oh, shit. Excuse me, this shawl is bothering my neck. That was better, wasn't it?"

Hatch bit down on his lower lip so he wouldn't burst out laughing. "Are you sure you want to go to the Jockey Club for dinner? There are other places. Places where you might feel more comfortable."

Nealy reared up in her seat. "With or without my shawl?"

"The way I see it, it's your call. If you get cold, I could give you my jacket or I could put my arms around you."

"Oh, yeah. No, no, no, that kind of thing leads to . . . you know. I bought one of everything in Victoria's Secret. I had so many of those pink bags people were staring at me."

This time Hatch did laugh. "Was it a good feeling?"

Nealy rocked back and forth laughing. "Yeah. Oh-oh, you were supposed to turn back there. We're there. Here. At the Jockey Club. You drive like Smitty drives, on two wheels. That was exciting turning around in the middle of the road like that with the tires screeching. I would never do that."

"Why not?"

"Because I always obey the rules, that's why. It's no fun, though. When you do everything that is expected of you, it makes you boring. Ruby said I was really boring. It's too soon for you to know if I'm boring. You'll probably have a better idea after dinner. Do you want to sit on the front porch and watch the stars when we go home?"

"I'd like that, Nealy."

"I like putting my feet up on the banister. I don't like sitting and crossing my ankles. You should try that sometime. It sucks."

"I bet it does. Sit still now and I'll come around and open the door. Can you do the seat belt?"

"Just as soon as I uncross my ankles, I will do the seat belt. I wish you'd hurry and open the door. I'm choking here."

Hatch scurried around to the passenger side of the car. Half of the luscious pink shawl was dragging on the ground and was filthy dirty. He opened the door.

"Arwk," Nealy gasped. "Now I can breathe again. We made good time, didn't we? It seems like we just started out."

"That's what happens when you're having fun," Hatch said with a straight face.

"Isn't that the truth? I cannot tell you how worried I was about this date. Is this a date or just dinner? I need to know so I know what to eat."

"Huh?"

"You know. If it's a date, you're nervous. You already know I'm nervous about all of this. That means I have to eat something soft so I can just swallow it. I can't drink anything sweet or sticky or I'll get sick. I usually order six desserts. Ruby said I can't do that. If I do that, you won't think I'm classy."

Hatch threw his hands in the air. Was this the same Nealy Diamond Clay who had been married to his best friend? Right now she seemed more like a nervous teenager than the formidable Nealy Diamond Clay of legend. What the hell. When in Rome . . . "*I'm* going to order six desserts!"

"You are!" Nealy said, her eyes almost popping from her head. "I can't. I promised I would do everything they said."

"I'll share mine with you then."

"I love sweet stuff. I have a real sweet tooth. Do you have a sweet tooth, Hatch?"

"I have a whole mouth full of sweet tooths. Or is that sweet teeth?" He lifted his shoulders and looked to her for an answer.

"I don't know. Probably teeth. That's one thing we have in common then."

"I think we have more than that in common, Nealy," Hatch said, taking hold of her elbow, steadying her.

Nealy stared at the Jockey Club emblem on the door. "This club was started by men and has always been maintained by men. There are no waitresses, only waiters. My mother was a waitress," she said, her mind taking a momentary detour. "Not here, of course, but in a small Texas town. They don't like women here but they have to let me in because I belong to the Jockey Club. They stare at me. I beat them. All of them. Me. Whataya think of that, Hatch?" Nealy said, sashaying over to the little podium. "I would like a table by the window in the smoking section, Franklin."

"Certainly, Miz Clay, just follow me."

"You have to hold your head up and pretend not to see all these people. I have to keep up what they perceive to be my nasty image."

Befuddled, Hatch nodded.

Nealy looked around. "Do you like this place, Hatch?"

"It looks kind of stuffy, or maybe I'm mistaking that with steeped in tradition. Don't you like it?"

"You're right on both counts. It's very stuffy and there's lots of tradition—tradition that doesn't include women. I don't like the people." She looked up when the waiter approached. "I'll have an Old Grandad on the rocks. A double."

"Ice tea," Hatch said. "I'm driving."

Nealy smiled at him. Was he always so in control? Probably. "That's right, you are driving."

Nealy stared across the room at the picture wall. The Derby wall. Her picture hung there with all those who had gone before her. She stared at it, wondering if the club would have a second picture to hang next year.

The restaurant was quiet, with just a handful of guests. She let her gaze rake past the tables but not long enough so she would either have to nod, smile, or mouth a greeting. It was dim, with the only light coming from sconces lined up around the walls. A small candle sat in the middle of each table. They gave off just enough light to read the menus. The tables and chairs were dark mahogany, the tablecloths a deep burgundy. The bar was dark mahogany with polished brass, the barstools were high and upholstered in dark red leather. The carpet was old and probably the most important thing in the dining room. The pattern in the center was the racetrack at Churchill Downs. Woven into each corner of the rug were the most famous Triple Crown winners of all time, Secretariat, Citation, Seattle Slew, and Whirlaway. Definitely a man's room.

"Is your picture hanging up there?" Hatch asked.

"Bottom row, third from the end. Next year they'll have to start hanging the pictures on the next wall. I'm honored to be here." She wiggled her bottom into the cushiony softness of the chair, the same way she did when she was trying to get her seat in a new saddle. "What should we talk about, Hatch? I can hold up my end of the conversation if we talk about horses or the kids. I'm not real good with that chatty stuff. Do you want to talk about Hunt and Sela so we can kind of go on from there? It's okay with me if you do. You have such sad eyes."

Hatch looked down at the table as though deciding what it was he wanted to say. "Sometimes I feel like I want to talk about Sela and my son, but I always feel if I do that, then they won't be mine anymore. I'll have shared them. They were my life. Everything I did, every thought, every action was for them. I couldn't wait to get home at night to be with them. I miss them with every breath I take. I've let go. I packed away all their things. I suppose I should have given them away, but I wasn't ready to do that. I try to do what Sela wanted by getting on with my life. When Nick showed up, it was like it was meant to be. I plunged into that with all my might. Believe it or not, he helped me get over the last hurdle. I'm okay now."

Nealy looked at him over the rim of her glass. "That's good, Hatch. I mean really good," she said with sincerity. "Life is for the living. I wish I had been more worldly when Hunt came into my life. I was so sheltered it was pitiful. At least you're going forward without regrets. I have a bushelful. Let's talk about something else. Like what we're going to order." She opened the menu and studied the entrees.

"Six desserts," Hatch reminded her.

"I'm going to have the macaroni-and-cheese casserole. It has little onions in it. Nick loved it. It's soft. That's what I'm having. I have to watch my weight. It's okay if you want to go over and look at the pictures. I'll just sit here and drink and smoke a cigarette. I quit, but sometimes I smoke when I'm nervous. I'm nervous, so I'm going to smoke. This is the smoking section. Do you smoke?"

"On occasion," Hatch said, getting up to walk over to the picture wall. "I'll be right back." Nealy heaved a sigh of relief as she gulped at her drink and signaled for another. Another hour and they could leave. She wondered if she could hold out that long.

Nealy stared across the room at Hatch. He was a big man. A gentle man. Yes, he had sad eyes, but there was laughter in those eyes, too. She wished she knew what he thought of her.

"Your picture is awesome. How did it feel, Nealy, when you were in the winner's circle?"

Nealy stared into her glass as she tried to come up with the answer. "Like a thousand Christmas mornings." She paused, reliving the moment, then looked up and met his gaze. "The best part, though, was when Flyby found that tiny little hole and made his run for it. At that precise moment I thought we really were flying. It was like this giant explosion of sound and sunlight and exhilaration. I don't have the right words to tell you. I won the Preakness and the Belmont, but they can't compare to the Derby. For me it was the Derby. I hope I can do it again next year. They're already talking about me being too old. I worry a little about that. I'm training. Tonight is . . . I'm smoking and drinking because . . ."

"You're nervous." Hatch smiled.

Nealy's head bobbed up and down.

The waiter appeared to take their order.

"I'll have the macaroni-and-cheese casserole. Coffee, too."

"Apple pie with pecan ice cream. Banana cream pie, praline pie, peach cobbler, chocolate thunder cake, and crème brûlée," Hatch said. "And coffee for me, too."

"No entree, sir?"

"Only if I'm still hungry. You know what they say. Life is short, eat dessert first."

Nealy grinned at him as she felt a warm glow flow through her.

Two hours later, Nealy looked across the table at Hatch. "I can't believe we ate all that food. We talked, too. Ruby was right. Maybe it was Smitty. I'm ready to go now."

"I'm ready if you are."

"Didn't I have a shawl with me?" Nealy said, bending down to look under the table.

"We left it in the car."

"Okay. I guess we can go then. Are we going to sit on the front porch and look at the stars? Sometimes I give them names. Do you ever do that?"

"All the time," Hatch said, cupping her elbow in his hand to lead her from the restaurant.

"Remember now, don't look at anyone."

"There's no one here to look at, Nealy. Everyone's gone. We're the last to leave."

"How'd that happen?"

"We had six desserts, they only had one."

"Oh."

In the car, with her ankles crossed demurely, her seat belt secure, the dirty shawl on her lap, Nealy fell asleep. A smile settled on Hatch's face and stayed there until he brought the car to a stop by the back door of Blue Diamond Farms. He exited the car and loped down to the barn, where he found Ruby and Metaxas.

"Our friend is . . . a little under the weather. If you show me where her room is, I'll carry her upstairs."

"Carry her upstairs!" Ruby bleated. "What's wrong with her?"

Hatch laughed. "She just got nervous."

"Nervous? What's that mean?"

Hatch threw his hands in the air. "I don't know. I never did understand women. She said she had to cross her ankles and then the shawl was choking her and she said she had to eat soft food and nothing sweet or sticky and she always does what she's told to do and a lot of pink shopping bags. I tried to keep up but gave up when I had to eat those six desserts."

"Was it a fun evening?" Metaxas asked carefully as he watched his wife for her reaction.

"Hell, yes. I haven't laughed like that in a couple of years. Well, that's not quite true. I wanted to laugh, but I didn't laugh. She's funny. I have to say, I had a good time."

"Did Nealy have a good time?" Ruby asked.

Metaxas rolled his eyes, a warning that Hatch should think before he responded. The big Indian missed the message.

"I don't think so. She was too nervous. Why she was nervous is a mystery. I guess women get nervous for no reason."

"Shut up," Ruby said as she marched toward the house.

"What did I say?" Hatch demanded.

"You said Nealy was nervous. Don't you know anything about women, Hatch?"

"Not a whole hell of a lot. How much do you know?"

"Probably less," Metaxas groaned. "I guess we aren't supposed to use the word *nervous*. I learned a long time ago not to ask questions. Women stick together. Like glue," he said, rolling his eyes. "Where are you sleeping, big guy?"

"I thought I was sleeping here. I guess now I'm not. I can go back to town and get a hotel room."

Metaxas placed a hand on Hatch's shoulder. "Sleep here in the barn. I'll fix you up a stall. We used to sleep in a stall until Nealy let us have a cottage. Still do occasionally. Trust me, you'll love it. We get up at four. We work till seven, and then it's breakfast. So, do you want to stay or not?"

"Sure."

"Well, it's bedtime as soon as Ruby gets back."

"It's only nine o'clock," Hatch said.

"Yeah, I know."

"I think I'll go up and sit on the front porch for a while. Show me which stall is mine."

"This one," Metaxas said, pointing to a stall three doors down from the one he and Ruby used every once in a while. "There's a bathroom and shower at the end of the breezeway. There's a ton of beer in the fridge in the kitchen. Help yourself."

Upstairs in Nealy's bedroom, Ruby struggled with a sleepy, limp Nealy. "So, how did it go, Nealy?"

"Pretty good I think. I did everything you and Smitty said to do. I really was nervous, though. Did Hatch say anything?"

"Just that you were nervous. Did you start to twitch or something?"

"I don't know what gave it away. I was trying to be so careful. He said he knew I was nervous because he's Indian and he could tell. I think that's bullshit. I didn't swear. I don't think I did anyway. Can I go to sleep now, Ruby?"

"Sure, honey. I'll see you in the morning."

"Night, Ruby. Thanks for all the advice. He's a nice man. Maybe he'll come back sometime when I'm not so nervous."

"Sleep tight, honey," Ruby said, turning off the bedroom light.

Nealy woke with a start. She knew instantly where she was and what time it was. Her head pounded as she rolled from side to side. She knew she had to get up to take some aspirin, and she also knew there would be no more sleep for her on this night so she might as well make some coffee and sit on the front porch and wait for the sun to come up. Should she shower or not? Maybe the steam would help clear her head. She walked down the kitchen stairway, plugged in the coffeepot Matilda had gotten ready before bed. She hiked back upstairs to wash down four aspirin and showered.

Feeling almost human, she pulled on some of her new Victoria's Secret underwear and her old ratty chenille robe. She'd timed her descent into the kitchen just as the coffee finished brewing. She poured a mugful and carried it out to the front porch.

"Hatch! What are you doing out here?" she asked in surprise.

"I don't know. I wasn't sleepy. I didn't feel right going upstairs and picking out a room. Metaxas fixed a stall for me in the barn, but I had a few beers out here and dozed off. My sleeping habits aren't the best. The big question is, what are you doing up at this hour?"

"I just woke up. I'm only up an hour ahead of schedule. Four o'clock is my normal time for waking up. I have a terrible headache, so that has to mean I had too much to drink. Normally I don't drink. Tonight I was . . ."

"Nervous. I was, too. You were my first date since . . ."

"Maybe that's where we went wrong. You know, thinking it was a date. Maybe if we had thought of it as just two friends going out to dinner, some of the anxiety would have been alleviated. At least for me."

"You're absolutely right. The stars are beautiful, aren't they? When I was a kid on the reservation I gave them all names."

"I used to do the same thing. I always looked forward to that one peek out the window before I went to bed. Sometimes, if I'm not too tired, I still do it. I had a mean, bitter childhood. Anything make-believe, naming stars, wishing on stars made the days and nights a little lighter if you know what I mean.

"There was this one time I named three stars because on a really clear night it looked like they were hugging each other. I called them Diamond, Ruby, and Emerald. I didn't even know what those gems looked like. I just used my imagination. I think I named Emmie for the Emerald star. Then Maud Diamond came into my life. Then Ruby. So, maybe wishing and naming stars wasn't such a waste of time for a little girl."

"I don't even remember what I named mine," Hatch said. "Medusa, the woman who runs my office, tells me that when you pass over, a star forms in the sky. I hope that's true because it would please me no end to know Sela and my son are up there winking down on me. All those who have gone before us are up there. Do you believe that, Nealy?"

"I think so. Thinking about it like that gives one a measure of security. They're gone, but they aren't gone."

"Do you miss the place where you grew up? Sometimes I miss the reservation and I have to go back and walk around."

"Sometimes. Sometimes months go by and I don't think about it at all. Sometimes I positively dwell on it. I'm so glad that my brothers and I have reconciled. I always wanted them to be these big, tough guys, and they aren't like that. They could never be like that. They're warm and shy and caring in their own way. To other people they probably seem cold and aloof. We were never around people much growing up. Yes, we went to school, but that doesn't mean we were around people. We had to get up early, do our chores, get on the bus, go to class, get back on the bus, and go home to more chores and schoolwork. By eight o'clock I was dead on my feet, and all I wanted to do was go to bed. I'm afraid I did just enough to get by. I let that attitude carry over into my life here. Let's not go down that road, okay?"

"Okay. You love this farm, don't you?"

Nealy sighed. "God, yes. Love, though, is too tame a word. I don't know what the right word is. It's part of me, it's in my blood. I guess I'm trying to say it's my life. To the exclusion of all else. I know, I know, that's not good. It's the way it is. Maybe someday things will change. Maybe someday Emmie will come back and want to raise her daughter here the way I raised her. I've accepted the fact that Nick won't come back."

"If that were to happen, Nealy, what would you do?"

"That's just it, I don't know. I guess I could travel, read books, go to the movies, shop. Maybe plant a garden and watch it grow. Take up flower arranging. I might take some cooking lessons, but I don't know if I would be happy doing those things."

"Are you happy now, Nealy?" Hatch asked quietly.

"Yes and no. I would be a lot happier if my kids were here. Let's just say I'm content. What does it feel like to be really happy? Do you know, Hatch?"

"God Almighty, yes, I know. It's a wild, euphoric feeling. Like if you flapped your arms you could fly, that kind of feeling. You're ecstatic, you're invincible and giddy all at the same time. Nothing or no one can rain on your parade. You want to hold on to the feeling forever and ever.

"I never knew, never expected anyone to love me the way Sela and my son loved me. Take a good look at me and tell me women would stand in line to date a big ugly Indian like me. There were no lines. The day I met her I knew. She said she knew, too. That was the magic of it.

"I had that feeling twice and held on for dear life, but it got away from me. That short time in my life was so wonderful, so cherished by me that I thought I was like God. As quick as it came, that's how quick it was taken away."

Nealy reached for his arm. "I'd stand in line for you. You're a nice man, Hatch Littletree." She withdrew her hand and clasped it around her empty coffee cup.

Hatch smiled in the darkness. "I suspect you're a rather nice lady yourself. Life is to be lived. It should never be a duty or all black or all white. Life is the whole spectrum, bright colors, laughing faces, work, happiness, sadness. It's just life. I think I'm trying to tell you I like you."

Nealy could feel her neck grow warm. Obviously, he was expecting her to make a comment.

"I like you, too. I'm not very good away from here as you probably noticed this evening. Last night actually. I . . . if I tell you something, will you promise not to laugh?"

"I would never laugh at anything you said, Nealy, unless it was a joke."

"I feel inferior around people. I feel like they're all looking at me and talking about me. That's why I never go to the Derby Balls. I make an appearance and then leave. Smitty said I had to start doing good deeds so we came up with this idea to have *our own* Derby Ball and sell tickets with the monies going to different charities. We raised, these past few years, almost ten million dollars. Everyone came. I was so stunned. I stayed the whole night because I was the hostess. I even had a good time.

"Smitty said I would have had a good time at the other balls if I had given them a chance. Back then in the beginning, I did give them a chance, and they all thumbed their noses at me. You only have to do that to me once, and then you go on my short list.

"Then when I won the Derby and the Triple Crown, things changed. For them. That's when they all wanted to get to know me, to have their pictures taken with me, to buy stud from me. If I wasn't good enough for them in the beginning, I didn't want them in my life after I became famous. The ball Smitty arranges is for charity. It's a big dinner with a lot of speeches and then the actual ball itself. I soak them what I think they're willing to pay just to come to one of my balls. I pay for the affair out of my own pocket, but I give the proceeds away. I don't know what that makes me in your eyes, but it's what I do."

"Does it work for you, Nealy?"

"Yes, it does."

"Then the way I see it is that's all that is important. If you're wondering if I'm judging you, I'm not. I understand exactly how you feel. I went through the same sort of thing to a lesser degree when I went off to college. I was this big, dumb Indian. It hurt. Sometimes it still hurts." He reached for her hand and squeezed it tight. This time she didn't let go.

Nealy looked up at the stars, trying to find Diamond, Ruby and Emerald. "I wonder if Emmie and Nick ever named the stars. If they did, I don't know about it. I asked Smitty to search out the best detective agency in the country to try and find Willow, Nick's wife. She literally fell off the face of the earth. In hindsight, maybe I shouldn't have told her I was cutting off Nick's access to the trust fund I set up for him with Hunt's insurance money. I don't know if it was my imagination or not, but her eyes were so cold and hard. I don't care what anyone says, she wasn't the right choice for Nick. And, yes, I know, it was none of my business. He made a mistake, Hatch, and I know he's never going to forgive me for that."

"In time he will. Willow left Nick of her own free will. She had choices, go or stay with him. She didn't give it a chance. She cut and ran. I have a little trouble with that part of it myself. Don't blame yourself entirely for her departure. Most women, and I'm the first to admit I know nothing about women, would have insisted Nick call you to tell you they were married. A brand-new daughter-in-law wants to start off right. She had a strike going in by getting married without telling you. She could have made it right. Medusa told me that, as did Bode's wife, Brie. Just don't be too hard on yourself where she's concerned."

"Okay. But I'm still going to try and find her. The night is so velvety, so serene, so peaceful. It's like the world and life take a little break when it gets dark. It's kind of secretive if you know what I mean."

"I agree."

"Hatch, I admire your philanthropic work. I think it's wonderful what you do. I should have done the same thing a long time ago. Life got in my way. I'm trying now. Smitty is helping. Hunt always said you were generous to a fault. He admired you so much."

"I hope I lived up to his expectations. Tell me what it's like to train for the Derby."

Nealy laughed. Where to begin? "I have to eat right and exercise to get myself in top physical form. And at the same time, I have to get the horse, in this case, Shufly, in top physical form, too. Then, there's the racing side. I'm not running him in any prep races because I want to keep his ability secret. So, I run him here, on our track against some of our own stock." She could go on and on but remembered Ruby's words about how boring she was. "Let's just say it's a lot of physical and mental work, a lot of dedication and a whole lot of sacrifice. But I wouldn't have it any other way. If it came too easy, it wouldn't be worthwhile."

"I don't know if I could do that. You said you were boring. You're not boring, Nealy. You're interesting as all get-out," Hatch said in awe.

"I'm not?" Nealy's eyes widened in surprise. "Horses and kids . . . they're all I've ever known. They're my life."

"So, what's wrong with that?"

"Well, most people do more, see more of the world. They're worldly. That means they have interesting things to talk about. Take tonight. I felt uncomfortable. Inferior. Take me away from this farm, and I'm out of my element. I wish I could be like Smitty and Ruby. The two of them have been all over the world. They're worldly people. I can never be like them. Tonight I tried because they wanted me to. I guess I was a bit of a mess, huh?"

"You should never try to be something you aren't. I had a good time this evening. I really did. You're good company. I'll have to bone up on horses so we have more to talk about the next time. I have horses at my ranch. Cutting horses. I ride Western, not English."

There was going to be a next time. "I can ride Western and I can ride bareback."

"Show-off!"

Nealy laughed. "Does that mean I have to study up on the law?" she asked, staring out into the velvety night.

"I could give you a couple of crash courses. I'd like to come back here if you're agreeable. I could talk to you about my love for the law, the old days, these days, and what the future holds. Hell, there's a lot of things I'd love to talk to you about. I want to know everything about you. I hope that doesn't scare you. Sometimes I talk too much. Guess it's the lawyer in me."

"You can come back anytime you want. I'd like to hear about all those things you just mentioned. I really would. It's going to be light soon," she said, changing the subject.

Hatch looked down at the glowing numerals on his Tag watch. "I'd say in about twenty minutes. Are you going to work Shufly today. If so, do you mind if I hang around to watch? I don't have to leave till four this afternoon."

"By all means, stay. Yes, Shufly works today. That means headache or not, I work, too. Training has to be consistent. That horse knows when something is out of whack. Today he'll let me know I wasn't here yesterday to work him. He'll pitch a fit right off the bat. Then he'll refuse the mint and his apple. When he sees that it isn't bothering me he'll try to make it up to me by nuzzling my neck, snorting, pawing the ground. He does everything but talk. He's just like Flyby but better. Maybe three times better. I never thought I'd ever say that, but I'm saying it."

"Will you have any competition like Shufly when you run the Derby?"

"Two or three. That's according to Smitty, who's on top of all this. There's a horse called Navigator that looks to be pretty good. Fast Track is supposed to be a real runner, and then there's Jake's Thunder. According to Smitty, Jake's Thunder is the one that will probably go the distance. It's a crapshoot. You never know till you run it. I've seen horses come from behind and win a race, horses with crazy thirty-to-one odds. It happens."

"Don't you get nervous?"

Nealy laughed. "You mean like tonight? No. When I'm on that horse I'm as calm as I can be. I don't know why that is. I wish I did."

"Was it me that made you nervous or just going away from here into town and eating in a public place?"

"It was you. I'm sober now, so you're talking to the real Nealy here. I wanted you to like me. I didn't want you to think I was . . . God, I don't know what you thought I was. Some hateful woman who was unkind to Hunt, to my children. I don't want anyone to think that of me. I only know how to be me. All I've ever done is work. It's all I know. If I slack, then I feel guilty and feel like I'm not worthy of what Maud and Jess did for me. Maybe that's wrong. Even if it is, I can't change.

"Everything I have, everything I own is because of Maud and Jess. When my . . . Josh Coleman booted me and Emmie out, I stole his truck with my brothers' help and it got me this far. I was sick, Emmie was sick, and they found me lying in the dirt. They took me in, got a doctor for both of us, and took care of us. They loved me and Emmie. Back then I didn't know what love was. I breathed it in like it was oxygen. They fed us, put a roof over our heads, bought us clothes, and paid me to work. More than a fair wage. I don't know what would have happened to us if Jess hadn't found me that day.

"I lived in fear those first few years, afraid they wouldn't need me anymore. I saved every penny thinking I might have to go it alone. I think I worked harder than I had back at SunStar just so that wouldn't happen. It never did. Every night when I say my prayers, I thank God for letting me find this place. A few years later, they legally adopted me. When they died, they left everything to me and Emmie. I've been putting Emmie's share of the profits in an account I set up. Now do you understand why I do what I do, why I act like I act? I'll probably still be trying to prove my worth until the day I die. Does that make sense in some cockamamie way? I went off on a tangent there. What I was saying was, I wanted you to like me."

"Of course it makes sense. And for the record, I wanted you to like me, too. Hunt said you hated me and the guys. Some small part of me always wondered how that could be since you didn't know us. I know you thought the duck egg was silly business, and you're right, it was. However, it got the four of us through some bad times. Laughter is the best remedy. I don't think there's been much laughter in your life, Nealy Clay."

"You're right about that."

"Then it's time we did something about it."

Nealy smiled. She was aware suddenly that it was now light out, and the stars were disappearing. "Yes, let's do something about that."

10

Nealy and Hatch were halfway to the barn when Nealy noticed the head groom leading Shufly out of the breezeway. The colt was wound up about something and required a second groom on his right shank to keep him under control.

"That's some horse!" Hatch exclaimed. He'd grown up around horses, mostly mustangs, who were small and wiry compared to the tall, sleek colt who stood before him.

Nealy laughed at Shufly's antics. She knew he was upset with her because she'd broken her routine and hadn't visited him in his stall last night.

Pride marched through her. "He's magnificent, isn't he?"

Hatch nodded, his gaze never leaving the colt. "I have to say, Nealy, he's the finest piece of horseflesh I've ever seen."

Shufly whinnied and would have broken away if the grooms hadn't been prepared for his antics and kept a tight hold.

"Careful, Nealy," Hatch warned. "Something's got him spooked." He reached for her arm to pull her toward him.

Nealy smiled. "It's okay. He's just a little annoyed with me because of last night." With a confidence born of having raised Shufly from birth, Nealy sprinted toward the colt, leaving Hatch a safe distance away. She reached for his halter, brought his head down to hers, and whispered in his ear. He immediately calmed down and became a docile pet, nuzzling his massive head against Nealy's arm.

Hatch thought his eyes were going to pop right out of his head. If he hadn't seen what he just witnessed, he never would have believed it. Nick had told him about his mother's uncanny way with horses. Years ago Hunt had told him the same thing, but he never fully appreciated what it was they were saying. Later, when he thought about it, he decided Nealy had cast a magic spell over Shufly.

Awed at what he had just seen, Hatch walked over to the now-calm Shufly and rubbed his muzzle. "Just out of curiosity, what did you whisper in his ear to calm him down?"

Nealy tilted her head to the side. "I simply told him if he didn't behave himself I wouldn't take him out to the track. I told him he had to behave like a gentleman."

Hatch grimaced. "And you're telling me he understood what you said?"

Nealy laughed. "He calmed down, didn't he?"

Hatch's eyes narrowed with disbelief. Was she putting him on? She looked serious and was watching him carefully for his reaction.

Something in him clicked. Suddenly he had the overwhelming desire to know everything there was to know about Nealy Clay. He wanted to know her strengths, her weaknesses, her likes and dislikes. He smiled. Nealy smiled back.

"He's rarin' to go, Miz Nealy," the groom said.

"Give me a leg up, will you, Hatch?"

Hatch bent down and cupped his hands together. She was light as a feather. Of course she would be. She was a jockey, and jockeys had weight limitations. He watched her wiggle her rear end into the slip of leather that passed for a saddle. She probably weighed around 110 pounds, less than half his weight and about a tenth of what Shufly weighed.

Hatch watched as she secured her booted feet in the irons. She reached down for the hat the groom held out to her. With one deft movement she had her hair piled on top of her head and the hat in place. She wasn't classically pretty, but there was a certain look about her, something that set her apart from the other women he'd known over the years.

"Hatch, stand over there by that platform and watch us," Nealy said, pointing to her left.

Hatch nodded. "You take care of yourself out there, okay?"

He wasn't afraid for her, was he? "Don't worry, we'll be fine," she said as she reined Shufly around.

Hatch headed for the platform, where he took a seat on the wooden bench. A groom handed him a pair of binoculars so he could watch Nealy walk Shufly on to the track, where they would be joined by two other jockeys and horses. He could see an ear-to-ear grin on Nealy's face as she joked with the riders.

She's in her element, he thought. *This is her life, her love.* He was beginning to understand why Hunt had been so in love with her and why her children were so in awe of her. She was special, from the top of her head to the tips of her toes. It was going to take a team of wild horses to keep him away from her.

"Okay, baby, let's show off a little bit for Mr. Littletree." She forgot everything and anything then as she waited for the gate to clang open.

Shufly ripped through the gate and thundered down the track, his running mates four lengths behind as Nealy urged him on. "You can do it, you can do it! Keep it up. You're doing good, baby! Come on, stretch those legs. Let's see you cross that line six lengths ahead of those slugs behind you. Good boy, good boy," Nealy said, leaning as low as she could get and still not be over his head. Dirt flew up in her face, blinding her, but still she screamed, "Go! Go! Go!"

And he did!

"Oh, baby, I'm so proud of you I could just bust. You've got it! Just like your daddy had it. Your day is coming, and you're going to run that track just like your daddy did and by God, you're going to win," Nealy said, wiping the dirt from her eyes and face.

She risked a glance at the platform, where Hatch was standing. She waved. The woman in her preened, knowing he was watching her.

As far as Hatch could tell, there had been no contest between Shufly and his running mates. He ran the mile with energy to spare. His time, according to the groom's stopwatch, was 1.34, which was close to a track record.

* * *

"It was a nice visit, Nealy. Perhaps a little too short to my way of thinking. I'd like to do it again sometime. However, my calendar's pretty full right now, and I know yours is, too. My head is still reeling with all you cram into one day. I can see why you love your life. It's beautiful here with all the bluegrass, the board fencing, the stone house that's a home and not just stone and mortar. There's something so graceful, almost ethereal about seeing the horses in the pasture. I think that's probably the Indian coming through in me. I love the land," Hatch said, shading his eyes from the late-afternoon sun. "I've never seen greener pastures or bigger trees."

"If you could have just one wish or if you could have anything in the world, what would you wish for?" Nealy asked softly.

Hatch frowned and then smiled. "Is that one of those trick questions that will allow you to take my measure?"

"No, it's just a question."

"No one ever asked me a question like that. Do you need the answer right now?"

"No. Take all the time you need." Nealy laughed. "Listen, I apologize for last night. I was just . . ."

"Nervous! It was an interesting evening, and I enjoyed it. I almost forgot, Emmie called me last evening on my cell phone."

Nealy's hand clutched at Hatch's arm. "Is she all right?"

"Yes, she's fine. She was just feeling a little down."

"About what?" Nealy whispered.

Hatch shrugged. "She gets that way sometimes. She misses you, Nealy. Nick does, too."

"Has either one of them said that to you?" Nealy asked, her eyes locking with his.

"No."

"Then you don't really know, Hatch," she said, waving her hand in dismissal.

Hatch grabbed her hand in midair. "Yes, Nealy, I do know. Just like I know that you miss them, that in spite of what happened, there isn't a day that goes by that you don't think of them and that you don't long to see them and to know Gabby. A person doesn't have to say the words aloud, Nealy. You should know that." His expression softened. "Tell me something. Are you going to contact Nick and Emmie before you ride in the Derby next year?"

Taken off guard, Nealy could only stammer. "I . . . I haven't given the matter much thought." She took a deep breath. "The Derby is a long way off. Almost a whole year. But it is something I will think about. Did you tell Nick or Emmie that you were coming here?"

"No. I didn't think it was any of their business, to be honest with you. My personal life is my own. I really enjoyed my visit, and I can't wait to come back again. Well, I better get going."

"Perhaps we can do it again when I'm not so . . ."

"Nervous?"

"Yeah, when I'm not so nervous."

"How about this weekend?"

Nealy burst out laughing. "Okay."

"Saturday morning. I should set down around midmorning. Is that okay with you? I'll pick up a rental car at the airport."

"Of course it's okay. But Saturday is just like any other day around here. Weekends are not days of rest or for play."

"I'll dress appropriately. I like picnics. Do you think we could squeeze one in?"

Nealy laughed again as she pushed the Stetson farther back on her head. "I can almost guarantee it. You do mean the kind of picnic where you have a basket of food and a blanket and sit under the tree, right? Yes, I'd like that, Hatch." She couldn't remember the last time she'd been on a picnic. The yearly barbecue was a far cry from a picnic.

Hatch leaned out the window of the car. "Being able to walk around with my hands in my pockets whistling without a worry in the world. You know like Opie and his dad in that Mayberry show."

"Gotcha," Nealy said, grinning from ear to ear. "I'll see you Saturday." She shoved her hands into her pockets.

"You can give me *your* answer on the weekend," Hatch shouted as he swerved the car around to head out to the road. Nealy waved till he was out of sight.

She watched the car until it turned onto the main highway at the end of her drive. For long minutes she stood there, looking at the empty driveway, thinking about her empty life. When had she ever felt this alone? The answer was immediate. When she'd taken Emmie and left SunStar Farms.

She closed her eyes for a moment and remembered the stormy night when her father had threatened to take her baby to an orphanage. With her brothers' help, she'd packed up her belongings and left SunStar, in the middle of the night, with a sick baby while she herself was on the verge of pneumonia. It was all so long ago. A lifetime, actually.

Smitty appeared at the top of the steps with two bottles of beer and a pack of cigarettes. "You get one cigarette and one beer. That's it."

Nealy sat down on the steps. She stretched her neck and shoulders before she reached out for the beer and cigarette. "He's coming back again this weekend, and we're going on a picnic."

"You don't say! For a big guy, he moves fast. Do you like him, Nealy?"

"I do, Smitty. I really do. He's easy to be around. He doesn't talk bullshit. Everyone down at the barn hit it off with him right away. Shufly even liked him. Flyby now, that's a different story. I think he was jealous. He'd take that big head of his and push Hatch backward, away from me. Hatch just laughed. He has a gentle touch with the horses, and they responded. He told me about Nick and Emmie. I didn't ask, Smitty. I swear to God I didn't. He volunteered everything. I thought my heart was going to leap right out of my chest when he started talking about the kids."

"That's wonderful, Nealy."

"Yes, it is wonderful. When Hatch and I were sitting on the front porch last night he told me Emmie is writing a book on the history of horse racing. He told me she has the cover all mapped out. She showed him a picture someone took of me when we crossed the finish line at the Derby. Hatch said I was full of mud and was so far over Flyby's head I looked like I had wings. My daughter wants to put me on the cover of her book! I almost lost it right then, Smitty. He said Emmie does her writing when Gabby is napping. She has a computer and everything. That computer you have scares the hell out of me."

"You know, Nealy, when you've been around as long as I have you develop instincts where people are concerned. Everything with your kids is going to work out just fine. In the last few days I think your destiny caught up with you. You always said you were waiting for your white knight to show up. He showed up, girl!"

"I was thinking the same thing. I really was." She thought about the conversations they'd had, the looks, the little touches that had made her tingle with awareness. She wouldn't be fooling anyone but herself if she tried to deny the attraction she felt for Hatch Littletree. She wondered if he was as attracted to her.

She turned her gaze to the stallion barn, her mind in turmoil. Realistically, Hatch's first and second visits had probably stemmed from a sense of duty to Hunt. But what had prompted his request to visit her again, if not attraction? "Time will tell," she muttered.

"How about one more cigarette, Smitty?"

"No more, Nealy. Matilda has your dinner ready. Salad and chicken. Why don't you take a nice hot bath and relax a little? Dover and I are going to some mud-wrestling thing in town tonight. I can't believe I agreed to go, but I'm going. Everything is caught up in the office, all the bills are paid. Things are so normal it's scary. I'd almost relish a little excitement around here."

"Not me. I like it just the way it is. Have a good time. Mud wrestling, huh?"

"Yeah."

Nealy laughed.

Summer passed and then fall and winter, and before Nealy knew it, it was spring again. Maud's morning glories climbed the trellises and the front porch was alive with scarlet geraniums in their white-wicker baskets. The rockers sported a new coat of fresh white paint, their flowered cushions just as vibrant as the geraniums.

It was the last weekend in April, and if Hatch could get away, he would attend the farm's annual barbecue later in the day. She looked forward to his visit, but this visit was going to be different.

He'd visited eight times so far, and she usually looked forward to his visits, but this time she wished she hadn't asked him to come.

Had it been any other week, she probably wouldn't have any misgivings. The next seven days were going to be stressful enough without having to worry about Hatch. The Saturday after next was Derby Day. She felt giddy at the thought.

Nealy sucked in her breath as past memories assailed her. She leaned back in the rocker and closed her eyes. To this day, all these years later, she could run *the race* in her mind. That's how she always thought of it, *the race.* Could she do it again? Metaxas and Ruby thought she could. So did Hatch. *I should be able to do it. I haven't done anything different. I'm just older. My weight is good, perfect actually. Shufly responds to my every touch.* Maybe what she was missing was Hunt's encouragement. He'd been a pillar of strength that first time. This time she was going it alone. Tears burned her eyes. She closed her eyes and sat back.

"You're not alone, Nealy. You can do it. You ran four races. You won each time because you're the best. Five if you count Santa Anita. None of those other jockeys can hold a candle to you. I want you to believe that."

"Okay, I'll believe it because when it came to the horses you never lied to me. That other stuff, the personal stuff is a different story. What am I really up against, Hunt? How do you see it?"

"The same way you see it. Navigator is good in the stretch. He can come from behind like a lightning bolt. You'll have to watch him. Hard Money is a real fireball, but he'll burn out in the stretch. Jake's Thunder is going to be your biggest competition. The best jockey in the world is riding him. He's going to go to the front early. There's going to be a shitload of speed in that race, Nealy. I think you have it aced, but you can't count on it. If Sweet Pete takes that first turn, he's going to save valuable ground. It's Jake's Thunder you have to worry about. He was bred to go long, Nealy. I'm happy that you've been studying your competition."

"The truth, Hunt, who's the better jockey, me or Mickey Lyons?"

"I think you're evenly matched, but you have a slight edge, Nealy, but not much. Mickey rides for hire. He's only twenty-six, and he's going to flaunt his youth at you. You ride for the love of it and because Shufly is Flyby's son. That makes a big difference. He'll try to rattle you, and so will the others. They're going to call you things like 'old lady' and worse. Roll

with it, Nealy. You being a woman eats at them. Don't fall for it. Give the bunch of them the finger if you have to. I'll be watching over you."

"I'll miss you at the walkover, Hunt. I hope I draw gate 15."

"I hope you do, too, Nealy. Those roses belong to you. You deserve them."

"That's one of the nicest things you ever said to me."

"So, how's it going with the big guy?"

"That's none of your business, Hunt. He's nice. I like him. He's become a good friend. It's an easy, comfortable friendship. He doesn't make demands, and neither do I."

"That's it, a friend? I was hoping for a little more than friend."

"I've been kind of busy, Hunt, in case you haven't noticed. He lives in New Mexico, and I live in Kentucky. I don't want to talk to you about Hatch. It's . . . it's immoral."

"You wearing the purple silks?"

"Absolutely. You gave them to me, Hunt. Of course I'm wearing them. Purple was Maud's favorite color. I hope they bring me luck. Do you have any inside . . . you know, firsthand . . ."

"No."

"You don't have to get snippy. Is something wrong, Hunt?"

"It's you, Nealy. Not me. You're starting to get nervous. That's not good. You have to shift into neutral."

"You're right. I'm sorry. I really am going to miss you on the walkover, though."

"I'll be there, Nealy."

"Will you give me a sign so I know you're there?"

"You bet."

Nealy rubbed at her eyes. She must have dozed off. For some reason her shoulders felt lighter. She thought about her children. Would they come home for the Derby? Did they know she was riding Shufly? Hatch hadn't mentioned anything to her on his last visit. She hadn't asked either. Maybe they didn't know she was riding. Emmie might know if she was researching her book. "I miss you both so much," she murmured.

"Ruby, do you think Hatch really likes me? Or do you think he comes here to give me little tidbits about the kids? You know, out of a sense of duty. I enjoy his company tremendously and I always look forward to his visits. He's only kissed me once, and it was just a little light peck. Hey, I was ready . . . for you know . . . *more.* We get on so well. Tell me if I'm wrong here. I'm thinking, he's thinking that he's being disloyal to Hunt. I don't know how Indian people think about stuff like that. Is it possible he just wants to be friends? I catch him looking at me in certain ways, I get all breathless, then nothing happens. Am I supposed to hit on him? Maybe I'm not giving off the right signals. He's been here eight times, Ruby. I don't need another Kendrick Bell in my life. Do you understand where I'm coming from?"

Ruby plopped down on the top front porch step. She was wearing a fuzzy pink robe and matching slippers.

"I'll tell you what I think. First of all, Hatch is no Ken Bell. I think he respects you. Yeah, Hunt may play a little part in it. Eight visits isn't all that much. Hell, you didn't even know the guy the first visit, so that doesn't count. I'd be real disappointed in him if he had tried to drag you off to his lair. Personally, I think that he thinks you are not ready for a relationship, and for now he's being a friend to you and a mentor to your children. For some reason I don't think he can separate the two. So, you might have to wait a bit longer. It's not a bad thing, Nealy. Actually, I think it's a good thing. It was like that with me and Metaxas at first. Then we really got to know one another. The bottom line is, he wouldn't be coming here if he wasn't attracted to you."

"I do like him. You look tired, Ruby. Are you okay?"

"I am tired. No, no, it's nothing like that," Ruby said, seeing the immediate concern in Nealy's eyes. "It's coming down to the wire. I feel like I have a load of fire ants in my undies. How can you be so calm? The race is just days away. All things considered, Metaxas is relatively calm. He loves that horse, Nealy. I'm talking about *real* love here. Shufly is like a child to him, his flesh and blood. I know that sounds stupid, but that's how he feels. In all honesty, I truly believe he doesn't care if the horse wins or not. He won't love him any less. Do you understand that, Nealy?"

"Of course. That's how I always felt about Flyby. I still feel that way. It's that family thing. Are you ready for the barbecue and the horde of Secret Service men that's about to descend on us? Tell me again why the vice president is coming here to my house. I'm in awe over that."

"He's coming because Metaxas invited him. The vice president and his wife are very active in some of the charities you sponsor with your Derby Ball. Plus, everyone wants to come to the Kentucky Derby. Oh, Nealy, you don't know half the people my husband knows. He knows the president, too. Think of Metaxas as a kind of Ross Perot.

"Allowing us to stay here and work all this time was just what we both needed. Metaxas has been able to keep his hand in his business and still help you out. I just love being around the horses and doing whatever I can do to help. Neither one of us is getting any younger, and I think Metaxas is actually ready to put down some roots. I'm not sure about this, but I think he has his eye on the Goldberg farm next to you. I think he might finally want to settle down and take life easy. I hope so."

"It would be wonderful to have you and Metaxas for neighbors. So, are you ready to meet the vice president?"

"Yes, but I voted for the other team, you know. When the vice president comes to town, so does the Secret Service. They have to make sure everything is safe and secure. Metaxas spent half the night talking to those guys. According to him they were actually thinking about confiscating the hoof picks and riding crops because they could be used as weapons. They shouldn't bother us too much. It will be dusk, and the barbecue will be over. I am going to stuff myself until those ribs come out my ears. How about you?"

"Can't put on even one ounce, Ruby. I'll have some of the barbecued vegetables. I ate light this morning, just yogurt, and for lunch I had broiled fish and a sliced tomato. When the races are over, I'm going to chow down for a solid week. Right now I would kill for a slice of praline pie and fresh whipped cream with strawberries dipped in milk chocolate all around the plate and a big glass of ice-cold milk."

Ruby groaned. "Are you looking forward to Hatch's visit?"

"At first I regretted inviting him because so much is going on, and I didn't think I would have much time to spend with him. I'll work it out, and now I'm glad he's coming. He's very easy and comfortable to be around. He likes sitting on the front porch and just talking. He's a very kind man, a gentle man. Fun, too. He can make me laugh. He told me Nick is going to ace the bar. When that happens he gets to sit in his father's chair and gets his name on his desk. I am so proud I could just bust."

"You never told him why you sent the kids off, did you?"

"You mean Hatch? No, I never told him."

"Maybe both Nick and Emmie will come for the race. I hope for your sake that happens."

"I do, too, but I have to be realistic. What have the papers been saying, Ruby?" Nealy asked, abruptly changing the subject.

"You don't want to know, Nealy. It's all garbage."

"No, I do want to know. Yesterday I didn't want to know. Today when I dozed off, I had a dream about Hunt. He said the other jockeys were going to try to rattle me. I'm prepared. So, what are they saying?"

Ruby was a long time in answering. "Somehow or other they found out you're a grandmother. Use your imagination." When Nealy rolled her eyes, she said, "I told you it was garbage."

Nealy smirked. "What they can't see, they can't write about. Hunt always used to say that. They're forced to pick on me. That's okay. This way Shufly remains a mystery, which is just the way I want it."

"Are you ready for your big Derby Ball tomorrow, honey?"

"Oh, God, you had to say that, didn't you? Now my heart is pounding," Nealy said, her face going white.

"Things this year will be better because you have a date." She tilted her head and looked past Nealy. "I bet Hatch is going to be impressive in his tux. I mean he's impressive anyway but in a black tux . . . woo-ee!" Ruby's eyes were bright with excitement. "And the very fact that the vice president of the United States is attending as your guest along with the secretary of state, thanks to Metaxas, I might add, will have everybody buzzing for weeks to come."

Nealy felt sick to her stomach. "If you're trying to make me feel better, it isn't working."

Ruby sighed with exasperation. "Don't be ridiculous. Everything is going to be perfect. You are going to be perfect. You have a gorgeous, spangled dress to wear, outrageous shoes, a classy new hairdo, and when you load on all those diamonds, honey, you are going to make an entrance like no one has ever made an entrance. The best part is now you know how to dance. Metaxas taught you well. It's taken us a solid year but you can hold your own now. All you have to remember is not to look down at your feet and don't mutter, 'one, two, three, one, two, three.'"

In spite of herself, Nealy laughed. "Just cross your fingers that I don't trip on the dance floor. I think we're going to have a sold-out crowd."

"Sweetie, we were sold out ten minutes after Smitty sent out the invitations. Checks were hand-delivered within an hour of receipt of the invitation. Smitty clocked it all. She got a kick out of it. A hundred grand *each*. Nothing shabby about that. I can hardly wait. I wish you'd get more excited." She stopped rocking and sat forward. "Listen, I probably shouldn't tell you this, but I don't want you getting all pissed off at the eleventh hour and blowing it, Nealy. Dagmar had this wonderful idea, and her paper is going to go along with it. She wants to run a picture of you in the paper all *duded* out in your slinky, sparkly dress and those diamonds. And right next to it she wants to run that famous picture or should I say *infamous* picture of you crossing the finish line on Flyby. You know the one where you look like you're flying and are covered in mud."

Nealy's knees started to buckle. "Oh, my God!"

"I think it's a great idea. It's going to make anyone who calls you a Derby-riding granny look like a fool. It's not going to hurt to have *your* picture taken with the vice president and the secretary of state either. Derby-riding granny, my ass," Ruby exploded. "I bet the vice president asks you to dance. God, it doesn't get any better than that. It isn't going to hurt for Hatch to see you looking like that either. I bet you are going to have the time of your life."

"Ruby. You make me sound like I'm on the auction block at Keeneland. I sure hope you're right," Nealy said over the cannon-ball-sized lump that lodged in her throat.

"Oh, pooh, you just don't know how to have a good time. This is a good thing, Nealy. The ball is raising millions of dollars for your animal causes, women's shelters, children's charities, and hospices. Metaxas said that's the reason the vice prez is coming. He's big on children's causes and the elderly. It isn't going to hurt *him* to have his picture taken with *you* either."

"Okay, okay. Time to get back to the barn. What are you doing up here at this time of day, Ruby? I thought you were going to sleep in for a change."

"Came for some of Matilda's coffee, and she made brownies this morning. Metaxas wants some. Sugar high. It's that time of day. Did I thank you for letting us stay in the cottage?"

"You have thanked me five times a day for the last three years. The cottage was just sitting there empty, Ruby. I'm surprised, though, that you lasted as long as you did sleeping in the barn."

"Two months was a long time." Ruby giggled. "It was that old devil sex that turned the tables. Metaxas, sweetheart that he is, didn't want to have sex with the horses listening. Even now, sometimes, he gets up in the middle of the night and sleeps in one of the stalls after he checks on Shufly. One other thing, Nealy, a roll in the hay is not romantic."

Nealy whooped with laughter. "That's pretty funny, Ruby." She turned serious after a moment. "I envy you two," she said. "You have the kind of romance Maud and Jess had, the kind I've always wanted."

"Speaking of what you've always wanted, Hatch is falling in love with you," Ruby said out of the blue. "I don't think he knows it yet, but this is going to be a momentous week for you both."

Nealy felt her emotions start to flounder. Was she right? Ruby was a romantic and looked at everything through rose-colored glasses. She shook her head to clear her thoughts. Her hands in her pockets, she crossed her fingers that Ruby was right about Hatch falling in love with her. Suddenly she felt so happy and giddy she wanted to sing.

"Let's go check out the barbecue pit so I can drool. Hatch should be here soon if he's coming."

"Speak of the devil," Ruby said, pointing toward the farm entrance.

Nealy turned around to see Hatch's rental car pulling in the drive as a dizzying current raced through her. "You're late," she shouted. "I was starting to worry." He smiled, and she felt warm all over.

"I ran into one hell of a head wind," he said, staring at her as if he was seeing her for the first time. "I guess I should have called, huh?" Nealy nodded. "Sorry, I wasn't thinking." He reached into the car for his duffel bag. "You know it just occurred to me that this may not be the best time for me to be here. It is Derby week. You can tell me to go, and it won't hurt my feelings."

"If I didn't want you here, Hatch, I wouldn't have invited you. I just don't know how much time I'll be able to spend with you. I don't want to hear another word about leaving. Doesn't the barbecue smell wonderful?"

"It sure does. Wait here while I run my stuff up to the apartment. You sure it's okay for me to stay there? Are you sure you won't be having other guests?"

"I'm very sure, and no, there will be no other guests. It's clean as a whistle." Nealy looked around. "Sometimes I think I should do more for the workers. I do this barbecue, then we do a big Thanksgiving dinner and we have a Christmas party and give presents to the kids and give generous bonuses to the guys. We pay well, the guys have a good health plan, and we started a pension fund when Smitty suggested it. Back then I didn't know much about stuff like that. Do you think I'm doing enough? How much is enough to show them I appreciate their hard work and loyalty?"

"You're doing plenty. No one has left your employ for years, and they all seem happy."

"I'm so relieved. I worry about stuff like that. Listen, I have to get down to the barn. You can help if you want. We do ninety-minute shifts so that everyone gets a chance to eat, have a drink or two, and dance. Right now it's my shift. I see you're dressed for work, so let's get to it." She reached for his arm and smiled up at him, her eyes sparkling. She couldn't remember the last time she'd been this happy.

"Wait a minute," Hatch said, pulling her toward him. "There's something I want to give you."

"What?" she asked, looking up at him.

"This," he said, kissing her.

"Hmmmm," Nealy said, melting into his arms. "Hmmmm."

"What does hmmmm mean?" Hatch grinned.

"Oh, that . . . well . . . I liked that. A lot. Would you mind doing it again?"

"Ma'am, I wouldn't mind at all," Hatch chuckled, as he clamped his lips down on hers. He almost fell backward with Nealy's ardor.

"Lady, don't do this to me here in public. Can we pick up later where we're going to leave off right now?"

Nealy, her face pink, felt flustered beyond belief. Her head bobbed up and down. "Name the time and the place."

"The apartment over the garage. When you get there. I'll be waiting."

"I'll be there," Nealy said.

Nealy's feet left the ground as Hatch picked her up and twirled her around.

Nealy's mind and emotions were on the stellar evening she'd spent with Hatch. It was everything she wanted, everything she expected. She knew now for certain that she was in love. She could still, if she concentrated, feel the tingle running through her body. No, that wasn't what she was feeling. She was *throbbing* with anticipation for it to happen again. She gave herself a mental shake as she started for the stallion barn.

Nealy looked down at the hands on her watch at the same moment all hell broke loose on Blue Diamond Farms. She could hear Smitty's screams, saw clouds of dust, and a caravan of eleven black cars. "What? What's going on?" she bellowed at the top of her lungs as men in dark suits, sunglasses, and handheld two-way radios invaded the barn.

"What's going on? Who the hell are you? Get your asses out of my barn and do it *now!*" Nealy ordered.

"Stand down, ma'am. That's an order!"

"Stand down! What does that mean, stand down? Who are you? You're upsetting my horses. I gave you an order, too. You aren't listening to me—get the hell out of my barn."

The gun in his hand was gray and deadly looking. "Stand down means don't move."

The hair on the back of Nealy's neck stood at attention. She grabbed her riding crop out of her back pocket and took a step forward. Behind her, she heard a horse whinny in fright. She glanced over her shoulder to see one of her grooms fighting to keep El Jefe, a million-dollar two-year-old colt, from rearing. Her fear turned to anger. Brandishing the riding crop she made for the man. "Whoever you are, don't take another step. You're scaring my horses."

"Stand down, ma'am. We're Secret Service agents."

"What? Your people were here all night securing the farm. How many men does it take to do that? Nothing's changed since last night. You need to be a little more quiet. This isn't good for the horses. There aren't any bombs in here, your people cleared it all early this morning. Where's the vice president?"

"There was a change in plans, ma'am. The vice president is in Washington. The secretary of state is sitting in his car along with the president until we give the all-clear signal. An hour at the most, ma'am."

"*The* president of *the* United States!" Nealy said in awe, her jaw dropping. "The president of the United States is here, and he's actually sitting in my driveway. How'd that happen?"

"The vice president couldn't make it at the last moment. The president just happened to be free and agreed to stand in for him. The president and the first lady admire you, Ms. Clay."

"Fancy that," Nealy said, her eyes full of shock.

"We need to check these stalls, ma'am."

"I wouldn't do that if I were you. These horses don't know you. They'll stomp you to death. I mean that." Out of the corner of her eye, Nealy watched dark-clad men moving in all directions, gun in one hand, two-way radio in the other. They looked fierce and deadly. She felt herself grow light-headed.

Nealy's mind raced. "Wait a minute. President or no president, you get on that radio and call your men back here stat, which means on the double. Hear me?"

The agent's eyebrows shot upward. "I beg your pardon."

"My horses are worth millions of dollars and no one goes near them without someone from my employ going along. You got that, Mr. Secret Service Agent?"

Hatch stood leaning against the paddock fence, chuckling, his eyes bright with amusement and admiration. His girl was giving them what for. He felt like shooting his fist in the air.

From the entrance to the breezeway, Metaxas and Ruby watched the proceedings, their jaws dropping when the agents bowed to Nealy's demands.

"We need to check these stalls," the agent said again. His eyes looked wary, though.

"If you all clear the barn, we'll lead the horses out to the paddock. Make your search quick. Just for the record, Mr. Secret Service Agent, I did not invite the president here. Technically, that means you are all trespassing. What that means is nothing better happen to one of my horses. Now be quick about it."

The agent jerked his head to show his fellow agents they should leave the barn.

"That means you, too. I'm not taking these horses out until you are all out of the barn. *You stand down, Mister.*"

An hour later the horses were back in their stalls, the workers agog at what was transpiring in front of their very eyes.

"You're free to go about your business now, ma'am. This might be a good time to welcome the president and perhaps serve some refreshments," the steely eyed agent suggested.

Nealy looked down at her hands . . . hands that were covered with hay, and green horse saliva because she had just checked a mare's teeth. She rubbed her hands on her jeans and hoped for the best.

There was no such thing as walking up the path to the house alone. They were a parade—Nealy, Ruby, Metaxas, and Hatch flanked by a bevy of agents whose eyes were everywhere.

"We're good to go here," the agent said quietly into his hand-held radio with the flashing lights. "Escort the president and the secretary into the house. Send a detail into town to sweep the ballroom, and report back to me. The motorcade will leave here at six-fifteen. The police have been alerted. Make sure everyone is inside and seated when we arrive."

Nealy looked down at her hands again. She rubbed them on her jeans. Again.

"Miz Clay, it's an honor to meet you," the president said, loping toward her, agents at his side. "My wife sends her regards. She also wants to know if it's possible to get a picture of you, me, and the horse you're riding in the Derby next week. I hope you don't object too much to me taking the vice president's place."

He looked and sounded just like one of her neighbors. He was dressed in denim, but then he came from a ranching family. "No, I don't object at all. I think we can arrange for the pictures, Mr. President," Nealy said, extending her hand. "I'd like to introduce Mr. and Mrs. Metaxas Parish and my friend Hatch Littletree."

"We've met," the president said, extending his hand to Metaxas and then Hatch. "It's a pleasure to meet you at last, Mrs. Parish. Metaxas has told me a lot about you over the years. Fine man, your husband. He's helped out the country many times, as Mr. Littletree has."

"Call me Ruby. Everyone calls me Ruby."

"Can I offer you gentlemen some coffee or perhaps a drink?"

"What I'd really like is a tour. I'd like to see the horses. I've been a Thoroughbred horse enthusiast most of my life even though I ride Western. Not as well as you, Ms. Clay. Why don't we get that picture business out of the way so you ladies can get ready for this evening. My wife told me not to interfere with what's going on. It doesn't make a difference if you're the president or not, you always listen to your wife." The president chuckled.

"You ride Western?" Nealy asked. "Hatch rides Western, too. We can do the pictures first, Mr. President, and please, call me Nealy. There's a camera in the barn we can use."

It was a precision drill all the way, with the Secret Service agents in charge. Nealy led Shufly from the stall as one of the agents positioned the president and Nealy next to the horse.

"He's magnificent," the president said, as Nealy led the horse out to the paddock. Nealy beamed. "Take more than one, Josh," he ordered. They posed, they smiled, they said cheese. "This big fellow reminds me of some of the pictures I've seen of Man O' War. Is he as good?"

"We'll know that for sure on Saturday, Mr. President. Everyone who has met him says the same thing. I agree, though. Like his daddy, he was born to run. Metaxas and Hatch can show you around. Would you like to see Flyby? Maybe you'd like to have your picture taken with a Triple Crown winner."

"Flyby? Hell, yes. That would be great."

Nealy handed Shufly over to his groom, then led the president out to the number three pasture. "There he is," she said, feeling so proud she thought she was going to bust wide open. Hatch came up behind her and gave her shoulders a gentle squeeze. She knew that life couldn't get any better than this.

"Here, Mr. President, give him this. He loves mints," Nealy said, raising her arm to reach inside her pocket. The agent named Josh had his hand in her pocket in the blink of an eye. He nodded curtly. The president rolled his eyes. Nealy, her hand trembling, held out the mint.

"I'll . . . I'll see you later, Mr. President."

"Would you mind if later on we sat on that lovely front porch of yours? Before it's time to leave for the ball?"

"I would be honored, Mr. President. The front porch is my favorite part of the house. Make yourself comfortable."

"I will. It feels like home around here," the president said wistfully.

Back in the house, upstairs in her bedroom, Ruby and Nealy fell into each other's arms. "The president of the United States is in my house. Well, in my barn. He's going to sit on my front porch. Ruby, did you hear me?"

Ruby's head bobbed up and down. "When we knew the vice president was coming we were in awe, and now we have *the man* himself. He said he wanted a picture of you and him and the horse. My God, Nealy, it doesn't get any better than that. Does it?"

"No. God, no! Did I act all right? You know how stupid I can be sometimes. Tell me the truth."

"You were just fine. I can't wait for tonight. Can you see the faces of all those horse owners when you walk in with the president of the United States? Oh, God, this is just too much. You have to call Dagmar Doolittle and make sure she's there so she gets the scoop, Nealy. Swear her to secrecy."

"Okay, I can do that. I will do that. When people talk about special moments in time . . . this is one of those moments, right, Ruby?"

"This is definitely one of those moments. Did you see Metaxas and Hatch? They were grinning and talking shop with the president. They just rolled with it. Now aren't you glad you got that ass-kicking outfit I made you buy?"

"Yeah," Nealy said in a jittery voice. "I have to call Dagmar."

The moment the reporter picked up the phone, Nealy went into her spiel. "Just be inside the door with your photographer. Be by the first table, and you'll get the first shot. Have your photographer run to the paper with the picture and I'll see what I can do about getting you a few words with the big guy. I always pay my debts, Dagmar. No promises now. You'll beat all those jackals with your story first thing tomorrow morning. I'll see you tonight. Yes, yes, it is so exciting I can't stand it. Bye."

"I need a drink, Ruby. I mean, I really need a drink. This is all so . . . I need a drink."

"Me, too. You go ahead and run your bath. I'll scoot downstairs the back way and get us something. Just one, right?"

"Yeah," Nealy said, remembering her first date with Hatch. "Maybe we should have tea."

"Maybe we shouldn't. This calls for a real drink. I'll put a lot of ice in yours."

"I can do this. I really can do this. I can, can't I, Ruby? I feel like Cinderella going to the ball."

"You are!" Ruby giggled. "I'm your lady-in-waiting."

"We better get a move on. We only have five hours to get beautiful. I'm allowing for an hour on the front porch. We probably won't need that much time on the porch, but an hour sounds right. Maybe thirty minutes."

"Be right back," Ruby said.

* * *

Nealy looked at herself in the mirror. It's me. This ravishing creature is me. She leaned over to peer closer at her reflection in the vanity mirror, Ruby behind her.

"Nealy, you look fabulous. In a million years I didn't think you could pull this off but look at you. You look like one of those gorgeous runway models. That dress is pure dynamite. You glisten and sparkle like a rare jewel. You aren't overdone either. It's just perfect and you smell heavenly. We made good choices. I think we are going to blow everyone's socks off tonight."

"Ruby, you look beautiful, too. That dress fits you like a glove. I want a picture of you tonight."

"Someone's at the door," Ruby hissed.

"It's probably Matilda. Come in!" Nealy shouted.

"I'm just checking the rooms," one of the female Secret Service agents said.

The agent nodded and closed the door. Nealy shrugged. "We'll go down the kitchen stairs. I haven't thought about horses all afternoon, Ruby. Or Hatch."

"Me either." Ruby grinned. "The ball starts at six, with dinner and speeches, even though everyone gets there at five-thirty. At least that's the way it's been the past two years. We're leaving here at six-fifteen. That means we will be fashionably late. I don't know when I've ever been this excited. You look so calm, Nealy."

"I'm not calm at all. I'm numb. Maybe I'm in shock."

The same agent who had poked her head in the bedroom door appeared in the kitchen. "The president asked me to ask if you and your escorts would like to ride to the ball with him and the secretary. The president said he spoke to Mr. Parish earlier this afternoon, but he wanted me to check with you ladies to be absolutely certain."

Nealy and Ruby both nodded.

"Good. The president enjoyed himself this afternoon. May I say you ladies look very grand."

"Thank you," Nealy and Ruby said in unison.

"Here come our dates. Metaxas always sounds like a herd of cattle. Hatch isn't a featherweight either."

"Ta da!" Ruby said, swirling around for her husband's benefit.

"Sweet baby, you're prettier than a summer day."

Nealy smiled at Hatch but stood rooted to the floor.

"You look pretty, Nealy," Hatch said. "I want a picture of you to take home with me."

"Okay. You look . . . you look, handsome, Hatch. I'm nervous. No, no, I didn't have a drink . . . Well, I did but . . ."

"It wore off two hours ago. We're both fine. Look, this was a shock! It isn't every day the president of the United States shows up in your barn. What did you guys do this afternoon while we were prettying up?" Ruby asked.

"We walked the farm. Took some pictures, drank a few beers. The president is a regular guy. He said he's going to try to come for the Derby with his wife, but he did say it's one of those things where crowd control has to be taken care of and the Secret Service doesn't like it when he springs things on them at the last minute. He called his wife and that was about it. Guy stuff. Then they left to get cleaned up and now they're back. I think it's safe to say the president enjoyed himself," Metaxas said.

"He ate three of Matilda's brownies," Hatch said. "She's fixing up a box for him to take back to his wife. He said they were the best he ever ate."

Twenty minutes later the Secret Service escorted the two couples to the long, waiting limousine. "The president will be along in a minute. He's talking to your housekeeper. She's wrapping a package for him," the agent named Josh said.

Conversation was general. Mostly how worrisome the weather would be for the Run for the Roses. "Shufly does real well on a sloppy track, Mr. President. I've trained him for all conditions. If you can't make it here for the race, will you watch it on television?"

"Absolutely." The president smiled.

"If I win, I'll give you a thumbs-up, Mr. President," Nealy promised.

"I'll be watching for it."

The presidential motorcade slowed to a mere crawl to pull alongside the long awning over the Derby Ballroom in town. Secret Service agents flanked both sides of the long walk to the door.

Other agents were scattered everywhere, a virtual army of dark-clad warriors.

The small black boxes in the agents' hands squawked to life. Nealy watched the flashing buttons, heard bits of the conversation. "All the guests are seated. Area's snow-white. The president can depart the limousine."

The president stepped out of the limousine, followed by Nealy and Ruby, and then Metaxas and Hatch. "Single file until we're inside. The president goes first," Josh ordered.

Inside the foyer, Nealy noticed that the wide, dark, teakwood doors were closed tight, agents flanking both sides. She knew there were at least *five dozen* more agents inside the ballroom. Some dressed as waiters, others as guests, and still others as reporters or photographers.

"Take the president's arm, Ms. Clay."

Nealy's eyes apologized to Hatch as she stepped forward. He nodded, a wide smile on his face.

"Mr. President, don't walk fast. I'm not used to walking in four-inch heels," Nealy whispered.

"You sound like my wife, Nealy. She has shoes for sitting, shoes for standing, and shoes for walking. Are you okay?"

"I'm okay, Mr. President."

"Then let's *do it!*"

The wide teakwood doors opened to a short drumroll followed by one of the agents announcing loudly and clearly, "Ladies and gentlemen, the president of the United States and Nealy Diamond Clay!"

Nealy saw Dagmar grinning from ear to ear as her photographer shot the first picture of the evening—the picture that would flash around the world within hours and the World Wide Web in minutes. She saw the stunned faces in the room, watched the guests rise to their feet in amazed disbelief. "This is kind of like the feeling I had when I crossed the finish line at the Derby, Mr. President," Nealy whispered.

The president stopped in mid-stride. He looked down at Nealy, and said, "No kidding!"

Nealy laughed. "No kidding, Mr. President." He hugged her then for all the room to see. She felt ten feet tall and invincible.

Later, Nealy said to anyone who would listen, "I don't remember a thing after I danced with the president. The rest of the night was a blur."

11

She was a golden-haired cherub, a whirlwind of activity. Emmie looked up from the computer she was working on and smiled. "Is it time for our tea party yet, Gabby?"

The little girl nodded, her blond curls bouncing. She pointed to the small table and chairs and the place setting for three. Emmie nodded. "Uncle Nick will be here soon. He said he was bringing chocolate ice cream." The little girl clapped her hands in anticipation.

A fat puppy named Cookie whirled around her feet as he attempted to catch his tail. Gabby shook with laughter as she bent down to hug him close to her chest. The puppy wiggled and in the end gave up and licked her face, happy to be cuddled and loved.

A door opened and closed. "I'm here!" a voice rang out. "Where's my girl! Guess what I have! Chocolate ice cream! Hi, Emmie," Nick said, scooping Gabby into his arms and hugging Emmie at the same time.

Emmie walked around her computer desk. "You look . . . like someone who has the world by the tail, Nick. What happened?"

"I'm done. I'm done, Emmie! I have a life now." He twirled Gabby around and around before he set her down. "I can sleep till ten in the morning or I can sleep the clock around. I have time to take you and Emmie out to dinner or lunch or even breakfast. I have time to sit down and read a newspaper if I want." He started dishing ice cream into Gabby's miniature bowls. "I can drink three bottles of beer, one after the other. All I have to do is take the bar and God Almighty, if I pass, I'm a real lawyer. A lawyer with a job! It doesn't get any better than that."

Gabby placed two cookies on each plate while Emmie poured lukewarm tea into tiny cups.

"I cooked them, Uncle Nick. Me and Mommie cooked them just for you."

"I'm impressed. See, I kept my promise, and you promised if I came to your tea party, you would take a nice long nap for Mommie and me. Then when you wake up, I'm going to take you and Mommie out to dinner. You have to get all dressed up and wear your shiny shoes and your socks with the pretty ribbons. Do you have a party dress?"

"I have two party dresses. A pink one and a blue one. Can we bring Cookie to dinner?"

"No, Cookie has to stay here, but we'll bring him back something real good. Finish your ice cream, then it's nap time. This tea is delicious." Nick grinned as he picked up the tiny cup.

"Are you going to sleep at our house today, Uncle Nick?"

"You bet. I brought my pajamas and everything. When you're ready, Mommie will clean you up and I'll carry you upstairs on my shoulders. Howzat?"

Gabby's eyes brightened. "Oh, goodie. Can Cookie sleep with me?"

"Sure," Emmie said, wiping her daughter's face and hands. She smiled when Nick lifted the little girl onto his shoulders and proceeded to gallop up the steps.

Nick . . . a lawyer. Finally, after all this time, he was free to be who he wanted to be. Emmie felt so proud she wanted to shout her happiness. The only problem was, there was no one within shouting distance to hear.

The moment Nick sat down at the table she knew there was something else on his mind. "How about some coffee, Nick? I'm ready for a break. There's something else, isn't there?"

"Yeah, there are a few other things." Nick reached inside his jacket pocket and withdrew three airline tickets. "It's time to go home, Emmie. The Derby is on Saturday. Mom's riding. I have to be honest, I'm worried sick. When she was younger and ran, it was different. She's *old* now. You know as well as I do a jockey takes his life and the life of his horse in hand every time they race. What if something happens?"

"Nick, you make Mom sound ancient. She's only fifty-two. Plenty of jockeys run at that age and even older. I'm sure she's been training. She wouldn't do it if she wasn't fit. Shufly must be some kind of horse to make her do this."

"You want to go home, don't you, Emmie?"

"I do, Nick. I really do. I've missed Mom so much. She's never seen Gabby. I can never give her back those early years. I can give her the rest of them, though. What about you?"

"I miss the farm, I won't deny it, but my place is here. I know now this is where I belong, where I want to be. I can't wait to practice law, Emmie. The best thing would be if Mom welcomes us and lets me visit. Do you think she'll unbend?"

"I'm almost sure she will, Nick. She's going to be so proud of you she's going to burst. We're family. We need to be at the Derby to cheer her on. Maybe she'll invite us back to the farm."

"Okay, we're going home Friday. God, it's been so long."

Emmie almost swooned, but she steadied herself. "I'll call the management company and have them open the house and clean it. Is that okay with you, Nick? We'll stay at my house in case . . . You know, in case Mom doesn't unbend."

"Sure. Will you be okay going back to the house where you lived with Buddy?"

"I'm okay with it, Nick. And before you can ask, no, I'm not going to say anything to Buddy. Why should I? Think about it for just a minute. He's never once contacted me after he dumped me on the gangplank when we got back to port. He never wanted children because he was afraid they might turn out to be deaf like he is. He didn't even take the time to drop me a note after the divorce. He wasn't in court either. I didn't expect him to be, but it would have been nice. That part of my life is over. My new life includes Gabby and excludes him. When Gabby is older and can understand, I'll explain to her why she doesn't have a father. Maybe someday I'll feel differently, but I doubt it. Time will tell. What's the rest of it, Nick?"

"There's something else I didn't tell you. Don't ask me why. I had a bronze of Shufly made. They're going to erect the sculpture the day before the Derby. My dad commissioned the one for Flyby. It's only right that I do one for Shufly. Dover Wilkie took a picture and, let me tell you, it was scary. Shufly looks exactly like Flyby. Same coloring, same markings, same everything. Months ago, I got in touch with the people that sculpted and bronzed Flyby. It will be up and in place by midmorning on Friday, the day before the Derby. I thought that was kind of appropriate. I can't wait to see it."

Emmie's expression went from shock to excitement. "Mom will go over the moon, Nick."

"I hope so. You know how she is when she's pissed about something. She might knock it down. Who the hell thought she would boot our asses out of there? I wish now I hadn't been so muleheaded and defied her. She might have mellowed these past few years, but I don't know that for sure. I wish I did. God, I wish so many things."

As if reading his mind, Emmie asked, "Nothing on Willow, huh?" She poured fresh coffee into Nick's cup.

Her intuitiveness didn't surprise him. It was that same intuitiveness that made her so good with horses. "Yes and no. Hatch has some of the firm's investigators working on it. Hell, they've been working on it from day one, and no one has come up with anything. He called on Sunday to tell me he had a possible lead. He's following up on it. I'm not real hopeful. Willow is simply nowhere to be found. I'm also realistic enough to know if Willow *really* loved me, Mom wouldn't have been able to scare her off."

"I wonder if we'll ever know what happened," Emmie said, biting into one of the sugar cookies from Gabby's plate. "It's been such a long time, Nick. Do you still feel the same way you did when she disappeared?"

"I don't know what I feel. I still dream about her. Sometimes when I allow myself the luxury of thinking about her, I get damn mad. One night I had this really bad dream. She was laughing at me and calling me a foolish young boy. It wasn't a nice laugh. She was mocking me, mocking my feelings for her. I don't want to talk about Willow because it makes me crazy. Look, I'm going upstairs to pack, and then I have a few errands to run. Let me throw this out to you, Emmie. These are first-class plane tickets, so we could switch up and leave today if we wanted to. I can help you open the house and clean up instead of the management company doing it. How do you feel about that?"

"Oh, Nick, yes, let's do it. Let's go home. Call the airlines and see if you can switch. I can't wait. We have to take Cookie with us. Gabby will be devastated if he doesn't go with us."

"We'll carry him in his little carry bag. He only weighs seven pounds and I don't want to put him in cargo. I'll take care of everything. See about emptying the fridge and all that stuff you have to do when you go away for a week. I'm thinking a week, Emmie. Anything more will be a bonus."

Emmie twirled around like a ballet dancer. "We're going home. The banished children are finally going home." Tears of happiness rolled down her cheeks.

"Yeah, we're going home," Nick said softly as he wrapped his arms around Emmie. "Don't have high expectations, Emmie. If things don't go well, we won't be disappointed. We're making the first move. After that, it's up to Mom."

Nealy stared down at the envelope on the kitchen table. She saw her name in dark ink across the front. Her heart thumped in her chest as she looked around the empty kitchen. It was seven o'clock, breakfast time. Where was Hatch? When he visited, he was usually the first one at the table, coffee cup in hand.

Smitty breezed into the kitchen swinging her voluminous tote bag. "I'm so hungry I could eat a bear," she grumbled good-naturedly. "What's that you're holding?"

"A letter. It was on the table when I came up from the barn. It might have been there earlier, but I didn't see it. I don't know who it's from."

Smitty grimaced as she poured coffee into two cups. "There's a way for you to find out. Open the damn thing, Nealy."

"What if it's bad news of some kind? It must be from Hatch."

"I see," Smitty said thoughtfully as she fired up her first cigarette of the day. "You finally discovered that you're more than just a little fond of the gentle giant, and you're afraid you might be holding a Dear John letter. Or, you think this might be bad news and right now you can't handle bad news. How am I doing so far, sweetie?"

"As always, on the money," Nealy groused. "Do you always have to be right?"

"Being right is better than being wrong. You like him a lot, don't you?"

Nealy knew Smitty wouldn't let it go. Sometimes she was like a dog with a bone. "Probably more than I bargained for. He . . . he makes my ears sweat, Smitty."

"Whoa," Smitty said, her eyes popping wide. "That's heavy-duty stuff." She grinned. "And such a wonderfully romantic way of putting it."

"I didn't . . . wasn't expecting to feel . . . friends was one thing . . . then . . . then somehow, it changed." An unwelcome blush crept into her cheeks. As old as she was, she was still embarrassed to talk about sex.

"And . . ."

"And nothing. Right now there is no room for anything but the upcoming races. Once they're finished, come what may, I'm seriously thinking of retiring and letting the workers run the farm. They're good people and they've all been here for years and years. I'm just in the thinking stage, Smitty, so don't read something into this that isn't there."

"Open the envelope, Nealy."

Nealy ripped at the farm stationery.

Dear Nealy,

I'm sorry about this but I got a call a short while ago that demands I leave immediately. It was late, and I didn't want to wake you. I hate leaving notes for people. I'll try to call later today or tomorrow. I promise I'll be back in time for the race, probably sometime Friday so I'll be able to travel with you to Churchill Downs.

I miss you already and I haven't even left.

Hatch

"I really thought it was going to be something, you know, awful," Nealy said, relief singing in her voice. "You don't think it has anything to do with the kids, do you?"

"No. He would have told you if that was the case. You told me yourself he travels all over. Business is business. Where's Matilda?"

"The milk and egg man's delivery truck broke down out by the main road. She took the golf cart to go pick up the eggs and milk. She'll be back in a minute. She fried bacon. Help yourself."

"What are you having, Nealy?"

"Yogurt and a slice of toast. Half a banana. I'd kill for blueberry pancakes and scrambled eggs."

Smitty sipped at her coffee and smacked her lips. "So he makes your ears sweat, huh? Tell me more." She winked slyly.

Nealy rolled her eyes. "Smitty, do you think I'm too old?"

Smitty feigned innocence. "Do you mean are you too old to have your ears sweat or are you too old to ride the Derby?"

Nealy threw the dish towel at her.

Aruba, the hub of the Dutch Caribbean.

Hatch stepped from the taxi, jacket in hand, his shirt and collar soaked with his own perspiration. He paid the driver, turned his travel bag over to a porter, and mopped at his brow.

Hatch took a moment to survey his surroundings. He loved Aruba because it was filled with pastel-colored buildings, windmills, divi-divi trees, golf courses, modern resorts, romantic restaurants, garden courtyards, and sugar-colored sand. A wonderful place to kick back and relax. Not a place to vacation alone.

Aruba, a desert island cooled by winds so strong that the island was dotted by the famous wind-bent divi-divi trees. Hatch looked over his shoulder. He could see the beaches to the southwest part of the island and the palm-lined oases washed by crystal-clear waters. He'd jogged the seven long miles of incredible white-sand beaches hundreds of times, his eyes on the calm waters that were so perfect for windsurfing, parasailing, jet skiing, sailing, and diving. All of which he'd done each and every time he'd visited the island.

Hatch closed his eyes, trying to picture Nealy and himself in these lush surroundings. Maybe when the Belmont was over he would suggest coming here for a little R & R. He blinked. This was no time to get sidetracked. He was here on a mission: to find Willow Bishop, who, according to the latest monthly report from the firm's detective agency, was working as a master chef at the island's most prestigious hotel and resort, managed by a friend of his.

He needed to get into some island attire so he would blend in, but first he needed a shower. Then he would call down to the manager, whom he'd represented several times over the years. Claude Yokim loved to talk and no doubt would share what he knew about his new chef.

"Hatch, is that you?" a man every bit as tall and muscled as Hatch said as he clapped him on the back. "What are you doing here, buddy? Why didn't you call ahead? Listen, the penthouse suite is yours. How long are you staying?"

"A day and a half at the most. This was a last-minute business thing. Figured I'd come myself and save the firm a lot of hours. I was going to shower and give you a call. How about a drink, in say, thirty minutes. I'll meet you at the Tiki Bar."

"Sounds like a plan to me," Yokim said. "Do you have dinner plans? We have a five-star chef."

Bingo! A familiar rush of excitement coursed through Hatch's veins. "You're kidding me! How did that happen? What's his name? Anyone I know?"

"He's a she, and her name is Willow Ryan. She was cooking at the Ritz Carlton and I snagged her away on orders from two of the owners of this fine establishment. I had to pay her some big bucks, but it was the best move we ever made. We have reservations months in advance. So, are you free for dinner?"

"I am now. See you in thirty minutes."

Yokim snapped his fingers. A bellhop appeared out of nowhere. "Take Mr. Littletree and his baggage to the penthouse." The minute Hatch stepped into the elevator he motioned to the concierge. "In thirty minutes I want you to send up our biggest fruit basket, a case of Foster's beer on ice, and a dozen yellow roses."

"Yes sir. I'll take care of it."

"I'll be in the bar if anyone needs me."

"Yes sir."

Instead of heading for the bar, Yokim detoured and made his way to the kitchen. "Willow, I'm having a guest for dinner. I've been bragging about you to him. I want him to leave here eating his heart out. Tell me, what can you create that will make him drool and blow his socks off at the same time?"

"Can you give me fifteen minutes to plan something, Claude?"

"Take all the time you need. I'll be in the bar with my friend. Just have one of the cooks bring me out a menu when you have it ready. By the way, how's that playboy husband of yours?"

"Just as indulgent as he was the day I married him two and a half years ago, and I wish you would stop calling him a playboy. He's on my case, Claude. He wants to sail around the world and wants me to go with him."

"I'll double your salary. I'll kill myself if you leave. Anything you want, a Porsche, diamonds, a tiara. Name it."

The chef smiled. "Now look what you did. You didn't wait for the rest of what I was going to say. I get seasick. That means I'm not sailing around the world, Claude. I like that double my salary business, though, and a new Porsche sounds lovely. A girl can never have enough diamonds. However, my husband gives me those, so you're off the hook on that one."

Claude stared at the young woman standing in front of him. He forced a sickly smile to his face. "Done. Shall we add ten more months to your contract to safeguard my investment?"

"Whatever you want, Claude. Drop the contract by the kitchen before I leave this evening and I'll sign it. You have to get out of here now so I can think and plan a menu for you. This friend must be pretty special."

For the first time, Claude noticed how cold and calculating his chef's eyes were. They became more so as he expounded on his and Hatch's friendship. His stomach turned into a giant knot when she asked, "Just how rich is rich? Richer than my husband?"

A devil perched itself on Claude's shoulders. "Ten times over, Willow. And he's a widower."

"How interesting. You'll have to bring him back to the kitchen after dinner. I'll look forward to meeting him."

"Yes, I'll do that. Work on that menu, Willow."

The chef made shooing motions with her hands. Claude retreated from the kitchen to make his way to the bar, where he ordered a double scotch on the rocks. How in the hell was he going to explain the salary increase and the Porsche to the owners?

"Hey, buddy, you look like you're at a wake. Did something happen in the last half hour?" Hatch asked, sitting down at the table across from Claude. "C'mon, we have some serious drinking and catching up to do here. Foster's," he said to the bartender.

"In a way, I suppose. I think I just caught my dick in the wringer. The owners aren't going to be too happy with me, but they're the ones that insisted she be hired in the first place."

"Who? What are you talking about?"

"The chef. I screwed up. She's a money-grubbing bitch, but I can't afford to lose her. You know this is a dog-eat-dog business. This is what happened . . ."

"You're not kidding you got your dick in the wringer," Hatch said, signaling for a second beer. "Where in hell did the Ritz Carlton get a five-star chef anyway?"

"Hell, I don't know for sure if she's a five-star chef or not. The owners said she was. She said she was. She cooks like she's one."

"Don't you have to have certificates, diplomas, and attend those fancy cooking schools in Europe? Aren't they supposed to hang all that stuff in the kitchen?"

"Yeah, they are. When I asked about them, she said she kept forgetting to bring them in. When I brought it to the owners' attention they told me to leave it alone. Everything is the bottom line, you know that. I know when not to rock the boat, and I know who signs my checks and hers, too. The woman brings in customers by the drove. I told you, our dining room is booked six months in advance because of her. Because of her this resort is the best on the island. If she goes, we become just like the rest. It's amazing how important good food and wine are to some people. That's another thing, she's an expert on wine. Listen, you'll judge for yourself tonight at dinner."

"She's married, huh?"

"Yeah, some land developer. He's well-off but not as well off as you. I'm not even sure he's rich. She says he is. She married him here at the resort. Didn't know him long at all. He was coming here every night to eat and finally asked to meet her and wallah, three weeks later they got married. She says he doesn't want her to work but that's bullshit in my opinion. She's got a story, but I don't know what it is."

"What was her name before she got married?" Hatch asked, draining his second bottle of beer.

Claude shrugged. "Some long Polish-sounding name. Willow Wojoloskey or something like that. Why?"

Hatch reached inside his shirt pocket and pulled out a photograph Nick had given him. "Is this your chef?"

"Yeah. Yeah, that's Willow. Where did you get that picture?" Hatch told him.

"Oh, Christ, does that mean you're taking her back to Santa Fe? If you do that, I might as well start looking for another job."

Hatch shook his head. "No, that's not what it means: I just want to be able to tell the kid where his wife is. What he does with that information is up to him. You said she got married here. Was the minister real?"

"Hell, yes, he was real. Man, we went all out, compliments of the house."

"That makes her a bigamist then. The kid doesn't know this, but his mother told me when Willow went to see her she told her she was cutting off Nick's trust fund. Willow worked at that farm, knew and heard what was going on. She probably set her sights on Nick and thought she'd hit the mother lode. When she found out his ma was cutting him off, she split. The kid has a right to know, Claude. He needs to get on with his life."

"You're right about that. Jesus, I hate the thought of updating my résumé. I'm too old for this shit," Claude said, ordering another round of drinks.

"I can steer you onto something if you're interested, Claude. A friend of mine, Metaxas Parish, owns among other things, six restaurants. Real high-end. I told you about him. He's one of the richest men in the world. I know for a fact he's looking for someone to take over and manage the restaurants. If you're interested, I'll put in a good word for you."

"I'm definitely interested. Thanks, Hatch."

"Do you by any chance have any of the pictures from your chef's wedding? You guys must have taken pictures."

"We have a whole album. Now that you mention it, she didn't like the idea, but the owners insisted. It's in the office. Do you want to see it?"

"Not right now. Have someone take it up to my room. I'd like to borrow it if you don't mind. I will return it to you."

"Sure. Wait here a minute. I'll be right back."

Hatch leaned back and closed his eyes. He felt sick to his stomach. What was this going to do to Nick? The kid was tough. He'd been a real trouper these past few years. He never once complained, even when he was dead on his feet. The big question was, how tough was his heart? Willow was his first real love. He'd be wounded to the quick. How astute of Nealy to see through the girl. It was that woman thing. His wife had had it, too. She'd seen through her rich childhood friend Callie, but none of her other friends had. Sela was always on the money. Just like Nealy. Damn, they were alike in so many ways and yet unlike in others.

Claude returned to the bar at the same time as one of the chefs bearing a single sheet of white paper.

"Ah, our menu. Let's see what culinary delight our little witch is going to prepare for you. By the way, this might be a stupid question, but does she know about you? On the off chance she does, shouldn't we come up with another name when I introduce you?"

"I don't know if Nick ever mentioned my name to her. We've never met face-to-face. Introduce me as Hank Mitchum. Hank is one of my partners. On the other hand, Nick might have talked about the firm and the partners to her. Introduce me as Steve Alexander to be on the safe side. So, what's for dinner?"

"She's giving us choices. We check off what we want. How does this sound? Salat pilpelim. That's a sweet pepper salad. Kallaloo. It's a green soup made with young green leaves of plants like tannia and taro. Basically a seafood and pork dish as a main course or boiled fish with onion sauce and fungi. It's a Caribbean dish and real popular here. Fried plantains, pigeon peas with rice served with little meat pies. Another Caribbean dish. Persimmon pudding with fresh whipped cream for dessert or Charlotte à la Framboise. It's a raspberry Charlotte. Oh, here at the bottom she added saumon aux poireaux. Filet of salmon with stewed leeks. Does anything appeal to you?"

If he hadn't been sitting in exactly the position he was sitting in, half-turned to the doorway of the Tiki Bar, he wouldn't have seen the kitchen door crack open just enough for someone to peer through the narrow opening. Willow?

"Not really, Claude. I'm not into all that fancy-dancy cooking. What are our chances of getting a good T-bone steak with a twice-loaded baked potato and a green salad?"

"I'd say they're pretty good." Claude scribbled their choices underneath the chef's menu before he drew a large X through the rich dinner choices. He added the words "FOR TWO" at the very bottom of the page, then signaled the bartender to take the menu to the kitchen. "Now what?"

"Now we wait for dinner," Hatch said, holding up his empty beer bottle for the waiter's inspection.

In the kitchen, the chef looked at her watch. "I have an errand to run. You all have your assignments. Even if I'm late, you know what to do until I get back. How many times do I have to tell you, John, do not cut the ends off the string beans. If I have to tell you again, you'll regret it."

Her heart beating trip-hammer fast, Willow removed her white chef's coat, hung it on a hanger, and walked out the kitchen door, where she took great gasping breaths of fresh air. She walked around the building to the entrance, walked into the lobby and over to the registration desk. "Henry, I need some help here. I think there's a guest who might have just registered, a big man, sort of Indian-looking, high cheekbones. I think I know him. If I do, I'd like to surprise him at dinner with something special."

"Oh, you must mean Mr. Littletree. He's a personal friend of Mr. Yokim. They're in the bar right now."

"Yes, that's him. Don't let on I asked, okay?"

"Sure, Willow. No problem."

No problem my ass, Willow thought as she made her way across the lobby and out into the bright sunshine. She was going to miss this place. Hundreds of times, at the end of the day when all activity on the island paused for a few moments, she had taken the time to look over her balcony, to view the desert-type sunset when the sky was awash with fiery reds and yellows giving way to deep purple, which in turn became pastel pink glowing on the horizon, until the sun finally plunged into the water. Which just proved it didn't pay to get too comfortable, for you never know when it will come to an end.

She climbed into her open-air Jeep. She loved the nightlife here. Loved the surge of energy that rivered through the resorts. She loved to watch the people milling about, shopping, ducking into the funky bars, or sampling the local foods from the great restaurants. She would miss the rhythm that kicked in each and every time she hit the casinos with the live bands and the beat of the discos and nightclubs that were always jammed with dancers until the wee hours of the morning. Most of all, she would miss the divi-divi trees.

She thought about Jack Ryan. She wouldn't miss him at all. Time to move on. On the drive to the house she shared with Jack, she thought about Hatch Littletree, Nick Clay's idol. How had he found her? Well, she wasn't going to hang around long enough to find out. It would take her twenty minutes to pack her jewelry, throw some of her favorite things into a suitcase, clean out Jack's safe, and do a wire transfer out of the local bank to a bank on the mainland. Thirty minutes and she would be on her way to the airport, a far richer woman than when she arrived. Her only regret was this time she would be leaving her pots and pans behind. She had to hurry, or she would miss the last flight of the day.

This was the part of her life that she liked the best. Flight, with its adrenaline-pumping excitement.

12

For the first time in his life, Hatch Littletree was nervous. His shoulders felt heavy with the information he'd gleaned on his trip to Aruba. To compound the problem, when he returned from Aruba and called the office, he was told Nick and Emmie had left for Kentucky. Did Nealy know? Did they go to the farm, or were they just going to show up at Churchill Downs? He wished he knew. He hoped it wasn't the latter; Nealy didn't need any last-minute surprises. She needed to focus all her attention on the race. Now, after a bumpy flight to Kentucky, he was driving to Emmie's old house, hoping against hope that he was right and both young people would be there.

Maybe all this was none of his business. Maybe he needed to keep his snoot out of Nealy's and the kids' private lives. He argued with himself. How could he stay out of it when he loved Nealy? He'd come to love her children as well. Would seeing the kids bring anxiety to Nealy? Would it throw her off her stride and cause problems with the race? He choked up at the thought of her having an accident on the track. God, how he loved her. He wiped at the sweat forming on his forehead. This was not something he could control, and he knew it. Hell, he couldn't even control his emotions when he was around Nealy. All he wanted to do was sweep her up into his arms and carry her off.

How was he going to tell Nick about Willow? *Just pretend you're in the courtroom and you're stating facts,* an inner voice suggested.

No, no, that won't work. The kid has a heart. He would have to soft-pedal the whole thing somehow. The kid might just decide to take a poke at him. He fingered his jaw, thought about all the pricey dental work he'd had done over the years. *I'll put some distance between us when I tell him,* he thought.

Hatch squared his shoulders as he ran his hand through his hair. It still rankled that Willow had disappeared before he'd had a chance to talk to her. He must be slipping. He'd give anything to know what had tipped her off. The way his luck was running, he'd probably never know.

Hatch parked in front of Emmie's house and made his way up the flower-bordered walkway to the small front porch and pressed his finger to the bell. Inside, Gabby's little dog Cookie yipped. Emmie opened the door, a huge smile on her face. "Hatch! Shhh," she said, putting her finger to her lips. "Gabby's napping. What are you doing here? Is something wrong?

"Nick, come quick, Hatch is here!" she called over her shoulder in a controlled whisper.

"I'm not sure, Emmie. I need to talk to Nick." Hatch bent down to pick up the little white dog to cover his nervousness.

"He's out on the patio studying the racing form. Go on out, and I'll bring you some coffee when it's ready."

"What's up?" Nick jumped to his feet, his hand extended. "I heard you talking, but I didn't hear you answer Emmie's question. You said you weren't sure if something was wrong. What does that mean? Did something happen to Mom or the horses? What? What are you doing here?" His voice was so anxious-sounding, Hatch cringed.

"I've been coming to Kentucky a lot this past year. Your mother and I have become very good friends. Although, I have to admit, we got off to a rocky start. I wasn't sure in the beginning if I should tell you and Emmie about those visits. I didn't want to stir something up for both of you. I went the first time for Emmie's sake, to show Nealy pictures of Gabby. I could have mailed them I suppose. I wanted to see for myself, to understand, why she booted both of you off the farm. Your mother, as I found out, was nothing like what I expected her to be. I have to tell you, kid, no one was more surprised than I that we actually hit it off. Your mother and I both had preconceived notions about each other that proved to be unfounded. It's time for me to tell you a few things. Some things you might like, and other things you aren't going to like. It's time."

Nick slouched down on a chaise longue. "You've been keeping Mom up to speed on me and Emmie. I'm okay with that, Hatch. Emmie will be okay with it, too. I guess I have to wonder why you didn't keep us up to speed on her."

"You had enough on your plate, Nick. It's a little more involved than bringing the two of you up to speed. That day when your mother told you and Emmie to leave . . . she did that on purpose. She had a plan in her head. She was waiting for just the right time to . . . to put it into play. Smitty clued me in the first time I came here and swore me to secrecy. I never let on to your mother that I knew. I guess it's something she isn't comfortable talking about. Look, it doesn't matter why or how or any of that stuff. Your mother did what she felt she had to do. It was the only way she could get you both to stand on your own feet. Especially you, Nick, because she knew it was what your father had wanted. She's the first one to admit she didn't make the best choice. She knows now there were probably other, better ways. She seized the moment and ran with it. No one is perfect, Nick. She loves you both so much. She understands the farm isn't the right place for you. Just because she's tough and hard doesn't mean she has no feelings. She does. When she talks about you and Emmie, her face softens and her voice gentles. This is a new day, Nick. The past is prologue. Trust me when I tell you your mother's arms will be open wide."

Nick was on his feet pacing, the racing form slapping at his leg. He nodded, relief written all over his face. "I thought about . . . driving by later this morning. They're going to erect the statue of Shufly this morning. My dad and the workers gave Mom the one of Flyby for her birthday a long time ago. I thought . . ."

Hatch grinned. "You are so much like your dad you spook me, boy. Your mother is going to bust with pride. I think she is about ready to step down from the saddle. She'll ride her three races, and then I've been hoping she will turn things over to Emmie. She wants to be Gabby's grandmother so bad she can taste it. I'm hoping, if things go right, that Nealy and I . . . can move forward.

Become close. Hell, boy, I want to marry your mother. There, I said it out loud. I want to show her the world outside this farm. I don't know if she wants that or not, but I'm prepared to bust my gut trying to get her to see things my way."

Nick rubbed at the stubble on his chin. "I'll be damned. You and Mom. Yeah, yeah, I can see it! I really can. I'm okay with that, too. I'm really okay with it, Hatch. Just be sure you make her happy. Emmie will jump at the chance. She's going to be okay with the you and Mom thing, too. This is where she wants to be. Where she wants Gabby to grow up. There's more, though, isn't there?"

"Yeah. There's no easy way to say this except to just come out and say it. I found Willow. She was in Aruba cooking in a big resort. Somehow she found out I was there and put two and two together. In a matter of hours she was gone. This might explain things a little better," Hatch said, handing Nick a thick, padded envelope that contained Willow's Aruba wedding album. "While you're looking at that, I'll just sit here. Your mother told Willow she was cutting off your trust fund. You have to deal with that, too." Hatch placed a comforting hand on Nick's shoulder and gave it a gentle squeeze.

Ten minutes later, Nick shoved the contents back into the padded envelope. Hatch noticed that his hands were shaking. He looked across the patio at Hatch, his eyes full of questions.

"You asked me to find her, kid, and I did. I used all the firm's resources. I know it wasn't what you wanted to see. I'm sorry as hell about that. It hurts like a son of a bitch when you get your heart broken. It hurts even more when you realize you were a fool and you *still* got your heart broken. My guess would be this, Nick. She latches on to rich men and takes them for what she can get and then she splits. She thought you were rich. She took off when your mother told her she was cutting you off. I know you aren't going to want to believe this either, but your mother saw right through her. My wife used to be able to do that. It's a woman thing, and us men need to pay more attention when they tell us stuff like that.

"Look, I can keep looking for her. Your mother hired all kinds of private dicks to search her out because she knew you loved her.

She tried, Nick, she really did. Jesus, look how long it took me to get a bead on her. Then she gave me the slip."

Nick stared off into the distance, the padded envelope still in his hand. "She must have had a good laugh over this dumb old horse handler. Christ, I poured my heart out to her, and she lapped it all up. I was just some dumb kid she had to teach how to make love."

"Nick, don't do this to yourself. I'd bet the firm she goes from place to place, sets guys up, marries them, takes what she can get, and splits. You were one of the lucky ones. Real lucky. All you lost was a little piece of your heart."

Nick nodded. "Emmie's calling you. I think I'd just like to sit here for a little while. I'm okay, Hatch. Don't worry about me."

"Did you hear, Emmie?" Hatch asked, closing the kitchen door behind him.

Emmie's face wore a mixture of emotions. "Yes. The kitchen window is open. Is it really okay for us to go to the farm? I guess I should be more concerned about Willow and Nick, but I suspected something along those lines myself. I guess I am Mom's daughter after all. If you're sure she won't boot us off the farm, I'm going out there as soon as Gabby wakes up. She was exhausted with the flight and the excitement. She got up, ate, and went back to sleep. I'm so excited, so jittery I can't see straight. My stomach is in knots. It's going to be all right, isn't it, Hatch?"

"Yes, it's going to be all right," Hatch said, watching Nick through the kitchen window.

"Poor Nick. Of all times for this to happen. No, no, I don't mean that the way it sounds. I just meant he's finished with school now and everything should be coming up roses as they say. We're home, Mom's racing, and now this. He looks . . . so stunned."

"It's a kick to the gut, that's for sure. At this point, knowing what I know, I'm not even sure their marriage was legal. Yes, they went through a ceremony, but what if this is a pattern with her? If she was already married, then they aren't really married. It makes Willow a bigamist. The firm will intensify the search into her background. He'll be a little rocky for a while, but Nick is tough. I'm counting on that toughness to get him through this. Everything happens for a reason, Emmie."

"I know but look at him. He looks . . . *whipped*."

"Life goes on, Emmie. You moved forward after Buddy. Nick will, too, in his own good time. I'll take that coffee now."

Emmie smiled, her eyes on her half brother Nick.

Twenty minutes later, Nick entered the kitchen. He handed the thick envelope to Hatch. His eyes miserable, his voice husky, he said, "If I'm married, I want to file for divorce. If I'm not married, I want to know that, too. Can the firm help, Hatch?"

"Absolutely. I'll call the office later and put the wheels in motion."

"Good. I hear Gabby stirring. I'll get her ready, Emmie, and we can head out to the farm. What about Cookie?"

"Cookie is family. He goes where we go. You know how Mom loves dogs. Take your time, Nick. Hatch hasn't finished his coffee."

Emmie turned to Hatch. "Are you and Mom . . . you know, seeing each other?"

"Seeing each other is a good way of putting it. We're very good friends. The truth is, I love your mother."

Emmie smiled. "Mom needs someone. Everyone needs someone, and I hope that someone is you, Hatch. I hope someday I find that special person who will love me and Gabby both. Mom used to tell me when I was little that she would wish on a star at night and say a prayer that someone would find her and love us both. She said she knew it wouldn't happen, but she kept on wishing and praying. When Hunt came along I wasn't little anymore. You know, like Gabby."

"Today is a new day, Emmie. For you, Gabby, and Nick. I have a good feeling about all of this. It's an old Indian thing," he said, winking at her.

"That's good enough for me." Emmie twinkled in return. "Oh, I'm going home. I'm really going home. We're *all* going home. Oh, Hatch," Emmie said, throwing her arms around the big man, "I'm so happy I can hardly stand it."

It was like the last time, Nealy thought as she walked down the breezeway. The air of excitement that maybe, if things went right, she would bring back a second Derby winner to Blue Diamond

Farms. She looked around, half-expecting to see or hear Hunt. His absence was the only thing that was different this time.

Nealy turned when she heard Ruby call out to her. "Nealy, we have to do something. Metaxas is going to give himself a heart attack over this. I have never, in my entire life, seen him so excited, so agitated, so damn wired. He's combing that horse's tail one strand at a time. Then he messes it up and starts all over again. Shufly just stands there and lets him do it. I caught him trying to brush his teeth this morning. Shufly let him do that, too. I don't know how he's going to handle the next twenty-four hours. Don't you have something else for him to do?"

Nealy placed both her hands on Ruby's shoulders. "I was like that the first time, Ruby. No, there's nothing you or I can do. Metaxas's bond with Shufly is stronger than I ever anticipated. That's a good thing. He's having the time of his life. This is an important day for all of us. All the training is over. All the big guy has to do is run for the roses tomorrow. I swear he knows what it's all about. I think Flyby remembers, too."

"Listen to me, Ruby. There is every possibility that I won't win tomorrow. Jake's Thunder and Navigator are right up there with the best of the best. No one has seen Shufly, so they aren't really talking about him. They don't know what he can and cannot do. I can lose, Ruby. I can come in fifth or sixth or finish last."

"Oh, Nealy, Metaxas and I truly don't care if you win or not. It's the fact that the big guy is good enough to get his shot at the roses with the best jockey in the world riding him. That's all we want. Win or lose, it doesn't matter."

"I'm old, Ruby. I can't run up and down these barns the way I used to. Mentally, I'm fine. I'm full of confidence. All this training has proved to be a little harder than I anticipated. The plain, unvarnished truth is, I'm not as agile as I used to be. Hell, I'm a senior citizen! By the way, that was the headline in the morning's paper. Another one said, Granny running for the roses. Smitty showed them to me. Dagmar's paper had the only decent article and headline. The others said I don't have a snowball's chance in hell of winning the Derby twice."

"Oh, baby, baby, is that what this is all about? Your age! Get those thoughts right out of your head. I don't want to hear another word about age, senior citizens, or those other yahoos running in the Derby. You have them all beat by a furlong. Shift into neutral, Nealy. Better yet, why don't you take a walk over to the cemetery and do some palavering with the . . . you know. Take Flyby with you."

Nealy's face brightened. "I . . . I'll do that, Ruby."

Nealy was leading Flyby down the breezeway when she saw them outlined in the bright sunshine. She brought her hand up to shield her eyes. It was Emmie who broke ranks and ran to her, her arms open wide. Nealy dropped Flyby's halter and ran the last few steps. "Oh Emmie, I'm so glad to see you! You came back! God, I missed you!

"Nick!" Tears rolled down Nealy's cheeks as she embraced her son and daughter. "I'm sorry. I'm so sorry about so many things. I wanted . . . I did it all wrong . . . I can't believe you're here. Can you stay? Are you going to the Derby? You look so wonderful. Taller, leaner, and you look tired. You both look tired."

"We aren't tired, Mom. We were worried you wouldn't want us here," Emmie said. "Oh, Mom, we missed you so much. Can I stay, Mom? I won't let you down again. I promise."

"You never once let me down, Emmie. Of course you can stay."

"Not me, Mom."

Nealy cupped her son's face in both her hands. "I know, Nick. You're where you belong now. Your dad would be so proud of you. I'm proud of you, too. Hatch said you're going to be a wild-ass lawyer. I am so glad you came back. I wanted to go after you a hundred times, maybe a thousand, but I couldn't. I had to give you your chance. I'm sorry it took me so long, Nick. Can you ever forgive me?"

"There's nothing to forgive, Mom. We're here. Whoa, what's this? He remembers me," Nick said in awe, as Flyby used his big head to butt him. Nealy slipped Nick a mint that he held out to the horse.

For the first time Nealy noticed Hatch. She grinned her thanks. He nodded. "Where's the baby?"

"Up at the house with Smitty."

"Mom, do you want me to take Flyby out to the pasture?"

"That would be nice, Nick. I was going to take him out to the cemetery to work off some of my nerves. I can do that later. I want to see my granddaughter right now."

"I'll stay down here with Nick for a while, Nealy," Hatch said.

Nick wrapped his arms around his mother. "I missed you, Mom. I never stopped loving you, not for a minute. I used to write little notes to you on my legal pads. Writing them made me feel better. I love it here, Mom, but I don't belong here. I need to hear you tell me you understand and that it's okay."

"It's okay, Nick, and yes, I do understand. I wrote a thousand letters to you and to Emmie in my head. I love you, Nick. Nothing will ever change that. I'm truly sorry about Willow."

"I know, Mom. I just don't want to talk about her. Maybe later on but not now, okay?"

Nealy nodded. "Okay, Nick."

"Go see your granddaughter, Mom."

"I'm going, I'm going," Nealy said, sprinting for the house.

"Mom, this is Gabby. Honey, this is your grandma," Emmie said.

Nealy dropped to her haunches. "Hello, Gabby." She cupped the little girl's face in her hands and kissed her forehead. "I've waited a long time to meet you. You look just like your mommy when she was little. Who is this little guy?" she said, pointing to the frisky pup.

"Cookie. Him sleeps with me."

"Is he nice and warm and cozy? Does he wiggle under the covers and keep you warm?"

"Uh-huh."

"Would you like to sit on the front porch with your mommy and me? You can play with Cookie on the porch."

"I brought some toys with us, Mom. They're in the car."

"You can bring them up on the porch, but I'm going to hold this little angel on my lap and tell her a story about the Rainbow Queen. Would you like to hear about the Rainbow Queen, Gabby? Later, when I have to go back to the barn she can play with the toys." Gabby nodded and allowed Nealy to pick her up.

"Once upon a time there was a beautiful queen named . . ."

"Gabby," the little girl chortled.

Nealy's gaze locked with her daughter's. "Ah, I see your mommy has already told you this story."

"She knows it word for word, so don't change anything." Emmie laughed.

Gabby snuggled into the crook of Nealy's arm. It felt so right, so good, she felt light-headed with the feeling. Cookie took that moment to hop onto her lap and wiggle his way close to Gabby. Now it was complete.

Thank you, God.

It was all behind her now. All the hard work, the sleepless nights, the weary hours, the cold, the heat. She was here again, running for the roses.

With Metaxas's help, she settled Shufly into his stall. "This is your day, baby. All I want is for you to do your best and remember this old lady is on your back. You know me and I know you. When we walk into that gate, we are *one*." Nealy whispered to the horse as she stroked his head. "God, I wish I knew what you were thinking. If there was only some way you could give me some kind of sign that you understand what today really means I would appreciate it. Part of me wants you to do better than your daddy and another part of me doesn't want that. I feel so disloyal even thinking such a thing, much less saying it aloud. You have wings on your feet, baby. I want you to use them today." She continued to whisper as she ran her hands over the mass of quivering horseflesh. In the moment it took her heart to beat twice, Shufly lowered his massive head and nuzzled her ear. Nealy giggled. "I'm going to take that as my sign. Okay, big fella. Here comes your human daddy. Stay calm. I'll be back in a bit."

"Nealy, where are you going? It's the middle of the night?" Ruby said, her voice filled with anxiety.

"I just want to walk around a bit. The last time I was here Hunt was with me. I need to stretch my legs and do some thinking. Where is everyone?"

"Hatch took the kids to the hotel. He'll be here bright and early with coffee and the morning paper. This is it, Nealy. You okay?"

"I'm very okay. Are you and Metaxas okay?"

"You bet. We'll be right here. Go ahead and do whatever you need to do. Shufly is in good hands. He knows, doesn't he, Nealy?"

"Yes. Yes, he does, Ruby. Flyby knew, too. That's why everything is okay. See you in a bit."

Nealy walked out into the dark, misty night. The soft night breeze tickled her face and fanned her hair. She brushed at it with an impatient hand. She was happier at that moment than she had ever been in her entire life. Her kids were home, her world was right side up, and Hatch was there. She looked up at the rolling cloud cover. Rain was in the forecast for tomorrow. She wondered if it would hold off till after the race. In the end, it wouldn't matter. Shufly was just as good on a sloppy track as he was on a hard, dry one. The only downside was if it rained, her hair would frizz up. She laughed as she dropped to her rear end, her back against a thick, old tree. A perfect spot to sit and watch all the activity. She'd sat there years ago and done the same thing. She smiled as she closed her eyes and relaxed for the first time in days.

"What's so funny, Nealy?"

"Hunt! I'm here. It's just perfect, Hunt. The kids are home and that grandbaby is something special. She felt so good, all soft and warm. My cup runneth over. Hatch is here, too. Guess you know that, huh? I'm going to get all choked up on the walkover. I'll be remembering the last time when you were with me. How's it looking from where you're . . . ah . . . perched? I can do this, can't I, Hunt?"

"Is this the Nealy Diamond Clay I know showing something less than full confidence? That's not the Nealy I know."

"Knew. That's the key word, Hunt. Things are a lot different this time around. They keep reminding me how old I am. I'm starting to believe them. You didn't answer my question."

"They scratched two horses an hour ago, just as you arrived. It's an eighteen-horse field now. The only horse that can give you trouble is Jake's Thunder, and he's as good on a sloppy track as Shufly. It's going to start raining hard in about an hour, so be prepared. You can do it, Nealy. If you

doubt yourself now, you're dead in the water. You've got the mystery horse this time around. You, Metaxas, and Ruby are the only ones who know what Shufly can do. The odds are out of this world."

"I wish you were here, Hunt." When there was no answer she said his name again. "Hunt? Are you still here?"

"I wish I was, too, Nealy. I'll be there in spirit every beat of the way. Nealy, listen to me, I want you to go back to the shed row NOW. Now, Nealy. There's something coming down, and there's nothing I can do to help you. Get up and run. Do you hear me?"

"What's wrong?"

"Do what I tell you."

The second Nealy's eyes opened she saw four blurred figures coming toward her. In an instant she was on her feet, running toward the shed row.

They were after her. By their size and weight she knew they were either exercise boys or jockeys. Her heart lurched as she calculated how far she had to run. Too far if their intentions were what she thought they were.

"Get her," she heard one of them yell. "Get her before she gets away."

Afraid she might not be able to outrun them, Nealy put her first two fingers in her mouth and blew. An earsplitting whistle raced through the thick, misty night.

From her far left she heard wood splintering and the sound of hard pounding hooves.

"Jesus!"

"What the hell!"

"Fuck."

"Holy shit!"

Shufly skidded to a stop next to Nealy. He snorted and blew like a demon from hell. Nealy grabbed onto his mane and vaulted up onto his back. Knowing she was safe, she said, "Boys, meet the next Kentucky Derby winner! This is Shufly!" Her voice quivered with fear. "Now get your asses out of here before I turn this big guy loose on you."

"What's going on here?" Metaxas boomed as he ran up to the group, Ruby in his wake, Dover bringing up the rear.

"All I know," Nealy said, "is that I was sitting under a tree, minding my own business, and when I woke up these four *little* twits were stalking me. That's what's going on." Nealy clenched and unclenched her teeth so hard she thought she'd chipped her front teeth.

"I'm going to report this. You could be banned from racing for pulling something like this," Metaxas bellowed.

"For what?" one of the four blustered. "We were just walking around, and she was sleeping under the tree. We were going to wake her up. In case you haven't noticed, it's raining. We were just being thoughtful and concerned about the old lady."

"My ass you were going to wake me up. I was already awake. You were going to *do* something."

"Prove it," a second youth said. "You look okay to me. We didn't come anywhere near you. You probably had a bad dream and spooked yourself. Old people do things like that all the time."

"Get the hell out of here," Metaxas warned.

The bad moments were over. Nealy's eyes narrowed as she watched the little group scurry away. "I guess I was asleep, but Hunt warned me to get up. He said *now* like in right now, right this second to *run*. I was doing what he said, but they closed in on me. That's when I whistled for Shufly."

She slid off Shufly's back. "Good boy," she said, rubbing him behind the ears.

"Good boy is right," Metaxas said. "You should have seen him. The big guy heard your whistle and went berserk. He did a real number on his stall door. God Almighty! I never saw anything like it."

"C'mon, baby, not these buttons, too," Metaxas said. "I only have one more shirt left with buttons. Ruby, you need to buy a case of buttons. He doesn't even eat them, he spits them out. I think he just likes to see my manly, hairy chest."

"You ready to go back, honey?" Ruby said, putting her arms around Nealy's shoulders. "Tell me what Hunt said," she whispered.

"It was just a dream, Ruby. Maybe it was that unknown seventh sense that kicked in. I sat down, you know, just to think, to relive the last time I raced here. I guess I closed my eyes and dozed off. Every time I try to catch those forty winks Maud always used to talk about, I dream of Hunt. I was thinking about him when I sat down. He did the walkover with me the last time. Dover is doing it this year. It . . . it won't be the same. He said it was going to rain in about an hour. I already knew that because it was misting when I sat down. Jake's Thunder, according to Hunt, is going to be my big competition because he's as good on a sloppy track as Shufly. Of course it could stop raining, and the track could dry out. Unlikely but still a possibility. Then Hunt said to get up and run. That's when they came up to me. I think, if anything, it was going to be a verbal thing. They wouldn't risk anything physical that would keep them away from this racetrack. At least I don't think they would. Young people are different today. It's over, it's done with. Let's just go back to the barn and try to catch a few hours' sleep."

"You're shaking, Nealy," Ruby said, alarm in her voice.

"A little. Come on, we're getting soaked out here."

The barn was quiet even though grooms and workers scurried about. Nealy looked in on Shufly, satisfied herself that he was none the worse for stomping down the gate to his stall, something she would hear about when it got light out. She shrugged.

"I'm all right, Ruby. A few hours' sleep and I'll be fine. I wonder if my brothers are here yet."

"Metaxas said they arrived. They're with Hatch and the kids. They'll all be here by sunup."

"Who's watching Gabby?"

"Emmie's old neighbor. Good thing, too, since it's raining. I was hoping for bright sunshine and a dry track."

"Me, too, but Shufly will do just fine. You've seen him run in slop and glop. Doesn't change a thing where he's concerned. I'm going out to the truck and curl up for a while. I'll lock the doors. Relax, Ruby, it's okay. I hate that word *old*. I really do. I wanted to jam it down their throats. I will, too, tomorrow."

"Attagirl," Ruby said.

"See you in a few hours. Ruby, wait a minute." Nealy reached into her jeans pocket and pulled out a wad of cash. "Dagmar Doolittle should be here bright and early with a copy of her paper.

Give her this and tell her to bet it on Shufly. She can pay me back with her winnings. If the odds stay as high as they are, and I think they will, she can retire if we win. If I lose, tell her she doesn't owe me a thing."

"Consider it done."

Holding one of the horse blankets over her head, Nealy sprinted for the Ford Ranger. She was just too tired to go to the van, too tired to go back to the motel. She could just curl up and sleep stretched out across the front seat. She locked the door and curled into a ball, covering herself with the blanket. She was bone-tired, but she was wide-awake, her adrenaline pumping at an all-time high.

They had rattled her. Not with their words but in the way they surrounded her. She'd never experienced fear like that before. Would they have done something to her? She would probably never know.

"Hunt," she whispered.

"I'm here, Nealy."

"Thanks for the warning. Now I'm nervous. This isn't good, Hunt. I should have calmed down by now. Tell me what to do. Tell me how to get over this."

"Find that inner core where you draw your strength from. Take long, deep breaths. You used to tell me to do that all the time. Practice what you preach, Nealy."

"Dammit, Hunt, I was scared. I've never been scared like that before, not even when I lit out from SunStar with Emmie. On the other hand, I was young and dumb back then. Four against one. Not good odds."

"You have good instincts, Nealy. They helped you. By the way, that's some horse you have there. You were kind of busy, so you probably didn't see the expressions on their faces when Shufly thundered to your defense. If I tell you they were scared witless, will you believe me?"

"Yes. I always believed you except there at the end. I don't want to talk about it. Let's talk about Nick. You must be very proud of him."

"Proud doesn't begin to describe the way I feel. I bawled like a baby when I saw that bronze of Shufly."

Nealy's mouth drew up in a smile. She rested her head on her arm and sighed. It had been a long day.

"When it's all over, Nealy, what are you going to do?"

"I think I'm going to see the world. It's time. I don't want to end up like Maud. I don't know, something happened to me this last year. I guess it's Hatch. He keeps telling me about the big, wide world and what I'm missing. I think he's right. So, with that thought in mind, I'm toying with the idea of letting Emmie run the farm. That's if she wants to take it over. Gabby will love growing up here."

"See the world? No kidding."

"Hard to believe, huh? It's Nealy time now."

"Nealy, don't read the morning papers."

"Okay, I won't read the morning papers. Hunt?"

"Yeah?"

"Ride with me."

"You mean the actual race?"

"Yes. You're weightless, right? I don't know anything about that . . . that spirit stuff. You're here somewhere because you talk to me. I owe you, Hunt."

"You don't owe me anything, but I accept. Go to sleep now, Nealy. I'll watch over you tomorrow, I'll be right there with you."

"You always wanted to know what it felt like to cross the finish line and win the roses. Together we can do it. I would be honored, and so will Shufly if you agree. You'll do it, then?"

"I'll do it."

"You won't spook Shufly, will you?"

"Nope. He won't even know I'm there."

Nealy laughed and Hunt joined her.

"Sleep tight, Nealy. I'll see you at the gate."

13

The sun was creeping over the horizon when Nealy woke with a start. Five-thirty. She hadn't slept this late in . . . she couldn't remember the last time.

The Day!

She lay still for a moment trying to decide if it was raining or not. Earlier, the rain pelting the top of the truck had lulled her into a sound sleep. The rain and Hunt. She propped herself up on her elbows to peer out the foggy windows. The rain had stopped but it was going to be a wet, miserable day. She thought about all the times she had raced Shufly on a muddy track. He'd always done well, better than she ever anticipated. His daddy, Flyby, wasn't half as good under the same conditions, even in his prime.

A knock sounded on the truck window. Nealy turned and opened the door. "Nick! What a nice way to wake up. You're here early. Is something wrong?"

Nick's arm reached out to help his mother. "Not a thing, Mom. I wanted to be here, to experience it. If you win today, I'm coming back for the Preakness and the Belmont. I don't know what good I'll be to you, but I want to be with you. Do you have the jitters? Are you okay?"

"If I was nervous, Nick, I wouldn't belong here. To answer your question, no, I'm not nervous. I'm not even anxious. Shufly can fly on a wet track. I have that cup of courage all jockeys need. Let's get some coffee, just me and you." She closed and locked the door of the truck. "I'm so glad you and Emmie came, Nick. I prayed and wished for it, but I never really allowed myself to believe you would forgive me and come back." She jammed the keys into the pocket of her jeans and then reached for Nick's arm.

"I love you, Mom. There's nothing to forgive. Coffee sounds good. I got all the papers. I saw that reporter, the one you like, the big Swedish lady. She said to tell you not to read the papers. Except for hers."

"I know. I promised your dad I wouldn't . . . What I mean is, I had this dream and he said not to look at the papers this morning."

Nick tilted his head back and looked down his nose at her. "You talk to him, don't you?"

Nealy looked everywhere but at him.

"It's okay to admit it, Mom. It always appears like it's a dream, but then it seems to be real. That's the way it is with me anyway. I think it's real, Mom. I really do. There were days when I wanted to quit, to bail out, and he always convinced me to hang on just a little longer. I told Hatch about it, and he said the same thing. I think Dad is watching over all of us. You aren't laughing at me, are you, Mom?"

Nealy bit down on her lip before she burst out laughing. "If I tell you something will you promise not to laugh at me? I don't want to see you raise your eyebrows or grimace. I need to hear you promise."

"I promise. What? Come on, Mom, you can trust me. What is it?"

Nealy took a deep breath and straightened her shoulders. She hesitated another moment before she said, "Your dad is riding with me today. I asked him, and he said yes. Am I crazy, son?"

"God Almighty! No, no, you aren't crazy. He . . . Dad promised to sit in with me when I take the bar. If you're crazy, then so am I. Boy, I feel better already. There were days there when I thought I was starting to lose it. Overload. I know you're in good shape, Mom, but you're older than all those guys riding today. You know it and you are worried and nervous, so don't pretend with me."

Nealy sighed. "All right. All right. In the past, I didn't give a tinker's damn about what people thought of me. Now that I'm older, I care in a cockamamie kind of way. It's the word *old*. Why do they go after me like this? What do the papers say, Nick? I don't want to read them, I just want to know what they say."

"It's the same old garbage, Mom. You're too old, you're a grandmother, you inherited the farm, you stepped into the golden pile of dung. That kind of stuff. Your friend wrote a straightforward article. Great pictures, the whole front page is yours. The other stuff is tabloid fodder. There might even be some libel in there if we take a better look. Hatch is checking that out. You have to ignore it. For now. If it goes legal, that's when you pay attention."

"Okay, Nick, I'll ignore it." She linked her arm with her son's. "I need to get a quick shower and do a few things. It stopped raining, but it's still going to be a sloppy track. We can live with it," she said happily.

"Hatch is worried about you, Mom," Nick blurted.

Nealy stopped in her tracks. "Why on earth is he worried?" Her voice was full of surprise.

"Because he loves you, Mom, that's why. He didn't understand how dangerous racing is until Emmie clued him in. She meant well, but she did make it sound gory. He asked me, and I told him the truth. Do you love him, Mom?"

Nealy dug the heel of her boot into the soft soil until she had a hole that was deep enough to plant a sapling. There didn't seem to be any point in hiding her feelings. "Well . . . I . . . I have . . . feelings for him and I like him a lot but . . . the answer is, yes, I guess I do. Your father approves. At least in my dreams he approves." Nealy smiled. "We'll see."

"You and Dad always used to say that to me when I was little. 'We'll see' wasn't a flat-out no, but it wasn't a confirmed yes either. I think the rain is over. What do you think, Mom?" Nick asked, looking up at the heavy gray clouds.

Nealy shook her head. "The air's too thick. More rain is coming and then the sun will come out around noon or so. I hope it's before post time. Oh-oh, I spoke too soon, here it comes. Listen, Nick, the coffee will have to wait. I'll see you later. I have some things to do right now."

Nealy drove to the motel where Emmie, Nick, and Hatch were registered. She needed to take a hot shower to work the kinks out of her neck. She also needed to reassure Hatch about the race. Nick had said Hatch was in love with her. Did she love her husband's best friend? The answer was yes. Suddenly she felt like singing.

Her head down, Nealy ran through deep puddles toward the motel entrance. She was soaked to the skin when she heard a familiar voice, "Whoa, Nealy."

"Hatch!" How joyous her voice sounded. She started to laugh right there in the pouring rain. His "Whoa, Nealy" had sounded a lot like, "Whoa, Nellie."

"Yep, it's me."

Nealy looked up at him through the rain. "Nick said you love me? Do you?"

It took Hatch a full twenty seconds to recover from his shock. "Nealy, I was going to . . . you know, take you out on the town after the race and tell you myself. I feel kind of silly standing here answering such a serious question."

"Imagine how I felt when Nick told me that. Then he asked me if I loved you."

"What did you say, Nealy?"

"I said yes I loved you. I do, Hatch. That's what I would say if you took me out on the town after the race."

Rain sluiced downward. Oblivious to the elements, Hatch scooped her up and planted a solid kiss on her lips. "I say we save this for tonight after the race," she whispered. "Are you of the same opinion, Mr. Littletree?"

"Yeah, yeah. Tonight." He looked so befuddled, Nealy burst out laughing.

"I have to get moving, Hatch. I need to take a shower to work the kinks out of my neck. I slept in the truck last night," she volunteered, her gaze locked with Hatch's.

"Nealy . . . about the race. I knew it was dangerous, but Emmie really filled me in. I don't suppose they'll call it off because of the weather, will they?"

"It will never happen, Hatch. I don't want you to worry about me. I'm a good rider, and I don't take stupid risks. Will you feel better if I tell you something?"

"It depends on what you tell me. No, no matter what you tell me, I'm going to be a basket case watching that race. What?"

"Hunt's riding with me."

Hatch rolled his eyes. "Oh, well, that's different."

He didn't believe her, but she had no intention of explaining. He would probably worry even more if she told him she had regular conversations with her dead husband. "Damn straight it's different. I have to run now. Bet the poke on me, okay?"

"The whole damn wad, Nealy. Damn, I do love you."

"Damn, I love you, too."

"See you in the winner's circle."

"Yep, that's where I'll be." Nealy laughed as she blew him a kiss before running off.

Hatch stood in the rain for a good five minutes mumbling over and over, "She loves me. She said she loves me. She really loves me. I heard her say she loves me. I knew I liked that kid for a reason." Stunned at what had just transpired, he felt like a twenty-year-old as he made his way back to the motel room, where he changed his clothes from the skin out.

Fully dressed, he called room service and asked for a fresh pot of coffee and a package of cigarettes. When they arrived he tackled both with a vengeance as he sat down to contemplate how his life was changing before his very eyes. When his room turned cloudy with cigarette smoke, only then did he move. Outside, he was startled to see the rain had stopped and miracle of miracles, it looked like the sun was struggling to peek through the clouds.

His gaze swept the parking lot. Nealy's truck was gone. Once again his gaze raked the parking lot as he struggled to find the exact place where the two of them had been standing. It seemed to him, at that precise moment in time, that he should mark the spot somehow.

"Hatch! Wait up," Emmie shouted from the second-floor balcony. "Is something wrong? What are you staring at so intently?" Hatch told her. Emmie clapped her hands in glee as she ran down the steps to wrap her arms around him. "Wait right here, I have just what you need."

Hatch watched as Emmie ran to her car and popped the trunk. She rummaged for a few minutes before she returned with a small box in her hands. "Indelible markers for Gabby's clothes. They like things marked at the day care. Take your pick," she said, offering the box of colored markers. "I forgot to tell you, they glow in the dark." She giggled. Hatch burst out laughing. "I'd go with yellow."

"Yellow will stand out at night," Emmie said. "You know, glowing in the dark, if you decide to come back here tonight. You're rich enough to buy this place, Hatch. If you owned it, you could build a fence around the spot and preserve it forever and ever. I am so very happy for you both."

Hatch laughed, a great booming belly laugh. "I just might take that under consideration, Emmie. I've done stranger things in my life. I'll see you and Smitty at the track."

"It's almost time, Nealy."

Nealy nodded. "I know, Dover. The last time I was here I was so euphoric I didn't know the announcer's name. That's not quite true. I knew it, but I couldn't remember it. I thought it so strange at the time and now I know his name as well as I know my own. Jim McKay." She smiled. "He's saying the same things he said the last time I was here. Listen, Dover."

"None of the horses running today have gone a mile and a quarter—and except for those going on to the Belmont—none of these horses will ever go the mile and a quarter again.

"When you handicap a race you usually look backward to see the best performance. Not so with the Derby—you have to anticipate who is going to run their best race today—for that reason Jake's Thunder, Navigator, and Sweet Pete still have their best shot yet to fire.

"Shufly, sired by Dancer's Flyby, a Triple Crown winner, is owned by Metaxas Parish and trained by Cornelia Diamond Clay. Ms. Clay will be in the saddle when he leaves the gate. Shufly is our mystery horse today with staggering odds. Ms. Clay will be the oldest jockey racing today. In fact, Ms. Clay is a grandmother."

"He had to say that, didn't he?" Nealy snapped.

"They have to say stuff like that to make things interesting," Dover said, pulling a face that made Nealy laugh.

"April Fool is not the favorite on this first Saturday in May, but he made it here. It will be interesting to see how his jockey handles him. He balks at the gate and has a rough exit."

"Nealy, twenty minutes to post time. I'm glad those silks still fit you. Shufly looks stupendous. The big fella knows this is his day. Look at him, curious as all hell."

"He knows, Dover. Trust me on that."

Metaxas crushed her to him. "I'm going to wish you luck even if you don't need it," he said. His gaze was intent and shiny bright. "I don't give a rat's ass about the win, Nealy. I just want you to get out there and let the big guy do the rest. Those creeps that keep harping on your age don't know you. I know you. Shufly knows you. That's all you have to remember."

Nealy nodded. She opened her arms to Emmie and Smitty, resplendent in crisp linen and wide-brimmed hats. Nick gave her a thumbs-up as he, too, hugged her. Ruby stepped into her arms, and whispered, "Listen, Granny, you go out there and kick some ass and don't look back. You're ten times better than any of those upstarts. You can take that to the bank, too."

Nealy hugged her and whispered in return, "Hunt's riding with me, Ruby, so wipe that look off your face. Tell Metaxas when you get in your box. It might make the next few minutes easier on him."

"Merciful God," was all Ruby could say.

And then it was Hatch's turn. "I don't know what to say. Good luck doesn't quite seem to cut it. Where should I meet you after the race?"

"How about the winner's circle?" Nealy quipped.

"The winner's circle it is then."

The announcer's voice sent all of them scurrying for their box seats.

"We're now bringing you a live look at the walkover that starts in the barn and then out onto the track. Here comes Shufly with his trainer and jockey Cornelia Diamond Clay along with Dover Wilkie, who is also Shufly's trainer. Right now he's on the first turn—walking toward the paddock to be saddled there and then there will be the call for Riders Up after the Post Parade and then the race itself. While that's going on, we're going to visit the jockeys' room and talk to a few of the jockeys to see what they're thinking and feeling before this momentous race. We tried to get a few words with Cornelia Diamond Clay but weren't successful. That alone only adds to the mystique of her magnificent horse Shufly. Everyone here in the stands is wondering if she can bring home the roses for a second time. As the only female jockey riding today, she opted to stay away from the jockeys' room I'm told. She's wearing purple silks, the same silks she wore when she won the roses the first time. We're told purple was her mother's favorite color. Ms. Clay's mother, by the way, was Maud Diamond who was a Derby winner in the past."

Nealy stared at the bright sunshine. It looked almost the same as the last time she was here. The famous twin spires. The grandstand. Even the track itself. She felt her adrenaline kick in. She spoke soothingly to the big horse at her side. Dover looked straight ahead.

Nealy listened as the announcer spieled off the gate numbers. Someone up above was smiling on her. Shufly was at 15, the same gate Flyby had rocketed out of years before. Shufly would do the same thing today. There was no doubt in her mind. None. This horse was going to fly, mud and all.

"Where are you Hunt? Are you here?" Nealy muttered under her breath.

"I'm right here, Nealy."

"Stay close, okay."

"You got it."

"How are we looking, Hunt? The track is a real mess, isn't it?"

"It sure is, but the big guy will do just fine. The others are going to have some problems. I'll report as we go along. You okay, Nealy?"

"I'm okay, Hunt. I don't want to do this for a living anymore."

"That's the smartest thing I've heard you say in a long time. You're going to go down in history, Nealy."

"Am I going to win today?"

"I don't know."

The sharp retort Nealy was about to offer up was cut short when she heard the call from the announcer.

"Riders Up!"

"This is it, Nealy, girl," Dover said, patting her hand. "You ready?"

"I'm as ready as I ever will be."

"That's good enough for me."

"This is the moment at hand," the announcer blasted into the microphone.

Dover gave Nealy a leg up, then mounted his own horse, whose tail and mane were decorated with purple violets. Side by side they fell into line behind Jake's Thunder and Navigator, the favorites to win.

The freckle-faced jockey riding Jake's Thunder looked over at Nealy and smiled as he gave her a thumbs-up. "A cup of courage to you, Miz Clay. Fine-looking horse you're riding today."

Nealy smiled and returned the thumbs-up.

The jockey riding Navigator wasn't quite as generous. "Shake it, Granny, we ain't got all day." He looked disturbingly like one of the young men who had tormented her last night. A dozen sharp retorts rose to her lips but a hard nudge to her ribs stifled them. "Good luck," she said with a straight face.

The walkover was just as she remembered, perhaps a little longer, under the main stand and out into the sunshine. The roar of the crowd thundered in her ears. "What do you think, Hunt? You comfortable back there?"

"Awesome. Absolutely awesome."

Six minutes to post time.

Nealy listened to the announcer. His words seemed to run together, or maybe it was the roar of the crowd that made it seem that way. He was using words she would never forget, words that had been carved into her brain the first time she raced. "Thunder in his stride, victory in his heart. I can see the warm steam coming up from the horses' backs. This crowd is from all over the world and now they're here to watch the most famous race of all, the Kentucky Derby. Everyone wants to know who is going to take home the roses. Will it be Triple Crown winner, Cornelia Diamond Clay riding Shufly or will it be Adam Witcheson's Jake's Thunder? Then again it could be Dillon Roland's Navigator. We don't know. What we do know is there is going to be a lot of speed in this race, and that's what will determine the winner.

"Ladies and gentlemen, please rise for the playing of 'My Old Kentucky Home.'"

Just as the last note sounded, Nealy said, "Hunt, if I win, remind me to give a thumbs-up to the president of the United States. I promised him I would do that."

"The president! Of these United States?"

"Yeah. I even danced with him. I can dance these days, Hunt. How'd you miss that? No more talk."

Nealy looked across at the jockey riding Navigator. Navigator was owned by Dillon Roland, the same Dillon Roland who had gotten her pregnant when she was seventeen and then threatened to blow her head off with a shotgun if she ever told anyone. Dillon Roland, Emmie's father. *Don't go there, Nealy. Not now.*

Nealy shook her head to clear away all thoughts of Dillon Roland and his horse Navigator.

Nealy leaned over and whispered into Shufly's ear. "Just do your best. That's all I ask. I taught you to walk into the gate like a gentleman. I want you to *fly* out of it like your daddy did. Wait for your opening. We've done this hundreds of times. You know what to do. This is your race. I'm just here for the ride. If you win this race for Metaxas, he is going to buy you a hundred shirts with buttons sewn all over them. We have one minute. Please, God, don't let anything happen to this beautiful animal, to any of the animals racing today. Keep all us jockeys safe in Your hands."

"Hang on, Hunt. I'm going to give you the ride of your life!"

The gate clanged open.

"And they're off in the Kentucky Derby!" the announcer blared.

"Shufly blasted out of the gate and takes the lead—on the inside is Jake's Thunder. Down on the outside is Navigator—Kriss-Kross and Little Tee, then on the rail is Red Max followed by Hard Money. Up and on the outside is Sweet Pete and by the stand for the first time is Jake's Thunder, showing the way by a length and a half.

"Navigator is now moving to the inside and looking for room. Sweet Pete is up on the outside—then on the rail is Kriss-Kross followed by Logan's Luck and Fire Walker—followed by April Fool and Fast Track, then Bright Star."

With each new call, McKay's voice rose an octave. "On the outside is Navigator followed by Shufly, the twenty-to-one-odds mystery horse, followed by Jake's Thunder and finally Sweet Pete. Moving to the clubhouse turn is the leader, Jake's Thunder leading by two and a half lengths, Kriss-Kross is second by a length, Navigator alongside. Sweet Pete is fourth on the outside and two lengths back and then Little Tee."

Blinded by the mud and deafened by the roar of the thundering hooves all around her, Nealy flattened herself out over Shufly's neck. "Now, baby, do it now!" she screamed.

McKay came back on the horn. "Oh-oh, what do we have here? Shufly has made a sudden move and is now sixth, then it's Fire Walker and Money Bags followed by Blue Streak, who is starting to move up. Hard Money and Hell Raiser are moving and right behind are Red Max and Bright Star.

"They're in the turn and bunching up for the lead with Jake's Thunder still the leader by a half length—on the outside challenging is Kriss-Kross and he now has a heavy front. Jake's Thunder responds to the challenge and those two are heads apart. Navigator is third followed by Sweet Pete who is fourth and rolling on. Money Bags drops back. Shufly is moving up on the outside and is now third and moving up to the leaders as they come to the stretch."

There was no other feeling like this in the world, Nealy thought, as she squeezed her thighs against Shufly's body. "This is it, baby! This is what you like, three across. This is your place," Nealy screamed at the top of her lungs. "Make up the ground. Come on, stretch those legs. Go! Go! Go!" She knew he heard her and understood a second later. She could feel his strides lengthen, stretch out. She continued to scream as hooves thundered in her ears and mud flew all around and over her. "Stretch those legs, baby. Go! Go! Go!"

The public address system fairly vibrated with McKay's call. "Jake's Thunder is the leader by a length. Shufly is in the center of the racetrack and that horse is a raging fire. Jake's Thunder drops back, Navigator is in the stretch on the outside. Now on to the homestretch is Shufly—a lightning bolt as he takes the lead. Jake's Thunder is holding at second and Navigator is third. Shufly is moving away by two lengths, two and half lengths, three lengths while Navigator moves on the outside, but he's lost his speed and Shufly is now four lengths and it is Shufly on this sloppy track who takes home the roses and wins the Kentucky Derby by four lengths. The grandmother from Blue Diamond Farms is the winner today, ladies and gentlemen!" McKay screamed to be heard over the roar of the thundering crowd.

Gasping for breath, Nealy whispered, "How was it, Hunt?"

"*Ass-kicking. Thumbs-up for the prez, Nealy.*"

"Oh, yeah." Nealy looked for the nearest camera and raised her thumb and mouthed the words, "For you, Mr. President."

"We did it, Hunt. We did it!"

And then she was in the winner's circle and a blanket of roses was being draped over Shufly's neck. She strained to see her family, but the crowd was too thick. They would find her. She heard her name called but couldn't make out where the call came from because the sun was in her eyes.

Nealy looked down at the man holding the microphone. "How'd it feel, Miss Clay?"

"Pretty darn good." She patted Shufly's rump. "He knew what to do, and he did it."

"You riding the Preakness and the Belmont?"

"You bet. This big guy is Triple Crown material, don't you think?" Nealy said proudly. "Here's his owner now," she said, pointing to Metaxas Parish.

"What do you have to say to all those people who said you were too old to pull this off?" The man pushed the microphone into her face.

Nealy swiped at the mud on her face. She wanted to say so many things, angry retorts, nasty things, but she bit down on her tongue. "I guess my answer would be, I'm here, and they were wrong."

The jockey leading Jake's Thunder passed by. He stopped long enough to hold out his hand. Nealy grasped it. "It was a hell of a race, and that's one mighty fine horse you got there. I'll ride against you anytime, Miz Clay."

"You did okay yourself. See you around."

"You're in good hands, Nealy. I'm outta here. I think you got yourself a date, and he's heading this way."

"You're spying on me again, Hunt."

She turned to Metaxas. Tears rolled down the big man's cheeks. Ruby's, too.

Metaxas bit down on his lower lip. "I swear to God, I don't know who I love more, you or this horse. What I mean is after Ruby."

"I'm happy with third place, Metaxas. Listen, you guys can take care of things, right? I got myself a date with my fella, and here he comes," Nealy said, pointing a muddy finger toward Hatch.

"Nealy. Nealy. Nealy . . . I . . . I never saw anything like that in my life. I've seen horse races, but I didn't know a single thing about the horse or the person riding it. This was . . . awesome. Are you sure you're all right?"

"Never better! This senior is taking home the roses. Boy, if I could have just one wish it would be that they put me on the cover of that magazine *Modern Maturity*. Maybe I could be like a . . ."

"Role model. An inspiration." Hatch grinned.

"Yes. Just because you reach a certain age doesn't mean you should crawl away and do nothing. It's a number. I bought into that number stuff for a little while. Until last night I still kind of believed it. That doesn't mean people should run out and ride a horse. That's not what I mean. They should challenge themselves to their own limit. Maybe someday I'll give a speech about that. Oh, look, there's Dagmar."

Grinning from ear to ear, the reporter held out a sheaf of bills. Nealy grinned at her. "So, are you going to retire?"

"Yes, but not until you run the Preakness and the Belmont. I'm going to go back home and live like a queen. I put down every cent I had in the bank on you, Nealy. Plus yours. Thanks."

Nealy hugged her, mud and all. "My pleasure."

A long time later, after many handshakes and well-wishes, Nealy finally spotted her brothers, Emmie, and Nick.

"As soon as you get cleaned up, Nealy, we're taking you out to dinner to celebrate. Metaxas flew in a chef from somewhere, and the dinner is on him. What's wrong? Are you too tired?" Rhy asked as he hugged her, then held her out at arm's length, then hugged her again.

Nealy looked at her brother and smiled. It was wonderful that he and Pyne had come to the race. Normally it was like pulling teeth to get either one of them away from SunStar. She realized now, after all these years, just how much she meant to her brothers. She knew also that they would never be a daily part of her life but she could count on them and they'd always be there for her. For that she would be forever grateful.

"No. No, not at all. I guess I'm just surprised. No one said anything about celebrating."

"I'll hustle her back to the motel, get her cleaned up, and we'll meet up back here. Is that okay with all of you?" Hatch asked. To Nealy, he leaned over and whispered, "We have the rest of our lives. They want to do this for you, and you deserve it."

Nealy nodded. "It sure is okay. Make sure you ask Dagmar to come along. Dover and Smitty, too."

Hatch asked, "What was it like, Nealy? There for a while all we could see was flying mud. Did Hunt ride with you?"

"Yep, all the way. I can't describe it, Hatch. My heart was pounding almost as loud as those thundering hooves. That's all you really hear. I was screaming and I couldn't hear my own voice. Shufly, just like his daddy did, waited for his moment and when he saw it he took it. That's the thing. He knew. Flyby knew, too. Shufly is real comfortable in that three-horse-across position. He likes being in the middle, and that's exactly where he put himself. I was just along for the ride. I would like a beer and a cigarette, Mr. Littletree." She took a deep breath and sounded like a deflating balloon when she let it out.

"While you're getting cleaned up, I'll get them for you. I guess I will never understand how you couldn't be scared out of your wits."

"If you're scared, you don't belong in the business, Hatch. Your horse reacts to you. When I'm on his back we are *one*. It's not him and me. It's . . . I don't know the word. It's like he absorbs me by some kind of osmosis or something. I don't know if it's like that for the other jockeys or not. Oh, Lenny, the jockey riding Jake's Thunder, congratulated me. None of the other jockeys did, though."

"Jealousy is the answer."

"Whatever. I just want to see Shufly before we head back, okay?"

"Sure."

Everyone was waiting for them at Shufly's stall. Nealy stood back and watched Metaxas for a moment as he continued to wipe his eyes on the sleeve of his white-linen jacket. *The love of an animal,* Nealy thought, *is a wondrous thing.* She inched forward. "Hey, big guy, you did real good out there today. You made me proud to ride you. You rest now." She held out a handful of mints and watched them disappear. She laughed a moment later when he snapped the buttons off her shirt and spit them out. "I'll see you later. Metaxas, are you okay?"

"I'm just in shock. I'm stunned. I can't believe what I saw. I'm damn well overwhelmed is what I am."

"Yeah, it's kind of wonderful, isn't it?" she whispered. She leaned over to kiss his cheek. "I'm gonna get cleaned up now. I'll meet up with you all back here in an hour. Okay?"

"Nealy, I honest to God love you." Ruby beamed. Nealy nodded as she walked down the length of the shed row to where Hatch waited for her.

She turned halfway down and looked back. This part of her life was almost over, she realized with a feeling of sadness. She turned and smiled at the second half of her life waiting so patiently.

14

It was a festive dinner, the food exquisite, the orchid centerpiece breathtaking, the china and silver elegant beyond belief. But it was the camaraderie and the laughter that made all the difference to Nealy Diamond Clay on her night of victory.

Nealy leaned back in her chair and remembered another time when she'd been at another celebration dinner, almost in the same position as she was now but with Kendrick Bell. She couldn't help but wonder if Ken had watched the race on his television set. Every time she thought about him, which wasn't that often anymore, she imagined him sitting in his recliner, a remote control in his hand.

She shrugged away the vision, dropping her hand from the edge of the table to reach for Hatch's hand. He squeezed hard. How good it felt. How right and wonderful. She couldn't ever remember being as happy as she was right this very minute.

"We need one more toast before we call it a night," Metaxas said, standing up and clinking his wineglass with his dessert spoon.

"Not another one, Metaxas," Nealy groaned with good nature. She'd consumed more wine tonight than she usually drank in a year. She hated to think about how she was going to feel in the morning.

Metaxas looked down his nose at her. "Absolutely, we need another one. This one is for Shufly!" he boomed.

As one, the occupants sitting at the long table stood up, their wineglasses aloft! "To Shufly!"

"Hear! Hear!" Nealy shouted. The others joined in.

"Now can we go back to the motel?" Nick pleaded.

Metaxas raised his hand. "No, not yet. I have to make a speech."

Playing with him, Nealy said, "*Then* can we go back to the motel?"

Metaxas stood up and put his hands on the table in front of him. "Now listen, everyone. I practiced this speech for weeks on the off chance that I would get to present it and, by God, I'm going to give it so pay attention. There is no hint of limit to Shufly just like there was no hint of limit with Man O' War. Maybe he didn't win the Derby, but Man O' War was one hell of a horse. When he crossed that wire, he had more to give if needed. Like Secretariat, Shufly showed the greatest exhibition of speed and stamina ever seen. McKay was right when he said he was a lightning bolt when he blazed down that track. Shufly popped out of that gate like a champagne cork and didn't let up. The whole world remembers Citation and his jockey Eddie Arcaro. I stand here before you with stars in my eyes and a humbleness I've never experienced in my entire life. I want you all to know that Nealy Clay is every bit the jockey Eddie Arcaro was. They called Citation the brightest star in the galaxy, but that was because Shufly wasn't around back then. They said Citation had no faults. He could sprint, he could go two miles, he could go in the mud, and he could go on a hard track. They said he could do it all. Shufly did all of those things today. He belongs up there with the greatest of the great.

"Seattle Slew," he droned on, "entered the twenty-first century as the only horse to win the Triple Crown while undefeated. I want you all to listen to me very carefully because I'm telling you, right here, right now, that Shufly is taking it home to Blue Diamond Farms."

"Wind it up, honey," Ruby said, twirling her index finger in the air. "We all want to get some shut-eye, especially Nealy, who looks like she's going to fall asleep any minute."

"I didn't get to Affirmed or Whirlaway, not to mention Spectacular Bid yet," Metaxas grumbled. At his wife's warning look, he said, "Okay, okay. Shufly's the best. Let's leave it at that."

On the drive back to the motel, Nealy asked, "Hatch, what did we have for dinner? Whatever it was, I ate it, but I can't remember. I must be really tired." She yawned as if to prove her point.

Hatch glanced over at her. "I think you're beyond tired, Nealy. I know I'm damn well exhausted, and all I did was *watch* the race. I think I remember what we had to eat. There was so much to choose from. I think I had a goat cheese and walnut soufflé on mesclun. The wine was some kind of Merlot. Forest Glen Barrel, I think. Ruby had chorizo and potato empanaditas, it's a kind of sausage and potato miniturnover with guacamole and fresh tomato salsa. I remember because it looked so good I wished I had ordered it. I think she had a mango cactus-pear sorbet for dessert. She was drinking watermelon margaritas. I do remember that. Metaxas had grilled garlic-marinated skirt steak with lime, poblano strips with onions, and cream-grilled shrimp with ancho pasilla sauce, fresh tomato salsa, warm tortillas filled with steak and salsa, grilled spring onions, and chopped avocado."

Nealy could only stare at him. "How can you remember all that?" she asked sleepily.

"I'm a lawyer, remember. I memorize everything. One of my better traits. Plus I'm used to eating stuff like that."

"What did my brothers have?"

Hatch laughed. "Steak and potatoes. Apple pie for dessert. They drank beer."

"'Night, Hatch," Nealy muttered as she curled into the side of the car seat.

Laughter rumbled in Hatch's throat. "Good night, Nealy."

Late the next morning, Nealy made her way downstairs to the smell of frying bacon and fragrant coffee. She smiled when she saw Hatch sitting at the table. "You're up early. Are you going somewhere?" She eyed the sizzling bacon knowing she couldn't touch it if she wanted to maintain her weight. Just smelling it was enough to make her crazy.

"I'm heading back to Santa Fe this morning. The office called me late last night. They say my presence is required in the office. I'll be back this weekend if that's okay with you."

"It's very okay. I miss you already. Hatch . . ."

Hatch held up his hands, palms outward. "Remember what I said, we have the rest of our lives. Right now I would only be getting a part of you, and that's not what I want. I want all of you,

Nealy. You have a commitment to Metaxas and yourself. I came along afterward. I can wait my turn."

Nealy reached for his hand across the table. "I have to wonder what I did to deserve you even if we got off to a rocky start. I'm really sorry I fell asleep on you the other night. That's the second time I did that. Did I snore?"

"Uh-huh. A gentle, ladylike sound. Everyone snores, they just won't admit it."

"You always know just the right thing to say. Will you call me tonight?" She couldn't help but marvel at his patience and understanding.

"Absolutely. The morning papers are full of you, Nealy. They're calling you the Kentucky phenomenon. Some of the articles sounded a little brittle to me, but for the most part I think everyone has taken a step backward. I wouldn't be a bit surprised to find them all camping out here. With a change of heart, of course. If you bring another Triple Crown winner to this state, you will be on one lofty perch."

Nealy shrugged. "So what do you think of these gorgeous flowers, Hatch?" she asked, leaning forward to sniff at the fragrant bouquet. "They're from the president of the United States and the first lady. The card said, 'I received your message. Well done, Ms. Clay.' And he signed it 'with affection.' I'm going to save the card and one of the flowers."

"They're beautiful. They mention the flowers in the morning papers. I would assume the florist alerted the paper that you got flowers from the president."

"I guess he watched the race. He said he was going to. I thought he might just be saying that, but I guess he meant it. It makes me feel special." She stuck her nose in one of the roses and breathed deeply. "Heavenly."

"You are special, Nealy. I don't think you have any idea of just how special you really are."

Nealy shrugged again. It wasn't that she didn't like compliments, she did. Sometimes, like now, she felt uncomfortable with the praise because she wasn't sure how to respond.

"I have to get down to the barn and get to work. I don't want

Shufly stiffening up, so I'm going to take him out for a breeze. I'll look forward to your call tonight, Hatch."

He kissed her then. It was a kiss that spoke of many things—desire, passion, and sweet tomorrows. She tingled from head to toe, not wanting to let him go. Not now, not ever.

It was Hatch who stepped away. "I'll call you tonight," he said gruffly.

"Okay." In her life she'd never been this shaken. "You make my ears sweat," she blurted.

Hatch stopped in mid-stride. He turned around and with one long-legged stride he was next to her again. He touched her ears. "I'll be damned," he said, his voice full of awe.

"What . . . what happened to you?"

"Me? Oh, I just got a hard-on the size of Mount Rushmore."

Nealy laughed all the way to the barn.

Two weeks later, on a balmy, sun-filled day, Nealy Diamond Clay rode Shufly to victory in the Preakness, her second win in the second jewel of the Triple Crown. Following the win and elated at the horse's prowess, Nealy fell back to light training for both herself and Shufly. Three days before the Belmont Stakes, she stopped everything to prepare for the trip North.

The Belmont Stakes.

The Triple Crown.

Shufly.

Hatch.

The start of a new life.

Nealy settled herself comfortably in the cab of the Ford Ranger, Hatch behind the wheel. Metaxas and Ruby drove Shufly and the horse trailer, while Dover Wilkie and Smitty followed close behind. A day of traveling, a day of rest, and then the race.

"Three days from now and it will all be over, Hatch. We'll drive home after the race, rest up for a few days, and then it's Nealy and Hatch time. Where are we going again?" She was on top of the world, and that's where she intended to stay.

"For starters, we're going to Hawaii. I'm going to teach you to swim, to sail, to scuba dive. You are going to love snorkeling. When we aren't playing in the Pacific Jewel, we'll be making love on our own private beach. We'll stay there for about three weeks. We'll island hop. After Hawaii, I thought I would take you to Santa Fe for a little while. Nick will be taking the bar around that time, and I thought you might want to, you know, be his mother while he's acing the three-day ordeal. After that, I thought we'd do Japan, Hong Kong and maybe scoot on to Australia and New Zealand. From there Africa, maybe Egypt and then back to the States and Colorado, where I'm going to teach you to ski. I have a house there with a giant fireplace that burns *whole* six-foot logs. I'm going to lace up your ice skates and we'll twirl around a pond I know of. We're going to get out my old Flexible Flyer and do some belly whopping and then back to Hawaii for a week or so. In short, Nealy, we are going to do all the things you never got a chance to do while you were growing up. It's called Fun 101. I hope you're looking forward to it as much as I am. We'll come home for Christmas."

"It sounds wonderful, Hatch. I should tell you, I'm not very coordinated."

"Are you kidding? You don't think it takes coordination to ride a horse, especially a racehorse at what is it . . . forty miles an hour? Trust me, Nealy, you won't have any trouble learning to ski and snorkel. But in case you're worried, we'll start off slow. I'll teach you in a private pool attached to the estate I rented. I want you to be a really strong swimmer before we attempt the ocean. The Pacific is like a jewel. Trust me when I tell you that you will love it. You have to really let go, though. You have to be free to experience everything I want for you. It's a whole other life, Nealy."

"Maggie Coleman Tanaka lives in Hawaii," Nealy said.

"So do thousands of other people. It's unlikely we'll see her."

"Cole Tanner lives in Japan."

"Millions of people live in Japan, Nealy. It's also unlikely that we'll see him either. Are you worried?"

"No." Nealy turned to look out the window. "I don't know why their names keep popping into my head. It is something to think about, though. Hatch, where are we going to live when we settle down?"

"Where would you like to live, Nealy?" he said, answering her question with a question. "It's up to you."

Nealy thought about it for a moment. "That's just it, I don't know, Hatch. If Emmie is running Blue Diamond Farms, she's going to want to do it her way, not my way. That's the way it should be. I think I'm going to be more or less homeless. Ruby and Metaxas are talking about buying the Goldberg farm. It used to belong to Buddy's family. If that happens, they'll be able to help Emmie and vice versa. Nick will be settled down in Santa Fe. I want to visit often with Emmie, so Gabby gets to know me. We can do that, can't we, Hatch?" Just the thought of little Gabby made her smile.

"Absolutely. We can stay in Kentucky if you like. Hell, Nealy, I don't care where we live as long as we're together. Don't worry about it. Where we live really isn't a problem. Between the airlines and my plane, we can be anywhere we want to be in a matter of just a few hours.

"We can take Gabby for whole summers if Emmie allows it. We'll work everything out. Where should we get married? At the farm?"

"In a church. I want to get married in a church. I want to walk down the aisle and I want Gabby to be my flower girl. I want Smitty, Ruby, and Emmie to stand up for me. How about you?"

"Bode, Hank, Nick, and Metaxas," he responded without hesitation. "We got it covered, Nealy. Just one question, though. Are you as happy as I am?"

"I'm so happy I could just bust wide open. I'll be even happier when this last race is over. I had this dream last night, Hatch. You aren't going to believe it especially the way I've been moaning and groaning about being a senior. In my dream I had stationery printed up that said, Nealy Littletree, Senior Citizen."

Hatch laughed so hard the truck rocked underneath them. He continued to laugh until tears rolled down his cheeks.

"Wait, there's more," she said, reaching out to touch his arm. "I wrote a letter to the president and the first lady on that stationery thanking them for the beautiful flowers." She doubled over, laughing hysterically. Hatch gasped as he wiped at his eyes with the back of his hand.

"When was the last time you laughed like that, Nealy?"

"Probably never." Nealy wiped at her eyes with a tissue from the glove compartment. "You are so good for me, Hatch."

"And you're good for me."

They talked about everything under the sun for the next few hours. She realized suddenly that she knew very little, if anything, about Hatch's childhood. "Tell me what it was like growing up on a reservation, Hatch. You know all about me, and now I want to know all about you."

"Do you really want to know, Nealy?"

"I do, Hatch. I want to know everything about you. Don't leave anything out either."

"My earliest memory is running with my friends. I was barefoot and half-naked. . . ."

"Are you feeling good about this, Nealy?" Metaxas asked as he stroked Shufly's big head. "He knows, Nealy, that today is different, just like he knew the Derby and the Preakness were different. See, he's not going after my buttons. That means something to me. That means he knows. He knows, Nealy."

"You're babbling, honey," Ruby said, linking her arm with his.

"They always know," Nealy said gently. "There's the call for Riders Up. Gotta go. Wish me luck."

Dover stood next to Shufly, waiting for her. "You pulled gate 9, Nealy. That's good. Just let Shufly find his place. He does love that three-across spread. Bring it home, Nealy," Dover said, hugging her tightly and then cupping his hands to give her a leg up.

Nealy wiggled down into her seat. "I'll do my best, Dover. You *know* Shufly is going to do his best. See ya, Dover."

The crowd roared with excitement when Nealy in her purple-and-white silks, rode into view.

"My God," she whispered, then bent to pat Shufly's mane. "I think they like us. Look at them, Shufly. Turn your head and look at them." He did just that: turned his head toward the crowd, perked his ears, then rolled back his lips in what Nealy could only describe as a smile. "You are a ham, Shufly." She started to laugh, catching the attention of the jockey behind her.

"What's so funny?" he called to her.

"Trust me, you wouldn't believe it even if I told you," she called over her shoulder.

In the gate, Nealy stroked Shufly. She bowed her head and said her prayer. "Please, God, keep all the animals and jockeys safe in this race."

She snuggled down into her seat and prepared herself. "You back there, Hunt?"

"*I'm hanging on, Nealy. You okay?*"

"I'm very okay, Hunt. How's it look from your vantage point?"

"*Tight as a duck's ass. Smoky Joe is the one you have to watch out for. He's got some speed in those legs. Cherokee Charlie can come from behind and into the stretch like greased lightning. Hiz Honor is in gate 8. He's hot spit, Nealy. You're the odds-on favorite, and we both know that can mean squat on the homestretch. This horse can do it. I know he can.*"

"Okay, okay. Enough. I need to talk to my horse now. Like me, you're just along for the ride. Remember that. Don't go confusing me." Putting Hunt out of her mind, Nealy leaned over Shufly's withers.

"*Then why didn't you say so.*"

"I just did."

"Listen to me, big guy, it's all the mints you want if you do this for Metaxas. All I want is your best. I know you're tired because I'm tired, and I'm just sitting on your back. You win this and it's bluegrass pasture, mares, and the love of the nicest man in the world. Okay, it's time, sweetie. Blast out of this gate and show all those slugs you mean business."

The bell rang, the gate clanged open. "And they're off in the Belmont Stakes!" The announcer blared over the public address system.

"Smoky Joe broke slowly and breaking on the lead is Cherokee Charlie on the inside, Hiz Honor showing speed on the outside. Next to him is Shufly, the odds-on favorite to bring home a second Triple Crown to the state of Kentucky and ridden by Cornelia Diamond Clay.

"Hiz Honor gets the lead, but Cherokee Charlie is taking over by two lengths. Smoky Joe is moving up and here's Shufly moving up on the inside and has moved to capture the second position. Smoky Joe is dropping back. Bringing up the rear is Bee Bop, followed by Starlite, Secret Sam, and Bell Wether. On the far outside is Silver Streak and Loveboat."

Nealy allowed herself a quick glance at Cherokee Charlie, whose jockey had a reputation for taking unnecessary risks. Other than that, she felt they were in a solid position. "Keep it up, boy, you're doing just fine," she shouted.

She could hear the excitement building in the crowd when the announcer blared on the horn. "Bee Bop is starting to nose up as Hiz Honor moves on the outside, and here come Fast Track, Silver Streak, Secret Sam, and Lord April. Moving into the turn it's Cherokee Charlie ahead by half a length with Shufly on the rail right behind him."

Out of the corner of her eye Nealy saw Cherokee Charlie's jockey rein his mount toward her. She needed to get out of the way before Shufly got pinned to the rail.

"Flying on the inside is Secret Sam, who is three lengths back from third and is now quickly making up ground. Smoky Joe is attempting to get through and is also moving up.

"Moving at breakneck speed is Cherokee Charlie, who moved up as Shufly blazes alongside. Smoky Joe is in third, a gap of two and a half lengths. Here comes Bee Bop, followed by Starlite and Secret Sam and Bell Wether. On the outside is Silver Streak and Loveboat. On the inside is Oscar and moving on to the backstretch is Lord April and on the inside, ahead and in front is Shufly in second and ahead by four lengths. Cherokee Charlie is third and ahead by four and a half lengths. Smoky Joe is in fourth place by a length and a half. Beginning to nose up is Bee Bop. Hiz Honor moves on the outside and here come Fast Track, Silver Streak, Secret Sam, and Lord April. Moving into the turn is Cherokee Charlie, Smoky Joe by half a length.

"Blazing along on the inside is Secret Sam, who is three lengths back from third and is now quickly making up ground and is fourth on the outside. Smoky Joe is attempting to get through along the railing and is also moving up and it's back to the next horse Bell Wether and into the stretch for Shufly, Cherokee Charlie, and Smoky Joe."

"Now, Shufly, go now! There's enough room," Nealy screamed, so loud she thought her tongue was falling out. "Get out now before you get pinned in." She could hear Hunt screaming in her ear as the sound of the racing horses thundered all about her. "Go, baby, go! This is it!"

"It's Shufly and Cherokee Charlie battling it out together and here comes Smoky Joe closing ground fast and moving into third. It's Shufly ahead at the stretch and he is taking over. Shufly is moving away by a length, by two and now it's two and a half lengths. Look at that horse fly! He has wings on his feet, and they aren't made of gossamer.

"Smoky Joe drives up on the outside and into second, Cherokee Charlie closing off on the inside. Going down to the wire is Shufly by four lengths, Cherokee Charlie is in second, and Smoky Joe is third." Screaming over the thunder of the crowd, the announcer blared, "Shufly straightened out his tail and is heading for the wire and it's Shufly who wins the Belmont Stakes and takes home the Triple Crown to Blue Diamond Farms!"

Nealy lifted up and off the saddle and stood in the irons, waving to the crowd, who, almost as one, shouted her name. When she came back around and in front of the grandstand, she gasped when she heard the announcer say, "Here she is, ladies and gentlemen, the woman of the moment, Nealy Diamond Clay, the first woman to win the Triple Crown not once but twice!"

As one, the crowd rose to their feet to give her a standing ovation.

"Hell of a race, Nealy. That crowd loves you. Thanks for inviting me!"

"My pleasure, Hunt. Is this some kind of horse or what?" she gasped, sitting back down into the saddle.

"He's the kind of horse he is because of you, Nealy, and don't you ever forget it. I'll see you around."

"Hunt, wait. What does that mean, you'll see me around?" Nealy asked, struggling with her breathing.

"I'm saying good-bye. You don't need me anymore. Here comes the big *guy. I told you he was your destiny. Be good to him, and be happy, Nealy. You deserve it."*

Nealy ripped off her goggles and cried into Shufly's mane. Her face streaked with dirt and tears, she trotted into the winner's circle. A lump the size of a golf ball settled in her throat. She watched as Metaxas Parish dropped to his knees and kissed the ground next to Shufly for all the world to see.

"I would have done a cartwheel, but I'm too damn old," he said getting up and wrapping his arms around Shufly's neck. "Congratulations, Nealy. Two Triple Crowns by father and son. You're going to go down in history."

"Watch this, Metaxas," Nealy said. To the roar of the crowd, Nealy swept her hat in front of her in a sitting curtsy, acknowledging their well-wishes. "Your turn, Shufly," she said, and the Triple Crown Winner bowed to the crowd.

"Is it my turn now?" Hatch said later, when the amenities were over and Shufly was being led away to be cooled down.

"No. It's *our* turn." Nealy burst out laughing. "I am now going to eat until food pours out of my ears. I am going to drink four bottles of beer and smoke as many cigarettes as I want. I'll quit smoking tomorrow. Can you fill that order for me, Hatch? By the way, Hunt said good-bye to me. He said I didn't need him anymore. He said you were my destiny."

"Did he now?"

"Yep. And you know what, he's right. Hunt was always right except on the rare occasions when he was wrong." Nealy smiled at her declaration.

"Nealy, you won two Triple Crowns! No woman in the world has ever done that."

"Yeah, I know. But I can't ski, snorkel, or ice-skate. Hell, I've never even had on a pair of roller skates. The truth is, the Triple Crowns belong to those magnificent animals I raised and trained. It doesn't seem right that they should be given to me. I understand the process, it just doesn't seem fair."

"You made Thoroughbred racing history today. You, a senior citizen."

"Fancy that." Nealy laughed. "I am now officially yours, Mister Littletree."

"Metaxas has some wonderful dinner party planned. We need to get 'gussied up,' as Ruby put it, for the festivities. It's a celebration and a send-off for Dagmar. She's returning to Sweden tomorrow with, as she put it, her poke filled to the brim."

"I just want a bath. But first I want to see Shufly."

"Then let's go."

In the barn, where Shufly was being catered to like a brand-new father, Nealy walked over to him, hands on hips, and stared at him with unblinking intensity. "You are the marvel in marvelous. There are no words, and if there are, I certainly don't know them, to tell you what a fine horse you are. You are your daddy's son. That's probably the greatest compliment I can give you. I love you with all my heart, but you belong to Metaxas. From this day forward, you're going to have the most wonderful life imaginable. I'll come back to see you from time to time. Just don't forget about me, okay?" Nealy said, wrapping her arms around the horse's neck.

Shufly pawed the ground and snorted as he pushed Nealy to the side to rub his muzzle against her. "What? What do you want?"

"He wants you to get on his back," Metaxas said quietly. "Here, I'll lift you up. Don't ask me. This horse has a mind of his own. I think he wants to do his parade strut. He knows it's over now. He's doing it for you, Nealy. Go for the ride."

Tears streaming down her cheeks, Nealy sat tall as Shufly trotted the length of the barn and then back. When he returned to his stall, his front legs bent so she could slide off his back, he reared back and let loose with a sound that was neither a whinny or a whicker.

"It's his roar of approval for *you*, Nealy," Metaxas said. Nealy bit down on her lower lip until she tasted her own blood. She managed to nod, the tears still streaming down her cheeks.

"See ya, big guy!"

Nealy ran from the barn.

This part of her life was now over.

The dinner was a colossal gourmet delight. The bushel basket of roses in the center of the table smelled heavenly. Nealy looked around, her champagne glass aloft. "I want to make a toast to the two finest horses in the world. To Flyby and Shufly!"

"Hear! Hear!"

Nealy swallowed the contents of her glass in one gulp. She held it up for a refill and locked her gaze with Mitch Cunningham.

"I know I wasn't invited, and I won't stay," the cinematographer said. "You did say I should look you up after you won the Triple Crown. You didn't say, if, you said when. So, will you do it?"

Nealy looked across the table at her daughter. "Emmie, they want to make a movie about me. They want to film it at Blue Diamond Farms. What do you think?"

"Go for it, Mom!" Emmie said.

"Can you shoot your film around me? I'm going off with my fella here for a little while."

Cunningham could only bob his head up and down. She said yes. That meant she agreed. Christ, he'd been prepared for everything under the sun but the word *yes*. "I have the contracts in the car," he said.

"Send them to my lawyer. If he says it's okay, Emmie, my daughter, has my power of attorney. By the way, my attorney is my son, so that contract better be real good. With one condition."

Cunningham groaned. "What?"

"You get that studio of yours to put my picture on the front cover of *Modern Maturity*. And the horse's."

"Done!"

"Okay, everyone, Hatch and I are leaving. You'll see us when you see us. Six months or so. Maybe sooner. Maybe later. Bye!"

"Smitty! Come quick. I got a letter from Mom. Hurry, Smitty!" Emmie shouted as she ran up the steps of the back porch and into the kitchen. She ripped at the envelope. "Ohhhh, it's a nice long one. We're going to need coffee with this one. A cigarette would be nice," she cajoled.

"You're worse than your mother. One cigarette, that's it. Where is she? Read!" Smitty ordered.

"Japan. Okay. Here goes."

My Dear Emmie,

First things first. I miss you, Gabby, and Smitty. I think about all of you and the horses every single day. Without you running things, Emmie, I wouldn't be able to be here with Hatch.

Hatch and I spoke to Nick several days ago. He passed the bar. I was so excited, I almost fainted. I think I was more excited than Nick was. He now sits in his father's chair, in his father's office. I am so happy for him. I hope you are just as happy running Blue Diamond Farms, Emmie.

I don't know where to start. Everything is so wonderful. I've learned to swim in the ocean and snorkel. In my wildest dreams I never thought I would do half the things I've been doing. I can ski a little on the bunny hills. My rear end is sore from falling on the skating rink. I loved every minute of it. Hatch is such fun. People look at us because all we do is laugh and hold hands. I'm looking forward to spending the rest of my life with him.

I'm having my wedding gown made in Hong Kong. Hatch knows this tailor who will measure me and make the dress in two days. He also knows someone who will take a mold of my feet and make me shoes to match the wedding gown. They will mail it home, so be on the lookout for it. I hope Smitty reserved the church and that plans for the reception are under way. Imagine me getting married the day after Christmas. The tailor is also making Gabby's flower-girl dress. I'm so glad I had the size with me. Make a note, Emmie, to find a special little basket for the flower petals. One she will be comfortable carrying down the aisle.

Tell Smitty and Ruby I'm happier than I've ever been in my entire life. I am literally seeing the world I only read about in a newspaper or saw on television and I am loving every minute of it.

And now for the biggest surprise of all. Hatch persuaded me to look up Cole Tanner and mend my fences, one board at a time. I did, and we met for dinner the other night. At first we stared at one another, neither of us sure what we should say. Hatch took matters into his own hands and got the conversation going. Cole has a wonderful family. His children are as precious as Gabby. It will be nice for her to have cousins even though they are so far away. We parted friends, and Hatch invited all of them to the wedding. Wouldn't it be wonderful if they could come? I'm okay with it all. I realize now I can't live my life full of bit-

terness and hatred. Hatch helped me with that part of it. That part of my life is over. We have to start somewhere, and this was a beginning. In the end, nothing is as important as family. Cole agreed.

Give everyone my love, and if things work out according to plan, we'll be home the week before Christmas. We're leaving for Hong Kong later today. I'm enclosing the balance of my itinerary should you need it. Give Gabby a hug from her grandmother.

All my love,
Mom

"Wow!" Emmie said.

"Wow is right," Smitty said.

"I think she's finally happy, Smitty. When I think back, I hardly ever remember Mom laughing. She smiled, but she never really laughed. I always wanted to make her laugh, but I didn't know how."

"I think she's making up for lost time," Smitty said. "I can't believe she invited the Colemans to the wedding. I wonder who's next on her list. I might as well get to it. Do you need anything, Emmie?"

"Nope. I have a ton of work to do. I'll be up when it's time to pick Gabby up at the bus. She does love preschool. She thinks she's hot stuff riding on the bus. I used to be like that. The only difference was, I couldn't shout with glee when I got off and ran to Mom. She was always waiting for me. Always. She never missed a day. God, I'm so glad she's happy."

"Now we have to work on you," Smitty said.

"I'm happy."

Smitty snorted. "That's what your mother always used to say. She lied."

Emmie grimaced as she turned to leave the kitchen, coffee cup in hand.

Smitty watched the young woman lope her way down to the barn. "Honey, you have no idea just how much like your mother you really are. You don't have a clue."

PART III

15

Miles away, at Sunbridge Ranch in Texas, Riley Coleman sat staring at his cousin Cole, a stack of ledgers and financial reports in front of him. He stared at them with glee in his eyes. "See this," he said to Cole. "This is a record of the money we owe Nealy Clay. "This," he said, waving a paper in the air, "is the current bank statement. It's time we paid her back."

Cole bit into a thick roast beef sandwich, then washed it down with a swig from a bottle of Sapporo beer. "Doesn't it seem a little strange to you, Riley, that we'll be paying her back with monies we won placing bets on her in Vegas?"

Riley threw his hands in the air. "Money is money. Hell, half the world probably bet on those three races she ran. However, the payback money is coming from the first gusher we brought in last year. You invested it, Cole. It's all there. You've been investing our winnings from those races these past few months. I know it's just six months since the last race, but when you invest millions and your return is eighteen percent, I'd say that's pretty good. We talked about this until we were blue in the face, Cole. We agreed not to touch the principal. It's there as a reminder to both of us. The day may come when we're called on to help a member of the family the way Nealy Clay helped us. I hate talking about this because it forces me to remember what assholes we were. We're on steady ground now. We all bit the bullet and you turned Rising Sun around in a little over two years. We brought in two gushers and a third is on the way. We have a magnificent herd of cattle, the drought is over, and we have a reserve in the bank. We paid off Sawyer and your aunt Maggie. Forget the fact that I no longer know what a night's sleep means."

"So what's our game plan here?" Cole uncapped a second bottle of Sapporo, his favorite Japanese beer.

Cole waved Nealy Clay's wedding invitation in the air. "By the grace of God, and Nealy Clay, we turned it around. It's not something you or I will ever forget. There was a point there when I just wanted to lie down and die."

"I was right there with you, Riley," Cole said. "Send her a cashier's check and a handwritten thank-you." He twirled the beer bottle around and around on the kitchen table. "So," he said, looking around, "will Ivy and Moss be back for Christmas?"

"It depends on Ivy's mother, who isn't doing as well as they expected after her hip replacement. Ivy feels she has to stay there with her mother. I was going to fly down for Christmas Day and then fly on to Kentucky for the wedding. What about you, Cole?"

"I'm heading back to Japan tomorrow night. I'll fly over for the wedding. I'm not sure about Sumi and the kids. She is petrified to fly, so that's the hang-up. She always insists we take separate flights and I can say for certainty she won't allow the kids to fly." He shrugged. "Sawyer and Adam are going and so is Mother. This side of the family will be represented. We can either pay her before the wedding or send the check to her attorney. My own personal opinion is we should do it before. I'd kind of like to thank her face-to-face and shake her hand."

"Then that's what we'll do. You must have been stunned when you heard her voice on the phone. How did you handle it?"

"Very carefully. That plant over the sink needs watering, Riley. Ivy will be pissed if you let it die. Sumi is like that, so I know."

Riley got up from the table to rummage under the sink for the watering can his wife always used. He watered the plant. "I really took care of this plant when she left me that first time. It was like it was a sacred trust or something. When Ivy came back her first words were, 'Good, you didn't let my plants die.'"

"Women are like that. What do you say we wash up and head for town. I could use some good Japanese food about now."

"You're on, cousin."

*　　*　　*

Hatch Littletree stared around at weary travelers as they waited for their luggage to appear. Almost all of them carried straw hats, colorful shopping bags, and gaudy jewelry attesting to their vacation in the islands. The red dome light above the carousel flashed and beeped as the first bag made its way up the ramp and down onto the conveyor belt. He reached for Nealy's hand and smiled down at her when he saw one of his bags tumble out of the top opening. Passengers pushed and shoved as they elbowed their way through the crowd of waiting travelers to reach for their bags. He sighed. He couldn't remember ever being as happy as he was right then.

Nealy shifted her shoulder bag to her right shoulder, at the same time kicking her travel bag between her feet. "I wish you were coming with me, Hatch."

Hatch shoved his baseball cap farther back on his head as he scanned the bags passing before him. "It's just two days, Nealy. There's a bunch of stuff I have to sign off on. I'll be back before you know it. We have to start off clean with no trailing baggage that's going to make us worry. When we leave on our honeymoon, I want both of us to be as free as the wind. No clocks, no timetables, no telephones except one cell phone for emergencies. Two days, tops." Nealy nodded.

"I'm glad we're home. The last leg of the flight was really frightening with all that turbulence. The weather outside looks . . . ominous. Promise me you'll call as soon as you set down in Santa Fe. Promise, Hatch."

Hatch reached for a large black-leather bag, at the same time nodding to a porter. "I promise. I'll see you to your cab, and then I have to take off." He grinned. "We started out with one bag each six months ago and we're returning with seven, counting our carry-on luggage."

"Presents, souvenirs. We covered a lot of territory in the past months. I had to buy presents from each place. Not to mention the stuff we bought for ourselves that we'll probably never use." Nealy reached for his arm as they trailed behind the porter to head for the taxi stand. She shivered inside her light windbreaker.

Hatch draped his arm around her shoulder. "What's wrong, Nealy?" He followed her gaze as she looked around, a frown building on her face. He, too, shivered in the brisk air.

Nealy shrugged as she settled the straw hat she'd bought in Hawaii more firmly on her head. "There's a storm brewing. I can almost taste it. Look at the sky, Hatch."

"I'll be flying above it, Nealy. Or is it the horses you're worried about? Don't go spooking me now."

"Both, Hatch. The only word I can think of is *ominous*. Maybe I'm just tired. Go ahead, I'll be fine. Make sure you call me as soon as you set down."

Hatch settled Nealy in the backseat of the taxi. He leaned over to kiss her lightly on the lips. "Five days and you'll be Mrs. Littletree." He grinned, and Nealy smiled. For one brief moment she forgot about the strange-looking sky overhead. She watched until Hatch's long-legged stride took him out of her line of vision.

Nealy settled herself into the corner seat of the cab, grateful for the humming heater. She was also grateful that the driver wasn't in a talkative mood.

A chill washed through her. She felt frightened and she didn't know why. Was she having a premonition of some kind? She wished the taxi could sprout wings and soar away to drop her by the front porch of Blue Diamond Farms. She wished for so many things of late. Maud had done the same thing in the later years of her life. Damn, where were these strange thoughts taking her?

She'd been so happy these past months. Almost too happy. Maybe that was the problem. At one time she thought she could never be happy anywhere but at the farm. Now she knew that was a myth. She'd been joyously happy with Hatch. And while she thought about the farm and the horses, she hadn't been consumed by those thoughts. She had Hatch. Hatch made all the difference.

Nealy continued to stare out the taxi window at the scudding clouds overhead. Not only did it still look ominous, but it *felt* ominous. Damn it, what was it? She'd experienced storms before. Terrible storms, wicked storms, god-awful storms. It was cold enough for snow. Maybe that was it. A white Christmas. A white wedding.

Her whole body started to shake. She curled into herself, fighting the urge to cry, not understanding where such odd feelings were coming from.

She saw the entrance then. "This is it," she told the cab driver as he pulled into the farm's driveway a long time later. She sighed in relief at the majesty of Flyby and the copper glory of Shufly standing guard over the entrance to Blue Diamond Farms. Such majesty, such glory, such presence. She sighed again, grateful that she was finally home.

The urge to bolt from the taxi and run the rest of the way to the house was so strong that Nealy found herself clutching at the door handle.

The moment the taxi came to a full stop her family appeared. She saw it all in one glance—her daughter's happy face, Gabby's chubby legs pumping furiously, Smitty's ear-to-ear grin, and Dover and the grooms waving. But the dark, swirling clouds overhead still bothered her. She held out her arms, her laughter forced, words tumbling from her mouth in short little bursts. Somehow, between hugs and smiles she managed to ask, "What's with the weather? It looks kind of scary."

Emmie and Smitty both shrugged. Gabby hung on for dear life as Nealy pretended to be a horse and galloped up the steps and into the house. "I could use a good cup of coffee. I really missed our coffee," Nealy said. "I really missed this place. No, that's not quite true. I thought about it a lot. Actually, I didn't miss it as much as I thought I would. I just love this kitchen. Kitchens mean home. No matter how nice a hotel or suite is, it isn't home."

"I'll be down in a minute, Mom. It's Gabby's nap time. Actually, it's past her nap time, but I let her stay up so she could greet you." Emmie scooped up the squealing toddler and started for the stairs.

Nealy smiled as she opened her travel bag. "This is for Cookie, so he has a friend," she said, presenting a small, white, stuffed dog. "And this is for you, Gabby," she said, holding out a small island-made rag doll. "Her name is Mary Lou. See, her name is stitched on her dress. Sweet dreams, Gabby. I'll give you the rest of your presents when you wake up." She ruffled the toddler's curls as she kissed and hugged her.

"Did you miss me, Smitty?" Nealy asked as she reached for the cup of coffee Smitty held out to her. She sank down gratefully into her favorite kitchen chair. The same chair Maud always used to sit in. "I feel in some ways like I've been gone forever. So, Smitty, did you miss me?" she repeated.

"Who had time to miss you?" Smitty said, tongue in cheek. "As you can see, nothing has changed. Somehow or other we managed to muddle through without you. Of course we missed you, Nealy. Ruby and Metaxas will be back Christmas Eve. They take possession of the Owens farm on January 2. Damn, I mean the Goldberg farm. Metaxas had some loose ends he said he needed to tie up before he became a farm owner full-time. The Goldbergs moved up North at the end of October. The whole place is just sitting there empty waiting for Ruby and Metaxas."

Nealy tried to stay focused, tried to pay attention to what Smitty was saying. "I don't like this weather, Smitty. It feels . . . *deadly*. I know that's a strong word, but that's how it feels to me. What are they saying on the weather station?"

Smitty poured more coffee into her cup. "About what you would expect. A bad storm later today. Nothing out of the ordinary. What's got you so skittish?"

Nealy got up to stand before the kitchen window. "Maybe it's just being home again after being gone so long. Maybe I'm tired. In all the years I've lived here, I've never seen a sky that looks like this one does. Summer and fall were so dry everything was brittle. When we landed, it was really cold. By the time I got here, the temperature must have gone up ten or fifteen degrees. When we landed, it felt like snow. Now the air just feels *thick*. To me that means thunder and lightning but not necessarily rain. I don't like what I'm feeling right now. Make some more coffee, okay? I want to change and go down to the barn."

Emmie bounded down the kitchen stairway. "I'm glad you're home, Mom. I really missed you. Ah, coffee. I am my mother's daughter," Emmie said as she poured coffee into a thermal container. "I gotta get back to the barn. This weather has the horses spooked. Boy are they going to be glad to see you, Mom."

"I'll meet you down in the barn. I want to change," Nealy said.

It was almost pitch-black outside when Nealy strode across the kitchen, grabbing her coffee and bolting down to the barn. She looked around; all the sensor lights were blazing. It was even warmer now than it had been when she'd climbed out of the taxi an hour ago. What did it mean? A hurricane? In December? Impossible. Tornado? A definite possibility. A gust of wind slammed into her back, forcing her to run the rest of the way to the barn.

The horses were uneasy, skittish. She headed straight for Flyby's stall, where she nuzzled the big horse, her face dreamy as she let her hands caress the animal. "I'm here, baby. I'm here. Nothing is going to happen to you." She turned at a sound. Shufly. "Hey, big guy, how's it going? Missed me, huh," she said, doing the same thing to him she'd done to his daddy. "You're lookin' good, baby. Guess Metaxas is taking good care of you. Okay, okay, here we go," she said, holding out a handful of mints. She filled her other hand and held them out to Flyby.

Her gaze swept the stallion barn. The grooms and workers were doing double duty trying to calm the skittish horses. Every single light in the barn blazed. Outside it seemed darker—if that was possible. She looked down at her watch—3:25. It was way too early for darkness to fall.

Nealy ran to the tack room and turned on the portable radio. She couldn't hear anything but static.

"Mom?"

"Emmie, what's wrong?"

"I don't know, Mom. I *feel* something. I think I'm starting to get scared. I've never seen anything like this. It isn't even three-thirty, and it's black as tar outside. I'm so glad you're home." Relief rang in her voice.

"Me, too, honey. We need to keep the horses calm. Are you okay being down here with Gabby sleeping up at the house?"

"Sure. Smitty dotes on her. She can tell to the second when Gabby wakes up. Then, again, it could have something to do with Cookie barking. She's fine. Smitty is like a second grandmother to her. It sure did get warm." To prove her point, Emmie removed her flannel shirt. She yanked at the neck band of the white tee shirt as she stretched her neck. "Is something going to happen, Mom?"

"I don't know, Emmie. All we can do is keep the horses calm and wait it out. Whatever *it* turns out to be."

"I can't believe those cameramen are out there filming. The past few days they've been working around the clock. Tomorrow or the day after, you have to sit down with them and do some background stuff. Mitch said they want some *insight* on you."

"Mitch, is it?"

"We've gotten to be good friends. Don't look at me like that. We're just friends, Mom. The whole crew has been real good about listening to me. They understand the horses come first. When I say no to something, they back off. Mitch says it's going to be good enough to be up for an Academy Award. Can you imagine, Mom?"

"No, Emmie, I can't imagine it. Right now all I can think about is this storm."

Ruby Parish stepped out onto the lanai of her island estate. She felt jittery and out of sorts. She looked down at her bare feet. They seemed wider to her these days. Maybe it had something to do with the hard leather boots she'd been wearing for the past couple of years. She'd always had nice feet when she was younger. She couldn't remember the last time she'd had a pedicure or had bought sexy sandals. Not that it mattered. She plucked a vibrant hibiscus bloom from the bush nearest her and stuck it behind her ear.

"That flower is almost as pretty as you," Metaxas said, wrapping his arms around his wife. "You seem pensive. Is something wrong, sweet baby?" The concern in her husband's voice startled Ruby.

"I'm not sure, honey. Do you remember that time we took off in the snowstorm to find Sunny and Harry? I called you because the chickens were restless. I had such an awful feeling that night. I knew something was wrong. I don't know if it was a female thing or not. I just knew something was wrong. I had that same feeling again when Fanny Thornton's mountain was on fire. That's the kind of feeling I have right now. I'm thinking it has something to do with Nealy. She and Hatch are due back today. I'm sorry I can't explain it any better than that, Metaxas."

"That's good enough for me." Metaxas had the portable phone in his hand and was dialing Blue Diamond Farms before his wife could finish speaking. His face ashen, he said, "The lines are down. Get your shoes on, sweet baby, we're outta here."

Minutes later, Ruby fiddled with the dial of the car radio as Metaxas guided the open-air Jeep up one hill, down another, and around hairpin turns. "They're saying it's some kind of unexplained freak storm that was spawned in the Gulf. It already ripped up through Alabama and Tennessee and is now headed straight for Kentucky. The announcer clarified it and said it is headed straight for Kentucky's horse country. So far there have been nine tornados, but they haven't been able to calculate the loss of lives yet. This storm just keeps getting stronger and stronger. They say the lightning is the worst that's ever been documented. They're calling it the storm of the century, honey. We can't possibly fly in this kind of weather. They won't let you off the ground. They won't even let you file a flight plan."

"We can skirt around the storm, that's not the problem. It's landing somewhere close that is going to be the problem. We're going to do our best, sweet baby. This is some homecoming for Nealy. She needs us, honey. We have to try, Ruby."

"Okay, honey."

"I don't know about you, Riley, but I'm ready to hit the sack," Cole Tanner said. "Let's get the ten o'clock news highlights and head off for bed." He switched channels. "Oh, oh, what have we here? Riley, I think you better come over here and look at what's on the screen. God Almighty!"

Both men stood staring at the sixty-one-inch television screen, their eyes wide. "Jesus!" Riley said.

"Get your gear together. Bring your cell phone."

Riley pulled on his boots. "The weather conditions aren't the best, cousin."

"They plain old sucked when we hit those Swiss Alps, but we did it anyway. Move, move!"

"I'm moving! I'm moving!"

*   *   *

Hatch was brushing his teeth when a sound like someone kicking in his front door reached his ears. He ran to the door and opened it. The toothbrush still in his mouth, a towel wrapped around his middle, his hair wet and on end. His eyes popped wide at Nick's wild appearance.

"We have to go to Kentucky," Nick yelled as he looked for the remote to turn on the television.

Hatch swallowed the foamy paste in his mouth as he watched Nick fiddle with the buttons. "Why? What the hell happened?"

"*That's* what already happened. Listen to the commentator. That killer storm is headed straight for Lexington. Blue Diamond Farms is in the path of the storm."

Live video cam shots of massive destruction in Alabama appeared on the screen. "Damage is estimated in the billions. Stay tuned for further live coverage."

"My God," Hatch said, his face draining of all color. "Give me five minutes to get dressed. I talked to your mother around four o'clock and all she said was they were bracing for a storm. When was the last time you tried calling?"

"Around six-thirty or so, but I couldn't get through. I was watching the evening news. The lines are down," Nick shouted so that Hatch could hear him in the bedroom. "You can fly us there, can't you, Hatch?"

"I can try." Hatch bent over to tie the laces of his sneakers. He felt light-headed, dizzy, and suddenly sick to his stomach. *Please, God, don't let anything go wrong. I can't lose her. She's my life. Please, please, don't take her the way You took Sela and my son.* When he straightened up he got a sudden head rush. He held on to the edge of the chair, shaking his head to clear his thoughts. "Okay, kid, let's go."

In Las Vegas, Sage Thornton took his eyes off the closed-circuit television to risk a glance at the incoming bulletin on the television set on his desk. He blinked once, then twice. "Birch! Come look at this!"

"Oh, my God! How soon can you be ready to leave?"

"I'm ready right now. Call Mom and Marcus and everyone else.

Put the word out on the street. I'll tie things down here and meet you in the garage."

"I swear to God, sometimes I think this family is cursed," Birch muttered as he picked up the phone. He closed his eyes, remembering the day Sunrise Mountain burned. His shoulders straightened when he remembered how Metaxas Parish had shown up, along with every able-bodied man from the Strip, to rebuild his mother's beloved mountain. As he spoke into the phone he heard the television announcer's high-pitched words; *lightning strikes*. His insides started to shrivel when he thought of the horses that could be killed or injured if fires broke out.

Ten minutes later he was riding the elevator to the basement level, where his twin brother Sage waited for him, the engine of his Range Rover racing.

"They were talking about lightning strikes, Sage. All I could think of was the day Mom's mountain burned. All those magnificent horses."

Sage nodded grimly as he peeled up the ramp and out to the access road that would take him to the main road and the private airfield where he kept the company's corporate jet.

Nealy stood outside Flyby's stall, rubbing the big horse's head. Emmie stood next to Shufly doing the same thing. They spoke soothingly as they watched the weather through the opening at the end of the breezeway.

"What kind of storm is this, Mom? There's no rain. Just wind and thunder. We never had a storm like this that I can remember."

"Those winds, according to Dover, are close to fifty miles an hour. Small hurricanes usually have winds like that but with rain. I simply don't understand. Just hours ago it felt like it was going to snow and now this."

It was twelve minutes past midnight when mother and daughter saw the first lightning strike. It hit the main barn with such force the ground trembled under their feet. The second strike hit minutes later—the mare barn. The third and fourth strikes followed minutes apart. A tongue of flame licked up from the eaves and quickly set the roof on fire.

Nealy ran through the barn, Emmie on her heels, as they struggled against the driving winds. Holding on to one another they fell repeatedly as they fought their way to the main barn. Crawling forward, Emmie hanging on to her ankle, Nealy reached the barn, where they scrabbled to their feet to get inside and lead the horses to safety. "Call the fire department," someone could be heard shouting. An answering response was that the phone lines were down and Blue Diamond Farms was the last and farthest farm from the firehouse. Off in the black night, hundreds of fires could be seen lighting up the dark sky.

"Get those horses out now!" Nealy screamed as she banged into one of the stalls to lead a frightened horse out to the breezeway. "We have to get them away from the barns. They're frightened, and that makes them dangerous. Be careful."

"Keep filming! Keep filming! Get everything. Shoot as much as you can. Jesus, this is just like Tara burning!" Mitch Cunningham shouted. "Get those horses on film!"

"I told you to get out of my way!" Nealy shouted. "Move those damn cameras and help us! Don't just stand there! Do something!"

"Yes, ma'am! Keep filming but stand back. What can I do, Ms. Clay?"

"Find some goddamn water," Nealy shot back.

"Mom, there's no water to fight the fires," Emmie cried as she, too, led a horse to safety outside the barn.

"We can rebuild barns. We can't breathe life into a dead horse. Move, people! Move!" Nealy shouted as she did her best to drag a balking horse into the swirling wind. "Just get them outside. We'll be able to round them up later."

They worked steadily, hour after hour, as the barns burned around them. Exhausted, soot-blackened, Nealy raced from barn to barn, always keeping her eyes on the main house and the stallion barn where Flyby and Shufly were safe inside their stalls.

She saw them coming, men carrying ropes and gear, but she couldn't tell who they were. Nor did she care. Help was help. She looked up, saw the lightning bolt rip downward, and knew immediately that it was going to hit the stallion barn. She ran then, wings on her feet just as the front end of the barn crashed downward.

Someday when this was all over, she was going to try and figure out how the barn literally split in two. She heard her beloved horses, heard their agonized and frightened cries, or were they her own? Her arms up to shield her face, she ran inside, through the flames, calling out to the horses. She reached Flyby first, opened the stall door, reached for his halter, and struggled to pull him toward Shufly's stall. More frightened than his daddy, Shufly balked at being led from the barn. It was then that Nealy realized her clothing was on fire, and her hair was burning. Flames shot upward as she shouted to the horse to follow her. Shufly reared back, pawed at the ground and at the wooden slats, but he did move, racing past her and out into the night. She tried to beat at the smoldering shirt covering her arms and knew it was melting into her flesh. She had to get Flyby outside. Her hands were black and raw with blisters. All she could see were flames around her. There was no way out but through the raging fire. "Down, boy, down. I have to get on your back. Do it, Flyby, do it for me." The horse lowered his head as he bent his front legs for her to slide on his back. "Now *RUN*!" she screamed, with her last ounce of strength.

"Are you getting this? Don't stop! Tragic as this is, it's the stuff movies are made of," Mitch Cunningham shouted at the top of his lungs. "Oh, God, oh, God! It's Ms. Clay. Keep filming. Get everything." He waved to his film crew to indicate they were to keep working. "I have to help out here. You know what to do."

She was aware of swarms of people, strong, cold winds, and a familiar voice. "Nealy! Oh, Jesus God!" Riley Coleman said, his voice catching in his throat. "Cole! Over here! It's Nealy!"

"Is Flyby okay? Did he get burned?" A moan of pain escaped her lips.

"He's okay, Nealy. Just scared. We'll take care of him. We have to get you to a hospital." He watched, his eyes wide with disbelief when the stallion dipped downward so Nealy could be lifted off his back. Satisfied that her beloved horse was safe, Nealy allowed herself to be taken off the horse's back. Her head rolled to the side as she lost consciousness.

"Mom! Mom!" Emmie screamed over and over. She fell to the ground to stare at her unconscious mother, afraid to touch her. She looked up at Riley and Cole. "We have to do something. What? I don't know what to do. Tell me what to do. Please tell me what to do."

"Where's the nearest hospital? What's the name of it?" Riley asked, flipping open his cell phone.

"Twenty miles away. Kentucky General."

"Oh, Mom, I'm so sorry. Hang on, please. We're going to get you to a hospital. Please don't die, Mom. I won't know what to do without you. Please, Mom."

The cell phone snapped shut. "All their ambulances are out on calls. We have to take her there ourselves. Which vehicle is best? Tell us where it is so we can make a bed in the back. Give us directions. We'll take care of your mom."

"Who are you?" Emmie asked, staring up at the soot-blackened face, the voice familiar yet unfamiliar.

"Does it matter?"

"No. No, it doesn't matter." Emmie sobbed.

The family arrived, one by one, and then the others came from far and wide—friends of the family, business associates—to help with the animals and fires.

Everywhere, as far as the eye could see, fires dotted the sky. The air was thick with black, choking smoke. The animals, frightened out of their wits, hugged the fencing in the pasture as they herded together, the grooms and workers doing their best to calm them.

"All we can do is let the barns burn to the ground. Where the hell is the fucking rain?" Metaxas roared. As if in answer to his plea, the skies opened up as the wind kicked up several notches.

"Where's Mom?" Nick yelled to be heard over the crackling flames and howling wind.

Metaxas whirled around to focus on Hatch, who was standing next to Nick. "They took her to the hospital. Emmie and Ruby went with her. I . . . what . . ."

"What?" Hatch thundered.

"She . . . she . . . was badly burned. Riley Coleman and his cousin drove them in to the hospital. There were no available ambulances. That's all I know. She was unconscious, Nick. Go ahead, the two of you go to the hospital. The horses are out, and all we can do is wait and hope this rain douses the fires. If not, they have to burn themselves out. Take a look around," Metaxas said, pointing to all the blazing fires that could be seen off in the distance. "What are you standing here for? Go! We're doing everything that can be done on this end."

Nick wiped a sooty hand over his face. "Metaxas, how bad was Mom burned?"

Metaxas choked on his words. "Real bad, son." He swiped at the tears running down his cheeks.

Hatch stood rooted to the ground. He made no move to follow Nick.

Metaxas shoved him backward. "You stupid, goddamn Indian! Go! Didn't you hear me? There's nothing you can do here. Nealy needs you."

Metaxas sat down on the ground outside the pasture fencing to stare at the devastation in front of him. His gaze swept up and around at all the fires lighting the sky. Behind him he could hear the restless animals. He thought of Nealy and how badly burned she was. He wanted to pray, but he couldn't remember the words he'd learned as a child. His head dropped to his hands. He cried. Great, shoulder-racking sobs that tore at his body. When the words finally came to him, he prayed because there wasn't anything else he could do.

Riley roared up to the front of the emergency entrance to Kentucky General Hospital. He hopped out, the engine still running, to run through the open doors leading to the emergency room, shouting all the way. "I have a burn victim out here. I need help!" He watched, his eyes filling with tears as Nealy was lifted onto a gurney. He saw Cole wipe at his eyes as his arm reached out to pull Emmie close to him. Ruby stood in a trance, her body black from head to toe. Her sobs tore at his heart.

A nurse in a crisp white uniform approached him. "I need to gather some information from you, sir. Will you come with me please?" Cole nodded, his hold on Emmie secure. Ruby trailed alongside, her face a mask of misery.

"I can't tell you much other than her name is Nealy Clay. I don't know anything about her insurance or anything like that. Look, if you need money, I can leave you a check or a deposit. Whatever you want. Her daughter is outside, but she's in no shape to talk about something like this."

"*The* Nealy Diamond Clay from Blue Diamond Farms?" the nurse asked in awe.

Riley nodded. "There's nothing left of the farm now, though," he muttered.

"Wait right here, sir."

Riley leaned back and closed his eyes. He wanted to pound his feet on the floor and shake his fists. It seemed like light-years ago when Nealy Clay had walked into his kitchen and told them she'd paid off the loans on Sunbridge. He thought about her daily from that day on. She'd become his savior. Something he didn't take lightly. She'd literally given him back his and his family's lives. And she'd asked nothing in return except to be left in peace.

The charge nurse ran down the hall to the administrative offices shouting, "Mr. Olmstead, we just admitted Nealy Diamond Clay. You might want to take over here. Miz Clay is burned over half her body."

The pudgy man was off his swivel chair in a heartbeat, his glasses jiggling on his nose as he made his way to the emergency room while the charge nurse returned to the admitting desk and Riley Coleman.

"Miz Clay is in good hands, sir. I suggest you and your party return to the farm and clean up. You might be carrying some infectious germs," she said primly. "We do everything humanly possible to safeguard our patients. For now, we'll waive the paperwork until Miz Clay's daughter can do it. Don't look at me like that, young man. We have an excellent burn center here at Kentucky General. Everything possible is being done for Miz Clay. I can assure you of that."

Riley looked down at his torn and blackened jeans, at his right boot whose toe seemed to be missing. He knew he was black from head to toe, as black as Cole and Emmie looked. He nodded wearily as he started down the long hall that led to the outside emergency door, where Cole, Emmie, and Ruby waited.

"What did they say? How's Mom?" Nick demanded as he hopped out of the car that squealed to a stop next to Emmie's 4-by-4.

"I don't know anything. They took her into the room and left me standing there. The nurse said they have an excellent burn unit." He jerked his head backwards, and said, "That nurse said we had to go home and clean up because we might be carrying germs."

Hatch staggered around the front of the car. "Didn't they tell you *anything*?"

Riley felt the urge to cry all over again. "No. They just rushed her into the room. I think, and this is just my opinion, it's going to be a while before we hear anything. I hate saying this, but she was burned pretty bad. Her shirt . . . her shirt . . . the sleeves, they were burned into the skin on her arms. She was unconscious when we brought her in. I wish I had something better to tell you, but I don't. I'm sorry."

"Her hair was fried right off her head." Emmie sobbed. "All her beautiful hair was gone."

"Did she say anything before she lost consciousness?" Hatch's voice pleaded with Riley to tell him something he wanted to hear.

Riley nodded. "She wanted to know if Flyby was safe. That horse carried her out. I can't even begin to imagine how she got on his back. He ran through the flames with her on his back. Shufly made it out on his own."

Hatch looked down at his filthy clothes. "I'm not going any-where. If I have to, I'll sit out here all night."

"Me, too," Emmie said.

"That goes for me, too," Nick said.

"I'll go back with you," Ruby said. "They might need my help."

"I have a suggestion," Cole said. "We'll go back to the farm and bring clean clothes and you can wash up in the rest rooms. We'll send someone with your things and we'll stay and help at the farm. Is that okay with all of you?" The little group nodded in agreement.

"The farm's gone," Nick muttered, his eyes on the hospital windows. "On the way here we could see the other farms. None of them fared any better than we did. The whole thing was . . . *unholy.* It was like the Devil himself unleashed all his fury in one wild swoop. I am never, ever, going to understand what happened tonight. Never!"

Hatch sat down on an iron bench near the entrance and dropped his head into his hands.

"I hate leaving them here like this," Cole said, getting into the driver's seat of the 4-by-4.

"I do, too, but there isn't a thing either one of us can do. We'll be more help back at the farm, or what's left of it."

"It was like a holocaust," Cole whispered. "I never saw anything like that in my whole life. You at least rode out a tornado, and there was that time your grandfather pitched a fit in the garden, but no way does either one of those things compare to what happened tonight. The sun will be up soon."

"A new day," Riley said, rolling up the window. "The temperature is dropping."

"We have to think about getting some shelter for the horses. Every farm owner in these parts will be hitting the lumber stores as soon as they open. I suggest we call the people you deal with in Texas and have it airlifted here. People were coming in masses as we drove away. I thought I saw Birch and Sage Thornton, so that means they brought people. If we get the lumber, we can have some kind of shelter up by nightfall. What do you say, Riley?"

"I say we go for it. I don't know the first thing about building a barn, though. My talents run to working on the oil rigs and stretching fencing. Do you know anything about building a barn, Cole?" Riley's voice rang with anxiety.

"Nope. I think we're going to learn real fast. It's payback time."

"Do you think she'll make it?"

"I honest to God don't know. Her skin was . . . was *charred.* I don't know how you recover from something like that. I don't know anything about burns, just the way I don't know anything about building barns. I hope she'll be okay. It might take a long time but if she has the best there is, she might stand a fighting chance. Let's just hope for the best and do what we can at the farm to help out."

"Okay."

"She'll be okay," Ruby whispered. "I know she will. If I have to, I'll breathe my life into her. I won't let her die. I won't. Do you hear me? I won't let Nealy die!"

16

"Christmas," the Reverend Babcock said to his parishioners, "is a time of miracles. Let us all bow our heads in prayer that our rebuilding will continue through this holiday season and into the New Year. Let us give thanks to all those who have come to help us in our hour of need. And let us pray for Nealy Clay's full recovery."

Hatch wiped at his eyes with the back of his hand. Out of the corner of his eye he saw Nick put his arm around Emmie's shoulders to comfort her. Gabby sat quietly in Smitty's lap, sucking her thumb.

There was no finery, no flowers, no candles, no religious statues in the tent Metaxas's people had erected for the service. There was, however, a makeshift altar. In a matter of hours after the devastation, the tent had gone up, and now served as an office, a mess tent, and a church. Within minutes, the minister would remove his robes and go on to the next farm, where he would pray with another family. The Blue Diamond tent would once again become a command post.

Hatch couldn't remember a time when he'd been this tired. Just the way everyone else was tired. While the others snatched a few hours' sleep when they could, he went to the hospital to stand his vigil. When darkness fell, the workers, one by one, would trickle to the front of the hospital with lighted candles.

Others had come, too. The news media, the breeders, the jockeys, the mayor, and the governor to light their candles and to say a prayer. Dagmar Doolittle arrived on the third day and lived out of her car, refusing to leave.

According to the local newspapers, the hospital had to request extra volunteers to handle the flood of mail and flowers, all addressed to Nealy Clay. Perhaps the most poignant, the most visible show of emotion came when the president of the United States and the first lady spoke at a televised news conference, where they both bowed their heads and offered a prayer for Nealy's full and complete recovery. After the conference, pictures Dagmar Doolittle's photographer had taken of the president and Nealy appeared on the screen. Following the pictures there were live updates from the hospital administrator, who spoke guardedly of Nealy's condition. Nealy Diamond Clay was news.

A persistent reporter from one of the tabloids asked pointed questions, the kind the administrator dodged from long years of practice. "Nealy Clay is in critical condition," was all he would commit to. When the same persistent reporter demanded to know if Nealy was on the brink of death, Dagmar popped him with a wide swing of the string bag she always wore around her neck like a life preserver. Security was called out, and Dagmar made the front page of the paper.

It was midnight when Hatch settled himself on one of the blue sofas in the lobby of the hospital. In just a minute it would be December 26, the day he was supposed to have married Nealy Clay. His shoulders slumped. Dagmar joined him. She patted his arm.

"Aren't they saying anything, Hatch? Have you spoken to the doctors?"

"Every chance I get. It could go either way. She's unconscious. She has to be in severe pain. Between Metaxas and me we managed to fly in the best of the best. The burn unit is top-notch. They're afraid . . . of . . . pneumonia. I'm afraid, too. I don't know what I'll do if I lose her. We were supposed to get married today. We had such grand plans. Wonderful plans. We were going to grow old together."

Dagmar reached for his hand and squeezed it. "This might be just wishful thinking on my part, but I think she is going to pull out of this. Nealy is a fighter. She has everything in the world to live for, her kids, Gabby, the horses, and you. She loves you with all her heart. You must know that, Hatch."

"Sometimes it simply isn't enough. I loved like that once, and I lost my wife and son. I don't know what to do. I feel so helpless."

"There's a chapel here in the hospital. We could go there and perhaps we can find some solace."

"I've always believed in the white man's God. The missionaries used to come to the reservation and hold Bible classes. I found theology very comforting. I still hold to the old ways in some instances. I don't ever want to give that up. I am what I am. It's sad when you think about it. People tend to pray when there is nothing else to do. Why is prayer always a last resort? I just don't understand, Dagmar. I've tried to live a good life. I try to do good. I don't cheat, I don't lie, I don't steal, and I don't try to put things over on people. I look around at all those people who get away with murder, rape, and child abuse. They walk around free thumbing their noses at the rest of us. Why do children have to die before they have a chance to live? Why does a father have to bury his child? I want answers. I *need* answers."

"If I had the answers, I would give them to you, Hatch, but I don't. Come with me to the chapel. You don't have to pray. We can just sit there. It's very peaceful."

Hatch lumbered to his feet. He looked so whipped, Dagmar wanted to cry for him. "How are things going at the farm?" she asked.

"They managed to raise a barn in one day. The finishing touches will take a while. I think they got the second one up today. There was one barn left standing at the Goldberg place Metaxas bought, but thank God there were no horses in it. The house was destroyed, and three barns. Metaxas was able to take nine of our horses over there. Ruby is taking care of them. I never saw such devastation. The miracle is no one lost any horses. Aside from a few cases of smoke inhalation, and a few minor burns, no one was hurt but Nealy. I don't understand how that can be."

"Maybe you aren't supposed to understand. Maybe none of us is supposed to understand. You aren't supposed to question God. I used to get cracked on my knuckles when I would ask the nuns questions like that. I think that's why I don't go to church much and why I became a reporter. I want answers. Like you, I *need* answers. I hope I get them before I have to leave next week."

It was the day before Valentine's Day when Nealy Clay came out of her drug-induced haze and said her first word. "Aspirin." The private-duty nurse almost jumped out of her skin. She pressed a button to summon the doctor before she made her way to the bed. "In a minute, Ms. Clay. Tell me, do you know where you are?"

Nealy slipped back to the black void she'd lived in so long. Then she saw light and the pasture. She watched from the edge of her black void as Flyby ran, snorting and tossing his head in search of his owner. "I'm here. Over here, Flyby. Come here, baby." And he was there, nuzzling her, pushing her ahead and then sideways. She could feel his touch all over. "No, no, that hurts. Be gentle, baby. I don't have any mints. How could I forget them? I'll buy more. Look, there's Maud and Jess and Hunt. Oh, they came to see you. You act like a gentleman now. I tell them all the time how wonderful you are when I visit in the cemetery. No, no, that hurts. You would never hurt me. Why are you doing that, Flyby? What's wrong? Make him stop, Hunt. Maud, isn't he beautiful? Look, there's Shufly. I won two Crowns for you, Maud. Come closer so I can see you. Jess, did you come to get me?"

"Nealy, can you hear me? I'm Dr. Clancy. Open your eyes, Nealy."

"What did you say, Maud? I can't hear you. People are talking."

"Talk to me, Nealy. Open your eyes. Nurse, close the blinds halfway."

Nealy opened her eyes but could barely focus. "Aspirin," she repeated, coming into the light.

"I'll give you something for the pain in a minute. Do you know where you are, Nealy?"

"No. Yes. In the pasture. Maybe it's the paddock. Everyone is there. Aspirin."

"You're in the hospital. Do you remember the storm and lightning strikes?"

"No. It was green and beautiful. Very peaceful. Aspirin. Please."

She was back in the pasture with Flyby, only this time she was on his back, riding faster than the wind. "Oh, that feels so good. The wind is cold today. I thought I was burning up. You always make things better, Flyby. No one but me knows how much I love you. Where did everyone go?" She called out to Maud, to Jess, and to Hunt. From somewhere in the distance she thought she heard a dog bark. Charlie? No, not Charlie. Who? "I have to sleep, Flyby. I can't ride anymore."

"She's out of the black hole. For now. I'll call the family," Dr. Clancy said. "In the meantime, nurse, keep talking to her. Each time she opens her eyes she'll stay awake a few seconds longer. Don't stop talking. She can hear you. I know she can. Sooner or later she's going to join the world."

"And then, Doctor . . . ?"

"Then it's going to depend on Nealy Clay."

Smitty took the call in the kitchen, one hand on the coffeepot and the other on the phone. She dropped both and ran as fast as she could toward the new barn. "Nealy's awake. She talked. The doctor just called. Tell everyone!"

They came from everywhere to ply her with questions. "That's all Dr. Clancy said. She opened her eyes and asked for aspirin. She's awake. God, isn't it wonderful?"

Emmie ran to Smitty and hugged her. Ruby started to cry. Metaxas wiped his eyes on his shirtsleeve. Hatch dropped his hammer and ran to his car. The others followed.

Three weeks passed before Nealy was able to join the world. She woke, aware of her pain, and knew instantly where she was and what had happened. She called out, her voice weak and rusty-sounding. "How long have I been here?"

"You were brought in a few days before Christmas. It's the first week in March. Friday to be exact."

"Wedding." Tears burned her eyes.

"Your fiancé has been here every day since you were brought in. Your family, too. One of the nurses in the admitting office kept a record of all the people who stopped by to inquire about you. Tons of flowers came and sacks and sacks of cards. We had to add extra volunteers to help out. We even have a video of the president and the first lady saying a prayer for you at one of his news conferences. Here's your doctor now, Ms. Clay. He can answer any questions you might have. He might even say you can have visitors."

Nealy struggled to find her voice. Her tongue was thick in her mouth. She longed for an ice-cold glass of chocolate milk. Her memory returned in little puffs of vapor, or so it seemed. If it was March and the fire was before Christmas, that had to mean she was in serious condition. She struggled with her thoughts and the pain.

"Mirror," Nealy said.

The doctor's response was curt and sharp. "NO!"

"Yes." Nealy could feel her toes curl in anger at the doctor's strong verbal response. It had to mean something if he wouldn't give her a mirror. Was her face burned?

"Not now. Later." Maybe he didn't have a mirror. Her toes uncurled.

"Home?" The single word was a question.

The doctor shook his head. "Not for a while. Soon, though. Would you like to see your family? They can visit through the glass."

"Mirror." Hatch. Hatch could see her through the glass. Emmie and Nick, too.

The doctor shook his head a second time. "No."

"No visitors," Nealy said. Her eyes continued to burn. "Drink."

The nurse spooned ice chips into her mouth. Nealy savored each one. "More."

"Are you saying you don't want any visitors?"

"No visitors. Mirror." She turned her head and felt the bandage on the side of her face scrape the pillow. She moved her head again and again. She wanted to touch her face, her hair, but she couldn't find her hands. "Hair."

"Your hair is growing back. The burns on your head have begun to heal," the doctor said. "The bandages on your face will come off soon."

Nealy screamed and screamed. And then she was back in her black hole, where it was safe and warm.

The nurse turned away so the doctor wouldn't see how her eyes filled with tears. She mumbled an apology. The doctor nodded.

The days passed slowly after that, one after the other. Each time Nealy woke, she appeared stronger, more talkative. She'd left her black hole for good and would, according to the doctor, mend. He cautioned the road would be long and painful.

Nealy accepted it all because she had no other choice. She was adamant about not having visitors. She did agree to speak to her family and to Hatch on the phone. Two-minute calls left her exhausted.

It was the beginning of Derby week when the bandages finally came off and Nealy was given a mirror. The scream she wanted to let loose on the world died in her throat. All she could do was stare at the hideous creature she'd turned into. She didn't cry. She didn't say anything. Her silence alarmed the team of doctors standing by.

It took every ounce of courage in her body not to black out. She was so dizzy, so frightened at what she'd seen in the mirror that she closed her eyes and shoved the mirror away. "I want to go back to my room." The head doctor nodded to the nurse.

"Close the door when you leave," Nealy said quietly, as the nurse settled her in the high hospital bed.

The moment the door closed, Nealy leaned back into the nest of pillows the nurse had created for her. She closed her eyes and longed for the blackness she had slipped into during the past months. How could this have happened to her? How? Just when she'd finally found happiness. Hatch wouldn't want her now. Gabby would be afraid of her. Emmie and Smitty would look at her with pity in their eyes. Nick would hug her and say it didn't matter. Ruby would cry for her and Metaxas would wring his hands and call everyone in the world to come and help her. Could she handle all that? No. The horses would accept her. The workers would pretend not to stare. A superstitious lot, eventually they would say she spooked the farm. They'd talk among themselves, to other men working other farms, and she would be the topic of everyone's gossip.

Under those circumstances, life simply wasn't worth living.

She didn't hear the door open. Didn't hear the footsteps until she sensed their presence. Instinctively her arms went up to shield her face. "How . . . how did you get in here?" she demanded.

"We just walked in. No one stopped us," Riley Coleman said. He reached up to take her hand away from her face. To his credit he didn't blink; nor did Cole Tanner.

She did cry then. "You should have left me to die. Anything would be better than this."

"No, Nealy, no. Life is always worth living. It's how you live it that matters. Your family doesn't understand. Hatch doesn't understand. They want to come and see you. Give them a chance, Nealy."

"That's very easy for you to say. You aren't the one who . . . who . . . looks like a Halloween monster. I guess I should thank you for all you did." Bitterness rang in her voice.

"Thanks aren't important to us, Nealy. We came to say good-bye. When you go home, I think you'll find it looks pretty much the same. All the horses are safe. You have new barns. The farm is running well. We were glad to help. If you ever need us, call. We are family. You taught us a lesson we'll never forget. What are you going to do, Nealy? Is there anything we can do for you before we leave?"

"I was trying to figure that out when you came in. Today was the first . . . they wouldn't give me a mirror. I didn't know . . . I wasn't prepared . . ." A sob caught in her throat. "I don't want to live like this. I really don't."

"Plastic surgery and a lot of grit and spunk on your part will go a long way, Nealy," Cole Tanner said. "There is a very special man I know who lives in Thailand. He's said to be the best plastic surgeon in the world. In the *world*, Nealy. He specializes in reconstructive surgery and even takes on the most hopeless cases. I'm not saying your case is hopeless, I'm just saying he might be able to help you. It's possible he won't be able to. You would have to understand that going in. Do you want me to arrange a consultation for you? I'm sure he would come here. He travels all over the world. I want you to think about it. I'll leave my card on the night table. Call me any time of the day or night. By the way, the doctor's name is Sinjin Vinh. You might want to mention it to the doctors here to see what they have to say. Don't give up, Nealy. Don't ever give up. My grandmother Billie fought to the last ditch. My mother

Maggie and Sawyer said you were just like her. To be like her would be the greatest compliment in the world," Cole said.

"Thanks . . . thanks for . . . helping me. Emmie told me all you did. We're even now."

Riley spun around and walked back to the bed. "No. We'll never be even. We'll owe you until the day we die."

Out in the hall on the way to the elevator, Riley asked, "What was all that shit you were saying back there in the room, Cole? Who is that doctor you were talking about? Jesus God, did you see her face. How can that be fixed? I'll fucking well kick your ass all the way to Japan if you were just mouthing words."

"I wasn't just mouthing words. I'm not going to wait for Nealy to call me. I'm going to call Sinjin myself. Well, that's not true. I'm going to call Sumi to call him. She's the one who introduced me to him and became good friends with his wife Maline. Sumi does volunteer work at the hospital three days a week. That's how we met him. Do I know if he can help her? No, I don't know that. It's worth a try, isn't it?"

"Anything is worth a try if she's willing to go along with it. I'm thinking in terms of years, Cole. Skin grafts. Surgeries. Healing time. We're looking at years. If what you say is true, let's get this show on the road."

"And just where do you think you're going?" a belligerent nurse asked. "Did you just come out of Ms. Clay's room?"

"Who? Us? Who is Ms. Clay? We're lost," Cole said, stepping into the elevator.

Nealy spent the rest of the afternoon agonizing. While she had spoken to her children and Hatch on the phone these past months, she had held firm to the no-visitor rule. Now it was time for a visit. She clenched her teeth at the thought. She knew there was no way to predict their reaction other than to say they would be horrified. Hatch. She couldn't even begin to comprehend how he would look or what he would say. In the end, it wouldn't matter. What mattered was what she had to say and how she said it.

She closed her eyes and hoped that Hunt would enter her dreams and tell her what to do. It didn't happen because she couldn't fall asleep. When the burn specialist and a well-known plastic surgeon checked on her a few hours later she was staring at the card Cole Tanner had left for her.

They talked around her the way all consulting doctors do as they poked and probed and stared at her scars through thick magnifying glasses hooked around their heads. How blank and stoic their faces were.

Nealy waited until they finished making their notes on her chart before she asked, "Do either of you know a Dr. Sinjin Vinh?"

"No," the burn specialist said quietly.

"I don't know him personally, but I've heard of him," the plastic surgeon said. "The best in the field. Why do you ask, Nealy?"

"Do you think he could help me?"

"I don't know, Nealy. I've heard he is so much in demand he only picks and chooses the worst cases. The hopeless ones, I'm told. I don't consider you hopeless. I'm told he is scheduled years in advance. If there is a way to schedule a consultation, I'd be all for it."

Nealy handed the doctor Cole's card. "Send all my medical records to him along with all those pictures you've taken of me to my . . . my nephew. He'll know what to do. When will I be able to travel, and when can I go home?"

"Nealy," the doctor said gently, "we told you that you could go home two weeks ago. You refused. You said you weren't ready, and since you donated so handsomely to this burn unit, we had no other recourse but to let you stay." The chuckle in his voice did not go unnoticed by Nealy.

"How long before I'm able to travel? In an airplane? Or on a ship?"

The two doctors looked at one another. The plastic surgeon spoke. "At least another month. I'd recommend a ship as opposed to an airplane flight."

"Thank you. I'm going to go to sleep now. I'm having visitors this evening. I'll go home tomorrow."

"In that case I'll get started on your paperwork. I assume you want your records sent by overnight mail," the burn specialist said.

"That would be helpful. Thank you."

The two doctors walked down the hallway. "She's too brittle.

Too in control. She sees a ray of hope, and that's what she's holding on to. I'd feel a lot better if she had shrieked and wigged out when she looked in the mirror." The plastic surgeon nodded in agreement.

"I wish she had okayed the counseling we wanted to put in place. She's a very strong, stubborn woman. What amazes me the most is she never cried, she never complained. Not once. What's even more amazing is that she held firm to her no-visitor rule. I try not to get involved, but it's damn near impossible with a case like this," the burn specialist said. "I better get started on her paperwork. I'm assuming you're going to want to add your input. The last pickup for overnight mail is seven o'clock. You better hit the computer."

The plastic surgeon nodded as he headed for the doctors' lounge for a cup of coffee. "I'll have it to you by seven."

"Good."

In her room, Nealy picked up the phone and called the house. "Smitty, it's Nealy. If you all want to come to the hospital tonight, come along. I'll be coming home tomorrow. Will you tell the housekeeper to get my room ready. Smitty . . . I have to . . . tell you something. First things first. Don't let Emmie bring Gabby to the hospital. I don't want her to get frightened, and she will if she sees the way I look. It's bad, Smitty. Really bad. Today was the first . . . they . . . they . . . what they did was . . . they gave me a mirror. I wanted to die right there. All I could think about was how I could kill myself. I'm going to be scarred for the rest of my life. They talk a lot about skin grafts, plastic surgeries. Years of operations, Smitty. Years. I don't think I can do that. My worst nightmare now is letting Hatch see me. I was wondering if you would . . ."

"No, Nealy. I am not going to say a word to that man. You aren't going to recognize him. I think he's lost fifty pounds. He's drawn and haggard. He doesn't eat or sleep. He lives for those five-minute phone calls you make to him. I know what you're thinking, and I know what you plan on doing. I know you better than you know yourself. He loves you. It isn't going to make a difference. It didn't make a difference with Metaxas and Ruby. What makes you think it will be any different with Hatch?"

"It's my face, Smitty. My face is pulled to the side, my eye droops. My jaw is slack. I look crooked. The scar tissue is welted and ugly. I have bald patches on my head where my hair hasn't grown back in. What I'm trying to tell you is, I'm past ugly. Now do you understand? I don't care about the rest of the scars down my arms and side. I can always cover them up. It's my face for God's sake." Nealy sobbed. "It's my face, Smitty."

"Hang up, Nealy. I'm coming to the hospital right now. Don't even think about telling me no. I told you to hang up, Nealy."

"Okay, Smitty. I'll hang up now."

Nealy replaced the phone on the night table. All she had to do was wait for Smitty. Smitty was so much like Ruby. They both always said the right thing at the right time. The only problem was this time there were no right words, no perfect timing. She could feel her insides start to shrivel. Don't think about Hatch. Hatch is lost to you. Forever lost the way Hunt is lost to you. Think about Rhy and Pyne. Think about Riley and Cole and all the others who came to rebuild the farm. Did she thank them? She couldn't remember. She had so many people to thank for taking care of her horses and rebuilding her barns. The first thing she was going to do when she got home was to call each and every person to thank them personally.

She stared out the window. The day was almost over, the last of the afternoon sunshine fading to shadows. Her thoughts turned back to Hatch. How noble and gallant would he be? Would he be able to hide his revulsion? Probably. He was, after all, a lawyer, and lawyers were experts at not showing emotion. She closed her eyes and thought about Hunt and their life together.

Nealy's eyes snapped open when she heard loud voices in the hall, one of which was Smitty's. "I'm telling you, Miss Nurse, she asked me to come here. Go ahead, ask her yourself. I'll just wait out here while you're doing that," Smitty bristled.

"Yes, I did ask her to come. It's all right to let her in," Nealy said when the nurse poked her head in the doorway.

To her credit, Smitty didn't flinch. Her eyes did fill, though. A moment later she wrapped Nealy in her arms. "My God, girl, how much do you weigh? Seventy-five pounds would be my guess."

"Smitty . . ."

"Yeah, Nealy."

"Your best guess. What will Hatch do?"

"He'll probably want to blubber like I do, but he won't. He'll wish it was him instead of you. He loves you, Nealy. You need to give him a chance. How do you want to do this? I'm not going to be coming back this evening because I will have to watch Gabby. Do you want Hatch to come alone and be first or do you want him to come last? Emmie, Metaxas, and Ruby can come together. I say let Hatch come last after they leave. You two will need some private time, and since you're in a private room, he can stay as long as you want him to stay."

"Okay, last. Take a good look, Smitty, and tell me what you think."

"It's pretty bad, Nealy. I understand how you feel. We don't love people because of the way they look. Well, maybe some people do, but not our kind of people. I'm sure surgery can take away some of the scarring. They have this medical makeup for burn and scar patients that is supposed to be pretty good. You have good doctors. They'll do what's best for you. Whatever is left over you'll have to suck up. It's called life, Nealy. You play the cards you're dealt."

"It's so strange, Smitty. Earlier I was thinking about how my life parallels Maud's in so many ways. The last years of her life she was in constant pain. She drank much too much but it was the only thing that helped ease that terrible pain she lived with. Jess was such a wonderful man. He doted on her. Waited on her hand and foot. When she died, he wanted to die with her. She always said he was her white knight. I don't see Hatch doing that for me. I just don't."

"Well, I think you're wrong."

Nealy told her about the doctor in Thailand. "I'm going to look into it. If he can help me, I'll do it. There. Here. I don't care. Otherwise, Smitty, I don't want to live like this."

"That's pretty goddamn selfish, Nealy," Smitty blustered. "You were never one to think about yourself. Hell, most of the time you looked like shit. Did you care? No, you did not. Jeans, shirt, boots, no makeup, a haircut that looked like it was done with a lawn mower. That was you. All of a sudden you care? Hellooooo!"

"Shut up, Smitty! I'm sorry I let you come here."

"I'm sorry I came, too. So there, Nealy Clay."

"Oh, Smitty, I'm sorry, I didn't mean that."

"I know you didn't. I didn't either," Smitty said as she gathered a sobbing Nealy into her arms. "It's not the end of the world, Nealy. You're alive. The horses miss you, especially Flyby. No one can do anything with him. Shufly is pretty cranky, too. All the noise, the barn building, all the people, and then your absence. Life is going to go on, Nealy. Choose to be a part of it. For all of us."

"You've been such a good friend to me all these years, Smitty."

"And you've been a good friend to me. You need to call Nick. He had to get back to work and said to call him when you were ready for visitors."

"I will, Smitty. I promise."

"I have to get back to the farm. Nealy, it looks wonderful. You'd never know anything happened. All the burned grass was taken up and sod put down. The barns sparkle. It just looks wonderful. Make it a happy homecoming, kiddo."

"Thanks for coming, Smitty. Give Gabby a hug for me."

"I will not. You can do that yourself when you get home tomorrow."

"I'll scare her out of her wits. She's just a baby."

"It'll never happen," Smitty said over her shoulder.

She didn't cry until she was in her car. She had to warn them. Especially Hatch.

Nealy sat up in bed, the lamp turned low at her side. She made no move to hide her face when Emmie and the others walked into the room. "It's okay to cry," she said. "I'd join you, but I'm all cried out. Just do me a favor and don't try to cheer me up. Don't tell me I'm alive, and it doesn't matter. It does matter. Now, come here, all of you and give me a big hug. I missed you. Talk to me about the farm, about the horses and the front porch."

They babbled. They even found themselves laughing. "I'm getting kind of tired now," Nealy said an hour later. "I still have to visit with Hatch. I'll be home tomorrow, and we can talk more then. I'm looking forward to sitting on the front porch."

They hugged her, their eyes wet, their bodies trembling. And then they left quietly because it was what she wanted.

Nealy steeled herself for what was coming next. She wished she had the courage to turn off the lamp. *Fool,* her mind shrieked. *Just do it and get it over with.* The knock, while soft, sounded like thunder to Nealy's ears. She struggled to take a deep breath. "Come in," she called.

He stared at her from the foot of the bed.

"You need to say something, Hatch," Nealy said.

"I know, but I don't know the words. I think you're expecting me to say one thing while I want to say something else. I'm trying to find the words. I guess you being a woman, you want to know if you look ugly. I really don't know what ugly is, Nealy. To me, everyone is beautiful. I know what an ugly heart is. I know what an ugly attitude is, but I don't look at someone and think they're ugly or they're this or they're that. I'm probably not saying this right. I think I'm trying to tell you it doesn't matter."

"It matters, Hatch. I can't . . . I won't . . . I'm not me anymore. I don't know if I can ever be me again. Maybe I can try. I want to try. I don't want you to be noble and feel like you have to marry me. We had our time in the sun. I will always be grateful for that time, for your love, for all you did for my children. Make no mistake, I love you with all my heart, but I will not saddle you with me in this condition no matter what you say or how you say it."

"Nealy . . ."

"No, Hatch. If you love me, you'll let me go."

"How can I do that? You became a part of my life. We said we were going to grow old together. We promised to love each other forever and ever. I can't let that go. Don't ask me to do that, Nealy. Please don't."

"You have to, Hatch. I have nothing left to give you. I'm drained, physically and mentally. I have long years of operations ahead of me. Long years of pain and anger. I can't foist that on you. I won't do that to you. Now, what I want you to do is turn around and leave. I want you to . . . I want you to go back to Santa Fe. I don't want you to wait for me. I want you to . . . to . . . do . . . whatever you have to do to . . . to get past this. I don't want to cry because tears are salty. It's not good for me. Just say good-bye and . . . leave. No, no, no, don't come any closer. Please, Hatch, don't make this harder on me. Please go. Go! If you don't go, I'll . . . I'll call the nurse. Just tell me good-bye."

"No. I don't like good-byes."

"Damn you, say good-bye."

"No!" Hatch roared as he yanked open the door.

"I hate you," Nealy roared in return.

"Well, I love you, Nealy Clay," Hatch said, storming out of the room.

"Liar! No one could love me looking like this."

When there was no response to her outburst, Nealy buried her head in the pillow and wept.

17

Nealy could feel her insides start to shake as she made her way down the steps. She wished she hadn't agreed to the family visit. Somehow or other, Smitty, Ruby, and Emmie had convinced her to agree to a family meeting. Fanny Thornton representing the Thornton family, and Maggie Coleman Tanaka, representing the Colemans, were coming to visit. Her brothers were coming, too.

She wished there was someplace where she could hide so no one would ever find her. Such a silly thought. She looked around at the leaves on the trees that were slowly starting to turn. A new season would appear shortly, and then it would get cold. She wasn't looking forward to winter any more than she looked forward to anything else these days.

Would they stare at her? Of course they would. She would just have to grit her teeth, straighten her shoulders, and hope for the best.

She sat down on the top step and wrapped her arms around her knees. The sun was just about to creep over the horizon. Another new day. She waited.

Rhy and Pyne were the first to arrive. She bolted from the steps to throw herself into their arms the moment they got out of the car. She could feel them both trembling. *This is harder on them than it is on me,* she thought. "Don't be afraid to look at me," she whispered.

"Nealy, Nealy why wouldn't you let us come sooner? You preach all this stuff about family and then when it's time for family stuff you run away and hide. We started out twice to come here and both times we turned around and went back home because we knew you didn't want us here. We respected your wishes. We only wanted to help."

"I wasn't ready, Rhy. I'm not ready now, either. But I knew it wasn't fair to you and I know you want to help. Unfortunately, there's nothing anyone can do. I no longer believe in miracles. Come up on the porch. I like having coffee out here early in the morning."

"Coffee sounds good, Nealy," Pyne said, linking his arm with hers.

Nealy turned around suddenly, and said, "Take a good look. What do you think?"

They didn't gasp, they didn't shrink from her, and they didn't say anything. Their eyes did fill up, though. They reached for her and hugged her tight.

"Sit down, and I'll have Matilda bring us some coffee. Would you like some sweet rolls or maybe some toast?"

"Coffee's fine, Nealy," Rhy said.

The minute the screen door closed behind Nealy, Pyne was off his chair, his closed fist smashing into one of the white columns on the porch. His back arched and his head jolted backward with the pain ricocheting up his arm.

"We should have come sooner even though she said she didn't want us here. Who was here for her besides Emmie?" Rhy asked.

"Smitty and Ruby. I'm sure Nick traveled back and forth. Women are better at this kind of thing. I want to say something to her, but I don't know what I should say. 'Hey, maybe someday they can fix your face.' I don't think so. I guess the best thing to do is pretend you don't see it and that isn't exactly right or fair either."

"You boys talking about me?" Nealy asked, slamming the screen door behind her.

"Yeah. We were saying we don't know how to act. We don't know what to say. We wanted to come here many times, Nealy, but you said no. We talked it over and decided to respect your wishes. Why did you relent? What can we do for you?"

"Just be my brothers. No one wanted to be around me when I first came home. All I wanted to do was hide and stay in the dark. Life goes on, I know that. I'm doing the best I can under the circumstances. I'm glad you came."

"We're glad, too. Is there anything we can do?"

"No, not really. We can take a stroll down Memory Lane. Now with all this time on my hands, I'm going to really get going on trying to find the rest of Mama's family. I let all that slide because . . . life got in the way. How are those violets doing that we planted on Mama's grave?"

"Nealy, you wouldn't believe how they multiplied. It's like a blue carpet. We keep them trimmed back and when it's dry we take turns watering. That was a good idea you had. The big picture you had blown up is hanging over the mantel. It would be nice if you could come up to the farm to see it."

"Maybe in the spring. Fanny and Maggie are coming in this morning. It was so weird the way that happened. I had just called you asking you to come for a visit and then the phone rang and it was Fanny Thornton. Reed is her married name now. Anyway, she said Maggie had called her and said they should come to visit me. She wanted to know if it was all right. I said yes. They're going to be here for a few hours. They mean well."

"Family, Nealy. Family will never turn against you," Pyne said.

"Yes, Pyne, they will. Ours did. I understand the circumstances now."

"You made it right. That's all that matters now," Rhy said. "Oh, I hear a car."

"Guess our family is here," Nealy said, getting up from the rocker. She tucked her shirt into her jeans, jammed her hands in her pockets and waited.

They didn't gasp or shrink from her either. They held out their arms, and it was Nealy who burst into tears. Tactfully, Rhy and Pyne got up and went into the house.

"Shhh, it's all right, Nealy. Sit down, honey, here between Maggie and me. No, no, don't turn away. Please, don't do that. Is there anything we can do, anything at all?"

Nealy shook her head. "I'm sorry. I do this all the time. I don't want to hide, but I don't have much courage. The truth is, I hide out because people have a hard time dealing with what I look like these days."

"People or you, Nealy? Fanny and I don't have a problem. It didn't look like your brothers had a problem. We all wanted to come sooner, but we respected your wishes," Maggie said. "We're family, Nealy."

Nealy dabbed at her eyes. "I just wish there was something you could do." She waved her hands in the air. "It is what it is. I'll try to do better. I want us all to get to know one another better. I want Gabby to get to know her cousins. I just need more time."

"We have all the time in the world. The airplane and the telephone are such marvelous inventions. You pick up the phone and you can talk to someone almost instantly. You can laugh or cry, moan or groan to the person on the other end of the phone," Maggie said. "This is where my husband, wise man that he is, would say, when you get handed lemons, make lemonade. Yes, I know, easier said than done."

"We're all just hours away by plane, Nealy," Fanny said.

Nealy relaxed and leaned back into the softness of the rocker. "Tell me about your families. Tell me things I don't know."

"Go ahead, Maggie, you go first," Fanny said.

"I'll try to give you the short version because we would be here forever with the long version. My grandfather, your father, Seth Coleman, was a ring-tailed son of a bitch! He hated my mother because she delivered two girls before she delivered a boy. That boy, Riley, was killed in the war. Then my father died of leukemia. The old man blamed my mother for both deaths. God alone knows where my sister Susan is. She's a concert pianist and a bit of a free spirit. We don't hear from her for years, then suddenly she pops up. She had a disastrous marriage and a child who died quite young. I don't think she ever got over that.

"I was a deeply troubled teenager and managed to have a baby at the age of fourteen. Mom raised Sawyer. Seth hated her, too. He hated all women. He thought only men were good enough in the business world. He was absolutely ruthless. Then I married and had Cole, got divorced and married Rand Nelson. He died. I moved to Hawaii and married Henry Tanaka.

"My father, Moss, was a womanizer, but he always came back to Mam. When he died of leukemia, Mam grieved, but she hadn't loved him for a long time. Years later, she married Thad Kingsley, my father's best friend. It was such a happy marriage. Thad, even after all these years, still grieves for Mam. He dodders a bit now, but we all look out for him.

"You remember how Josh Coleman drove you out of the house. Well Seth did the same thing to my aunt Amelia. Like I said, he hated women. We've had our highs and our lows, but we managed to stay a family. Fanny's family helped us out many times, and we help her side when we can. Just the way you helped us. That's the short version." Maggie smiled across at Nealy and reached for her hand. "Someday, when you really have nothing to do, I'll fill you in on the nitty-gritty stuff that went on in our family. In telling you this, Nealy, it's to let you know we pull together and weather whatever is thrown at us."

"I guess it's my turn," Fanny Thornton spoke up. "Sallie Coleman was Seth's sister and your aunt. She was a saloon singer and a woman of the evening. A prospector left her, as she put it, his poke, and she ended up being the richest woman in the West. She literally built Las Vegas. She educated herself, married her teacher, and gave birth to two sons. I married both of them. Ash, my first husband, was just like Maggie's father. In fact, Ash knew Moss Coleman, and that's how Maggie and I found each other. I divorced Ash because he couldn't keep his pants on, and then I married his brother, who was a psycho if there ever was one. On his deathbed, Ash killed his brother to protect me from him. If you wrote the story of our lives in a book, no one would believe it.

"Ash and I had four children. Birch and Sage, the twins, Billie, named after Maggie's mother, and Sunny. Sunny has multiple sclerosis. She has two children but because of her health, Sage, my son, is raising them, making sure they know Sunny is their mother. It's a sad but doable situation. Sage and Birch run the casinos and Billie has her own family business.

"I married Marcus Reed, and we live very quietly enjoying our golden years.

"Ruby was my father-in-law's daughter. Born on the wrong side of the blanket so to speak. Ash denounced her when she first made her appearance, but I wouldn't allow that. I love Ruby. Ruby is real and as good as they come. Ash came to find that out, and he finally came around and acknowledged her as his sister. Ruby was so happy that day. She's done so much for all of us. You know the story of Metaxas replanting my mountain. Sage lives there with his wife, Iris, their children, and Sunny's children. The mountain is a wonderful place to raise children. There, now, that's my short version. But as Maggie said, sometime when you really have nothing to do, I'll tell you all the Thornton nitty-gritty stuff of our lives."

Nealy smiled. "Life isn't easy, is it?"

"Sometimes it is damn hard. Mam always said you have to pull up your socks and keep going, no matter what," Maggie said.

"You never give up, Nealy. Someone, somewhere, will be able to help you. I just know it."

Nealy nodded. "Neither one of you had an easy life, right? I can see it in your faces. And yet you weathered it all. How did you do it? I fell apart. I'm still unraveling like a loose strand of yarn."

"Think about the alternative. The here and now is always the best way. When there are people who love you and depend on you, how can you give or do less than your best?"

"Point taken." Nealy smiled. "Would you like a tour of the farm?"

"We would," Maggie said. "Later, I'd like to go for a ride if that's possible."

"We can do that, too. Let me call my brothers and we can check things out."

The call, when it came, was the night before Halloween. Nealy laughed, her voice edged with hysteria. "Do you see the irony, Smitty? Halloween! I need you to help me pack. Cole Tanner is on his way here to pick me up. He's personally going to hand-deliver me to the famous Dr. Vinh."

Smitty stared at Nealy, a mixture of emotions on her face. "You're going to Thailand? I don't believe what I'm hearing. Thailand is on the other side of the world. For how long?" she asked breathlessly.

"For as long as it takes. I have to give it a shot, Smitty. I have to try. Please don't try to talk me out of it."

"I won't, Nealy. I understand. You have to do what you have to do. For some reason I didn't think . . . I thought you would opt to have your operations done here. What about all the paperwork?"

"Cole took care of everything. I'm good to go. We leave tomorrow night. He said he'll grab a few hours' sleep and we'll leave. If . . . if it doesn't work out, I'll be back. Well, either way, I'll be back."

Smitty pulled clothes off hangers willy-nilly. "I think it's warm over there. Maybe it isn't warm. Do they have a winter? Oh, who cares," she mumbled as she shook out garments and folded them haphazardly, only to shake them a second time and refold them. "Are you going to tell Hatch?"

"No. Nick will tell him even if I swear him to secrecy. If I talk to him, I might waver. I can't take the chance of that happening. You must have noticed he doesn't call anymore."

Smitty screwed her face into a grimace. "I noticed. I also notice you stop whatever you're doing every time the phone rings. Admit it, you want him to call."

"That's not true, Smitty. That's over and done with. He gave up pretty damn easy if you want my opinion," Nealy snapped. "So much for undying love."

Smitty sat down on the edge of the bed. "That comment is so unworthy of you, Nealy. He did what you asked of him. I hope he finds someone wonderful who will love him the way you used to. He deserves the best. He's a kind, caring, generous man. You made the biggest mistake of your life sending him away. In your heart you know it. Sometimes I think you do have a black heart. Finish your packing yourself. Packing is not in my job description."

Smitty slammed the bedroom door and marched downstairs.

Maud's rocker beckoned. Nealy's gaze went to the window to see the soft evening shadows that were starting to form. Smitty said she was like a vampire these days, waiting for darkness before venturing out and down to the barns. She'd literally turned her days into nights and her nights into days. The moment full darkness descended, her day began. She worked in the barns, did what she'd always done, but under cover of darkness. Minutes before the sun started to creep over the horizon, she was back in the house and in her room, where she slept the better part of the day. Shortly before dusk, she would go downstairs, eat something, and sit on the front porch, weather permitting.

She watched the last of the late afternoon fade into darkness. Another thirty minutes and it would be time to go down to the barn.

She looked across the room at the phone. She had to call her brothers and Nick. She decided to wait. Maybe she would call them from the barn. Maybe she would ride over to see Ruby and Metaxas and tell them personally. Flyby might like a ride.

She rocked in the rocker, her feet tapping the floor. There was no comfort tonight, no solace. She thought about the hoard of pills she'd stashed in the toe of one of her boots. She had enough to take her into oblivion if the time ever came when she couldn't handle life any longer. The coward's way out. She wondered if she would ever have the guts to take her own life.

Black heart. Smitty had said she had a black heart. Hunt had said the same thing.

It was almost dark now. Almost time to go outside. She watched the minute hand on her watch. Time to see the horses. Time to talk to them, time to touch them. The horses were the only things that made her feel halfway human and gave her a sense of normalcy these days.

Nealy hesitated on the second step from the bottom of the staircase. She watched Smitty as she gathered up her keys, her cigarettes, and her purse. She wanted to say something but couldn't find the right words. She hated it when Smitty found fault with her. If there was one person in the world she truly loved besides her kids and Ruby, it was Smitty.

"I know you're there, Vampire Nealy. I heard you come down the stairs. It must be time for you to suck the life out of the night, eh? Well, go to it, honey. I'll say good-bye now. In case you forgot, I won't be here tomorrow. I'm having my bunion operated on, and I have to stay off my foot for a week. You have a good trip. I'll see you sometime."

"I'm sorry, Smitty. I know I say that a lot these days. You're right, I did forget about your bunion. I'm sorry about that, too. My head is so full of myself, there doesn't seem to be room for anything else. Maybe someday . . ." Her voice trailed off. She held out her arms, expecting Smitty to come to her. She didn't. Nealy's arms dropped to her sides.

"Not this time, kiddo. And by the way, I flushed all those pills you stockpiled in the toe of your boot right down the john."

Nealy blinked. "Damn you, Smitty!" There was no answering laugh, no good-bye. She heard the sound of the car engine, saw the headlights arc on the kitchen window, heard the car drive off.

Nealy turned around and ran up the steps and down the hall to her room. She rummaged in the back of her closet until she found her old boots. She upended them and shook them sideways. Nothing fell on the carpet. She sat back on her haunches. Instead of feeling anger she felt only a sense of relief that Smitty had been friend enough, wise enough to take matters into her own hands.

Nealy crouched in the corner of the closet and hugged her knees. Why was everyone so smart and she so stupid? Why?

"*Because you do stupid things, Nealy. You're too stubborn for your own good. You react to the moment. You don't think things through. It's always been your way or the highway.*"

"Ah, now you show up. Where were you when I needed you? Just answer me that, Hunt. On second thought, don't bother. Get out of my dream. I'm pretty damn sick and tired of everyone telling me what to do, what's best for me. I don't need or want your input. I mean it, Hunt."

"*You are one miserable excuse for a human being, Nealy Clay. I'm sorry you still carry my name. For the last six months you have shunned everyone who only wanted to love and help you. You don't even let your own grandchild come near you. You know what that makes you in my eyes, Nealy? A loser. A coward.*"

"Shut up, Hunt. You aren't walking in my shoes. You don't know the first thing about me or how I feel."

"*You're right about one thing, Nealy. I don't walk in any shoes. I'd give anything to be ALIVE and walking around in a pair of shoes. I wouldn't care if I was as ugly as a mud fence. Life is for the living. When it's gone, it's gone. You think about that. For a while I thought there was hope for you. So you won two Triple Crowns. Big whoop. What's that gonna get you, Nealy? The things that really matter, the things that held hope for you, you've managed to destroy. I'll never forgive you for what you did to Hatch. I'm not going to forgive you for ignoring that beautiful little granddaughter of yours either. By God, you do have a black heart. And now you drove Smitty away. Who's next, Emmie? Ooops, you already did that once. You don't do repeat performances. That must mean Ruby and Metaxas are next. Well, go to it, Nealy. Then when that fancy doctor fixes you all up, you'll come back and expect to pick up the pieces only there won't be anyone here and there won't be any pieces for you to pick up."*

"Go away. I'm too tired to fight with you. You shouldn't have come back. Leave me alone. Another thing, Hunt. Where were you when I needed you? When I first got to the hospital. I needed help. You weren't there for me."

"I was there, Nealy, but you were in the black hole. We were all there: Maud, Jess, and surely you heard Charlie barking. We were waiting. You should be thanking me that we didn't reach out for you. Thanks, Nealy. Not recriminations, not harsh words, not bitterness. What you did to Hatch was unforgivable. That's your M.O. Nealy first and the hell with the other guy. Now get off your ass and make it right."

When Nealy woke, the moon was riding high in the sky. The room was dark with only silvery moonlight winking through the slats of the plantation shutters. She strained to see the digital numbers on the small onyx clock on her nightstand: 10:35.

She was stiff and sore from sleeping in such a cramped position. Hobbling, bent over, until she could straighten up, Nealy made her way to the bathroom. She avoided looking in the mirror the way she always did. She brushed her teeth and wondered why she was doing it. Probably so she wouldn't have to think about the horrible dream she'd just had.

In the kitchen, Nealy reached for her jacket. Outside in the brisk autumn air, she took great, deep breaths. As she headed for the barn she remembered that she wanted to ride over to see Ruby and Metaxas, but it was too late now. She'd peeked in on Emmie and Gabby, and they, too, were sound asleep. Her announcement would have to wait until morning.

It was an hour before dawn when Nealy looked around the barn for the last time. Tears welled in her eyes. When would she be back? She hugged Flyby, whispered in his ear before she ran as if the hounds of Hell were on her heels. She flew into the house and up the stairs to her room, fell into the rocking chair, and sobbed. Hours later, when there were no more tears left, Nealy picked up the phone. She dialed Hatch's number from memory.

The phone rang and rang before the voice mail responded. She blinked at Hatch's flat emotionless recorded message. "I'm sorry I'm not here to take your call. If this is an emergency, call the office. If this is a personal call, leave a message and I'll get back to you in a year or so. I'm off to see the world and to try to recapture my soul. Don't try to figure it out, it's an old Indian thing. Thanks for calling."

Nealy leaned back in the rocker. *What did you expect?* she asked herself. *He did what you told him to do, he's getting on with his life. You blew it. You are so stupid, Nealy Clay. You cut your losses. You burned your bridges. You certainly are an expert at screwing things up.*

She reached for the phone again and dialed Nick's number. He picked up on the first ring.

"You got me just as I was leaving, Mom. What's up?" She told him. "I guess that's good, Mom. I'm trying to understand you going halfway around the world to have all that surgery. Are you sure you're doing the right thing? I hope it all works out the way you want it to. If you need me or if there's anything I can do, let me know."

"I will, Nick." She didn't want to ask but she did. "How is Hatch, Nick?"

"I don't know, Mom. He packed up and left in July. I asked him when he would be back, and he said a couple of years. The partners said he meant it. You broke his heart and his spirit, Mom. I'm not blaming you. I'm just telling you the way it is."

"Why didn't you tell me before?"

"Why? Because you told me not to mention his name to you ever again. You said that part of your life was over. Are you telling me now you changed your mind?"

"Yes. No. I don't know. If he should happen to call, tell him I called to say good-bye."

"You already said good-bye once. Are you trying to torture the guy, Mom? He won't call in. The partners said if he said he wasn't calling, then he wouldn't call. They know him better than I do, so I have to believe them. Listen, I gotta run, Mom. I have to be in court early. Call me when you're settled in over there and let me know how it's all going."

Nealy leaned back against the headrest of the old rocker. "All right, Nick. I love you."

"Love you too, Mom. Bye."

Nealy sighed, her face a mask of misery.

Nealy's good-byes were heart-wrenching and tearful. She kept hoping, right up to the last minute, that Smitty would somehow appear as if by magic. Smitty was a woman of convictions. "Tell Smitty I said good-bye. Tell her . . . tell her . . . she's right about everything."

"I'll tell her, Mom," Emmie said, giving her one last hug.

She didn't look back. It was too painful.

Thirty-six hours later, Nealy walked into Sinjin Vinh's private hospital, Cole Tanner at her side.

"I'm leaving you in good hands, Nealy. Call me if there's anything I can do. When it's time for you to leave, I'll personally fly you home."

"You're leaving?" Nealy asked in surprise. "But . . . I . . ."

"Don't be afraid, Nealy. There's nothing more I can do here. I have to get back to my family. Nose to the grindstone and all that."

"I don't know how to thank you, Cole."

"I'm just glad I could help. It's all up to you now. I ask only one thing of you, Nealy. Don't give up. They do things a lot differently over here, so don't be surprised at anything. Just accept it. They're very Eastern in all things. Take care."

He was gone, and she was whisked away for her first meeting with the illustrious Dr. Sinjin Vinh.

The moment the amenities were over, the doctor said, "Now it's time to get down to work. I had a case like yours once, many years ago. I made her whole again, but it was a very painful, long, hard road. She grew to hate me toward the end, but she didn't give up. There were so many operations even I lost count. Each one more painful than the one before. I imagine, you, too, will come to hate me. If you feel you aren't up to it, tell me now. I have many people waiting for me who need my help. For the time being, I am having all my patients brought here just so I can work on you. I don't want you to let me down halfway through because you are in pain. Are you up to it, Ms. Clay?"

She didn't stop to think. "Yes."

"Good. Then let's get started. Maline will take you to your room. Based on the information Mr. Tanner supplied us with, we tried—or I should say, Maline tried—to do everything she could to decorate your room so you wouldn't be homesick. I hope you approve."

"I love it when Americans come here," Maline said happily. "I did my nurse's training in the United States. I adore American slang and all the fast food. At home I wear blue jeans and sneakers. My husband does not approve. Oh, well, that's what makes the world go around. So, tell me, do you like this room?"

Nealy looked around in awe. A rocker just like Maud's sat in the corner. The draperies and the bedspread were the same as the ones back in her room in Kentucky. But it was the pictures on the wall that stunned her. Pictures of her sitting on Flyby and Shufly, pictures of her, including the one of her covered in mud crossing the finish line dotted the walls. Photographs of Emmie, Nick, Gabby, and Smitty marched across the dresser. On the night table a picture of Ruby and Metaxas with their arms around her brothers. She blinked at the small oval-framed picture of her and Hatch in Hawaii.

Nealy turned to the small, fragile-looking nurse. "You did all this for me."

"But of course. It was no trouble. It is part of your recovery. We want you to feel at home. You will spend many agonizing hours here. We wanted you to be surrounded by familiar things from your home. I'm so pleased that you like it. Your room opens into a small garden. There are benches outside, and in the morning and in the evening as well, the birds will sing to you. You may cut the flowers if you like. You can unpack later, Ms. Clay. Now you must change and meet Doctor Vinh in his examining room. A nurse will come to fetch you. Take all the time you need. We are very patient here. Ah, I see by your eyes you have questions. You may ask me one. The doctor will answer all the rest."

"The other patient, the one who was similar to me. Was . . . did she . . ."

"No, she was not perfect when she left here but she was comfortable with how she looked. She invited my husband and me to her wedding. She was a lovely bride."

"And her scars . . . ?"

"Some were visible, some were not. She used makeup made especially for her."

"And her husband . . . he accepted her without any problems?"

"But of course. He loved her very much. They now have three children. I must get back, and that was three questions, Ms. Clay."

Nealy smiled. "Thank you. And thank you for decorating the room."

"It was my pleasure. I admire you greatly. I must make a confession. I have never seen a flesh-and-blood horse, and you ran all those remarkable races. And you are so tiny, a little person like myself. Amazing."

"They're awesome creatures. Perhaps one day when you have some free time we can sit in the garden and talk."

"I would like that very much, Ms. Clay."

"Call me Nealy."

Maline Vinh knocked softly on the door to Nealy's room. When there was no response, she opened it slightly and called out. When there was still no response, she ventured into the room and called out again. She saw her then, sitting on a rattan chair with deep colorful cushions, in the garden. She drew a deep breath, knowing how much Nealy was suffering.

They'd become good friends during the past year, calling each other by their first names and sharing secrets. On the tray in her hands were two bottles of beer and a fresh package of cigarettes. Maline wasn't sure if it was a treat or a bribe. What she did know was that Nealy welcomed the bottle of beer and the one cigarette allowed her.

Maline walked into the garden. She picked a colorful scarlet bloom and placed it on the tray. "If I had a penny, I would give it to you for your thoughts, Nealy."

"I'll give them to you for free, Maline. I am in such pain even my hair hurts. I can't sleep, and I can't eat. Yes, I am complaining and yes, I hate your damn husband. I can't do this anymore. I want to go home."

"I see."

"Bullshit, you see. You don't see at all. You and Dr. Vinh say the words. That's what they are, words. Words aren't helping me. When I leave here—*if* I ever leave here—I'm going to be either a drug addict or an alcoholic. Maybe both. The worst part is that the drugs and the alcohol don't work. I go to the kitchen at night and sit there drinking beer, one bottle after another. If there was whiskey, I'd drink that, but there isn't any in the refrigerator. I stagger to my room and pray for sleep. Do I sleep? No, I do not. You didn't know about the beer, did you?"

"Yes, Nealy, my husband and I know about the beer. Sinjin is the one who put it there for you. Either I or one of the other nurses were watching you at all times to make sure you made it safely to your room. You do sleep. We do that every evening. Tonight, let us talk about something pleasant, something wonderful."

"And that would be . . . ?" Nealy snapped.

Maline reached into her pocket and withdrew a packet of letters. "Perhaps, if the letters aren't too personal, you could read them to me. I would very much love to hear what your family is doing. I know they must miss you as much as you miss them."

Nealy looked at the neat bundle of letters. Guilt rushed through her. How wonderful and faithful they were, writing once a week and calling when they could get the time straight. She hadn't written, but that was because of the bandages on her hands and fingers. She did talk on the phone, short little talks—I'm well, things are going all right. Short little spurts of conversation.

"I don't allow myself to miss them. This physical pain is all I can endure." As an afterthought she asked, "Who are the letters from?"

Maline looked down at the envelopes in her hand. She knew Nealy's family now and was comfortable talking about them. "There is one from Emmie and Gabby. Gabby's name is on the envelope also. Ruby has written and so has Smitty. Such a name for a lady. There is one also from your son Nick. Are you sure you don't want to read them now?"

"I'm sure. I can't do this anymore, Maline. I want to go home."

"You promised Sinjin you would see it through, Nealy. A promise is a promise."

"I lied. I've had eleven operations in twelve months. I'm scheduled for number twelve tomorrow. I'm looking at another six, possibly more. I'd rather be dead!"

Maline stared off into the distance, the delicate features of her face creased into a frown. "That is such a terrible thing to say, Nealy. You should be thinking of the time when you walk away from here. You should be thinking of the magic in my husband's hands and how far he has brought you. You should not be thinking of death. Shame on you, Nealy Clay."

"What magic? I know only what you tell me. There are no mirrors in this place. No clocks, no telephones. I'm in a goddamn time warp here. Why won't you let me see what those magic fingers have done for me?"

"Because it isn't time for you to see. We have done everything humanly possible to make you whole again. The mind and the spirit must cooperate. You need to let go, Nealy. You need to accept what is. When you do that, it will become easier."

Nealy picked the flower off the tray and held it up to her nose. "It smells wonderful. I couldn't smell anything last week. Oh, it's delicious."

"You see, you have progressed. Your sense of smell has come back. Sinjin will be so happy when I tell him. Shall we drink our beer now, Nealy? What shall we toast tonight?"

"My eyebrows finally growing back. Yes, that's a good thing."

Maline giggled as she uncapped the two bottles of beer. "Yes, I don't think I ever toasted someone's eyebrows before." She held her bottle aloft before clinking it against Nealy's. "I have another surprise for you."

"The only thing that could possibly surprise me is if you tell me Dr. Vinh canceled my surgery tomorrow," Nealy said.

"No, that is not the surprise, but the surprise does involve my husband. Nealy, Sinjin went to great lengths to get this for you. It is the videotapes of all your horse races. It took months for him to accomplish this for you. There is also a videotape from your family. We have not viewed these. There will be no one in the sunroom later, so you can view them in private. Sinjin thought it might take the edge off tomorrow for you. He is a very kind man, Nealy. That is why I love him so much. He does feel your pain, Nealy. My husband is the one who does not sleep at night. He is constantly reviewing your case, studying his notes, staring for hours at your pictures. He has more compassion in his little finger than a hundred people have in their whole body. He does care, and he does feel your pain. I hope you will thank him for going to all the trouble of getting these videos for you."

"I will, Maline. Today is a bad day. They're all bad, but today is worse. We'll talk of this another time. I'm going to walk down to the kitchen for some more beer. No, I don't want the cigarette. I think I finally quit. I should get a prize for that."

"I will see that you get one," Maline quipped. "Come, I will walk with you to the kitchen. Remember, you cannot eat or drink after seven o'clock. The videos are on the VCR in the sunroom. All you have to do is insert them and press PLAY. The machine does the rest." Nealy nodded.

"I'll see you before surgery. I think you will sleep well this evening, my friend."

"I hope so," Nealy said, uncapping the bottle of beer. "I'm going to stay here and drink it, Maline."

Maline waved as she closed the kitchen door. In the hallway, her tiny shoulders slumped. She headed for her husband's office, where he was reviewing the procedure for tomorrow's operation on Nealy.

It was a cheerful kitchen for a small hospital. It was quiet now, everything cleaned up and put away for the morning. Nealy could, if she wanted, make coffee or fix a sandwich. She'd never done that, though.

She liked the little kitchen, liked the butterfly nightlight, the bright red teakettle, and the bowl of fresh flowers on the little table. She thought she could smell peanuts. She sniffed again. The urge to smile was great, but it hurt too much. Perhaps after this next procedure she would be able to smile.

Nealy looked at the bottle of beer in her hand. She didn't really want it. Walking down to the kitchen and getting it was half the enjoyment. She poured it down the drain and set the bottle in the trash container outside the back door.

Nealy walked down the hall to the sunroom, her favorite spot other than the garden in the whole of the private clinic. The furniture was wicker, the tables teak with a high sheen. Fresh flowers were everywhere. Lush green plants filled in the corners. Vibrant watercolors dotted the walls: rainbows, butterflies, fluffy white clouds, and blue skies. All things to make you want to spread your wings and soar. Would she ever have wings to spread? Dr. Vinh said yes.

Once she'd come into this room hoping to see her reflection in the glass of the big-screen television set. She'd wanted to cry when her fingers traced the waffle weave of the protective screen.

Nealy slipped the video marked, "Family" into the VCR. She sat down to watch her self-conscious family talk to her.

"Hi, Mom. I miss you," Emmie said with a catch in her voice. "Everything is fine here. Flyby misses you. At the end of the video there will be some footage of him. Ruby has some of Shufly she's going to put on here. Gabby went trick-or-treating down at the barn today and somehow managed to get a bag full of candy. She wants to say hello."

"Hello, Grandma. This is Gabby, and this is my candy. Look," she said, holding up a paper sack. "It's all full to the top. I was a fairy princess."

"Hello kiddo. I think about you every day. You know I miss you. I'm going to get my other bunion operated on next week. Things are going nicely here at the farm. It's kind of cold today with a light rain. Ruby and Metaxas want to talk to you now. Take care of yourself, Nealy. We all love you."

"I miss you," Ruby said, her eyes full of tears. "I hope it's all going well for you, Nealy. I wish you were here. Things over at the Goldberg farm are good. I keep calling it the Goldberg farm even though it's ours now. We have nine horses. We're all well as you can see. Here's Metaxas."

"Hello, Nealy. I hope you're well. Shufly is doing great. We miss you and can't wait for you to come home. Take care of yourself now, you hear me."

Nealy waited through the static and the grainy tape until Flyby took front and center. She clapped her hands when he snorted and pawed the ground. It was as if he was performing for her. Her eyes filled with tears as she saluted him. She waited again as Shufly made his appearance. He stared straight at her before he tossed his head from side to side and then galloped off.

The next segment was of her two brothers standing side by side, clearly ill at ease and embarrassed. "We miss you," Pyne said gruffly.

"Yeah, we miss you," Rhy said just as gruffly. "Don't be so lazy, and write us a letter. We want to know how you are. We're okay here at the farm. You can call us on the phone if you want to."

Nealy sat forward. The last segment had to be Nick. She sucked in her breath.

"Hi, Mom. Hank Mitchum is videotaping me here in the office that was supposed to be Dad's office. See, Mom, this is his chair. Well, it's mine now. It's taken me a whole year, but I think I fit into it now. I'm real busy, we all doubled up taking over Hatch's work. It's all working out fine. I miss hearing from you, Mom. We still haven't heard anything on Willow. Oh, guess what, the firm got a postcard from Hatch. He was in Bora Bora when he sent it. Said he's brown as a nut and eating berries. He said he hasn't found his soul yet. Well, Hank has to get back to his desk so I'll say good-bye for now. I really miss you, Mom. Call me when you can. I love you."

Nealy leaned her head back into the tufted cushion of the chair she was sitting in.

Bora Bora.
Brown as a nut and eating berries.
He hasn't found his soul yet.

The next six months passed in a blur of pain and heavy seda-
tion. Nealy neither knew when the sun came up nor when it set.
She cried with the pain, with her inability to remain silent. And
then on a glorious morning in April, she woke knowing something
was different. She opened her eyes and for the first time, saw
everything in the room clearly, thanks to the permanent contact
lenses that had been implanted in her eyes. But more than that, she
felt no pain. She moved her head, her arms and legs. Everything
seemed to be working properly. She lay quietly, wondering if she
was dreaming. Her hands went to her face. It felt smooth to her
touch. Her heart leaped in her chest.

Was this the end of the road? Was it all over? Was it time to go
home?

She could hear the birds singing in the garden.

A knock sounded, and then the door opened. A pretty little
nurse with black shiny eyes and a fat pigtail going down her back
said, "Dr. Vinh thought you might like to have your breakfast in
the garden. I will set it up for you, Ms. Clay."

"Yes, thank you. Breakfast in the garden sounds wonderful.
Thank Dr. Vinh for me."

Nealy slipped into her robe before she headed for the bathroom.
She felt a little wobbly, but that was to be expected. She had spent
the better part of the last six months in bed. The miracle was she
was free of pain. Free of pain. Someone should write a song using
those exact same words.

Nealy laughed when she saw the breakfast tray. A bottle of beer,
a plate of cheese crackers, and a pack of American cigarettes. This,
then, must be a celebration. She laughed, a funny little sound, but
her lips did stretch into a smile. She could feel the pull and tug of
her facial muscles. A miracle. A wonderful miracle.

Her hatred for the surgeon disappeared, and she winced when
she thought about how she'd screamed at him, calling him a quack
and even worse. Would he ever forgive her? Obviously he had, she

thought, looking down at the tray. A celebration meant she should celebrate. She would smoke two cigarettes and throw the rest away. She would drink the one beer and make a mental resolution to have no more than one drink a day from now on. If that much. A new life and a new beginning didn't need to be cluttered up with tobacco and alcohol.

There was only one thing missing—a mirror. Perhaps today was the day one would be provided.

Would she miss this place? Yes and no. She would miss this small, private, walled-in garden with its exquisitely pruned shrubs and flowers. She would probably miss her room, too. It had been a haven for her all these months. She'd cried here, slept here, cursed here, vented her hatred here, and now, just maybe, she could rejoice here.

Was today the day?

Nealy looked up to see Maline standing in the doorway. She was dressed in street clothes. How different she looked without her starched white uniform and little cap perched on her dark curls. "Are you going somewhere, Maline?"

"You are not dressed, Nealy."

There was such dismay in her voice, Nealy smiled. "I didn't know I was supposed to get dressed so early. Why?"

"Today is the true test of Dr. Vinh's work. Quick, you must dress, for we have to be back here by noon for your scheduled appointment."

"Why? Are we going somewhere? No, I'm not ready . . . no one said . . ."

"Doctor Vinh's orders, Nealy. Hurry now."

"Tell me why," Nealy said.

"I told you, it is your true test. We are going shopping."

"Shopping?" Nealy said stupidly.

"Yes, for looks. To see if people look at you. You know, stare. When I am satisfied with what I see, then we will really *shop*."

Fifteen minutes later, Nealy was dressed, her hair pulled back in a ponytail. "Do I look all right, Maline?"

"You will look even better in minutes. Sit quietly now while I apply your makeup."

"That's the makeup?" Nealy said, looking at the jar Maline held in her hands. "It looks like putty. You know that stuff they use to fill in the cracks when something gets broken."

Maline giggled. "You're half-right. This will last for about six hours, and then you have to reapply it. Now sit still and don't move your facial muscles."

Her touch was light and sure. Twice she stood back to view her handiwork only to advance and dab and smear. "Yes, I think that will do it. You must wear a hat, Nealy. I brought one for you. We do not want any sun on your face. That is another reason why I want us to get out early."

Nealy plopped the wide-brimmed straw hat onto her head. "When can I see what I look like?"

"When Doctor Vinh says you can see and not one minute before. We are going to the market, where you will buy fresh vegetables and fruit. Here is some money. You will engage the vendor in conversation, and I will watch for his reaction. We will do this again and again until I am satisfied. You will not see any mirrors or windows where we are going. We must hurry."

Nealy could feel her heart racing as they arrived at the huge open-air market where Maline shopped. She did as instructed, watching each person she came in contact with. No one paid any attention to her. They wrapped her purchases, took her money, made change, and smiled. She was almost ready to jump out of her skin with excitement when they reached the last vendor, where Maline bought a small carving of a mermaid for her husband. She explained away her last purchase by saying, "There is little in Sinjin's life to make him smile. Everything is work and dedication. When he smiles he makes me so happy. I think the test worked and you passed, Nealy. Sinjin will be so happy. And you, my friend, what is it you feel?"

"I don't know, Maline. I'm excited. I'm wary. I'm afraid. I feel like I have glue on my face."

"You will get used to the way it feels in time. I think you look beautiful."

Nealy stopped in her tracks and reached for Maline's arm. "Is that the truth?"

"But of course. I would not lie to you about something so important. Now do you want to really *shop*?"

"I'm your girl," Nealy said happily. "I have so many presents to buy."

They arrived back at the private clinic with minutes to spare. "There is just enough time for me to remove your makeup and clean your face. Quickly now, Nealy, Dr. Vinh doesn't like to be kept waiting. He is most anxious to hear my report."

The moment.

That's how she would always remember it in the years to come. The moment when Dr. Vinh viewed his surgical skill with a clinical eye. The moment when he would shake his head, and, if she was lucky, he would smile. The moment when he would hand her a mirror. The moment when perhaps he would say something nice.

The moment.

She took her seat in the high familiar chair and closed her eyes when the bright magnifying lights shone down on her face. She waited, hardly daring to breathe for what he would say.

"How did your excursion go, Maline?"

"Very well, Doctor. No one paid the slightest bit of attention to your patient. The makeup worked superbly. I saw no problems."

"And you, Nealy, how do you feel?" the doctor asked, taking a step back from the chair.

"Scared out of my wits. I'm afraid to look into the mirror."

"You do remember what I told you about your expectations, don't you?"

"Yes, I remember. I remember every single word. Can I see now?"

"The mirror, Maline." The nurse reached for a large mirror with a bright blue handle. She handed it to the doctor who in turn handed it to Nealy.

Nealy stared at her red face. It was her, but it wasn't her. Her scarred fingers reached up to touch first her nose and then her cheeks. Both were smooth to the touch, but she already knew that. "I don't think Gabby will be afraid of me, Doctor. You exceeded my expectations. I don't know what to say. I need to say something. I'm sorry for my anger. Thank you for being patient with me.

Thank you for your marvelous skill. It doesn't seem enough to say thank you."

"It is enough, Nealy. It is what I do. Everyone I operate on is not as fortunate as you. I know it wasn't easy. In time some of the redness will disappear. It will never go away entirely. The makeup works wonders. We will send you home with a generous supply. This afternoon one of my nurses will teach you how to apply it. A total makeover if you like. A hairstylist will also be here this afternoon to add the finishing touches. Tomorrow you can go home."

Nealy froze in the chair. "Tomorrow? So soon? I don't know . . . I'm not sure . . ."

"Mr. Tanner is on his way as we speak. He said he made a promise to you to deliver you back to your home safe and sound. You will leave tomorrow at ten in the morning."

"But . . . my bill . . . I haven't called anyone. You want me to surprise them, is that it? Don't you think I need a few days to . . . you know . . . get used to looking in a mirror? I think I need . . ."

"A surprise is a wonderful thing. Think how happy everyone will be to see you. Your bill was paid in full the day you arrived by Mr. Tanner. And no, you do not need any more time. That's a polite way of saying we need your accommodations for someone else who needs my help."

"Oh, well, that's different. I understand, Doctor. Thank you for everything."

"Have a good life, Nealy Clay," Dr. Vinh said, shaking her hand.

"Men shake hands, Dr. Vinh. Women hug." Nealy wrapped her arms around the portly doctor and gave him a paralyzing hug. He laughed. Something she had never heard him do before. Even Maline seemed startled at the sound.

The rest of her day was spent in a frenzy. Seated in front of a portable mirror, she paid rapt attention to the nurse who instructed her on how to apply her makeup. Even she was stunned at the difference it made. She almost looked like her old self. She was no longer the hideous Halloween creature. *I'm me again. I am Nealy Clay.* She was even more convinced when they took a break for the hairstylist, who snipped and layered her curly hair. She actually looked fashionable when she was done. She felt like singing.

"I think I have it now," she said to the nurse an hour later.

"Yes, you have done very well, Ms. Clay. I will bring you several jars to take home with you. The rest will be sent through the mail. There will be enough to last you three months at which point, call us and another shipment will be sent. We'll adjust the tint as the redness fades. You look wonderful," she said shyly. "Can I help you with anything else?"

"No, but thank you for asking. I want to pack myself. Then I want to spend the rest of the day in the garden."

"Very well. Ring your bell if you want anything."

Fourteen operations and eleven skin grafts later and she was finally going home. *Thank you, God. Thank you.*

Nealy was waiting in the lobby when Cole Tanner stepped through the doors. She ran to him. "How can I ever thank you for bringing me here. How?"

"Tell me you forgive my family's stupidity. That's all I want, all my family, our family now, wants in the way of thanks."

"I forgave you the day I walked out of the kitchen at Sunbridge. It's a new day now. Life is too short to look backwards. I learned a lot here, Cole."

"I bet you did. You look wonderful. Are you happy with the results, Nealy? Does your family know you're going home?"

"I'm delighted with the results. Truthfully, I didn't think it would turn out this well. I was prepared for the worst and, no, my family doesn't know I'm going home. I didn't know myself until yesterday. I want to surprise them."

"I like surprises." Cole grinned. "Time to say good-bye."

Nealy looked around. Where was the doctor? Her eyes questioned Maline.

"Dr. Vinh is in surgery, Nealy. He said to say good-bye. I will miss you, Nealy. Have a good trip. Call me or write to me when you have time." They hugged one another before the tiny nurse fled down the hall.

Nealy and Cole walked out into the sunshine. She turned back to raise her eyes to the second-floor surgery unit. She waved.

Sinjin Vinh stood at the window watching his patient as she

walked away. Both his fists shot in the air, a wide grin stretching across his face.

"I saw that!" Maline said, entering the room. "You did well, my husband. Nealy Clay will have a good life now, thanks to you."

"I hope so, Maline. I could do nothing for the deep sorrow in her eyes. I hope she finds the happiness she seeks. I want her to be as happy as you and I are."

Maline smiled.

Aboard the corporate jet, Nealy leaned back against the seat and closed her eyes.

She was going home.

Epilogue

The dream was beautiful. She was riding Flyby, the wind in her face, and she was laughing. A joyous sound of happiness because she was back where she belonged. She half heard herself mumble something. The dream changed and she was back in Thailand and someone was poking her, getting her ready for more pain, more agony. "No. No more. I can't take anymore. I'm sorry I let you down. I want to go home. I need to go home. No more operations. I don't care anymore. Please, let me go home."

Cole Tanner placed a comforting hand on Nealy's shoulder. "Wake up, Nealy. We're back in the States. You were having a bad dream. Are you okay?"

Nealy shook her head. "You're right, I was dreaming, and it was a bad dream. I have a lot of those lately. We're home! My God, are we really home?"

Cole hedged and repeated, "We're back on American soil. It's okay for both of us to get off the plane now."

Nealy reared up in her seat. "How's my makeup?"

"You might want to touch it up. It looks like some came off on your sleeve the way you were sleeping."

"Will people stare at me when I get off the plane?"

"I don't think so. Hey, I'm a guy. You look great to me, Nealy."

Nealy looked out of the window. "This doesn't look like . . . where are we, Cole?" Her voice sounded so anxious she couldn't believe it was her own.

"Well, we aren't exactly in Kentucky. It's more like we're in . . . New Mexico," Cole said, looking everywhere but at Nealy.

"New Mexico! How'd we get here? Is something wrong? Oh, no, you didn't . . . you wouldn't . . . don't do this to me, Cole."

Cole dropped to his haunches. "Look at me, Nealy, and listen to me. I brought you here because of Hatch. He's back at work in the office. I got this from Riley who got it from Emmie who got it from Nick. The point is, he's back. You're back. If ever a man loved a woman it is Hatch Littletree. I saw that the night we met in Japan. You can get it all back, Nealy. You can. He'll never come after you, you need to understand that. You sent him away. Besides, I have it on good authority that Triple-Star can't finish the movie until you get married. They've been filming at the farm for months now. Think of all the money it costs to make that movie. Think about all the actors who will be out of work if you don't follow through. Everyone wants a happy ending. I want a happy ending for you, Nealy, because you deserve it."

"I can't . . . I'm not ready . . . This is all too much, too quick. I'm all wrinkled and messy. My hair, my makeup . . ."

"I don't think he'll care, Nealy."

"That's easy for you to say. I can't . . . what if he . . ."

"It won't happen. Trust me. You trusted me once, trust me now."

This was what she wanted, wasn't it? This was what she had dreamed about for a year and a half. "Can I at least change my dress and fix my makeup? I want to brush my teeth."

"The airport is riddled with rest rooms. I'll rent a car for you. Meet me by the Avis counter."

"Are you sure . . ."

"I've never been more sure of anything in my life. Just trust me on this, okay? You do love him, don't you?" Cole asked anxiously almost as an afterthought.

"You'll never know how much. Okay, okay, I'm going. Avis, you said."

"Yeah."

An hour later, Nealy drove out of the airport parking lot, Cole's directions to Hatch's office in her lap. Her heart was thundering in her chest, and her mouth was so dry she couldn't feel her tongue.

Maybe she should stop and get a drink. Two drinks. Maybe even some cigarettes. She shook her head, remembering her resolution. What was she going to say? What would Hatch say? What if he told her to buzz off. What if he didn't love her anymore? *You can do this, Nealy. You know you can. Cole said you could. Even Maline said you could do this if you wanted to do it badly enough.*

She turned on the radio, then turned it off. She longed for a cigarette. A cold beer. Maybe when she found Hatch's office she would see a restaurant nearby and she could stop in. She was so intent on her thoughts she almost missed the street where she was supposed to make a left-hand turn. She swerved just in time. On her left was the adobe building. Inside were her son and Hatch. She circled the parking lot and drove off, careful to remember the landmarks across the street.

She saw the bar and grill and pulled into the parking lot. She inhaled and exhaled five times the way Maline had taught her. When she felt calm enough to get out of the car she settled her straw hat more firmly on top of her head and marched into the bar, where she sat down in a booth and ordered a triple shot of Wild Turkey bourbon. She gulped at the fiery liquid and downed it in two gulps. She was tempted to order another one but changed her mind. She left a twenty-dollar bill on the table.

Back in the car, she drove out of the parking lot, crawled the one block at fifteen miles an hour before she turned left again, where she parked in the back end of the lot. She sat for a long time trying to get up the nerve to get out of the car. She got out, got back in. Hatch was there. His Range Rover was parked three cars away from her.

Inside the building, Nick heard the tinkling bells headed his way. Medusa entered the room and went straight to the window. She motioned for him to join her. Nick looked downward, then up at Medusa. "You knew?" She smiled.

Nick barreled out of the office and down the hall to Hatch's office. "Come with me. *Now*, Hatch."

"What the hell . . ." Hatch said, getting up from his chair.

"Do what he says, Shunpus," Medusa said as she tinkled her way back to Nick's office.

"Look out the window, Hatch, and tell me what you see."

"Cars. Mine, yours, the partners' and Medusa's buggy. A few strange ones, probably clients' cars. What am I missing?"

"That's what you're missing," Nick said, pointing to his mother, who was getting out of the car for the fourth time. "She needs more time. See, she's getting back in." Nick raised the window.

Hatch's face turned milk white. His breathing was labored as he stared down at the parking lot. Were his eyes playing tricks on him? Nealy. Was it really Nealy?

On her fifth exit from the car, Nealy looked upward to see them all staring at her.

"Hey, Hatch!"

"Yeah, that's my name," he said in a shaky voice.

"My ears are sweating! And I'm real nervous."

"Stay right there. I know just the cure for that!" Hatch boomed, before he sprinted from the room.

Medusa and Nick listened as he barreled down the steps, then watched as Hatch ran across the parking lot. He scooped Nealy up in his arms and whirled her around and around.

"It's you. It's really you! God you look . . . beautiful."

"Not under the makeup. I'm red and scarred, Hatch. I have to wear this junk for the rest of my life. It's like glue."

"Who the hell cares. You said something about your ears sweating and being nervous."

"Yeah, you said you knew what to do about it."

"I did say that. Yeah, yeah, I know what to do about it. Yes sireee, I do."

"Then let's get to it," Nealy said, as she was lifted off the ground again and twirled in the air until she begged for mercy.

"Carry on!" Hatch shouted to everyone gathered at the window. "You'll see me when you see me!"

"Don't count on it. He's all mine now!" Nealy shouted.

"Get in the car, Nealy," Hatch ordered.

"I'm in, I'm in. I'm a little nervous here. I had to stop for a drink before I got up the courage to come here. Not really nervous. You know, a little nervous. Well maybe a lot. It was a triple. It went right to my head."

Hatch threw his head back and laughed. And laughed.

"God, I love you," Nealy said.

"*Way to go, Nealy,*" Hunt said.

"What did you say?" Hatch asked.

"I didn't say anything," Nealy said.

"*On that thought, I am going to leave you now.*"

"Thanks, Hunt," Nealy murmured.

"I'll take care of her, Old Buddy," Hatch muttered under his breath.

"*Have a good life. Be happy.*"

For a sneak preview of
KENTUCKY SUNRISE
the final book in this trilogy—
coming from Kensington in October 2002—
just turn the page . . .

Kentucky Sunrise

Sage Thornton looked across the table at his twin brother Birch. His expression clearly said board meetings are deadly dull. Birch rolled his eyes as if to say, I agree, this is boring as hell.

Fanny Thornton Reed peered at her sons over the rim of her reading glasses. "I wonder, Sage, if you can tell me why the Emperor's Room has been operating in the red for the past two months. The Emperor's Room has always been the hottest ticket in town for fine dining. As far back as I can remember, we've always been backlogged for reservations. The way it stands now, you can walk in off the street and get a table without a reservation."

Sage leaned forward, better to see his mother. "The chef bailed out on us. She didn't give us any notice, so we shut down for ten days until we could find a replacement. One day she was here and the next day she was gone. Obviously the new man we hired isn't doing the job he was hired to do. I've been looking for a new chef since the day she left. Five-star chefs are not that easy to come by, Mom."

"Let's try to do better. I hate seeing all these red circles," Fanny said quietly. "I think we're adjourned unless any of you have some business you want to discuss."

Sage glared at the board members sitting at the long conference table. His gaze said there had better not be any new business.

"Then we are adjourned." Fanny shuffled her papers and booklets into an accordion-pleated envelope. The sound of the rubber band snapping into place was exceptionally loud to those in the room.

The twins waited until the room emptied out before they approached their mother. They both hugged her. "Nice to see you, Mom. You should come to town more often," Birch said.

Fanny twinkled at her sons. "What good would that do me, Birch? You're in Atlantic City all the time running Babylon Two. As for you, Sage, I only live fifty miles away. You could come to visit. By the way, you are going to Kentucky for the family reunion in June, aren't you? I think it's wonderful that Nealy is willing to hostess a family get-together. Marcus and I wouldn't miss it for the world. Sunny and Billie are planning to attend, as are all the Colemans. It should be quite wonderful."

"We'll be there," Birch and Sage said in unison. "Are you staying on, Mom, or heading back to the ranch?"

"Marcus is waiting for me. I have to get back. How's my mountain, Sage?" Her voice was so wistful, Sage felt his eyes start to burn. He stared at her for a long moment, his heart fluttering in his chest at how old and frail his mother suddenly looked. He blinked. Her hair was almost snow-white and the fine wrinkles were now deeper. Her smile was the same gentle, warm smile of his youth. He made a mental note to go out to the ranch at least once a week even if it was at midnight.

"It's as beautiful as ever and just as wonderful. The kids love it. I wish you and Marcus would come up and spend some time with us. Iris would love it if you'd come for an extended stay."

"If I were to do that, I might not want to leave. We'll be there for Christmas. I'll say good-bye now." Fanny gathered up her purse and coat.

"How about a trip to Atlantic City, Mom?" Birch asked as he hugged her good-bye.

"One of these days. I like to be close to home. You know I'm only comfortable around my own things in my own place. Marcus is having knee replacement surgery after the first of the year. Recovery time will be at least a few months. I will think about it, though. Be sure to call me. That goes for you, too, Sage."

"Okay, Mom. Do you want us to walk you to the car?"

Fanny laughed. "I think I can get there on my own. You can walk me to the elevator, though."

Even here, on the fourth floor of the casino, the noise from the first floor could still be heard as the slot machines whirred and clanked to the sound of silver.

"Oh-oh, here comes trouble," Sage muttered as soon as the elevator door closed. He made his way across the deeply carpeted hallway to greet two burly Las Vegas police detectives. "What brings you here at this hour of the morning, Joe? Noah, good to see you again," he said, pumping the second detective's hand. "You both know Birch."

"We're here to ask you about one of your employees. She's got at least twenty aliases that we know of. Willow, Willa, or a variation of that first name. As to her last name, here, take your pick," the detective named Noah said, handing over a sheet of paper. "We have no clue as to what her real name is. She's a cook. We were told she worked here at Babylon."

Sage looked at his brother, a frown building between his eyebrows. "If you're referring to Willa Lupine, yes, she worked for us in the Emperor Room. She's a five-star chef, but she quit a few months ago. She pretty much left us high and dry. Why are you looking for her?"

"Murder."

This time Sage's eyebrows shot up to his hairline. "Murder! Willa? Who is she supposed to have killed?"

"Her husband, Carlo Belez. Also known as Junior Belez. It was in all the papers. Didn't you see it?"

Sage threw his hands in the air. "Hell, it was on the front page of the paper every day for weeks. It didn't say anything about a wife or mention our chef by name. I would have remembered something like that. If this happened two months ago, are you telling me you just figured out Junior was married to one of our employees? I didn't even know Willa was married."

The detective looked sheepish. "So you did know Junior."

Sage jammed his hands into his pockets. "I never said I didn't know him. Every casino owner on the strip knows . . . knew Junior

Belez. He was a high roller. Never ran a marker that I know of. He won and lost money in all the casinos. Are you implying our old chef killed Junior?"

"It looks that way. We want to question her. The only problem is we don't know where she is. We have an all-points out, but nothing has come in. We just found out about her a few days ago."

Sage raked his hands through his hair. "Wait a minute. The guy was killed two months ago and you're just now finding out he was married? What the hell kind of police work is that?"

The detective clenched and unclenched his teeth. "Junior lived on his ranch way out there, maybe twelve miles or so past the Chicken Ranch. He liked privacy. He didn't have a housekeeper, but he did have a groundskeeper who sticks his snoot in the bottle from time to time and then has to dry out. He was drying out when this all went down. He came back expecting to pick up where he left off, only his boss is dead. He's the one who told us your cook was married to Belez. If it wasn't for him, we still wouldn't know about your . . . cook."

"She wasn't a cook. Anyone can cook. Willa was a chef," Sage said. "I don't know anything that can help you. She worked for us. She drew customers like a magnet. She was one hell of a chef. She quit and took off. That's the sum total of what I know. Feel free to go to the kitchen and talk to the people who worked with her."

"We'll do that. If you hear anything, call us."

"I will," Sage muttered. He looked at his brother. "Don't look at me like that, Birch. I don't know anything about the woman. The kitchen was strictly off-limits to everyone when she worked here. She was hell on wheels about people going in and out of her kitchen."

Birch shrugged. "You taking me to the airport or should I catch a cab?"

"Do you mind taking a cab? I want to talk to the kitchen staff myself. I have this . . . weird feeling I know something but I don't know what it is. It's like . . . something I heard. Then again, maybe it was something I saw and didn't realize it at the time. Christ, I hate when that happens. It makes me damn near nuts trying to figure it out."

"No problem. Let me know if I can help."

"Hey, wait just a damn minute, Birch. You're looking kind of smug. You didn't snatch her away, did you? Damn, it would be just like you to pull a stunt like that."

"Sorry. Never saw the lady, and I don't know anything about her. See you."

"One of our employees is wanted for murder. I can't believe this, Birch."

Birch bent down to pick up his briefcase. "He said she was wanted for questioning. There's a difference. She might be a suspect. That still doesn't prove she committed the murder. It's the elimination process to track down the killer or killers. Don't go off half-cocked here, Sage. I'll call you when I get home. We can do that word-association thing we used to do when we were kids. Maybe something will come to you. You could also call Sunny. She's great with stuff like that."

Sage watched the elevator door close behind his brother. He felt his stomach muscles bunch up into a knot.

Murder!

Fern Michaels likes to hear from her readers. You can e-mail her at *fernmic@aol.com*